Miss Julia Meets Her Match

Miss Julia Meets Her Match

Ann B. Ross

DOUBLEDAY LARGE PRINT HOME LIBRARY EDITION

Viking

This Large Print Edition, prepared especially for Doubleday Large Print Home Library, contains the complete, unabridged text of the original Publisher's Edition.

VIKING
Published by the Penguin Group
Penguin Group (USA) Inc., 375 Hudson Street,
New York, New York 10014, U.S.A.
Penguin Book Ltd, 80 Strand,
London WC2R 0RL, England
Penguin Books Australia Ltd, 250 Camberwell Road
Camberwell, Victoria 3124, Australia
Penguin Books Canada Ltd, 10 Alcorn Avenue,
Toronto, Ontario, Canada M4V 3B2
Penguin Books India (P) Ltd, 11 Community Centre,
Panchsheel Park, New Delhi – 110 017, India
Penguin Book (N.Z.) Ltd, Cnr Rosedale and Airborne
Roads, Albany, Auckland, New Zealand
Penguin Books (South Africa) (Pty) Ltd, 24 Sturdee
Avenue, Rosebank, Johannesburg 2196, South Africa

Penguin Books Ltd, Registered Offices:
80 Strand, London WC2R 0RL, England

First published in 2004 by Viking Penguin,
a member of Penguin Group (USA) Inc.

ISBN 0-7394-4286-4

Printed in the United States of America

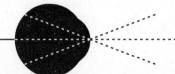

This Large Print Book carries the
Seal of Approval of N.A.V.H.

This book is for all the readers of the Miss Julia books, and for those who have a part in getting the books to them—Viking editors, copyeditors, artists, publicity managers (especially Cindy), marketing and sales forces, as well as for booksellers everywhere. My thanks to each one of you.

And to Kathy Morgan of Morganton, NC, many thanks for the use of your name and for your support of the auction to benefit The Children's School.

Special thanks, also, to Jennifer R. Ross, first-grade teacher and beloved daughter-in-law, for helping me put words in Latisha's mouth.

{Chapter 1}

"Where y'all gonna live?" Lillian asked, as she beat three eggs, one after the other, into a bowl of cake batter. "If you thinkin' 'bout tyin' the knot, somebody gonna be movin'."

"I'm not studying a move." I was at the kitchen table, folding towels taken from the dryer. The window rattled from a gust of late April wind, and I glanced outside to see more rain clouds moving across the sky.

"Huh. You better be studyin' on it, Miss Julia. 'Cause either Mr. Sam be movin' in here or you be movin' in there."

"That's too far down the road to worry about," I said, not wanting to worry about it either down the road or at the moment. "And, see, Lillian, that's part of the problem. Tying the knot. I don't know that I want to be tied to anybody, even Sam, who's as fine a man as I've ever known. But that's what happens when you marry. I've had a taste of doing things my way, you know, since Mr. Springer passed." I smoothed out a hand towel, smelling the packaged fresh air aroma rising from it. "Even if that freedom came too late in life to be of much use. Lillian, do you realize that I was married for almost forty-five years, and never had a moment's peace? Always fearful of what would set him off, what would displease him, what I was doing wrong, and on and on. Now, I don't have to answer to anybody, and I'm not at all sure I want to give that up."

"Mr. Sam, he seem like he pretty easy to get along with," Lillian commented as she greased three cake pans, then sprinkled flour in them. "I doubt he pull on that knot too much. 'Sides, he tied up, too. Least, the man s'posed to be."

"Yes, and isn't that the trouble?" I pushed aside the hand towels, folded, stacked, and ready for the linen closet. "Everybody expects a wife to toe the line, but a husband? I tell you, Lillian, the only change marriage makes in a man's life is he gets his food cooked and his laundry done."

"I don't know as I'd go that far," she said,

as she poured the batter into the cake pans, then shook each pan so the layers would bake evenly. "'Course, I jus' look at other folkses' marriage, not mine. 'Cause you hit the nail on the head when it come to mine."

"Oh, Lillian," I said, just done in by all the decisions that were piling up, waiting for me to get to them. Well, actually only one decision, but from that all the others would flow. "I don't know that I want to marry anyone again, much less have to decide where to live when, *if,* I do." I rested my head on my hand. "It's more than I want to deal with."

I lifted my head then, as more thoughts on the subject jumped up in my mind. "You know, it used to be that where a couple lived was never a question. The man decided, and that was it. The woman was expected to pull up stakes, leave her family and friends and everything else and go wherever he said. And be happy about it, too." I bit my lip, remembering my own wretched experience. "I don't think it was ever even discussed when Wesley Lloyd proposed to me and, Lord knows, it didn't occur to me to question whatever he said. I took it for granted that I'd leave my home and move into his. Not that I wanted to stay home, but still."

"I think that what the Bible tell a woman to do," Lillian said. She opened the oven door and arranged the pans on a rack, the heat making her brown arms glisten with perspiration.

"Well, that's where you're wrong, because it's the other way around," I said. "It says a *husband* should leave his father and mother and cleave unto his wife." She and I looked at each other, as we both recalled that while I'd done my share of cleaving to Wesley Lloyd, he'd done a good bit of his to somebody else.

But turning my mind back to the current problem, since Wesley Lloyd was dead and gone, I'd been up one side and down the other over it, and I still couldn't decide. Hazel Marie'd said she knew exactly what I ought to do, but her mind was filled with one romantic notion after another, so I wasn't a bit surprised by where she stood. Then she'd gotten serious and said, "Miss Julia, all you have to do is decide what *you* want, then just do it."

Well, of course that was the crux of the matter. I didn't know what I wanted—

whether to marry again and run the risk of another betrayal or to stay a single widow and run my life the way I wanted to. I don't mind saying it—I had thoroughly enjoyed doing just that the past few years since laying Wesley Lloyd in his grave, especially since I had free rein of half of his sizeable estate, Little Lloyd being the beneficiary of the other half.

Actually, I'd hardly ever made a decision based purely on my own wants. There'd always been responsibilites and obligations to other people that came into play and, as I am of a generous nature, I usually bowed to whatever somebody else wanted.

So, ever since Sam had come up with the idea of us marrying, I'd been keeping myself busy, trying not to think about it in hopes that I wouldn't have to give him a final answer. I didn't want to lose him, but I wasn't sure I wanted him full-time, either. The fact of the matter was, I was about half mad that he hadn't left things as they were. But, no, he had to bring up something that put my life in turmoil.

Well, Lord knows, he'd hinted around about it long enough, but when he finally got serious, the actual thought of being his wife, with all that that entailed, made my heart leap inside my chest. But I'd answered with my head, and my head said, "Don't rock the boat." Still, he'd kept on and on at me, telling me I'm not getting off the hook, that he's a patient man and sooner or later I'm going to give in and make him a happy man. And to tell the truth, the upshot of it all put me on edge so bad I could hardly stand it. I've prided myself on being a fairly decisive woman, but the agitation and indecision I'd been under made me ready to bite somebody's head off.

The one thing that did tempt me, though, was Sam's ability to make me laugh, which I did whenever he started rattling off his many admirable qualities. I don't think Wesley Lloyd made me laugh even once during all the years of our dour marriage. He made me frown a lot, cry on too many occasions, and nurse a sorrowful heart all the time.

Lord, I never thought I'd even consider such a thing as marrying again. Once you've done it and suffered from it, you're not all that anxious to get back into a similar situation. Of course, Sam was not Wesley Lloyd Springer, not by a long shot. I'd gone into marriage with Wesley Lloyd without an inkling that such a respected pillar of the church and the community could've ever done what he did—which was to enter into more than a decade of dalliance with Hazel Marie Puckett, produce a son and heir, and leave me to clean up the mess he left and end up with both mistress and son living under my roof. And if you think that's a strange arrangement, you wouldn't be the only one. But by this time I'd come too far to let what other people think bother me. Lillian says I'll have stars in my crown for doing it, and I don't doubt it, even though it hasn't been as hard as I'd feared or as one might think.

Still and all, I'm stuck with the conviction that men, as a general rule, can't be trusted as far as you can throw them. And I speak from painful experience.

I raised my head as I heard Hazel Marie's car pull in the driveway and, in a few minutes, she came through the back door, shrugging out of her raincoat. It was a wonder to me how much better she looked the older she got. Not that she was all that old, forty-something being an enviable age from my vantage point, but I'm talking about comparisions to what she looked like before she had the wherewithal to purchase suitable clothes and have her hair professionally done. Which was what she'd been doing that morning.

I smiled at her as she stuck her umbrella in the stand. "Your hair looks very nice, Hazel Marie." And it did, the highlighted streaks of blonde on blonde shone in the overhead kitchen lights. "Velma is finally learning how to do it right."

Hazel Marie pulled out a chair at the table and immediately began to fold towels, since I'd fallen down on the job. "Miss Julia, you'll never believe what I heard at the beauty parlor."

"There's no telling. What?"

"Well, oh, I'm sorry, Lillian," she said. "I didn't even speak to you, which just shows how stunned I am. I'm so full of the latest gossip that I can't think of anything else."

Lillian laughed, her gold tooth flashing. "Gossip do that to you sometime. 'Specially if it real good gossip."

"Well, this is as good as it gets." Hazel Marie took a deep breath, trying to calm herself before imparting her news. "Miss Julia, guess who's having an affair."

"I don't have any idea and, Hazel Marie, if

you heard it at Velma's, you ought to consider the source."

"Oh, I do, but everybody's talking about it. I mean, out loud and everything. This wasn't something whispered and speculated about. It was told as a fact, because she's been seen coming out of the Mountaintop Motel."

"Well, my word," I said, drawn into the story in spite of my natural aversion to gossip, having suffered considerable anguish myself from wagging tongues. "Who?"

Hazel Marie leaned across the table, smiling with the assurance that she was going to shock me good. "Miss High and Mighty, Norma Cantrell, herself."

"No!" I reared back in my chair, suitably shocked. Norma Cantrell was our Presbyterian pastor's secretary, and she ran his office like a third world dictator. I'd never had much use for her, but the pastor thought she hung the moon. "That can't be true." Then I thought about it, rubbing my fingers across my mouth. "Are you sure?"

"As sure as I can be. It was Mildred Allen who saw her at the Mountaintop."

"Well, I say." That iced the cake for me,

until I thought of something else. "And what was Mildred Allen doing there?"

"Collecting for some fund or another," Hazel Marie said. "She had to go twice. They kept putting her off and still didn't donate a thing. That's a pretty ratty motel, from what I hear. A perfect getaway place if you don't want people to know what you're doing or who you're doing it with. Of course, Norma didn't expect anybody she knew to be there. Velma said that Mildred said she didn't think Norma saw her because she hid behind a laurel bush when Norma came out of one of the rooms. And not once, but both times Mildred was there." Hazel Marie stopped and thought about it. "I expect it was a pretty big laurel bush, considering Mildred's size. But, anyway, Norma thinks it's still a secret."

"Well, now, Hazel Marie, there could be a perfectly innocent explanation, you know."

"Like what?"

"I don't know. Maybe she has a sick friend."

"At a place like that?"

"It does sound suspicious, and I'll admit I'm not all that surprised. Norma's always struck me as having more going on under-neath than she lets on."

"Yes," Hazel Marie said, "but it's hard to imagine that she'd get involved in a seedy affair since she's so particular about every-thing."

"Norma's been divorced almost all her life," I told her, as Lillian came to the table with cups and the coffee pot. She liked a little spate of gossip as well as the next person. "The way I heard it, she married right out of high school, but hardly a year later, her husband ran off with their next-door neighbor. Norma's been living off sym-pathy ever since. People think her heart was broken and that she'll never recover, but this just goes to show, doesn't it? So who is she supposed to be seeing at the Moun-taintop?"

Hazel Marie smiled. "You'll never guess."

"Just tell me, Hazel Marie," I said. "I can't imagine who'd even be interested in her. Her husband certainly wasn't."

"Well, nobody knows for sure, but the Honorable Clifford Beebee was mentioned. Can you believe that?"

"My word," I said again, mumbling it this time as I tried to absorb this turn of events.

"If this gets out, Clifford Beebee's political career is over in this town. To say nothing of his marriage, because I don't believe Gladys'll put up with it."

"Sound like to me it already got out," Lillian said, as she stirred sugar into her coffee. "But that man been mayor so long, he pro'bly think he b'long there."

"You're right about that, Lillian," I agreed. "Nobody's been willing to run against him for ever so long, so he probably thinks he can get away with anything."

"Well, not this time," Hazel Marie said. "Because I heard that Bill Denby's going to go up against him in the primary this spring. You know him, don't you? He's the service manager at the Chevrolet dealership. Somebody said his campaign slogan's going to be 'Fix It and Run It,' which is what he says the town needs, just like a car. Mayor Beebee just might get taken down a notch or two, considering how high-handed he is."

"I should say, high-handed. Why, it's gotten so that none of the commissioners dares do anything without his say-so. At least, that's what I hear. I'm not all that politically minded, myself. But what I want to know is why the mayor's name is being linked to Norma's? Did Mildred see him, too?"

"No, but she saw his car," Hazel Marie said, her eyes dancing with the image that produced. "You know that big ole thing he drives? You can't miss it, and everybody knows it. It was parked right outside the room, and Velma said that Mildred said that she waited as long as she could after Norma left to see if he'd come out of the room, too. But she had to go to the bathroom real bad and couldn't wait any longer.

"But," Hazel Marie went on, a smile playing around her mouth. "You haven't heard it all yet."

"I don't think I can stand much more. What else are they saying under the hair dryers?"

She put her hand on my arm and said, "Now, I'm not sure I believe this, but here goes. When Velma was combing me out, she whispered that there's talk going around about *Emma Sue Ledbetter.*"

"*What!* With the mayor?" I was stunned, having no idea that the mayor was man enough for two women plus his wife.

"No, no," Hazel Marie said, patting my arm. "I've changed subjects."

"Well," I said with some relief that our preacher's wife was not linked with another man. "Thank goodness."

I knew that Emma Sue would no more make herself a topic of this kind of gossip than she would fly. Although, as I thought about it, she had been trying out her wings a little here lately.

"Besides," Hazel Marie went on, "Norma's got the mayor all tied up. At least, I guess she has. A few other names were mentioned in connection with hers, so nobody knows for sure who all she's catting around with. But what I wanted to tell you is that Velma said that Emma Sue made an appointment to have a complete makeover. And I'm talking hair color, makeup, everything."

"No!" I scrunched up a bath towel in my hands, unable to believe what I was hearing. "Hazel Marie, that is more unbelievable than Norma Cantrell traipsing around in a motel room. Are you sure?"

"Velma showed me her appointment book because I couldn't believe it myself. And there it was, Emma Sue Ledbetter, Thursday at seven P.M. Velma's doing her a favor by taking her after hours, so nobody'll be there with her."

"Pour me some more coffee, Lillian," I said, holding out my cup, more shaken with this item than I'd been to hear about the preacher's secretary. The preacher's wife, on the other hand, was known far and wide for her outspoken views on the value of a woman's natural beauty. Which to me meant the way you look when you first get up in the morning, and as far as I was concerned, every woman in the world needed a little help.

"Why?" I asked. "Why would Emma Sue suddenly want to make herself over? Why, Hazel Marie, you remember when she criticized you for wearing eye shadow? And I've heard her say many a time that since there'll be no Avon or Mary Kay products in heaven, women ought to get themselves prepared to do without down here. And she can get downright vicious on the subject of lipstick." I stopped and smoothed out the towel. "Wonder what's come over her?"

"Velma thinks Emma Sue may be having an affair, herself," Hazel Marie said, which nearly shocked me out of my chair.

"The preacher's wife! Hazel Marie, what a

thing to say. No, not Emma Sue Ledbetter, no way in the world would she do such a thing."

"Well, all I know is that when a woman's thinking about it, the first thing she does is buy new underwear. And getting a new look may be along the same line."

Lillian started laughing then. "Law me, I never heard the like."

"One thing's for sure, though," Hazel Marie said, "if she starts using makeup, she's going to have to do something about all that crying she does. Her face'll be a mess if she starts overflowing. Can you imagine?"

"I certainly can," I said, recalling Emma Sue's tendency to cloud up and cry whenever she got her feelings hurt, which seemed to be about all the time. "Well, Hazel Marie, I don't know what's going on in this town, but we'd do well not to repeat any of this." I thought about it for a few minutes, then went on. "Of course, I'll have to tell Sam, and I know you'll tell Mr. Pickens, but that's all. Lillian, you won't tell anybody, will you?"

"No'm, I'm right bad to listen, but I don't do much passin' on." She got up and checked the cakes in the oven, then came back to the table. "Sound like to me, though, that they a awful lot of people not real happy with what they got an' they out lookin' for what they like a whole lot better."

{Chapter 2}

Well, wasn't that the truth. Which is exactly what I said to Sam as I told him the latest beauty parlor news when he made his usual visit that night. It had become our custom to retire to the living room after supper while Lillian and Little Lloyd watched television upstairs. I could occasionally hear their laughter floating down the stairs, a matter of comfort to me when Sam became exceptionally amorous. Not that he was anything but a gentleman, but there was always the unnerving possibility that things would get out of hand.

I mention that we had the living room to ourselves because we had in effect displaced Hazel Marie and Mr. Pickens. Before Sam had come up with the idea of marriage and begun showing up at my house everytime I turned around, the living room had belonged to Hazel Marie and that black-eyed Mr. Pickens. If I let myself think about it, I expect I would've had to replace my Duncan Phyfe sofa.

But now that we had claimed the sofa, Hazel Marie and Mr. Pickens had to find another courting place. I think they went to his house where they could have some privacy. But I never asked, not particularly wanting to know what they did nor where they did it.

"Well, what do you know," Sam said, momentarily sidetracked from inching across the sofa to where I was sitting. "Norma and Clifford. Hard to picture that." He shook his head, smiling at the thought. "Who'd ever guess those two would ever get together. Total opposites, I'd say."

"So would I. But, Sam, it might not even be the mayor. From what Hazel Marie heard at the beauty shop, it could be somebody else Norma's been meeting. All we have to go on is the big baby-blue Cadillac parked outside the room she came out of, although there's not another one like it in town."

"I'd say that pretty well confirms it," Sam said, a lazy smile on his face. "Although, who knows, Clifford could've been discussing campaign tactics with her. Maybe he's going to offer her a job."

"In a motel room? No, there's only one reason anybody would sneak around in such a place as the Mountaintop. The only question is who she's sneaking around with. Although, far be it from me to engage in speculation." I rested my hand on the sofa between us to preserve a little space. "I wonder if the pastor knows what she's up to."

Sam put his hand on mine and said, "I doubt he'd believe it if he saw them himself. He thinks Norma's the perfect secretary because she's a good organizer and runs interference for him all the time."

"She certainly does that. Hazel Marie called her particular about things. I'd call her downright peculiar. Everything has to be just right and in its place. I mean, just look at that hair of hers. Not a strand out of place and teased within an inch of its life. I just can't imagine her in the throes of passion enough to mess it up."

"Not like us, Julia," Sam said, picking up my hand so he could slide a little closer. "We don't mind getting messed up in the throes of passion, do we?"

"Now, Sam . . . ," I said, trying to get back my hand. If the man thought our sedate courting constituted the throes of passion, he was in a bad way.

He laughed. "Everybody says we were made for each other. And speaking of hair, nobody's turned a single one since we got together."

"I wouldn't exactly call us together, if you're comparing us to what Norma and the mayor, or whoever, are up to." I scooted closer to the arm of the sofa. "You won't catch me going in and out of a motel room with a married man. Or an unmarried one, for that matter."

"Oh, come on, Julia," he said, cocking his head to one side. "You wouldn't go in and out of a motel room with me? Of course, if I ever got you in one, you might not ever get out."

"Behave yourself. Now listen, I've got something else to tell you." And I went on to tell about Emma Sue's sudden decision to make use of some beauty aids. "That is much more worrisome to me than whatever Norma Cantrell's up to. As far as Norma's concerned, I've never liked nor trusted her. It doesn't really surprise me that she's leading another life underneath that prissy front she puts up."

"You're being a little hard on her, aren't you?"

"Well, you don't know what I've had to put up with. I'll tell you the truth, Sam, I've always thought she had a thing for the pastor."

Sam threw back his head and laughed. "Larry Ledbetter? Oh, Julia, the things you come up with."

"Well, he's human, too. Although sometimes it's hard to tell he is. But, Sam, Norma acts more like a wife to him than a secretary. She's very jealous of his time and gives the third degree to anybody who wants to see him. She takes his clothes to the cleaners and picks them up, brings a special brand of coffee that's just for him, and makes out like he can't make a decision without running it by her first. What I really think is that if he gave her the least bit of encouragement, she'd fall over backward for him."

Sam sputtered as he laughed again, though I didn't see anything funny about a preacher being in peril. "Well," he finally said, "you may have something there. Maybe that's why Emma Sue's so concerned about her looks. Maybe she's heard that Norma's seeing somebody, but she hasn't heard who."

I jerked upright, poking Sam with my elbow to give myself some room. "That's what it is! She thinks it's her husband that Norma's seeing. Wait till I tell Hazel Marie."

"Now, hold on," Sam cautioned. "We're just speculating here. Let's not start any rumors."

"Well, but it fits. Don't you see, Sam, Emma Sue thinks Pastor Ledbetter's seeing Norma, who is really seeing Mayor Beebee, but Emma Sue doesn't know that, so she's trying to beautify herself so she can win her husband back."

"I don't think . . ."

"Well, I do, and you're the one who brought it up. Sam, that poor, pitiful woman is trying everything she can to save her marriage. And if she thinks she can do it by slapping on a layer of makeup, she's in pitiful shape. I feel sorry for her, thinking she can keep a man just by improving her looks. Not that I'm against trying to look your best, but when a man's got eyes for somebody else, it's too late for a quick fix."

"All this is real interesting, Julia," Sam

said, as he slipped an arm around my shoulders. "But we've been talking about everything under the sun except what I want to talk about, which is when you're going to marry me. I spend my time going back and forth between our houses, and it'd be easier on my poor feet if we lived in the same place. Then we could talk all the time, and you could keep me up with the latest gossip as soon as it comes in."

"You know I don't gossip," I said. "At least, not to spread it around."

"Sweetie," he said, tightening his arm around me and embarrassing me to death with his tendency to use affectionate names. I was so unaccustomed to it, you know, and I didn't know another soul in the world who would think me sweet, so the word hardly applied to me. "Forget about gossip for now, and tell me what you're thinking is about us getting married."

"I don't much want to think about it, to tell the truth. I don't want to hurt your feelings, Sam, but don't you think we'd be upsetting the apple cart to change things? Who knows what we'd be getting into, and we're both too set in our ways to suffer such an upheaval at this time in our lives."

"Not me," Sam said. "I'm not set in my ways. I like a challenge, or haven't you noticed?"

"I've noticed a number of things, that motorcycle, for one, which you seem to be trying to kill yourself on." I picked at my dress, pleating and unpleating it, wishing he wouldn't put me on the spot, but thrilled, in spite of myself, that he was. "I just don't know, Sam."

Sam leaned his head against mine and took my hand. "You do realize what a prize you'd be getting, don't you?"

I smiled to myself. Of course he was a prize. I just didn't know if I could handle having one.

"For one thing, I've got money in the bank."

"I don't need your money."

"But I want to take care of you, Julia."

"I've been doing fine by myself."

"I know you have, but you could have a lot more fun with me. And think how people would envy you, getting a catch like me."

I covered my mouth to keep from laughing. He did love to carry on.

"Now, Julia," he said in a serious tone, although if I'd looked up at him I knew I'd see his eyes sparkling. "You know I'm a respectable member of the community, and I'm handsome enough to be admired by any number of widow ladies in town."

Well, I knew that to be a fact. They swarmed around him, which didn't at all set well with me. How could I ever know he'd be able to resist the temptation to stray? After what I'd gone through with one wandering husband, I didn't plan to take a chance on another one.

"Besides," he went on, "you have to admit that I'm a fine specimen of a man with no health problems to speak of."

"Oh, Sam," I said, loosening my hand from his to cover my face. I didn't know whether to laugh out loud or tell him I appreciated knowing that little tidbit, because I certainly didn't intend to nurse a sick old man.

"And another thing, Julia, in case you're worried." He stopped, then lowered his voice as he pretended to reassure me about a serious matter. "I don't want the state of my virility to concern you for a minute. Believe me, I am as fit as a fiddle and may even be getting better with age."

A thrilling shiver ran up and down my

back at the thought of the state of his virility. But I suppressed it, hoped he hadn't
noticed, and sat up straight. "Listen, Sam,
don't you think the pastor ought to know
what Norma's up to?"

"I'm not thinking about the pastor," he
said, pulling me back against him. "Are you
changing the subject?"

"It needs changing, so, yes, I am. What
I'm thinking, Sam, is that there'll be an up-
roar over at the church if the pastor hears
about her. I mean, he had to eat his words
several years ago when he hired her in the
first place. Remember that?"

"Of course I remember it. I was on the
session then, and it was something to hear
Ledbetter try to justify having her on the
payroll. It was just after he'd preached that
series on marriage and divorce—he was for
one and against the other." Sam laughed at
the memory, and I was somewhat relieved
to have distracted him from his earlier pur-
suit.

"I remember that," I said, smiling with
him. "Pastor Ledbetter made a big thing
of how we shouldn't encourage divorce by
overlooking the sinfulness of it. He reminded us that in days gone by divorced

people were all but shunned, that we should be polite and friendly to them, but also let them know that we didn't approve. And then he up and hired Norma Cantrell, the town's preeminent divorcée."

Sam leaned his head against the back of the sofa, a reminiscent smile on his face. "That was the most entertaining session meeting I ever attended. Some of those old-timers were fit to be tied because they agreed with his sermons. So he had a time convincing them that what he'd said in the pulpit didn't apply to his needs in the office."

"He got his way, though," I said, "and she's been ensconced outside his door ever since. You know, Sam, I think the pastor ought to be told what she's doing. Especially since it reflects on the whole church."

"You're not thinking of telling him, are you?"

"Well, no, but somebody ought to."

"He'll find out sooner or later, but it shouldn't come from us. He'll be defensive about her and angry toward whoever tells him. Besides, we don't know for a fact who she's seeing, or even if she's seeing anyone at all."

"Well, I trust Mildred Allen, and if she said Norma came out of a seedy motel room where the mayor's car was parked, it's good enough for me."

"Still, let's let things run their course. I don't want the pastor taking out after you."

"I don't need looking after, Sam."

"Yes, you do. Now, where were we?" He drew me close again just as we heard Little Lloyd's laugh ring out from upstairs.

"I've got to get that child in bed," I said, trying to untangle myself. "He has school tomorrow."

"Give him a few more minutes," Sam said against my cheek, and I decided a few more minutes wouldn't hurt the child. Or me.

{ *Chapter 3* }

The next morning, I awoke with a smile on my face and Sam on my mind. He had a way of filling me with good will toward any and everybody, even those people who vexed me half to death. Maybe it would be worth the risk of marriage to feel this benevolent toward the world for the rest of my life.

Throwing back the covers and reaching for my robe, I sat on the side of the bed, marveling at how well I felt. Even when I stood up, there wasn't a twinge of stiffness or an aching joint anywhere. Youthful was how I felt. Light on my feet and in my heart. I even twirled around in the privacy of my bedroom, thinking *Mrs. Sam Murdoch.* I'd have to order new stationery and put away all my monogrammed linens, but those were minor considerations. *Julia Murdoch.* Well, it didn't have the same ring as Julia

Springer, but it didn't have the same baggage as Julia Springer, either.

As I tightened the sash on my robe, the smile on my face widened, and I felt something inside myself click and fall into place. The thought of being Sam's wife suddenly seemed to be the finest thing in the world.

I reached for the phone beside the bed to call him, then drew back my hand. No, I thought, better to ponder this in my heart a while longer. I needed to try it and test it, and make sure it wasn't a rash and impulsive decision, one that I would regret for the rest of my days. For all I knew, a poor night's sleep would make a world of difference in how I looked at such a life-changing decision.

In spite of the surge of joy I felt at the thought of actually marrying Sam, my mind drifted to something Hazel Marie'd said the day before. While I dressed, it came to me that my undergarments could use some refurbishing and replacing. Lord, all I had were plain, unadorned cotton brassieres, slips, and step-ins, without an inch of lace or picot edging anywhere. Maybe, I thought, it wouldn't hurt to purchase a few lacy, see-through things. Not that I expected anybody to see, or see through them besides me any time soon, but there was always the possibility that I'd be in a wreck and have to be taken to the hospital. And Hazel Marie had once said that pretty underclothing made a woman feel confident and self-assured. I could use a little of both, so if all it took were a few flimsy items, it'd be money well spent. Maybe a silken gown and robe would help, as well. Even though there's nothing like flannel for warmth, I had to admit that it didn't do a whole lot for one's appearance.

I mentally shook myself as I headed down the stairs. Why in the world were such trivial matters cluttering up my mind? I was no Norma Cantrell, nor an Emma Sue Ledbetter, either.

I'd hardly gotten to the foot of the stairs when the doorbell rang, so I veered from my progress toward the kitchen and went to answer it.

A large man, bundled up in a tan raincoat with the hood pulled over his head, stood on the other side of the screen door. He huddled inside his coat, his hands jammed into his pockets, as a blustery wind blew rain across the porch.

"Mrs. Springer?" he sang out. "Sorry for

the intrusion so early in the morning. Wonder if I could take a minute of your time?"

I unlatched the storm door and held it open for him. "Come in. It's awful wet out there."

"Yes, ma'am, it is that," he said as he came into the living room and I closed the door behind him. He pushed his hood back, giving me a look at his florid face and brown, gray-streaked hair that was pulled back into a thin ponytail, of all things. His hands were large and chapped, the knuckles lined with grime. As he unbuttoned his coat, I could see his plaid flannel shirt straining at his midsection. A working man, I thought, a laborer of some kind, and I mentally prepared myself to tell him that my gutters had already been cleaned and that it was either too late or too early to do any pruning.

"And you are?" I asked, wondering why in the world I'd invited a perfect stranger into my house. The sounds that Lillian was making in the kitchen and Little Lloyd's voice talking to her reassured me.

"Name's Dwayne Dooley, ma'am, and I'm here on a mission to do the Lord's work in Abbotsville and environs."

"Well, I say," I murmured, somewhat taken aback. It was too early in the morning for door-to-door missionaries, and I didn't ordinarily accept pamphlets, newsletters, or tracts from them any time of the day. But I'd let him in, so it behooved me to at least listen with politeness. "Very commendable, I'm sure. But I support the Presbyterian church across the street, and I'm not interested in donating to any other cause at this time." To tell the truth, I'd about had my fill of donating to any and every cause, what with all the appeals that had come in the mail and on the telephone right before Christmas, a poor time of the year in my opinion to be asking for money when you had your own family to do for.

"No'm," he said with a quick grin that revealed yellowed teeth. "I'm not soliciting funds. I've come to see you about some property you own south of town, that twenty acres or so right off County Line Road. Now, I'm not in a position to buy it outright, but I was wondering if you'd listen to a lease arrangement."

Well, if it was a business deal he was after . . . "Have a seat, Mr. Dooley."

"No'm, I won't do that. I'm wet and I been

out tramping through the woods, gettin' the lay of the land, so to speak, and I don't want to set on your fine furniture." And with that, his milky brown eyes took a survey of the room.

"Well," I said, "that acreage has been sitting there for years just waiting for the right opportunity. What do you have in mind?"

A smile crinkled his face, although there were a gracious plenty of wrinkles on it already. I couldn't figure out his age, fiftyish maybe, or a little more, although I knew that hard work could age a man. But when he started talking, his words came out in the cadence of Lillian's radio preachers. I moved back a step.

"The Lord has called me to proclaim his holy name, and he has led me right to your property. It's near to town, it's here to stay, it's got room to spare. If I could only find the words to open up my vision to you, Mrs. Springer, why, you'd jump at the chance to be a part of what the Lord has put in my heart to do. I didn't want to at first, I'll be honest about it. I kept arguing with him, but he worked on my heart and since he's the boss, I'm doing what he wants. The Lord's working on your heart, too. I can see it in the kindness of your face."

Lillian poked her head around the kitchen door, attracted by the sound of preaching so early in the morning.

"Mr. Dooley!" I said, right sharply. "I'm a businesswoman, not a charitable foundation, so don't count on any trace of kindness you might see in my face. If you want to lease that property, I suggest you see my attorney, Binkie Enloe Bates, whose husband is Deputy Coleman Bates of the sheriff's department." I always liked to make my connections clear, in case anyone was thinking of taking advantage of me.

He shifted from one foot to the other, giving off a whiff of woodsmoke, or maybe tobacco smoke. "Well, I might of got ahead of myself a little, begging your pardon, but I already had a lawyer draw up a lease agreement. Just to save time and trouble, you understand." He reached into an inside pocket and pulled out two copies of a long, legal-size document. As he handed them to me, I recognized the wording of a standard lease, having seen many similar forms before.

"Now, see, Mrs. Springer," Mr. Dooley went on, pointing with a thick finger, "I took the liberty of making it a five-year lease with options to extend. But I left some places for you to fill in, like the amount you're willing to lease it for. I guess I might as well be honest and say I hope you'll see your way clear to giving a Christian enterprise a little break on what you'll take for it. But wait now." He held up his hand as I opened my mouth to assure him that I wasn't interested in giving breaks to any kind of enterprise, Christian or otherwise.

"I'm not here as a beggar," he earnestly assured me. "I got good people supporting me, so if it's not unreasonable, I can afford to pay a decent price. See, Mrs. Springer, the Lord's laid this on my heart some few years ago, and I been making my plans and savin' up for it."

"Just what do you plan to do out there, Mr. Dooley? I need to know that before I sign anything."

"I'm aiming to build a religious theme park, Mrs. Springer, one that'll bring Christian folk from far and wide to walk where Jesus walked. And that's what I'll call it— it come to me one night in a dream— The Walk Where Jesus Walked Christian Theme Park. See, first off, you'll come to the

manger and it'll be all set up with real ani-
mals and hay and so forth. Then there'll be
his earthly daddy's carpenter's shop in a
real-live village. And a temple, which'll be
the hardest to set up right, seein' as how I'm
not right sure what it looked like. Then
the streets of Jerusalem of course. One of
the highlights is gonna be the cave where
Lazarus was buried. Can't you see it now,
ma'am? The man who'll play Jesus will yell,
'Lazarus, come forth!' and out he'll come all
wrapped up in his burial clothes. I'm thinking of having some kinda sulfur mixture in
the cave with him, so all the folks'll get the
stench of the tomb, just like the Bible says.
Then I'll have the Lord fishing in a boat on
the pond, and we'll rig up something that'll
make a lot of lashing waves, with thunder
booming out over the loudspeakers, so that
folks'll feel like they're really there. Then
we'll have the hill called Golgotha with the
three crosses and . . ."

"Don't tell me you're going to hang somebody!"

"Oh, no'm, not exactly, just tied up, with
lots of fake blood running down. It'll be like
a outdoor play but, see, people can walk
along the highways and byways that Jesus

walked and pretend like it's all happening in the present day. I tell you, Mrs. Springer, it'll be just like being there, and, with your permission, I'm gonna put in some trailer hookups—it's all there in the lease. That way, whole families can come and spend a day or two getting close to the Lord. We're all living in trailers, ourselves, so it'd be mighty convenient for us, too."

I stood and stared at him, wondering if the man had good sense. "You certainly have some expansive plans, Mr. Dooley."

"Yessum, I do," he said with evident pride. "But when you're working for the King of Kings, you can afford to. Ask and it shall be given you, he says, and that's what I'm doing. Coming here and asking you about leasing to us."

"Well, I appreciate that, but my attorney usually makes these decisions for me," I said, and watched his face fall.

He shuffled his mud-caked boots and said, "Then I thank you, ma'am, for hearing me out." He reached for the lease in my hand. "Your property was our first choice, but there's another tract that'll probably do as well. I'll run on and talk to that owner."

I held on to the papers, not wanting to

lose an eager lessee and the income he represented. "However, since you've already gone to the trouble," I said, indicating the lease, "I don't know that I have any objection. Especially since that land has been setting there doing nothing but costing me tax money."

I took the copies of the lease to a table and looked them over carefully. "I assume the area you've mapped out here is correct? There's a lot of undeveloped land out there, you know, and not all of it belongs to me. I hope you know which is which, because I sure don't."

"Oh, yes ma'am," he said. "Walked it myself, from stake to stake, every step of the way. Now here's what I hope you'll let me have it for." He wrote a figure down on a scrap of paper again taken from his pocket. I frowned at it and wrote another one beside it. After a little more back and forth, we came to an agreement that pleased me since it would cover the taxes and a little more. And I'd be getting some improvements on the land, although the way he was proposing to improve it wouldn't have been my first choice.

I was, in fact, feeling quite pleased with

how I was handling the negotiations. Business dealings were not all that complicated and difficult to understand, even if Binkie, and Wesley Lloyd before her, thought I needed my hand held before signing anything. This would prove I knew how to manage a simple lease agreement to my advantage.

"One other thing you might consider," I said, as I signed and dated both copies of the lease and handed the pen to him for his signature. "What will the local churches think of this plan of yours? If you're going to do any preaching out there, especially on Sundays, you might have a problem on your hands."

"Oh, we'll work with the locals, don't worry about that. I already been going around to a lot of the churches in the county, letting them know what's gonna come along and help fill their pews. We don't aim to set up as a competition, 'cause we want to be a help and a support to all those who're laboring in the Lord's vineyard."

"You keep saying *we,* Mr. Dooley. Who all is working with you?"

"A small group of brothers and a few

sisters who've dedicated theirselves to taking the word of the Lord to those who need it, and we've got us a sponsor that's behind us every step of the way. See, we could preach and we could hold revivals and we could have conferences, but when I had this dream of walking where Jesus walked, every one of us saw it was something that would be mighty special to a lot of folks. So we give up our jobs and set ourselves to making that dream come true."

Then to my astonishment, he pulled out a wad of cash and peeled off enough hundred-dollar bills to cover the first six months. "Hope you don't mind cash," he said. "I like to pay as I go."

"Why, not at all," I murmured, taken aback at the curling bills he counted out in my hand.

"Well, Mr. Dooley, I wish you all the luck in the world," I said, pleased to be doing business with a man who paid up front, but wondering how he expected to build the land of Galilee on twenty acres of scrub land. "I expect you'll need it."

He smiled broadly, so much so that his eyes squinched together. "The Lord provides, Mrs. Springer, as he's proved time and time again. Now, I'll let you get on with your day, and may the Lord bless and keep you for the good deed you done for us." He folded his copy of the lease and put it in his pocket. Then he pulled his hood up before heading out into the rain again.

"Thank you, Mr. Dooley," I responded, quite satisfied with the morning's business. I figured that the property was so far out of town that I wouldn't have to see whatever mishmash he erected on it. And if I could realize a little profit on land I wasn't using anyway, then all the better.

I closed the door behind him and continued on my way to the kitchen.

"Lillian," I said, as I headed for the coffee pot, patting Little Lloyd's shoulder as I passed. "Looks as if this county's going to get exactly what it's been needing—another preacher with something to sell."

{ Chapter 4 }

I recognized the resonant voice as soon as I answered the phone a few days later.

"Miss Julia?"

"Why, Pastor Ledbetter, how nice to hear from you," I said, bypassing the truth for the sake of good manners. The pastor was not known for keeping close contact with the members of his congregation, leaving visitation up to a group of designated pastoral helpers. So to hear directly from him usually meant big trouble somewhere.

"Miss Julia," he went on, ignoring the pleasantries, "I wonder if you'd mind stepping across the street to my office. There're a few matters I'd like to discuss with you."

My word, I thought, had Pastor Ledbetter already heard of my dealings with Mr. Dooley and him hardly out of my house? Of course, I could name a number of other matters that might've prompted a telephone call, but I didn't know what the pastor thought I had to do with them. That hadn't stopped him in the past, however, for he and I had crossed words and swords several times before. I wasn't all that eager to face another counseling session.

"Well, it's raining out there again, pastor. Wouldn't it be just as easy for you to come over here? Lillian has made some Russian tea that I know you'd enjoy."

There was a pause as the phone line hummed between us. "I know I shouldn't ask you to get out in this weather," he finally said. "But this is a matter for privacy, and you have a lot of people in and out at your house."

Oh, Lord, I thought to myself, he's going to ask me about Norma, and what am I going to say? But then, that didn't make sense, for Norma would be right outside his office door, which was not exactly conducive to privacy.

My word, what if it was about Emma Sue?

"I'll be right over," I said, hung up and went to get my raincoat and umbrella.

After braving another spring shower, I

was glad to get inside the church building, but not so glad to see Norma behind her desk in the pastor's outer office. For once, though, she didn't give me the third degree about my presence. She busied herself at the computer, nodded toward the door to let me know I was expected, and barely had the courtesy to speak. Which suited me fine, for I couldn't imagine carrying on a conversation with her while images I couldn't control danced in my mind. The mayor, of all people. Why, the man was as arrogant as only a short, fat man can be. Who'd want him? But, as I'd long noted, there's no accounting for taste.

I nodded my head back at her and went through to the pastor's cherry-paneled office. He immediately stood and came around his desk to see me to one of the damask-covered wing chairs facing his desk.

"Thank you for coming, Miss Julia," he said, as solicitous as if he needed funding to meet the budget projections. But the Every-Member-Canvass was months behind us, so I didn't think it could be that. Besides, my pledge had been as generous as ever, so if he needed more he'd have to wrangle it out of somebody else.

I unbuttoned my coat as I settled in the visitor's chair and watched as he took a seat in his leather executive chair.

"One of the matters I want to discuss," he started, as he stacked some papers together and pushed them aside, "concerns this religious theme park that I understand you have something to do with."

That surprised me so that I couldn't help but laugh. "*I* have something to do with it? Not at all, pastor, other than leasing some unused land to them for the purpose of erecting it. You surely don't think I'd be actively involved in such a scheme, do you? Theme parks, in general, are hardly my cup of tea."

"That's what I was led to believe," he said, leaning back in his chair so that it swayed with the movement. "Although it certainly didn't sound like something you'd be interested in."

"Who led you to believe such a thing?"

"Ah, let me see." He leaned forward and searched his desk for a notepad. "I wrote it down. The man didn't have a card. Here it is, a Dwayne Dooley. He came to see me to let me know his plans for the theme park and to ask if I'd encourage my congregation to support it. Frankly, I'm somewhat skeptical of unorthodox groups, as you know. After we prayed together, though, I realized that at least Mr. Dooley's heart is in the right place. But when he said that he was hoping for your help, I thought I'd better caution you. You don't want to be too closely involved until you know exactly what they're up to."

"I had the same feeling," I told him, marveling at the notion that he and I could see eye to eye on anything.

"Well, then," he said, reaching for a pencil. He began tapping the eraser end on the desk, while studying the action with an intensity that it hardly warranted. Frowning, he said again, "Well, then. I guess there's not much we can do to stop it. It'll be outside the town limits, so no help from zoning restrictions. It's just that I'd hate to see gullible Christians taken in by scam artists, if that's what they are."

"I don't know about that, pastor," I said, feeling a thrill of pleasure to be able to turn the tables on him. "I admit that I think they're biting off more than they can chew, but you can hardly fault them for wanting to set up an area for people to Walk Where Jesus Walked. I mean, it's not exactly a unique idea. You know about that evangelical group that asks What Would Jesus Drive, which I'm here to tell you offends any number of pickup truck owners. Even Sam Murdoch has talked about buying a Dodge Ram, and he says he thinks Jesus would too if he was still in the carpentry business. And then there's that youth campaign that asks What Would Jesus Do, which sells bracelets and necklaces and bumper stickers and I don't know what all. Seems to me that Mr. Dooley is just jumping on the bandwagon."

Pastor Ledbetter shot me a dark look. We both knew that he'd been on the same bandwagon with that WWJD business, urging the young people in the church to ask that every time they turned around and before they did anything.

"The What Would Jesus Do movement is an entirely different matter," he said in a way that admitted no doubt in his mind. "Mr. Dooley may be setting up a money-making scheme to bilk naive Christians, while the WWJD movement aims to help young people find their way through worldly distractions, not to relieve them of their money."

"It sure does offer a lot for sale."

Pastor Ledbetter appeared not to have heard me, for his attention was now focused on the pencil which he was running up and down through his fingers. I'd had about enough of the conversation. There had been nothing of a private nature discussed, certainly nothing that required my coming out on a rainy day to listen to.

I pulled my coat closer and prepared to take my leave. "Well, if that's it, pastor, I'll be going now. I wouldn't be surprised if I came down with some kind of foreign flu after this little expedition, so I need to be on my way."

He straightened up then, put down the pencil and looked directly at me. "That's not all I wanted to talk about," he said, then bowed his head.

I determined right then that, if he intended to take off in a long-winded prayer, I intended to stop it in its tracks. I buttoned my coat and stood up.

"Miss Julia," he said, wiping his hand across his brow, his eyes fixed on the top of his desk. "Please don't go. I know you and

I have had our ups and downs, but I'm at my wit's end. I need some help and advice."

From *me?* I couldn't believe it. The man must've been in a sorry state to be willing to admit to me, his most adversarial member, that he needed help. I unbuttoned my coat and settled back to await whatever was forthcoming.

"I'll be glad to help any way I can," I said, my nerves zinging inside of me. Which would it be? Norma or Emma Sue? And what was I going to say about either one? Far be it from me to carry tales, even if half the town thought they were both carrying on extracurricular activities.

"This is difficult for me to talk about," he said, his shoulders slumping heavily.

"It's Emma Sue," he moaned, covering his face with his hands. "I don't know what's gotten into her. I can't talk to her anymore. She doesn't listen to anything I say, and she refuses to realize the consequences of her actions. I'm so worried about her, I don't know what to do. I thought, if you pointed out the error of her ways, she might listen. She thinks so much of you, you know."

That was news to me, but I nodded encouragingly.

"As you know," he went on, "Satan has many faces and exhibits himself in many ways. I fear for Emma Sue, but she's put up a stubborn wall between us. It would be a great blessing if you would find out what's going on and help me to help her. I'm afraid she's having some sort of spiritual break-down, and I need to intervene before it's too late."

I twisted my hands together in my lap, knowing this had to be handled very care-fully. "Just what are her symptoms, pas-tor?"

"I'm sure you've noticed some of them," he said, giving me a quick look. "That mo-torcycle Poker Run last fall, for one thing. That was the first time in all our years to-gether that she outright defied me and went against my wishes. It was a burden to my soul to see her flaunt herself in such a pub-lic way."

I pursed my mouth, waiting for what I was sure would come next, which was that he blamed me for getting her involved in that motorcycle fundraiser. But he surprised me by not mentioning my baleful influence at all.

"After that," he went on, "it was one

thing after another. She decided to go into a bridal consulting business with LuAnne Conover, and you and I both know there's not a lick of business sense between the two of them. Now they've spent I don't know how much money on business cards, stationery, and office equipment. And, Miss Julia, they don't even have an office, much less any clients. They're using one of our bedrooms, fiddling around for hours every day, making plans, deciding on color schemes and fixing up portfolios to show to prospective brides."

"Well," I said, "all that seems to be the way to proceed. I'm not sure that indicates any serious problem. I'd think you'd be proud of her for putting her talent to use."

"Her *talent!* She doesn't have any talent!" He ran his hand through his hair in his agitation. "The only thing she can do is make clothes on that expensive sewing machine nothing would do but I had to buy her. Now, she says she's moved past homemade clothes."

I, for one, was glad to hear it. Whatever Emma Sue's talent was, it certainly did not lie in fashion.

"One's interests do change over the

years, pastor. I expect that's all that's going on with Emma Sue, and I don't see that it's anything that should worry you."

"You haven't heard the worst of it," he said. The man was slumped so far over, I feared he was going to put his head on the desk and begin sobbing, the thought of which almost unnerved me.

"Well, let's hear it. What's the worst?"

"She's . . ." He stopped, swallowed hard and finally managed to say, "she's dyed her hair. And painted her face and shortened her skirts and bought spike-heeled shoes and tells me I need to smarten up." He rubbed his hand across his face again. "When she came home from that appointment last night, looking like a . . . a streetwalker, I had to get down on my knees and pray for her. But this morning, even after all my praying, she put it all on again!"

I didn't know whether to laugh or cry, but his anguish was so obvious that I made the effort to control myself. I let the silence lengthen as I sought for something reassuring to say. As for my own thoughts, I thought it was high time that Emma Sue tried to beautify herself. All that naturalness she was so committed to needed more help than it'd been getting.

But according to the pastor, she had made some major changes. I couldn't wait to see her.

"It may not be so bad, pastor," I said. "Most women like to look their best, and maybe that's all Emma Sue's doing. Trying to be fashionable doesn't necessarily mean she's on the road to wrack and ruin."

He rested both elbows on the desk and propped his forehead on the heels of his hands. "I don't want her to be fashionable. I want my wife back the way she was, not tarted up like a, like a *tart*." He raised his head, seemingly stricken with his own choice of words. "Forgive me, Miss Julia. I got carried away, but I'm so frustrated I don't know what to do. Emma Sue's gotten herself up to look like the wife of a television evangelist. Every time I look at her, it unsettles me something awful, and I'm her *husband*. We all know that it's incumbent upon every Christian woman to avoid circumstances that tempt men to sin. I ask you, Miss Julia, what if she stirs the loins of every man who sees her?"

My word, I thought with a jolt, is he saying that she stirs *his* loins, too? I fought back a mental picture of a commotion in Pastor Ledbetter's nether regions. But if that was his problem, what was wrong with being stirred, since their union was both legal and church sanctioned?

As I kept my silence, mainly because I didn't know what to say and was afraid I'd laugh if I opened my mouth, he straightened in his chair and said, "It makes me cringe to look at her and know what people must be thinking."

"Seems to me you'd be better off knowing what Emma Sue's thinking," I said with some asperity. "I wouldn't worry about other people."

"I have to," he moaned. "In my position, I have to worry about what people think."

I bit my lip before voicing my next thought, aware that I might be telling him more than he wanted to know. I went ahead and did it anyway. "Maybe Emma Sue's trying to get your attention. Have you thought about that?"

"She *has* my attention," he said. "She's my wife. What more could she want?"

"I'm sure I don't know," I said, since being his wife would be the last thing I'd want.

"Well, pastor, I'm not sure what I can do, but I'll try my best. Although I must admit that a woman's judicious use of cosmetics does not automatically send me into a tailspin. But since you feel so strongly about it, I would recommend that you pray about it. As you've told me so many times, prayer is our only recourse. Let go and let God, I believe is the way you put it."

He didn't look as if he believed me or appreciated my turning back on him the stock answer he'd always had to my problems.

I took my leave then, assuring him that I would exert every effort to reform Emma Sue and put her back on her former track. As I went through the outer office and past Norma, who was just too engrossed in paperwork to speak, I couldn't resist shaking her up a little.

"I expect you already know this, Norma," I said, knowing full well that she did not. "But the pastor is deeply concerned about the worrisome activities of somebody very close to him. I hope you'll put him on your prayer list as he wrestles with the problem."

A flash of fear blazed in her eyes as she glanced up at me, and I felt a flash of shame for what I'd said. But then, her mouth tightened and her eyes got hard. "There're a lot of people on my prayer list," she said, "because *some* more than others really need it."

I felt my own mouth tighten. "Well, Norma, for once we're in agreement." I pulled my coat together and sailed out of there.

{Chapter 5}

I went flying into the house, slamming the front door behind me. "Hazel Marie! Where are you?"

"In here," she called. "In the kitchen with Lillian."

I hurried that way, flinging off my coat as I went. Hazel Marie was sitting at the table, working on a piece of cross-stitch that she'd been struggling with for weeks. Home Is Where the Heart Is was the slogan on it, and she aimed to have it framed for Mr. Pickens if she ever finished it.

I'd told her that if she was going to spend that amount of time on stitchery, she'd do better to work in needlepoint, which would last ever so much longer. But she'd never been able to get the hang of the bas-ketweave stitch.

"Wait till I tell you what the pastor wants

me to do," I said, collapsing into a chair and patting my breast. I had a tiny tug of conscience about revealing what he'd called a matter of privacy. But then, he'd never said it was a matter of confidence. Besides, I was going to need help in deciding if Emma Sue really was headed for hell in a handbasket, painted face and all. Or if, as I suspected, the pastor himself was way off base.

So I decided to drag out the telling by starting out the way he had. "First thing he said," I said, "was to warn me off any involvement with that theme park it looks like we're getting. He thinks they may be fly-by-nights, and I totally agreed with him. Which was a wonderment in itself."

"Theme park!" Hazel Marie almost came out of her chair. "We're getting a theme park here? Oh, that's wonderful. I love those things, but I haven't been to one in years. Are they going to have big-name stars? Oh, I hope so." She grabbed Lillian's arm in her excitement. "Maybe Tim McGraw or, oh, maybe Kenny Chesney! I love that song about his tractor. He can sing the dog out of that one."

"Hazel Marie," I said, "it's not that kind of

theme park. The only stars they'll have are amateur actors playing Lazarus and the Samaritan woman. I don't believe they'll have any singing at all, much less any guitar playing. But listen, the theme park wasn't the main thing Pastor Ledbetter wanted to talk about."

Then, paying little mind to Hazel Marie's disappointment over no star billing at the theme park, I went on to tell her and Lillian what had really been on the pastor's mind and what he wanted me to do. "Now," I ended up, "how am I going to encourage Emma Sue to go back to being his meek little shadow, when I am absolutely delighted that she's making something of herself at last?"

"Did you tell him that?" Hazel Marie asked, putting aside her needlework.

"Oh, no, I wouldn't do that. The man was so upset and under so much strain, I wouldn't have attempted such a thing."

"And 'sides," Lillian said, "the preacher might be right. Don't nobody know but him how bad off Miz Ledbetter be."

"Well," I said, struck by Lillian's observation. "There's the voice of reason right there. I've been assuming that Pastor Ledbetter just feared losing his control over her but, for all we know, Emma Sue could be making herself over to look like the town harlot. Maybe we shouldn't jump to conclusions."

"Yessum," Lillian said. "I think that be best."

I shot her a quick glare, then turned to Hazel Marie. "What do you think?"

"I think we should invite Emma Sue out to lunch. That way, we can see how she fixes herself up to be in public. The Main Street Tea Shoppe's under new management, you know, and we can tell her we want to try it out."

"Good thinking, Hazel Marie. I'll call her right now and see if she can meet us tomorrow."

I noticed Lillian's look of disappointment, so I said, "We'll invite her back here after lunch. To see your cross-stitch, Hazel Marie. Maybe you'll have a question for her on how to frame it or something. She won't suspect a thing, and Lillian will be able to give us her opinion, too."

~⚜~

Hazel Marie and I arrived early at the tea shoppe and took a table toward the back so we could talk without being overheard. Not that the place was crowded, but most of the diners were seated near the front.

As Hazel Marie and I looked over the menu, a delicious thrill surged through me as the thought of becoming Sam's wife came to mind again. It was a possibility that I'd been turning over and examining in my quiet moments, trying to look at it in the cold light of reason, rather than in the hot flame of emotion. Which, in spite of what some people might think about aged people, was still a force to be reckoned with. Even though I'd had to expend so much time and thought dealing with Mr. Dooley, counseling with the pastor, and worrying about Emma Sue, I realized that the dream I'd only played with in my mind had apparently firmed itself into a decision.

My heart thumped so suddenly and so loudly that I thought surely Hazel Marie would hear it and ask if I needed a doctor.

I wanted so badly to tell her, but Sam deserved to hear it first. I didn't know when his proposal had changed in my mind from a laughing matter to a matter of serious import, but I knew it had. Maybe it'd been when I'd gotten out of bed the other morning so light on my feet that I didn't even moan when I straightened up. But for now, I intended to hold the secret close to my heart, and tell Sam when the time was right. Then I would announce it in the newspaper and tell everyone I knew and, if the preacher would let me, ring the church bells, too. I didn't know that I'd ever been so filled with joy and excitement, so it was all I could do to decide what to order for lunch.

When Emma Sue came through the door and stood looking around for us, I simply did not recognize her. My first uncharitable thought was that somebody'd had an appointment at the Good Shepherd Funeral Home instead of at Velma's.

I got a real jolt when I realized who it was. When I did, I whispered, "My word, Hazel Marie. Is that her?"

Emma Sue saw us and began weaving her way through the tables. Heads turned as she passed, most doing a double-take, unsure of what they were seeing.

I'll admit I was stunned. Emma Sue's hair was the honey-blonde color of Hazel Marie's and it was teased up in a bouffant 'do like Norma Cantrell's. Imitating Hazel Marie was one thing, but copying Norma was an entirely different matter. I couldn't help but think that Emma Sue suspected her husband of having a thing for Norma, which in and of itself was enough to split the church wide open, and this was her way of showing him that she could backcomb with the best of them.

As she came toward us, I could see that her face was splotched with purplish eye-shadow, rose blush, and shiny fuschia lip-stick. Her eyebrows had been darkened, and she had on the longest eyelashes I'd ever seen outside of a package in Eckerd's Drugstore.

When she got to our table, she took off her coat to reveal a tight pink turtleneck sweater above a pleated gray skirt that hit her right above the knees. A sight that shocked me, since in all the years I'd known her, I'd never once caught sight of them. Below that, she wore knee-high patent leather boots with heels that she'd not yet quite mastered. Her youthful attire would've been considerably improved if Emma Sue's figure had had any shape to it at all. The poor woman barely had a waist, very little bulk above it and too much below it.

She teetered to a stop in front of us and asked, "Well, what do you think?"

That was Emma Sue for you, blunt to a fault. I arranged my face from its shocked state and said, "Have a seat, Emma Sue, and give me time to get used to the change."

"You look lovely," Hazel Marie said, as kind and untruthful as only she could be.

Before anything else could be said, a waitress appeared beside our table. She couldn't keep her eyes off Emma Sue, since by now everybody had recognized her and, in this small town, knew she was the Presbyterian preacher's wife.

"I'll have the fruit plate," Emma Sue said. "I'm working out now and I have to watch my weight."

"Good for you," Hazel Marie said. "I'll have the chef's salad. What will you have, Miss Julia?"

"A decent lunch," I returned. "Give me a cup of mushroom soup and a chicken salad sandwich on toasted white with lettuce and plenty of mayonnaise."

With one last lingering look at Emma Sue, the waitress took our menus and left to place our orders.

Emma Sue leaned across the table and said, "Now, what do you really think? And I want your honest opinion."

No, she didn't. That was the last thing she wanted. So I tried to be tactful and helpful at the same time. "It takes a while to learn to use all the beauty products on the market nowadays. So if you really want my opinion, Emma Sue, I'd say a little more practice wouldn't hurt."

"I knew you wouldn't approve, Julia," she said through her teeth. "You're as bad as Larry, always wanting things to stay as they are. Well, you're just going to have to put up with it, because I like it. And I don't care what anybody says."

"Did I say I didn't like it? No, I did not, because I do. I think you're to be commended for trying to improve on your natural state. All I'm saying is that it takes a steady hand to use all those brushes and creams and colors."

"Velma showed me how to apply my makeup," she said, as if Velma were the last word in cosmetology, which, take it from me, she was not. Emma Sue leaned across the table at me, and almost hissed, "At least

I'm trying, which is more than I can say for you."

Well, I hadn't invited her to lunch to be criticized, but before I could remind her of that fact, Hazel Marie, who couldn't stand any kind of confrontation, said, "I'll tell you what let's do. As soon as we have lunch, let's go to our house and have a makeup party. I have a bunch of cosmetics, and we can try different looks. Emma Sue, I do love your hair."

Emma Sue turned a grateful face to her. "I told Velma I wanted your exact color. I hope you don't mind."

"Of course not. It is just gorgeous and quite becoming."

Hazel Marie had the warmest heart. Emma Sue's hair was neither gorgeous nor becoming, for she had a sallow complexion that did not lend itself to a honey blonde hair color. Still, I had to concede that it looked better than her previous mouse color that had sprouted sprigs of gray around her face.

When our plates were served, Emma Sue only picked at hers. She was more occupied with casting glances around the room, having become aware of the whispers and stares that were aimed at her. She put her hand along the side of her face to shield herself from view, and her shoulders began to slump in on themselves. Far from her head-high attitude when she first arrived, she was now sinking back into her usual self-consciousness. I saw tears gathering in her eyes, and wondered how much Kleenex I had in my purse.

"Larry hates it," she whispered, dabbing at her eyes with a napkin. "He hates it all. He says I've destroyed my testimony, and he doesn't know who I am anymore."

"For goodness sake," I said. "You are still Emma Sue Ledbetter, regardless of the outer covering." Unfortunately, that was true. It was too bad that all those makeover articles in magazines got things backward. As far as I was concerned, a makeover should be from inside out, not from outside in. But since I'd not tried either way, I wasn't all that firm in my opinion.

"Oh, phooey on him," Hazel Marie said, laying her hand on Emma Sue's arm. "What do men know anyway? I'll show you how to blend in shadows and we'll try some different colors to see what's best for you. Velma doesn't know but one way to do it, and you should've seen me when I let her do a makeover. Pink is all she knows. Just wait, Emma Sue, you're going to be a knockout, and if the pastor doesn't appreciate it, everybody else will."

I shot a frowning glance at her. She was getting too close to the rumors floating around about Emma Sue.

"Well, of course, she's only doing it for her husband in the first place," I said, then suddenly realized that I might've put my foot in my mouth, too. If Emma Sue feared she was losing her husband to another woman, it was not up to me to remind her of it. One thing I know for certain, when you don't know who knows what, anything you say can come back and smack you in the face.

Emma Sue sat up straight and looked me right in the eye as if my remark brought her purpose back to mind. "I'm not doing it for him at all," she said. "I need a change for myself. I'm tired of looking in the mirror and cringing. I'm tired of having people gravitate to Larry and overlook me. I'm tired of being a nobody, and looking like one, too. I want somebody to notice me, for a change. I'm a person. I have something to offer. I'm not just the preacher's wife who's not worth a second look. I can have a life of my own."

"You go, girl," Hazel Marie murmured, smiling.

"Well, but, Emma Sue," I cautioned, "you have to consider the fact that sudden changes take some getting used to." It came to me that she might really be undergoing temptation as the gossips had it and the pastor suspected. But whether it was from Satan, the mayor, or some unknown suitor lurking in the shadows, I couldn't say. What I could say was that, one way or another, Emma Sue was headed for trouble. And so was the pastor but, in my opinion, he pretty much deserved whatever he got.

{Chapter 6}

When we got back to the house, Hazel Marie led us down the hall to her bedroom. There, she told Emma Sue to sit at the dressing table, which was covered with every beauty product known to woman. I took a seat to the side so Hazel Marie would have plenty of room for her ministrations, and I would have a clear view.

Lillian came in on the pretext of offering refreshments, which we refused, having just finished lunch. Lillian stood in the door for a minute or so, watching as Hazel Marie draped a towel around Emma Sue's shoulders. After getting a good look at Emma Sue's pitiful attempt to recreate Velma's makeup application, Lillian cut her eyes over at me while her eyebrows went up to her hairline. Then she left us to it, since she knew that Emma Sue would not appreciate an audience. Lillian had a sensitive soul.

"First, we'll take all this off," Hazel Marie said, swabbing at Emma Sue's face with a cold cream–laden tissue. "Then I'll show you a few tricks of the trade."

Emma Sue's eyes filled and threatened to overflow as she watched the face she'd been born with begin to emerge as Hazel Marie mopped off the heavy covering and the false eyelashes. Hazel Marie pretended not to notice, just kept up a steady stream of reassuring patter. I was struck with her professionalism and the confident way she went about her work. I recalled that Hazel Marie had once intended to study hair dressing with a specialty in nails, and seeing her now in action, I thought it a shame that her education had been so rudely disrupted.

"Now," Hazel Marie said, throwing away the last tissue, "we have a clean face to start with. A little moisturizer, then we'll find the right foundation for you. I have several shades, because I get darker in the summer, but we can mix a couple if we have to." She began testing a few along Emma Sue's jawline until she was satisfied that she had a good match. As she began to smooth it on Emma Sue's face, Hazel Marie said, "You have beautiful skin. You must take real good care of it."

"I just keep it clean." Then Emma Sue began to cloud up again. "There's never been anything on my face but soap and water and a little lotion. Larry always said that a woman's inner beauty shouldn't be hidden with cosmetics." She sniffed, then went on. "The Bible college I went to didn't approve of makeup, either. So all these years I've thought it a sin to try to improve on what God made, but I don't think he ever intended me to look like this. I look terrible."

"No, you don't," Hazel Marie said soothingly. "Just you wait, the right color scheme is going to knock your socks off." She stood back and surveyed her handiwork. "That's good. Not too heavy, and it blends right in with your skin tones. Now," she went on as she searched through the jars and bottles and compacts on the dressing table, "I think a little blush on the coral side, something very natural looking."

As she applied the blush to Emma Sue's cheeks, she said, "Oh, you have excellent bones, Emma Sue."

"I do?"

"Just wait till I give you some shadows and do your eyes. You won't believe yourself. Now I'm going to darken your eyebrows just a little with a light brown pencil. See, you just feather it in like this. Now, some taupe eye shadow with a little white blended in here and here to bring out your eyes. Then a little liner and some dark brown mascara. Your lashes are so long, you don't need false ones. Just be sure you put mascara all the way out to the end. See, like this."

Hazel Marie worked as she talked, calming Emma Sue down with her compliments and making me marvel at what she was accomplishing. I declare, if Hazel Marie and Little Lloyd hadn't had more money than they knew what to do with, thanks to the child's inheritance, I would've set her up in the beauty shop business. She would've run Velma out of town within a year.

"Open your mouth just a little," Hazel Marie said and Emma Sue complied, opening up like a little bird. "I'm outlining your lips with a brown pencil, and we'll stay in that color range for your lipstick. I'll tell you right now, Emma Sue, pink tones are not for you. You are a true autumn, and you should stick to fall colors when you pick out your clothes. You know, like the golds and rusts and sage greens. What you want to do is wear a block of color, not break it up with one color on top and another on the bottom. A block of color will make you look tall and elegant."

I looked down at my gray shirtwaist and wondered if that qualified as a block of color.

"And," Hazel Marie went on, "if you don't mind my saying so, Emma Sue, I'd like to see you tell Velma to put a light brown color on your hair next time. Then she can pull some strands through to give you blond streaks and highlights. It'll go so much better with your coloring. I can wear my hair in this honey blond shade because I'm so fair, but you have a warm, healthy glow to your complexion, and you need something that will complement it."

I'd never realized how tactful Hazel Marie could be. Listening to her ramble on about Emma Sue's bones and complexion made me realize I'd never have made it in the beauty business.

Hazel Marie stepped back and cocked

her head, surveying her work. Then she said, "Now, look in the mirror and tell me what you think."

Emma Sue gazed at herself for so long I thought she was too stunned to say anything. She almost was. But then she almost ruined Hazel Marie's creation as her eyes glazed over with tears.

"Oh, Hazel Marie," she said, grabbing a Kleenex to dab at the tears before they ran streaks down her face. "I didn't believe I could ever look this good. Thank you, thank you." She turned and grabbed Hazel Marie's hand. "I take back all the things I've ever said and thought about you."

My eyes rolled back in my head at Emma Sue's utter lack of common sense or tact, but Hazel Marie just smiled and said, "That's all right. Now, let me show you a better way to wear your hair." She took a brush and began to unsnarl Emma Sue's teased hair, rearranging it so that it was looser and much more flattering. "Part it like this, and bring over some half-bangs, which Velma can cut for you."

"I want you to do it," Emma Sue said, having now put herself entirely in Hazel

Marie's expert hands. "You're better than Velma any day of the week."

So Hazel Marie cut her some bangs right then, poofed them up and lifted the hair around her face with a pick. I could see that Hazel Marie was a true artist, for she had transformed Emma Sue into a fairly attractive woman, something I'd thought hardly possible. At least, she no longer looked ready for viewing at the Good Shepherd Funeral Home.

But how was I going to explain this transformation to Pastor Ledbetter, who expected me to turn his wife back into the plain, unadorned woman she'd once been? Had Hazel Marie, with my approval, only made Emma Sue even less pleasing in her husband's eyes and more pleasing to roving ones?

"Miss Julia?" Lillian stood at the door and beckoned me into the hall. When I walked out to her, she whispered, "Miz Conover pullin' in the driveway."

"Oh, my word," I said, looking back at Emma Sue. "We better head her off. It'll be all over town if she finds out what we're doing, and I'd rather not take credit for it.

"Emma Sue," I said, sticking my head

around the door, "LuAnne Conover's here. Why don't you get your things together and sneak out the back door?"

Emma Sue jumped up and began gathering her coat and purse. "I've got to get out of here. Don't tell her a thing, Julia. Hazel Marie's got me looking so natural, nobody'll know I'm wearing makeup unless somebody tells. So don't tell."

"We won't," I said, cutting my eyes at Hazel Marie, who knew as well as I did that nobody would be fooled after one look at Emma Sue's face. It was such a pleasant change, you know.

As Lillian and Hazel Marie hurried Emma Sue through the back hall and toward the kitchen door, the front doorbell rang. I went to answer it and welcome LuAnne in.

"Julia," she said as soon as I unlatched the storm door, "I'm so full of news I can hardly stand it. Some good, some not so good. How are you, anyway. Let me sit down, I'm all out of breath."

"Have a seat, LuAnne," I said, gesturing toward the sofa. "Let me take your umbrella. I'll tell you, I'm ready for some good news for a change. What's going on?"

"Well," she said, plopping down on the

sofa, her hands all aflutter. "First off, have you heard about that Christian theme park somebody's putting up?"

"Yes, I have."

"Oh, shoo, Julia, you're no fun. But listen, it's going to be the grandest thing. I've always wanted to walk where Jesus walked, but as you know, Leonard wouldn't go overseas for all the tea in China. He is such a stick in the mud, but now I'll get to go to the Holy Land right here in Abbot County. It's going to be a big draw for tourists, and Mayor Beebee's behind it one hundred percent. Everybody's thrilled out of their minds."

"Not quite everybody, but I expect it'll draw a certain type of tourist. I just hope they don't create a carnival atmosphere in town. We don't need that."

"Oh, you always see the dark side of things. But, now, let me tell you what else I've heard. Emma Sue Ledbetter's going around town made up like you wouldn't believe. Somebody ought to show her how to put on makeup. The poor thing doesn't know how awful she looks."

I nodded. "She'll get the hang of it sooner or later."

"It better be sooner, or she's going to be a laughing stock. Listen, Julia, something's going on with that woman, and I hate to think what it might be. You've heard about Norma Cantrell, haven't you?"

I nodded again. "Just a word or two about the mayor."

"Well, don't believe everything you hear, because from what I heard, that's all off. It was never anything but a fling anyway." LuAnne brushed that aside, as if flings were beneath the notice of sophisticates such as herself. Then she leaned over to whisper her next piece of news. "They say she's really got her eye on the pastor. Can you believe that?"

"I've always wondered about her," I said, trying to be careful of what I said, knowing it would be relayed up one side of Main Street and down the other. "But I can't believe he'd look twice at her or anybody else. He's a God-fearing man, LuAnne, and we ought to be careful of linking his name with another woman."

"Julia," she snapped, "you don't need to lecture me. I'm not making this stuff up. I'm just repeating what everybody's talking about because I thought you'd appreciate knowing about it. I mean, he *is* our preacher, and we ought to be doing something about all the gossip swirling around him. And his wife."

"I certainly agree. So now that's taken care of, what else is going on?"

She looked down at her lap, where for once her hands were resting there without a twitch. Then she glanced up at me. "Well, I don't know if I ought to tell you this or not. I know it'll upset you."

"For goodness sake, LuAnne, don't start something you can't finish. If you didn't think I should hear it, why bring it up? But now that you have, just tell me."

Her eyes darted around the room, as she realized she'd gone too far to back out. "I want you to know that I don't believe it for a minute, but the rumor's already going around."

"What is it?" I said, trying to prepare myself since, with all this buildup, it had to be about me. Then I smiled, for I figured the word was out about Sam and me. Somebody must've put two and two together, especially if Sam had told somebody he'd popped the question. As for my answer, I was still keeping my decision close to my breast, wanting it to be my own precious secret for a while longer. "I think I know, LuAnne, but nobody knows what I'm going to do about it."

"I know what *I'd* do," LuAnne said with some heat. "I'd wring her neck."

"Who? What're you talking about?"

"That woman who's come to town with the Walk Where Jesus Walked outfit. I heard that she's living in a trailer with the man who's in charge of it. His common law wife, they say." She frowned. "I just hope that doesn't reflect on the spirituality of the theme park."

"It could hardly help, LuAnne. If it's true. But what does their living arrangement have to do with me?"

"Oh, nothing," she said, as her hands started fluttering. "Really. It's just, well, I might as well tell you since you're going to hear it sooner or later anyway. Now, don't get mad at me, Julia, but the word is that she's another girlfriend of . . . ," she leaned forward and whispered, "you-know-who."

{Chapter 7}

My heart lurched to one side and I gripped the arm of my chair.

"No, I don't know," I snapped, as pain clutched at my chest at the thought of Sam in the company of another woman. I didn't want to hear it, but I asked anyway, "Who're you talking about, LuAnne?"

"Well, you know." Then she scooted to the edge of the sofa and hissed, "Wesley Lloyd. Your *husband.*"

If I'd been standing, my knees would've given way on me, both in relief that it wasn't Sam and in anguish that more of Wesley Lloyd's unsavory deeds were coming to light. As it was, an icy chill seeped into my insides, and all I could think about was getting rid of LuAnne so I could crawl into a corner and cover my head. But I dared not show my consternation, for I knew she'd describe my reaction to the next person she met.

Could it be true? Well, yes, it could. But true or not, it hardly mattered. What mattered was the talk, and who the talk would hurt. I had to try to stop it before it spread throughout the town and ended up hurting Hazel Marie and Little Lloyd. Lord, the child could suffer lasting damage from hearing such a thing about his father, whether or not it was true. Once a person is tarred with the brush of adultery, people would say: He did it once, so it stands to reason he'd do it again. And we all knew he'd done it once. Little Lloyd was the proof.

"I know who Wesley Lloyd is, or was, Lu-Anne," I said, trying to disguise my sinking feelings and show her that what she'd passed on didn't bother me at all. "And I hardly think that he would've taken up with some town-to-town carnival woman. How in the world would he have known her?"

"Well, see, that's the thing," she said. "She used to live here. At least, that's what they say. She's a Mooney, and there're a lot of Mooneys out in the county."

"Yes, and not a one worth the rope to hang them. Now, LuAnne, I don't know how this rumor got started, but I don't think you ought to go around spreading it any further."

I knew that would make her mad, for she stiffened noticeably and said, "I should think you'd appreciate being told what's going around, but I see that you don't. All I'm trying to do is be a friend and let you know what everybody's talking about. And, believe me, they *are* talking." She stood up and pulled her raincoat together. "At least, *this* time you won't be the last one in town to know what he was up to."

That was a jab at my prideful ignorance where Hazel Marie and Little Lloyd were concerned, whom I hadn't known about until after Wesley Lloyd was six feet under.

"I do appreciate it, LuAnne," I said, standing, too, and hoping she'd take herself out of my sight so I could try to deal with this devastating news. "You are a dear friend and, as such, I hope you'll do everything you can to put a stop to these hurtful rumors. I, for one, don't believe them. And since Wesley Lloyd's been out of circulation for so long, I can't imagine why anybody'd be interested enough to listen to them. And I'll tell you this, I don't know why that woman doesn't stand up for herself and put a stop to them."

"Money, Julia," she said. "Which is another reason I wanted you to know about her. I mean, she has to know, like everybody else does, what a gold mine Hazel Marie fell into, and for no other reason than taking up with your husband. So why wouldn't she try for the same thing—especially if she claims to have a child? What other reason would she have to come back here? And to think that she's part of a Christian organization."

"I'm having my doubts about how Christian that organization is," I said, as another kind of dread swept through me. Wesley Lloyd's estate had already been rent asunder once, and I had no desire to see it divvied up again.

"Now, Julia," LuAnne said, as she tucked her pocketbook under her arm. "You can't blame a whole organization for the actions of one person in it."

"That's very true," I said, thinking of the church and the activities of some of its members.

"One other thing," LuAnne said, turning back. "People who remember when she used to live here, they're saying that she had a reputation then for being somewhat free with her favors. And not too picky about who she favored, either. So, if it helps, maybe Wesley Lloyd wasn't the only one." She got a far-off look in her eyes. Then she shook herself, and headed toward the door.

I bade her good-bye and thanked her for her thoughtfulness in passing along a stab in the heart, although I didn't put it quite that way. She left with a smile on her face, confident that she'd done her duty as a friend.

I closed the door and leaned against it. What in the world was I going to do about another of Wesley Lloyd's escapades? Lord, the man had been as randy as a rooster, except in his own coop, and all unbeknownst to me. That said a lot about our marriage. Distant was the best description of it. I just hadn't known how distant.

Now, I had to deal with another woman who'd popped up out of the past, long after I thought he'd been put in his grave and out of my hair. It had been all I could do to withstand the gossip when Wesley Lloyd's supposedly secret life became the town topic the first time. Now, I'd have to withstand it for Hazel Marie, as well as for myself. Again.

And Little Lloyd! My stomach tightened

up as an awful dread swept over me at the thought of what that child would have to endure if his schoolmates got wind of this. To say nothing of what he would suffer inside himself just by knowing of his father's inability to keep his trousers on.

The telephone rang, sending a jolt of fear through me. If it was someone else calling to tell me what I didn't want to hear, I just wouldn't answer it. Lillian could tell the caller that I was indisposed, which I certainly was. But the silence stretched out and I heard no summons to the phone. Feeling some relief to have a moment to myself, I collapsed on the sofa where LuAnne had delivered her news.

I sighed from the bottom of my soul, wondering if I had the stamina to go through it all again. It had not been easy the first time, but I'd managed to overcome my distaste of Wesley Lloyd's commingling with Hazel Marie for, as I got to know her, I'd begun to think that he'd fallen in love with her sweet disposition, in spite of himself. But I'd gradually become convinced that he'd thought no more of Hazel Marie than he had of me. Add another woman to the mix, and my conviction was more than confirmed.

With a burning ache in my heart, I pushed myself off the sofa and walked purposefully toward the kitchen. If I could spare Hazel Marie any of the anger and humiliation I was feeling, I would. The first thing I needed to do was to find out what I could about the Mooney woman and put a stop to whatever she had in mind. And, if she did come up with a child and expect me to recognize it as Wesley Lloyd's, why, I'd just show her his will, which made no mention of any off-spring, other than Little Lloyd. And *then,* I thought, as I stomped through the dining room, make sure the woman knew she wasn't due one red cent for having crawled into bed with Wesley Lloyd Springer.

I pushed through the kitchen door, figuring that if anybody could be of help it would be Lillian.

Before I could open my mouth, she said, "Oh, Miss Julia, I just got the awfulest news I ever heard, an' I don't know what we gonna do."

That shook me. "Who told you? I just found out myself."

She frowned. "How you find out? Janine jus' call me all the way from Detroit and tole me."

"Detroit? How . . . Oh, Lillian, we're talking about two different things. Your news couldn't be any worse than mine, but what is it?"

"It jus' terr'ble, Miss Julia. I wouldn't do this to you for anything in the world, so I got to move out somewhere real fast."

"Move out?" I was stunned. Lillian had been living in my guest room upstairs for the past several months while her house was being remodeled and updated. "Where're you going and why?"

"I don't know where, but the why is 'cause that no-good gran' of mine, you know Janine, she sendin' her baby for me to take care of. She say she got a job in New York City, an' can't take no chile with her. So who the first person she think of to help her out? Me, that's who, an' here I am livin' in yo' house an' I can't take no chile, either."

"Well, just tell her that having a great-grandchild is inconvenient now. She'll understand when you tell her your house isn't ready yet."

"No'm, she won't. I done tole her two dozen times I can't do it, an' she keep callin' an' keep callin'. Now, she already put that baby on the Greyhound bus, an' it comin' in tonight. I 'spect it already more'n half way here. That Janine done hook up with another triflin' man, you want my opinion."

"Well, my word, Lillian," I said. "I guess there's nothing to do but meet the bus. We'll work something out when the baby gets here. Surely somebody's with her on the bus. Maybe that person can be persuaded to help out."

"It not 'zactly a baby. I jus' say that. I think Latisha be 'bout five now. And, no'm, Janine put her on that bus by herself, an' the driver say he look after her." Lillian looked up at the ceiling and cried, "Lord Jesus, what I gonna do with another'n to raise, an' me here in Miss Julia's house?"

"Now, Lillian, there's only one thing to do at this late date. Bring the child here for the time being, then we'll see what can be done."

"Oh, Jesus," Lillian went on, tears shining in her eyes. "I don't know what I done to have a gran' like Janine, who don't have the sense God give a billy goat."

I patted her arm, trying to reassure her, but wondering how the rest of us would manage with a five-year-old in the house. It would be a temporary measure for us, but Lillian would have Janine and now, Latisha, as her cross to bear from now on. And it looked as if I was going to have Wesley Lloyd Springer, who I thought had been lifted from me some years ago, as my own never-ending burden.

Little Lloyd and I glanced at each other as we heard Hazel Marie's car pull into the driveway a little after nine that night. She had taken Lillian to the Greyhound station to meet the bus, while we waited to meet our new house guest.

As the car doors slammed, I began to hear the chatter of indistinguishable words going on and on. Hazel Marie came into the kitchen, her eyes dancing with amusement.

She put down the Samsonite suitcase she'd brought in and held the door open for Lillian. "Wait'll you meet Latisha," she said, barely holding back a wide grin. "She got off the bus talking, and she hasn't stopped since."

We could hear her rattling on before we got our first look at Lillian's great-grand-child. As we waited, in walked a tiny, brown-skinned girl with large eyes and a head full of plaits and barrettes. A rag doll of similar visage was clasped in one arm, while Lillian held the child's other hand. As Latisha stood in the kitchen, taking everything in with a serious expression on her face, she kept on talking, not at all abashed at being in a strange place. I don't think I've ever heard such a penetrating, piercing little voice in my life.

Lillian said, "Hush, chile, jus' hush for one minute. This here's Miss Julia, who kindly let you come to visit. Now, you behave yo'self in her house, an' show some manners, if you got any."

The child looked me over with those serious eyes and said, "How you do, ma'am. You got a real nice house somewhere down here in North Car'lina, 'cept I don't know where that is, but it's where I'm at now."

"We're happy to have you, Latisha," I said, but she'd turned her attention to Little Lloyd who was standing almost behind me.

"Who's that big ole boy over there, Great-Granny?" Latisha asked, surprising me again with the strength of that voice coming out of such a thin little body.

"That there's Little Lloyd, an' you better

not be botherin' him," Lillian said, looking about at the end of her tether.

"Lloyd? I never heard of such a name before in my life," Latisha said. "Lloydy Lloyd, he look pretty good to me."

Lillian frowned down at her and said, "Behave yo'self, Latisha. You know better'n that."

"Well, I don't think I do, but I'll try," Latisha said. "I don't think he likes me, 'cause he ain't said a word since I been here."

Little Lloyd stepped forward and rectified that right away. "I do like you, Latisha, and I hope you'll be happy here with us."

"Look like I'm gonna be," she said, as somber as a judge rendering an opinion. "These folks look pretty nice to me, Great-Granny, an' I specially like that big, ole boy name of Lloyd."

"*Latisha,*" Lillian cried. "You got to be nicer'n that. Now, come on upstairs with me. You goin' to bed, an' maybe you be calmed down in the mornin'."

"Well, I don't think I will be, Great-Granny. This pretty much my nat'ral self right here and now."

Lillian grasped her arm and practically

lifted the child off the floor, as she headed for the back stairs. "Girl, you got to behave yo'self better'n this. These folks won't know what to think of you. Now, say good night."

"Lillian," I said, seeing how embarrassed she was over the child's talkativeness. "Lillian, don't worry about Latisha. She is charming."

Lillian grunted and, walking the child up the stairs, said, "She a little too charmin' to my way of thinkin'."

Latisha was not at all deterred. We could hear her voice chattering on and gradually fading out as they gained the top of the stairs. "I think that Miss Julia pretty charmin', herself. An' that Miss Hazel Marie, she awful nice, bringin' in my suitcase and drivin' us an' all. But I still like that big, ole boy the best. I 'spect I'm gonna be followin' him around every where he go. He gonna think I'm his shadow, only colored in."

As silence descended in the kitchen, the three of us looked at each other and began to laugh.

"That child is wide open, isn't she?" Hazel Marie said, wiping her eyes. "I've never seen anything like her."

"She is certainly a precocious little thing," I said. "I think we've got our own built-in entertainment, but I'm not sure Lillian thinks so."

"She feels responsible for her," Hazel Marie said, still smiling. "And concerned about bringing her into your house. She told me so while we were waiting for the bus."

"I know," I said. "We'll just have to assure her that we don't mind. And I think Latisha will calm down when she gets used to us. In the meantime, I'm not at all averse to having a little comic relief around here." Turning to Little Lloyd, I went on. "What did you think of her, Little Lloyd?"

"She's pretty cute," he said. "For a girl. But I hope she won't be following me all the time. That could get old in a hurry."

"Just give her time, honey," Hazel Marie said. "I expect Lillian'll put her in kindergarten, and that'll take her mind off of you. I think I'm going to enjoy having her around. We need somebody to liven up the place a little."

And with that, my mind veered onto the Mooney woman and her claim of being one of Wesley Lloyd's women, of which there seemed to be a growing number if the two I knew about was any indication. So, if Hazel Marie thought we needed livening up, I feared we were in for more than any of us wanted.

{ *Chapter 8* }

When they were all in bed and silence filled the house, I sat in the living room alone, burdened with thoughts of my blindness to Wesley Lloyd's amorous activities. Lord, it was as if I'd never known the man. And obviously I hadn't, so taken up with living my own exemplary life that it'd never occurred to me to question his. I wondered why he hadn't put me aside legally so he could pursue his interests with no fear of a vengeful wife.

But, of course, he'd had no fear of me. I'd given him cover, something he could hide behind, and I now felt that was all he'd ever wanted of me. Even so, I'd had every right to expect fidelity and some semblance of respect from a husband, such as he was. Not that I'd ever been starry-eyed in love—

I didn't know what that meant—but I had devoted the best years of my life to him.

I sighed and leaned my head against the back of the chair. My chest ached, as I thought of how proud I'd been of being the wife of such an influential man. As I thought of how I'd allowed him to take over most of the years of my life, flashes of anger blazed through my mind, not only at him, but at myself, as well. I was as much to blame for my bleak marriage as Wesley Lloyd had been. Well, maybe not as much, but a good bit.

What it came down to was that I had not been able to keep a husband happy at home. Why in the world did I think I could do any better with another one, now that I was old and ugly and on my last legs? I would never be able to redeem the years frittered away on a wayward husband but, Lord knows, I didn't have to put myself in the way of peril again.

After a few more minutes of self-pitying reflection, I felt a growing conviction that there were still a few things I could do to preserve my dignity and to prevent any other man from pulling the wool over my eyes. And the first thing I did was go to the phone, I didn't care how late it was.

"Sam?" I said, when he answered, then hesitated to say what had to be said. "We missed you at dinner tonight, and you missed meeting Lillian's great-granddaughter. You have a treat in store when you do."

"I look forward to it," he said. "And I was about to call you, so I'm glad you beat me to it. I thought the Rotary meeting would never end. I kept thinking of you over there all lonely and despondent because you didn't have me to entertain you."

I started to smile at his carrying-on, but remembered my new resolve and the reason I'd called him. "You do entertain me, Sam, and I hope you'll continue to do so, but I want to tell you that I've made up my mind and there'll be no changing it."

"Well, that lifts my heart, Julia. It's the best news I've ever had. When do you want to do it? The sooner, the better, as far as I'm concerned. And I give you my solemn promise, you won't regret it."

"Regret what?"

"Why, marrying me. I'm going to make you happy, Julia. That is my dead-level promise."

I let the silence lengthen over the line, as I felt my own heart sink to the depths. Tears came to my eyes, and I had to clear my throat before proceeding. "Sam, the reason I called was to tell you that you might as well stop all this marriage talk. I'm not marrying you or anybody. I've had enough of that sad state of affairs to last me a lifetime and then some."

I hung up the phone, and stood over it, thinking that my heart was surely going to break in two. Then I turned off the bell so I wouldn't hear it ring when he called back.

I suffered through that night, tossing and turning and getting my gown in such a tangle that I almost strangled myself. When it was finally time to rise, I did it with a great deal of creaking and moaning, as I held onto the bedpost to get straightened up. But I did it with a new and firm acceptance of what I knew was the bottom line. There are some women, for whatever reason—upbringing, personality, basic characteristics, or something I couldn't think of—who just are not cut out to be loved and cherished. And if you find that you're one of those women, then the thing to do is accept it and concentrate on whatever positive qualities you can find.

I spent some minutes trying to dredge up a few positive qualities of my own, but nothing rose to the surface. I had to face the fact that I was no bargain for any man. But neither had Wesley Lloyd been for me, and neither was any other man I knew. Except Sam, maybe. But then, you never really know a man until you live with him, and by then it's too late.

Even though my heart was as heavy as a rock and my eyes kept watering up, I was firmly set in my mind not to give another man the chance to do me in ever again. So I girded my loins, so to speak, and went forth with my head held high. There're worse things in the world than living alone, and one of them is to live with a man who makes a fool of you every time you turn around.

Just as I figured he would, Sam showed up at my door bright and early. Trying to ignore the ache in my chest, I asked him in.

"Lillian has breakfast ready, Sam," I said. "Come on in and join us."

"We need to talk, Julia. I can't leave it at this, not knowing why. Is it something I've done? You know I wouldn't hurt you for the world."

"No, Sam," I said, shaking my head but unable to look at him. One look at his dear face might have persuaded me onto another course, but I knew the futility of that. "It's nothing you've done. It's all me, but it's not a good time to talk. Everybody's up, and we'd have no privacy at all. Come on in and meet Latisha."

"All right," he said, steering me with a hand on my back. "But you need to understand that I'm not giving up on you, or taking no for an answer."

I glanced up at him, steeling my heart against the pain I thought would be evident on his face. Instead, I saw a determined look and, to my amazement, a smile.

"I've made up my mind, Sam," I said, "whether you believe it or not. But I do want us to stay friends."

"We've always been friends, Julia, and always will be. And when you get over whatever problem you've dreamed up, we'll be more than that."

Well, it wasn't the time to argue with him,

which I would have to do sooner or later. As we walked through the dining room, I told him how and why Latisha had come to us, grateful for a neutral subject that kept my mind off a painful one.

As soon as we walked into the kitchen where Hazel Marie, Latisha, and Little Lloyd were having breakfast, Latisha turned her serious face to Sam. She pushed aside her cereal bowl and said, "Great-Granny, who that big ole white-headed man just come through the door?"

"Latisha!" Lillian cried, throwing down a dish towel. "That no way to talk to Mr. Sam. I'm gonna take a switch to you, you don't behave yo'self."

The threat didn't bother Latisha, as she continued to give Sam her solemn appraisal. "How you do, Mr. Sam."

"I'm doing fine, Latisha. Under the circumstances, that is. How are you?"

"I'm doin' fine, without no 'stances at all. Great-Granny, I sure do like these stewed apples. They the only kind I can eat. I haven't had no normal apples in two whole years."

Little Lloyd stared at her. "Two years? Why?"

She stuck her head up and stretched her lips in a grimace, revealing a snaggle-toothed mouth. "My teeth been comin' out every day of my life, that's why. I can't get no grip on a apple, 'less they been stewed to death like these here."

Hazel Marie covered her face with a nap-kin trying to choke back a laugh, while Little Lloyd regarded her with a bemused fascina-tion. Even Sam seemed entranced by her, in spite of my having so recently broken his heart.

"I got eggs and bacon, Mr. Sam," Lillian said. "Set down, if you can stand all that talkin', an' I bring it to you."

"Thank you, Lillian. I'll give your good cooking a try, though I'm not feeling too peckish today. Good morning, Hazel Marie. You're looking well this morning."

Hazel Marie smiled her thanks, and be-gan pouring coffee for us. Sam and I sat at the table, while Latisha kept her eyes fas-tened on him. "I'm not feelin' too peckish, myself," she announced. "I had to sleep with Great-Granny last night, an' she snored all night long."

Lillian whirled around. "I did no such a thing. Girl, you better watch what you say."

"Well, I didn't mind listenin' to that racket. I've stayed up all night long before. Take when Santy Claus come, I didn't get a wink of sleep, watchin' out for that big ole fat man."

"Did you see him?" Little Lloyd asked.

"Naw, he slipped by me again, but I'm gonna catch him one of these days an' I'm gonna jump out an' yell 'Ho-ho-ho' at him an' ast him where that dog I been asting for all these years."

Sam said, "If you catch him, let me know. I need to ask him why I haven't gotten what I want, either."

For the first time that I'd seen, Latisha laughed out loud. "I know why you didn't get what you want," she said between giggles. "You have to set on his lap an' you bigger'n he is. You'd mash him so flat he couldn't crawl in that ole sled he rides around in."

"Latisha," Lillian said, "Santy Claus won't come see you anytime, you don't eat yo' breakfast an' leave Mr. Sam alone."

"She's fine, Lillian," Sam said. "How's school going, Lloyd?"

"Okay, I guess," the boy said. "I'm in the

beginners' band now. I'm going to learn to play the trumpet, or maybe the saxophone, whichever the band director wants me to."

"Play the drums!" Latisha cried, waving her spoon. "That's what I'm gonna do. I'm gonna get me some drums and I'm gonna beat the hell outta them things."

"*Latisha!*" Lillian jumped a mile, dropping a pan with a clatter that almost drowned out our convulsed laughter. She jerked the child out of the chair and gave her a swat on the bottom. "You get yo'self up them stairs an' stay there till you can talk like decent folk. Miss Julia," Lillian went on, an anguished expression on her face, as Latisha scampered up the stairs, "I 'pologize for my great-gran', she ain't been raised right, but I gonna teach her better an' you not gonna be shamed by her again."

"Lillian, it's all right," I said. "I mean, the language isn't, of course, but don't distress yourself. She'll learn. And we shouldn't've laughed. It was . . ." I struggled to control myself, then wiping my eyes, I said, "It was just so unexpected coming from that little thing."

We didn't stay long at the table after Latisha's banishment. Little Lloyd ran upstairs to get his book bag, while Hazel Marie prepared to drive him to school. I knew Sam was waiting to get me alone so we could hash out my reasons for turning him down. So I lingered, helping Lillian clear the table, not at all eager to be put on the spot about my unwavering decision.

On his way out the door, Little Lloyd whispered to me, "I found an old coloring book and some crayons for Latisha. She told me she didn't know what she'd done wrong, but she now knew that her Great-Granny wasn't going to put up with whatever it was." Little Lloyd couldn't help but laugh as he told this.

"It was good of you to give her something to play with," I said, thinking again of how much Little Lloyd pleased me and how I needed to keep him safe from hurtful rumors. "And I hope you told her how unacceptable that word is. She'll learn that lesson from you better than from Lillian, since she's so taken with you."

He grinned. "I don't know about that, but I'll try. She's a smart little thing, and, boy, is she funny."

I patted his back. "Have a good day at school, sweetie." Then felt my heart wrench at saying the word that Sam had called me. There'd be no more of that, I reckoned, and looked across the room where he was waiting for me.

We walked to the living room, and I told myself to stick to my guns, regardless of how much I wanted to lean against him and hear him say that I was all he'd ever want.

But I never found out what he would've said for, just as he put his hands on my shoulders and looked me in the eye, Lillian stuck her head around the kitchen door.

"'Scuse me," she said, "but Mr. Pickens jus' pullin' in."

As I stepped away from Sam, he blew out his breath and said, "Well, damn, as Latisha might say." Then he pointed his finger in my face, and went on. "Now listen, woman, I don't know what kind of bee you've got in your bonnet, but you haven't heard the last from me."

Chapter 9

Mr. Pickens came in with his black eyes shining against his swarthy complexion, making him look like a maiden's fevered dream after reading one of those Harlequin romances.

He and Sam spoke and shook hands, but it wasn't long before Mr. Pickens asked for Hazel Marie, who was the reason he was there, as every one of us knew.

"She's taking Little Lloyd to school," I said, "and I think she has a meeting over at the church. She shouldn't be long, though. Did she know you were coming?"

"No, I was over this way and thought I'd take a chance on seeing her. Mind if I wait?"

"Not at all. I expect Lillian could have some breakfast for you, too, if you haven't eaten."

"That sounds good," he said. "I'm about

to cave in, it's been so long since I've had anything."

I raised my eyebrows, figuring he'd already had at least one breakfast. Mr. Pickens was no slouch when it came to pulling up to a table.

"Come on, Sam," he said. "Have some coffee with me."

Sam didn't look too happy about having a third party around, but he enjoyed Mr. Pickens's company so he put off taking his leave. We all trooped to the kitchen where Mr. Pickens picked up where he left off the last time. He walked over to Lillian and rolled his eyes back as if he were about to swoon.

"I smelled your good cooking a mile away, Lillian," he said, putting his arm around her waist. "And I knew you couldn't wait for me to get here."

"You a mess, Mr. Pickens," she said, laughing at his carrying on.

While we were sitting at the table, I saw Latisha peek around the door from the back stairs. Before long, she'd edged out into the room, her attention focused on Mr. Pickens. I declare, every female I'd ever known was just naturally drawn to him.

"Great-Granny," she said in that powerful voice, making Mr. Pickens swing around in his chair to see what it was emanating from. "Who that big ole black-headed man settin' over there drinkin' coffee like he b'long here?"

"Good God," Mr. Pickens said. "Who is that?"

"That Latisha," Lillian said with a resigned sigh, "who think she too big for her britches. Go on upstairs, girl."

"No'm, I think I like to look at that black-headed man some more."

Mr. Pickens grinned and said, "Well, come on over here and get a good look."

Latisha walked right over and let him set her on his lap. Mr. Pickens did have a way with children, as well as with women.

"Who's that you got there?" Mr. Pickens asked her, poking his finger at her doll.

"This here's Luwanda Lou," Latisha said. "But she don't blink her eyes or say Mama or wet her underpants or do nothin' but hang around me."

"Well, if I don't blink my eyes or say Mama or wet my underpants, can I hang around you, too?"

Latisha covered her mouth with her hand and giggled.

"Latisha," Lillian said, "jump down from there, an' let them folks do they own talkin'. You 'bout to wear me out."

While this was going on, an idea began to form in my mind, and it had to do with Mr. Pickens and his private detecting skills. Although my previous employment of him had resulted in having him under foot all the time as he pursued Hazel Marie, I resolved to get him alone somewhere and make him another proposition. This was a case that needed a professional, if there ever was one.

It took some doing to get him alone, because Sam stayed on and on, and Hazel Marie didn't return, and I thought Sam and Mr. Pickens were going to sit at the table until Lillian put lunch on it.

Finally, though, Sam gave it up, saying he had things to attend to. As I walked him to the door and out of Mr. Pickens's hearing, he said, "Julia, I don't know what kind of problem you're having with marriage. But keep in mind that you've never been married to me, so you don't know what you're missing."

"Oh, Sam," I said, smiling in spite of myself. "I have so much on my mind right now. I just can't take on another thing."

"Good. That means you're still up in the air. We'll talk this out and, before you know it, you're going to be the happiest and the luckiest woman in Abbotsville."

I smiled as he left, then felt a heart-stopping sense of loss at the thought of letting him go. He was so good-hearted, so kind and decent, and so easy to get along with. Wesley Lloyd would've flown off the handle in a minute, if I'd even hinted that I didn't want what he wanted.

With an effort of will, I pulled myself together and hurried back to the kitchen where Mr. Pickens still waited for Hazel Marie. I hoped to find him alone and, thank goodness, I did. Lillian was walking Latisha back up the stairs to get her dressed for the day.

"Mr. Pickens," I whispered as I pulled out a chair and leaned close to him. "I have need of your services."

His eyebrows went up and a smile played around under his mustache. "What services would that be, Miss Julia?"

"I want you to find out about a woman."

"Well, you've come to the right man. That's my specialty."

I glared at him, letting him know that I was in no mood for frivolity. "Settle down, Mr. Pickens. This could hurt Hazel Marie and Little Lloyd."

That straightened him up in a hurry, and I felt the sudden intensity of his black eyes. "Tell me."

"There's a woman, recently come to town, come *back* to town, that is, and there're rumors going around about her. I want to find out if they're true. Will you do it?"

"I need more to go on than that. Who is she? Where is she? And what does she have to do with Hazel Marie?"

I turned my face away, as I felt it burn with shame. "Well, to tell you the truth . . . I don't think I can, it's too mortifying."

"One thing at a time, then," he said, impressing me with his compassion for my distress. "What's her name?"

"She's a Mooney. That's all I know."

"What does she look like?"

"I don't know. I've never seen her."

"Where does she live?"

"The only thing I've heard is that she's

living in a trailer with a Mr. Dwayne Dooley, out on County Line Road where they're making a Walk Where Jesus Walked religious theme park."

Mr. Pickens's eyebrows shot straight up. "A what?"

So I told him about Mr. Dooley and his plans to recreate the Holy Land on my twenty acres. Mr. Pickens just shook his head.

Then he frowned again and said, "Okay, you want the Mooney woman investigated. What about Dooley?" He smiled. "Mooney and Dooley, that's a combination for you."

"Don't worry about him for now," I said. "He may not even know what's going on with her."

"Right. So what *is* going on with her? What's she got on Hazel Marie?"

"Nothing, as far as I know. It's just that if the gossip gets back to Hazel Marie, it will just do her in. But, more than anything, I don't want the sins of his father to be visited upon Little Lloyd's head. He could be damaged for life. So, I want you to find out if the gossip is true, and, if it is, I want you to get rid of her."

He reared back, then leaned in close. "You mean you want me to take her out?"

"Absolutely. Out of this county and out of this state." Then as I realized that he was ragging on me, I said, "Mr. Pickens, this is serious, and I expect you to take it seriously. Of course I don't want you to do away with her, I just want you to get her away from here."

"Okay," he said, "I got you. Now, here comes the hard part. Why?"

"Because," I said, and bit my lip. I leaned my head on my hand, wondering how to put it to him. "Because everybody's saying that she had a, well, an amicable relationship with my husband, which may or may not have produced a child. You know, like happened with Hazel Marie, and the woman's neither confirming nor denying it. And it may be because she hopes to benefit in the same way Hazel Marie has."

"Ah," he said. "I see." He ran his hand across his mustache and went on. "When was this, ah, amicable relationship supposed to've happened?"

"I don't know," I said, shaking my head. "I don't know anything, except it had to've been before Mr. Springer's demise. But the talk's going to get back to Hazel Marie and Little Lloyd if we don't do something. I don't want that child to know that his daddy was a lecherous old goat. I mean, anymore than he's going to eventually figure out for himself. And I'd like to keep it from Hazel Marie, if we can, to spare her the shame I've had to put up with."

"Yeah, I see what you mean." By this time, Mr. Pickens had his professional face on, and I could tell that he was considering all the ramifications of the Mooney woman's presence in our town. "I'll get right on it."

"Two more things, Mr. Pickens," I said. "I know I gave you a hard time before about your fee, but this time there'll be no quarreling. Whatever you charge, I'll pay and gladly."

"You think I'd charge to take care of Hazel Marie and Lloyd?" He tightened his mouth at the thought. "What's the other thing?"

"Well, we can discuss money matters later. The other thing is I want to take part in your investigation."

He was shaking his head before I even got it out of my mouth. "We've been over that before, too. I'll stay in touch, but I don't work with a partner, which you know as well as I do."

I nodded, but if he thought I was going to stand by and wring my hands while that woman tore us all to smithereens, he'd have to think again.

{ Chapter 10 }

I sat straight up in bed, wide awake and gasping for breath. The perfect solution to the Mooney woman problem had come to me in my sleep. I glanced at the bedside clock and saw that it was only four-fifteen, much too early to put my plan in motion. Still, I was so excited with the thought of it that I got out of bed and put on a flannel robe against the early morning chill. Then I slipped into the big, fluffy bedroomers that Little Lloyd had given me for one of the birthdays that I no longer acknowledged.

Tiptoeing so as not to wake the others, I went to the kitchen and started the coffee. The incessant rain we'd had all spring made the house feel damp and chilly, so I stood in the kitchen, shivering, while the coffee perked. I could see my reflection in the dark windows, but I turned away, unable to bear such a distressing sight for long.

I went to the refrigerator, thinking I would make a piece of toast, then decided against it. When the coffeepot stopped, I went into the pantry and got a handful of Oreos, then poured a cup of coffee, turned off the lights and went back upstairs.

It was not my custom to eat in bed, but this was a special occasion. I propped pillows behind my back, tucked the covers all around and proceeded to enjoy my coffee and cookies. Lillian would raise Cain about such a breakfast, but once in a blue moon wouldn't hurt anybody.

Going over and over it in my mind, I struggled to understand the Mooney woman and her reason for returning to the scene of her disgraceful actions. You'd think that she wouldn't come within a hundred miles of Abbotsville since, as I'd often told Little Lloyd, people may forgive a step out of line, but they don't ever forget it.

By this time, I had resigned myself to the fact that the Mooney woman had indeed been one of Wesley Lloyd's conquests. Or maybe it was the other way around, and he'd been hers. Whichever, though, the result was the same—they'd had physical congress, and her return to Abbotsville had revived the scandal. And I intended to put a stop to it one way or another.

My heart was working overtime as I watched the clock, waiting for a decent hour to get up and dressed. My plan was to call Binkie. Why hadn't I thought of it before? Here, I'd gone through agonies for an entire day over rumors that I could've brought to a screeching halt with one phone call. And it hadn't even occurred to me. I wondered if my mind was going.

By six-thirty I was fully dressed and on my way downstairs. I thought of calling Binkie at home, knowing she'd be up feeding the baby, but I decided I could wait one more hour. One must be considerate of others, although in this case it was hard to consider anything but what I needed her to do.

Lillian rounded on me as soon as I entered the kitchen. "Who been up in the middle of the night perkin' this coffee?"

"I was, and good morning to you."

"Good mornin', but what you doin' wanderin' 'round when you ought to be in bed?"

"I had things on my mind, Lillian, but I'm

happy to say that I solved them, and I was so pleased with myself I couldn't sleep."

"You gonna wish you had yo' sleep, come afternoon," she mumbled. "Now set down an' eat something 'fore you keel over."

"I'm feeling fine, Lillian. Don't go to any trouble for me, I had a little snack earlier."

"You don't s'posed to be eatin' no snacks 'fore breakfast. What's wrong with you?"

We both looked up at the ceiling, as the footsteps of Latisha and Little Lloyd rumbled overhead. They stomped from room to room, with Latisha calling to him, wanting to know what he was wearing to school and could she go with him and when would he be back and would he play with her when he got home.

"Law, that chile," Lillian said. "She be the death of me yet."

"Well, I'll tell you, Lillian, I never thought I'd see the day that this house would be filled with children. But, now that it is, I have to admit that I hardly mind it at all."

She grunted, but she didn't disagree. She set a plate of eggs and bacon in front of me and said, "What all goin' on with you an' Mr. Sam? He s'posed to eat supper with us las' night, an' he never showed."

"Now, Lillian, that's between him and me." I stirred my eggs, wondering if I could get them past the sudden lump in my throat. Here, I'd been feeling so good about ending the gossip problem, and Lillian had to bring up the very thing to send me into the dumps again.

"You better watch yo'self," Lillian warned. "You hurt that good man's feelin's, you gonna be left high an' dry without nobody."

"I know, I know. I don't need a lecture on the subject. There's something else going on that I've been meaning to tell you about, but . . ."

I got no further, for Latisha and Little Lloyd came crashing down the back staircase, laughing and talking and ready for breakfast. The commotion was too much for me, so I greeted them, then took myself upstairs so I could use the phone in some semblance of peace and quiet.

At one minute past eight, I dialed Binkie's office. "Mary Ellen," I said to her receptionist, "I need to speak with Binkie. It's urgent."

"She just got in. Hold on a minute and I'll see if she can take your call."

She'd better take it, I thought to myself, or she'll have me camping on her doorstep.

"Miss Julia," Binkie said, sounding out of breath. "What can I do for you this morning?"

"Binkie, I apologize for not asking how you are or how the baby is, but I don't have time to chat. What I need you to do is get me out of a lease I signed before I knew what it entailed."

"What kind of lease and for what?"

"For twenty, more or less, idle acres running between Berea Church and County Line Roads, and it's a five-year lease with two options to renew. And I know I should've consulted you, Binkie, but I didn't, and now I've changed my mind, and I want out of it."

"Well, I don't know, Miss Julia. If the lease is properly drawn up and you've signed it and accepted payment, you may be stuck with it. Unless, of course, the lessee has misrepresented himself or what he wants to use it for. Who'd you lease it to?"

"Some fly-by-night person by the name of Dwayne Dooley. He's planning to put a Christian theme park out there with all the stops that Jesus made when he walked the earth. Have you ever heard of such a thing?"

"No, but that doesn't mean anything."

There was silence for a minute, except for the breathing that I could hear over the line. She noticeably exhaled then and said, "Is all that covered in the lease? I mean, spelled out?"

"I'm afraid so. I read every word, Binkie, and I know I should've let you see it first, but he was so eager and he had money in hand, and all I could think of was getting some good out of that land."

"Sounds like you'll have to honor it, then."

"Oh, my goodness," I said, feeling the bottom drop from under me. "Binkie, think of something, because I really need to get out of it. I've just found out some disturbing things about that bunch of so-called Christians." I stopped, so undone that my perfect solution to the Mooney woman problem wasn't so perfect, after all. And all because I'd been so eager to make a little money on unused property. Greed is a terrible thing, and even worse when you find it flourishing within yourself.

Binkie said, "If they're doing something illegal, you can break the lease, no problem."

"I don't know if what they're doing is illegal or not. But I'm certainly going to have

Coleman and the whole sheriff's department go out there and check them out.
They could be doing anything. Binkie, the
truth of the matter is . . ." I stopped, not
ready to tell her what the truth was. "Well,
let's put it this way, I just don't like them. I
don't want to be associated with them, and
I want them gone, out of sight and out of
mind."

"My goodness, you do feel strongly about
it. Well, look, I can talk to Mr. Dooley and tell
him you've changed your mind. He might be
willing to cooperate, especially if I tell him I'll
find another place for him."

"No, Binkie, you're not understanding me.
I want them gone from Abbot County,
somewhere as far away as they can get.
Finding another place just won't do. I just
want you to get me out of that lease."

"Whew, that won't be easy, especially
since you have no good reason for breaking it."

"I have a good reason."

"Well, tell me and I'll go from there."

"I can't, Binkie. I can't tell anyone because I don't want it known." Any more than
it already is, I added to myself.

She was silent again, while I sat there

waiting for her to come up with a way to null and void that lease without telling everybody and his brother why I wanted out. "Binkie?"

"I'm thinking."

"Will it be that hard?"

"Pretty hard, especially since you've accepted advance payment."

"He can have it back. I don't want his money, and where did an itinerant preacher get the money to pay a half a year's rent in one fell swoop, anyway?"

"Miss Julia," Binkie said, sounding just the least bit exasperated, "it doesn't sound as if you have any evidence of wrongdoing on his part, and certainly nothing to take into court."

"Court? Who said anything about *court*?"

"*He* might, if we try to break the lease. And if he did, you'd have to show cause and, if you're unwilling to tell me, what're you going to tell the court? What I'll do is appeal to his sense of fair play and his desire for the good will of the community. And give him his money back, of course."

"Go further than that, Binkie, if you have to. Offer him something for his pain and suffering. You know, for the inconvenience."

"I can offer to buy out the lease, but it'll cost you."

"I don't care what it costs. Just get rid of him and the flatbed trucks he came in on. What I want to hear is that he's packing up today and taking that whole crew to Arkansas or somewhere."

After we hung up, I continued to sit there and wring my hands, knowing I was doomed to even more worry while waiting for his response. I just despised being at the mercy of someone else's willful decisions.

Mentally shaking myself, I got up and went downstairs. I knew I'd feel better after sharing my anxiety with Lillian, who was as trustworthy as anyone could be. And, when I told her, I'd have someone in the house who could help me bear the burden of protecting Hazel Marie and Little Lloyd. And who, also, could tell me if she heard more of that terrible gossip.

But wouldn't you know it? She was on her way up the back stairs with Latisha, telling her that she needed to get dressed and brush her teeth. It was the first time that I felt any resentment toward Janine for sending Latisha to us. I needed Lillian. I did not need her to be busy with someone else when I was in such dire straits.

As I poured another cup of coffee—my third or fourth of the day, and it not yet nine o'clock, I heard Hazel Marie's car pull in, back from taking Little Lloyd to school. Well, some things do work out, I thought. If Lillian had been available, I would've barely scratched the surface before having to stop so Hazel Marie wouldn't hear.

"Hey, Miss Julia," she said, smiling with her usual good spirits. "You'll never guess what I heard when I dropped Lloyd off at school."

My coffee sloshed out of the cup and spread across the table. "What did you hear?"

"Here, let me get a paper towel for that." She quickly wiped up my spill, then sat down across from me. "Well, I saw Amy Broughton just as I was leaving the school, and she pulled over and rolled her window down. Her husband is on the session and he told her about their meeting last night. Pastor Ledbetter alerted them—that's what she said, alerted them—that we're going to have a VIP visiting the church for the next few months."

"You mean somebody from the General Assembly? Are they checking up on us? I wouldn't doubt for a minute that we're not following their guidelines, but what can they do about it? They need the churches more than the churches need them, because we're where the money comes from."

"No, not from the General Assembly, nothing like that."

"Then it's probably somebody on a Pastor Seeking Committee from another church. Oh, Hazel Marie, maybe Pastor Ledbetter'll get a call from a bigger church, and he'll take it, I know he will. Then we can get a more agreeable preacher, one who won't fight me at every turn. Even though," I went on after thinking about it, "he's proven himself somewhat more amiable since having a few troubles of his own."

"No, no, wait a minute." Hazel Marie was half laughing at me, knowing how poorly Pastor Ledbetter and I got along. "I'll tell you if you'll give me a chance."

"Well, I'm sure I can't imagine who else could be so important."

"Somebody named Curtis Maxwell. You've heard of him, haven't you?"

"No, I haven't. So why is he so important?"

"Oh, you have. He's the Maxwell of Maxwell Household Products. You know, Dorene Miller and Jackie Crutchfield and, I think Etta Mae Wiggins used to, and anyway, a bunch of others, they all sell Maxwell Household Products—cleaning agents of all kinds, room deodorizers, washing powders, floor wax, furniture polish, and I don't know what all."

"Oh, for goodness sake," I said, shaking my head. "That stuff's not worth the powder it'd take to blow it up. I bought some once from Dorene, just to help her out because she was going through a rough patch, and Lillian hated it. We threw it out, and I didn't buy any more."

"Well, a lot of people like it. And that Curtis Maxwell makes it all, and he has housewives all over the country selling it for him. And a lot of men, too, especially those who've lost their jobs. He's worth a mint, Miss Julia, and he's coming to our church."

"What're we supposed to do? Roll out the red carpet for somebody who makes toilet bowl cleanser? It doesn't make sense to me that his arrival deserves to be announced to the session."

"Why, Miss Julia, he's coming in on his private jet, and he's renting a huge house just to be here for a few months. I think it's kind of exciting to have somebody in our congregation who can pick up and go wherever he wants to go in his own airplane."

"Maybe so, but anybody can buy a ticket and go off wherever they want to. Why in the world is Pastor Ledbetter so thrilled about having him?"

"Well, Amy, or rather her husband, thinks he's hoping to have some help with that new roof the sanctuary needs, so he wants everybody to make Mr. Maxwell feel real welcome. He's going to ask him to speak some of the Sundays he's here, you know, in the pulpit and everything, because he's known for his Christian testimony. He talks about how the Lord has blessed him with a successful business. We'll be getting a notice in the mail, asking people to entertain him and make him welcome any way we can."

They Lord, I thought to myself. The pastor was going to ask us to bend over backward for some man none of us knew, just because he had plenty of money and owned a private jet. It vexed me to think of it, for nobody had ever gone out of their way to give me any special treatment, and I had plenty of money. Of course, I didn't have a private jet airplane, but who in the world would want one?

Chapter 11

I spent the afternoon pacing the living room floor, worrying myself half to death while waiting for Binkie. I could hear the never-ending buzz of Latisha talking to, or rather at, Lillian in the kitchen. Little Lloyd was still in school and Hazel Marie was off running errands, still blithely ignorant of what was hanging over our heads. At the sound of tires scraping the curb, I looked out the front window and saw Binkie getting out of her car.

"Binkie," I cried as I opened the door for her. "Are they leaving? What did he say? Did you break the lease?"

"Whew, let me get inside," she said, as she checked the soles of her boots. "I hope I'm not tracking mud inside. Now, listen, Miss Julia," she said, as she plopped down on the sofa, "I did the best I could, but

Dwayne Dooley is not interested in letting you off the hook."

"What did he say? Did you tell him I'd buy him out?"

She nodded. "I told him everything I could think of, and offered him enough money to send you into orbit, but he just kept smiling and shaking his head. He said, 'A deal's a deal, and this'un's a done deal.' So, that's it, Miss Julia, you have to honor the lease."

"Oh, Binkie, this is awful! Isn't there some way . . . maybe there's a mistake, an error or something, when his lawyer drew up the lease. That would do it, wouldn't it?"

She shook her head. "It would, but he showed it to me and there's not a thing wrong with it. Unfortunately, in this case."

"This just makes me ill."

She flashed me a quick smile, which I was unable to return because of the sickness in my heart. "All we can do at this point is watch them," she said. "I talked to Coleman about it, and he said that's a prime area for growing illegal product. For that reason, he said the sheriff's glad the property's being developed because all the activity'll run the pot growers off. That's not much help to you, though."

I sank down in a chair, my perfect plan in tatters now that even the sheriff was smiling on Dwayne Dooley and his efforts.

Binkie brushed back her hair and leaned forward. "Let me tell you what they're doing out there. They've really been busy with bulldozers and equipment of all kinds. They've cut some roads and cleared a parking area for visitors' cars and trailers and motor homes. They've sunk a well to have running water, and got electricity hooked up. They're serious about this theme park business."

I rubbed the frown lines on my forehead. "Well," I said, half resigned to being the enabler of new gossip about Little Lloyd's father. "I guess all I can hope for is that the theme park will fall flat on its face. If nobody patronizes it, they'll have to move on, won't they?"

"I expect they would." She got up from the sofa and started for the door. "I better get back to the office. I've been gone too long already. Miss Julia, I'm sorry about all this. I wish I could fix it for you, but it looks as if you don't have any choice."

"It's all right, Binkie," I said, though clearly it was not. "I appreciate what you've done, and wouldn't have another lawyer if one came free of charge. But let me ask you one thing. If I find out that they're doing something illegal or underhanded, or that they're here under false pretenses or engaged in any other shady activities, I wouldn't have to honor the lease then, would I?"

"No, you wouldn't." She smiled like a conspirator. "If you hear of anything, let me know. We'll run 'em out of town on a rail."

I bade her good-bye, closed the door and sank down in my Victorian chair by the fireplace, just so put out with myself for getting into such a fix. That Mooney woman was out there creating havoc in our lives, and I'd done nothing but aided and abetted her in the doing.

Tiring of sitting and staring off into space, I made myself get up and go upstairs to find something to take my mind off the terrible troubles that Wesley Lloyd was still causing. You'd think that his being dead and gone would've put a stop to rampant rumors about his conduct. But no, they just went on and on, reaching out from the grave to distress and mortify me.

When I got to my room, I found Lillian changing the linen on my bed. She was holding a pillow under her chin while she slipped the other end into a pillowcase.

"Where's Latisha?" I asked.

"She busy colorin' 'cross the hall."

"Good. Lillian, I need to talk to you. Something awful's going on, and I need you to know about it."

She put down the pillow and turned to give me her full attention. "How awful?"

"Oh, Lillian," I moaned, sinking down onto the edge of the bed, "it's just terrible." And I went on to tell her about the Mooney woman and the stories about her and my late husband, and how everybody was talking about them and how she was doing nothing to stop the gossip. "I don't think," I went on, "that it would bother Hazel Marie all that much, except for the shame and mortification she'd suffer. It'd make her mad as fire, I know, just as it did me when I heard about her, but she could handle it. So I'd tell her, if it weren't for Little Lloyd, who I'm trying my best to protect from hearing the tales. Because, Lillian, you know Hazel

Marie couldn't keep a secret if her life depended on it."

Lillian's eyes had gotten bigger as I related the whole sorry tale. "Law," she said, "I thought all that be over an' done with, now Mr. Springer be buried so long."

"You would think, wouldn't you?" I said dryly. "But I guess we can't expect much from a man who was constitutionally unable to stay in his own yard."

"Well, but, Miss Julia, you know Miss Hazel Marie won't go tell that chile 'bout his own daddy's carryin's-on. I don't know why you say she can't keep a secret."

"Oh, I know she wouldn't deliberately tell him. She'd want to keep it from him as much as I do. But you know how smart Little Lloyd is, and he'd know something was wrong as soon as he saw his mother in an agitated state. Which she would be, believe me."

"Yessum, an' first thing you know, he figure out what it is."

"That's exactly what I'm afraid of, and the very reason to keep this to ourselves while I try to send that woman packing. And I'll do anything, Lillian, to keep that child ignorant of his daddy's unnatural proclivities."

"Well," she said, reaching for a fitted sheet, "I hate to mention it, but from all I know 'bout men, Mr. Springer be more nat'ral than un."

"And I hate to hear it, too. Still, they're not all like that." Sam, in all his big personality, shimmered in my mind. "Are they?"

"They's no tellin'," she said, with a rueful smile. "Now, get up from there an' let me get this bed made."

"Let me help," I said, going to the far side of the bed. "I need to busy myself with something."

"Yessum, an' me, too, after hearin' all that. It gonna worry my mind something awful from now on." She flipped the top sheet on the bed, while I took one end of it. "You need all them blankets on here?"

"I certainly do, even if they're so heavy I can hardly turn over."

We spread the blankets and, working in rhythm, soon had the bed made.

"Miss Julia?" Lillian was dusting the bedside table, and didn't look at me when she spoke. "You seen Miz Allen lately?"

"Mildred? Why, no, I don't guess I have. Well, I saw her in Sunday School but, come to think of it, that was a few weeks ago. Why?"

"I jus' wonderin' how she doin'."

"As far as I know, she's doing fine." I looked at her sharply, feeling that she was leading up to something but didn't much want to get to it. "Lillian, what's wrong with Mildred Allen?"

"Well, I hate to bring up something else on top of what you just tole me, and you know I don't like to carry no tales. 'Specially 'bout yo' friends."

"What? What else is happening in this town? Tell me what Mildred's doing, and I'll talk to her about it."

"Oh, no'm, don't you be doin' no talkin' 'bout it, specially not to her. I wouldn't hurt that nice lady for anything in the world."

I was about exasperated by this time, for I knew Lillian did not loosely talk about people. For her to go this far meant something dire had happened to Mildred.

"Just tell me, Lillian. What is it?"

"Well," she said, her eyes carefully avoiding mine, "you know that boy of hers and Mr. Horace's come home some few weeks ago?"

"Tony. Yes, I'd heard he had, and wondered why we haven't seen him in church."

"He not likely to be there any time soon. I tell you, Miss Julia, I never heard the like in my life."

"If you don't tell me what you're talking about, I'm going to call Mildred and get it straight from her. Is Tony sick? Is Mildred sick? What is it?"

"It like this. You know Mr. Tony been in New York City all these years? No tellin' what he been doin', 'cept he say he been in the ladies' dress business."

"Yes, I know, and he's done quite well, I understand. When he was a boy, Mildred used to take him with her wherever she went. We all knew that when we invited Mildred, we'd get Tony, too. Nobody minded, because he was so charming, and he loved to visit with her friends. He sat right down there in my living room many an afternoon, drinking tea and entering into the conversation like he was one of the ladies."

"Yessum, that just the trouble. He be one of the ladies now. Least I hear tell he is."

I frowned. "What do you mean, he's one of the ladies?"

"I mean he done gone and got a operation an' now he say his name Tonya, an' he wearin' dresses an' high heels an' nylon stockin's an' I don't know what all, an' his mama done took to her bed."

"They Lord," I cried, collapsing on a chair. "Surely not, Lillian. That has to be just false and baseless gossip. I know he used to be slightly on the precious side with all that curly hair, and he did like to wear a cape and walk around with a cane occasionally, but Mildred loved him to death and purely doted on him. Oh, this will just kill her. And his daddy! That man must just be crushed."

"What I hear," Lillian said, "is Mr. Horace be sulled up something awful. Won't even look at Mr. Tony, nor talk to him nor nothin' else. He jus' make out like nobody in the house but him and Miz Allen."

"Horace has always been a proud man," I said, thinking of the lumbering investment broker who kept his own counsel while making money for himself and the few clients who could put up with his uncongenial personality. "You know," I went on, "I've always wondered how two such large people as Mildred and Horace could produce such a dainty little thing as Tony."

"Yessum, it be a wonder."

I rubbed my forehead, trying to get my mind around this shattering news. I glanced up at her. "Where did you hear all this? Are you sure it's true?"

"It all over my neighborhood. Mr. Tony, I mean, Miss Tonya, been seen all over town. He got him one of them little sportscars, an' everybody want to know where he get his money. I mean, after payin' for that operation an' all. We figure it don't come cheap."

"I can't believe this. Maybe he's practicing for a part on the stage or something. He was always interested in acting, and did a good bit of it in school. That's probably what it is. He's been away from Abbotsville so long, he's forgotten how people talk. In New York, you can pretty much do whatever you please, and nobody'll look twice at you. That's all it is."

"Maybe so, but Miz Causey, her house next door to mine, if them workers ever get 'em finished up, she seen him, an' she say he got bosoms an' ever'thing. An' they real, too, 'cause she say he wear a dress cut so low, they almost flop out in her face. She didn't hardly know him, but he come right up an' say good mornin', like he real proud of how he look."

This news just about did me in, and I felt for Mildred, knowing that she might never recover from the blow. But the more I thought about it, the more I realized that it could work in my favor. People do talk, you know, but as soon as something new and outrageous happens, the old news is dropped like last week's *Enquirer.* I began to feel much better as I realized that Tony, or Tonya, Allen could take Wesley Lloyd's place in the headlines at the checkout counter. Not that I was happy to hear about his surgical transformation, you understand, but I was gratified that it had come about just when the town could use a new topic.

Chapter 12

Everybody knows that I'm not in the habit of passing along every bit of gossip that comes my way, but I was living in times that were trying my soul. Even though I loved Mildred dearly and fully sympathized with her on the loss of her son, I felt justified in telling Hazel Marie about Tony. I mean, Tonya. Sam needed to know, too, but he could wait.

I was counting on Hazel Marie being so entranced with the way he was said to be flaunting himself around, that she'd pay no attention to whispers about anybody else.

"Come on, Lillian," I said, fully resolved to do my part in spreading the word. "Hazel Marie needs to hear about this."

"Well, I don't know, Miss Julia. We might not oughta be talkin' 'bout it. I ought not of tole you, but I knowed you think a lot of Miz Allen."

"So does Hazel Marie. Besides, if Tony didn't want people to know, he wouldn't've come home. Where is Hazel Marie, anyway? She's going to just die when she hears about Tony. Tonya. Whoever he is."

"She cleanin' out her closet, see what she need for summer."

"Well, let's go." And off we went downstairs and through the back hall to Hazel Marie's room. She had winter clothes piled up on the bed, and she, herself, was on her hands and knees inside the closet with only her bottom sticking out.

"Hazel Marie," I said as we entered the room, "come on out here. Lillian's got a story to tell you that might end up on a rack in the checkout line at the Winn-Dixie. You're not going to believe it."

As Hazel Marie backed out of the closet, Lillian said, "Uh-uh, you tell her."

Hazel Marie stood upright without pulling herself up on anything and without a creak or pop in her joints. I vaguely remembered being able at one time to do the same.

She brushed the hair back from her face and said, "Oh, good. I haven't been to

Velma's lately, so I'm really out of the loop. What's going on?"

"We better sit down," I said, moving shoe boxes off a chair. "This is going to curl your hair. Tell her, Lillian."

So Lillian did, and Hazel Marie's eyes got bigger and bigger with the telling.

"You mean he was a man, and now he's a lady?" she gasped.

"Hazel Marie," I said, "he may be female, but he is certainly no lady. He was a perfectly lovely young man until he went up north, and it just *ruined* him."

"Yessum," Lillian said, nodding in agreement. "Jus' like it did Janine."

"Oh, I'd love to meet him," Hazel Marie said, her eyes dancing with excitement. "Or do you say her?"

"I don't intend to say either one, although for my money he'll always be a him. I watched him grow up, and I know people change, but they don't turn inside out."

"It's called gender reassignment, Miss Julia. I read about it somewhere, maybe in *People,* and you wouldn't believe the number of men who've done it. They don't even have to go to Sweden any more. They can get it done right here in this country." She her way to help me out of a sticky situation many a time. Maybe if we showed her that we accepted Tony, or Tonya, she might be grateful for our efforts. I mean, after one great, big coming-out party, so to speak, everybody would know and she wouldn't have to explain him ever again. It never works to try to hide anything, anyway."

"Miss Julia," Lillian said, glowering at me, "you ought not be thinkin' that way. Yo' pastor get all steamed up, you commence makin' out like they no diffrence 'tween a man an' a woman."

I smiled. "All the more reason to do it." But my real reason was one I was unwilling to share. A gala affair to introduce Tonya Allen to local society would bring out every woman in town who counted, socially speaking. No one would refuse an invitation to such a function. Not that anybody ever refused my invitations, barring the excuse of sickness or death, but this would be the highlight of the season, as well as several seasons afterward. For all I knew, it would enter the annals of Abbotsville lore, and be talked about for years to come. What Wesley Lloyd did or did not do when he was alive and kicking wouldn't be able to hold

frowned and shuddered. "Think of all
electrolysis they have to have."

"Better to think of hair removal," I s
"than of what else gets removed when y
gender's realigned."

But Hazel Marie wasn't listening. Her f
lit up with a sudden idea. "I tell you w
Miss Julia. Let's have a party. A receptio
something, and invite him and everyb
we know."

"Hazel Marie!" I cried, springing from
chair. "How can you suggest such a thi
No, Mildred would not want to draw att
tion to her shame. The thing to do is ov
look him, pretend nothing's out of the o
nary." Then, on a sudden second though
sat back down and considered how
tongues would wag at our audacity in h
oring the new woman in town. Maybe
party wasn't such a bad idea. "Of cour
he might not accept," I mused aloud, "ar
know Mildred wouldn't. She's such a stic
ler for the rules of etiquette, you know, a
I don't think Emily Post covers a situati
like this."

I tapped my fingers against my mou
my mind running through the possibilitie
"Still," I went on, "Mildred has gone out

a candle to the thrill of seeing this new woman in the flesh or to my boldness in making him the guest of honor.

"Oh, let's do it," Hazel Marie urged. "I'd love to see what he'd wear. I mean, if he's been in New York, he'd have the latest styles, wouldn't he?"

I didn't care what he'd wear. Well, yes, I did. If he showed up in a three-piece suit and tie, that would certainly put a crimp in my strategy.

"Let me think about it for a minute," I said, wondering if I dared go through with it. Although, if anything could send the Mooney woman to the bottom of the town topics list, Tonya Allen would.

"Miss Julia," Lillian said, "you gonna be talked about, you go an' have a party for such as this."

"I've been talked about before," I reminded her. "And, Lillian, you know you'd love to see him up close."

"I know I would," Hazel Marie said. "Although we ought to make it a morning function when Lloyd's in school. I don't think I could explain Tonya to him, and I certainly don't want to give him the idea that people can pick and choose whatever they want to be."

"Miz Causey say you can't tell no difference 'tween Mr. Tony an' a real lady," Lillian informed us. "'Less you knowed him 'fore his operation, which she did, so she could."

"Yes, but Hazel Marie's right," I said. "We need to protect that child as much as we can. What's the use of monitoring what he watches on television, if we bring it into our own living room? Now, Hazel Marie, we should put our heads together, and decide what we're going to do, who we'll invite, and how we'll approach Tony about it. I guess we ought to think about that first."

Lillian shook her head at me. "What you oughta be thinkin' 'bout is what Miz Allen think. You go an' hurt that sweet lady's feelin's, you bring shame on yo' own head."

"You're absolutely right, Lillian," I said, recalling the long friendship I'd had with Mildred Allen. "What I have to do is feel her out and see if she has any objections."

Lillian threw up her hands. "She not gonna like it! You know she won't. That boy be flauntin' hisself all 'round town now. You think she gonna want you to he'p him do it even worse?"

"Maybe we ought to rethink it," Hazel Marie said, more soberly than when she'd made her suggestion. She never went out of her way to hurt a living soul, which I both approved of and respected. She didn't, however, know what was burdening my soul. And it wasn't Mildred Allen, as much as I liked her, and it certainly wasn't that chameleon of hers.

"Neither of you know Mildred like I do," I said, unwilling to let the idea of a party that would be talked about for weeks, if not forever, go so easily. "She might surprise us. For all we know, she may have accepted what she can't change, and would appreciate us doing the same thing. Hazel Marie, I think we ought to pay her a call."

"You mean, like a condolence call?"

"We'll play it by ear. If she's all broken up, then, of course, we'll extend our sympathy. But if she's come to terms with it, then we'll broach the idea of a party. And if she doesn't want to draw too much attention to Tony's alteration, we won't make him the guest of honor. Just invite him as if he's like anybody else."

"Well," Lillian mumbled, "that the las' thing he be. I jus' don't want y'all to get in any trouble, en'ertainin' somebody nobody might not wanta look at, much less be pourin' tea for. What Miz Ledbetter gonna say, anyway? First thing you know, she start cryin' while she pourin'. An' handin' out Bible verses what say be happy in whatsoever condition you find yo'self."

"We'll cross that bridge when we come to it," I said. "Besides, she can't be too critical, since she's been undergoing a little transformation, herself, these days."

I got up again, figuring if we didn't strike while we had a mind to, I might think better of entertaining such an unknown quantity in my own house. Even if it did come from a good family.

"Get yourself together, Hazel Marie," I said, putting my qualms firmly aside. I had a higher good to accomplish, even if it meant doing something slightly underhanded to get it done. "We're going to see Mildred. Then we'll decide if a celebration of Tony's unexpected emergence as a woman is in order."

{ Chapter 13 }

"You have your calling cards?" I asked
Hazel Marie as I parked at the curb in front
of Mildred's house. "In case Mildred can't
see us?"

"In my purse," she said. Then taking her
lip between her teeth as she gazed out the
window at the large Federal-style house,
she went on, "I hope we're doing the right
thing."

"Yes, well, I'm a little uneasy about it, myself. Still and all, I expect Mildred will appreciate a visit from us. You know how people
are in this town. Let something out of the
ordinary happen, and they stay away in
droves, too embarrassed or shocked or
thrilled or something to extend the least little courtesy." I opened the car door. "That's
not my way, though. All she has to do is
refuse to see us, if she's not up to it. We'll

leave our cards so she'll know we cared enough to come by. Come on, Hazel Marie, let's go."

We went up the broad brick walkway to the front door and rang the bell. While we waited, I noticed that all the draperies were drawn across the windows, and no light was coming through the fanlight or the glass panels on each side of the door.

Finally, though, the door opened a tiny bit, and Ida Lee, Mildred's housekeeper, peeked around it. When she saw who it was, she fully opened the door, seemingly relieved to see someone she knew. She looked so neat in her gray uniform with its white collar and cuffs, but her face was drawn and sad-looking.

"Good afternoon, Ida Lee," I said. "Is Mrs. Allen receiving?"

"I don't know if she is or if she's not. Come in, Miz Springer, I'm real worried 'bout her. She been in bed ever since Mr. Tony come home, an' the onliest thing she eat be chocolate candy, one after the other. She real down in the mouth, 'cause none of her other friends been here nor called nor nothin'."

"That's why we came, Ida Lee. Run up

and tell her that Hazel Marie and I love her to death, and we want to see how she is."

"Yessum. Y'all jus' have a seat in the drawin' room, an' I be right back."

As soon as she scurried up the stairs, I looked at Hazel Marie. "See? I knew nobody'd come to commiserate. They're all acting like she has the plague or something."

"They probably don't know what to say," Hazel Marie said, worriedly. "I know I don't."

Ida Lee appeared in the door. "Y'all can go on up. She say she not dressed for comp'ny, but she too sick to get up."

Hazel Marie and I climbed the stairs, turned right and went into Mildred's large bedroom. My Lord, what a sight. The curtains were drawn, dimming the corners of the antique-filled room. Lamps on each side of the bed were the only illumination. Mildred, herself, was spread out in the middle of the four-poster bed, the canopy reaching almost to the ceiling. She was wearing a celadon satin bedjacket and was propped up by a half-dozen lace-edged pillows. Mildred was a big-boned woman to begin with, but sprawled out on the bed like she was, she looked as big as a mountain. She was always neat about her person, though, careful to have her hair and makeup in perfect order.

And so she did that afternoon, if you could overlook the red, swollen eyes, splotchy face and the crumbled Kleenexes that were strewn over the bed covers. A box of Godiva chocolates sat beside her, most of the spaces empty.

"Julia!" she cried, stretching out her arms toward me as soon as we entered. "Oh, you are so sweet to come see me in my time of anguish."

I walked over and endured her embrace, then stepped back so she could crush Hazel Marie to her ample bosom.

"How are you, Mildred?" I asked.

"Heartsick!" she cried, flopping back against the pillows. "Just heartsick. Pull up a chair, Julia, and you, too, Hazel Marie. Close to the bed. I just don't have the strength to raise my voice." She sniffed and pulled out another Kleenex. "I know you've heard about my dear, sweet Anthony. My darling Tony. Oh, Julia, has any mother suffered worse than this?"

"Not having any children, I wouldn't . . . ," I began, but she wasn't listening.

"I don't know how I'm going to live this down," she said, wiping her eyes. "I won't be able to go anywhere in this town ever again. I'll just stay in this bed till I die."

"Oh, come now, Mildred. Worse things have happened, and you'll get over this sooner than you think. You just have to get up and face everybody down. I mean, you can't say you've exactly *lost* Tony."

"That's what he says. He says he's still the same person he ever was inside, that just the outer appearance has changed. But, Julia, surely I would've noticed if he was a girl inside all the years he was growing up. Wouldn't I?"

"You would think so," I said, but I wasn't so sure. Thinking again of the young Tony, I recalled that he was always more comfortable in the company of women. He was never known to participate in the games that little boys seemed attracted to. Never played any kind of ball or engaged in rough and tumble activities that we normally associate with boys. He'd liked tea parties and gentle gossip and the latest fashions. I remembered his telling me once how much he liked a dress I was wearing, and I remembered being inordinately pleased, because he was known to have such fastidious taste. I knew a number of women who had consulted him when they had questions about their wardrobes.

Maybe we'd missed seeing his real self, even though it'd been right in front of our eyes all along.

"Mildred," I said, gathering my nerve, "Hazel Marie has had an excellent idea, and we want to see what you think of it. Tell her, Hazel Marie."

Hazel Marie jumped in her chair. "I don't think it was my idea. I think we all thought of it."

"Oh, I need all the help I can get," Mildred moaned, burying her face in a Kleenex.

I shot Hazel Marie a glare, then took a deep breath and plunged in. "Well, it's like this. We're thinking of having a reception or open house with Tony as the guest of honor. I mean, as a way of introducing him as Tonya, and . . . ," I trailed off, as Mildred lifted her head and stared at me.

"Introducing . . . ?"

Hazel Marie finally gathered her courage and stepped into the breach. "What Miss Julia means is that the only way you can get past the, well, the shock of it, is to act above it all. That's what she did when she took me in, and now nobody thinks a thing about her situation. And everybody's so nice to me, and they will be to Tonya, too, once they get to know her, and if you don't give them a chance to do otherwise."

Well, Hazel Marie certainly had more insight than I'd given her credit for. Of course, she didn't know that another round of shameful gossip was about to descend upon us. I clutched my pocketbook at the thought of it.

"You really think so?" Mildred's voice quavered as she looked from one to the other of us.

"Yes, I do," I said. "Hazel Marie's right. You let them know that Tony's alteration has brought you to your knees, they'll talk about you all the more. But if you show them that you accept him as Tonya, they'll soon tire of the topic."

Lord, I hoped they wouldn't, but I couldn't tell her that. It never ceased to amaze me how hard it is to carry out a devious plan with complete ease of heart, and without getting mixed up, for I am essentially an honest and forthright woman.

Mildred slowly shredded a Kleenex, the

diamonds in her rings glinting in the lamp-light. She seemed to be giving our proposal serious thought. "It could work, maybe. If I had the courage to go through with it." She stopped and looked up at me. "Julia, you've heard what they say when a son gets married? That you're not losing a son, you're gaining a daughter? Well," she gasped as tears overflowed again. She sniffed loudly, then went on. "I'm trying to comfort myself with that. I mean, I guess I now have both a son and a daughter, although he'll always be my darling Anthony to me." Her shoulders crumpled over, as sobs overtook her. "Even," she gasped, "even if he does have to wear a brassiere."

"That's something I've never understood," I ventured, since I couldn't help but wonder about it. "How did he get . . . ? Oh, forgive me, Mildred, I shouldn't ask such a personal question."

She waved her hand. "It's all right. I know everybody's dying of curiosity. Besides, I had to ask, too." She wiped her face again. "Hormones, Julia, that's what it is. And surgical implants, of all things, because he said the natural ones weren't big enough. *Natural.* Hah! If they were really natural, he'd take after me and they'd be bigger than he wanted." She reached for my hand and held on tight. "More than ten years that boy was in New York, and all that time he was saving his money to spring this on me, and saving the money I sent to him, too, because I couldn't bear the thought of him doing without what he needed. And he *thanked* me, Julia, for helping make his dream come true. Oh, if I'd only known." She flung her arm over her forehead and sighed loudly. "I had to be helped to my bed when he came home looking for all the world like an aging Britney Spears, only better dressed, without a bit of warning or even a hint of what he'd done, and he knows my heart can't take such sudden shocks."

"It's all right, Mildred," I said, hoping to soothe her. "I understand that he is a most attractive woman. You can take pride in that."

"You are the kindest of all my friends, Julia. And you, too, Hazel Marie. Do you know that the only person to befriend Tony has been Calvin?"

"Calvin?"

"Yes, you know him. He's worked for me for several years in the yard and around the house. He drives me sometimes, too. He's been so kind and considerate to Tony. They have a real affinity for each other. Of course, Calvin never knew Tony when he was a boy, so I guess it's not such a shock to him. I am so grateful to him for being such a friend." She glanced up at me. "Tony's still in the recuperative stage, you know, and he needs care and kindness, which Calvin goes out of his way to give him."

My word, I thought, Calvin and Tony? Of course, it was Calvin and Tonya, for all Calvin knew. Mildred, however, seemed not to have put two and two together, so I wasn't about to add it up for her. One's background and social class meant everything to Mildred, and I just couldn't see her welcoming a laborer in overalls into her drawing room. Still, a shocker like this, if that's what it was, would make Wesley Lloyd's additional escapades seem small potatoes, indeed. I smiled to myself.

"So, Mildred," I said, "what do you think about an open house to introduce Tonya? How would he feel about it?"

She sighed. "She would love it." She swiped again at her eyes as fresh tears welled up and spilled over. "More's the pity."

{ Chapter 14 }

Hazel Marie was uncommonly quiet on the drive home, but I was so busy chattering about our upcoming social coup that it took me a while to notice.

"We'll invite everybody in the garden club, Hazel Marie," I said, switching on the windshield wipers against another rain shower. "I'll get their names and addresses from Helen Stroud, and of course everybody in the Lila Mae Harding Sunday School class. I expect they all knew him when, and will want to see what he's turned into. I'll get out my Christmas card list, and we need to check the high school teachers, too. Some of them may have been there when Tony was coming along. I say we invite everybody who has the least interest in him, and some who wouldn't know him from Adam, but will talk about him anyway. Norma Cantrell for one, don't you think?" I glanced over at Hazel Marie as we approached our drive, but she was looking out the window. "Hazel Marie? Don't you think inviting Norma would be a good idea? I'd like to see if having an affair makes her look any different, don't you?"

"Hm-m-m? Oh, yes, I guess so." Hazel Marie was not giving the invitation list her full attention. In fact, as soon as I put the car in park, she was out of the door like a shot.

I followed her into the kitchen where she was asking Lillian, "Where's Lloyd? Is he home from school?"

"Yessum, he upstairs with Latisha, tryin' to do his homework while she talkin' to him."

Hazel Marie went to the foot of the back staircase and yelled, "Lloyd! I want you down here right this minute!"

My eyebrows went up, and Lillian and I looked at each other. Raising her voice was not at all like Hazel Marie.

Little Lloyd and Latisha, who was still lugging that bedraggled doll, came clattering down the staircase.

"Ma'am?" he asked.

Hazel Marie propped her hands on her

hips and demanded, "What are you doing in the house on this pretty day? Outside!" She pointed to the back door. "I want you out there right this minute, and I want to see a ball in your hands. Shoot some baskets, play pitch, hit a few, I don't care what. Just get out there and roll around in the dirt if you can't think of anything else."

Little Lloyd's eyes darted around, looking for some help. Latisha edged around behind him, staring at Hazel Marie like she'd never seen her before. I was just as dumbfounded as they were at this singular outburst.

"Ma'am?" Little Lloyd asked.

Hazel Marie pointed at the door with an arm so stiff that her finger trembled. "Out! You don't need to be staying in this house all the time with a bunch of women. Invite a friend over! Go see a friend, one of the boys from school. I want to see some *football* around here!"

"But, Mama, it's raining."

"A little rain won't hurt you. As long as there's daylight, I want you outside playing like any normal boy."

Little Lloyd sidled around her and headed for the door, Latisha right behind him. They both kept their eyes on Hazel Marie, wondering what would come down on them next.

Latisha piped up, "I think he pretty normal, far as I can tell."

"Latisha," Lillian cautioned her, but quietly.

As the children left, I sank down into a chair, realizing what was troubling Hazel Marie. I wiped my face with my hand.

"Hazel Marie, I don't think you have to worry about Little Lloyd. He may not be much interested in athletic activities, but he's not at all interested in fashion."

Hazel Marie's eyes flashed. "I'm taking no chances."

"Law!" Lillian cried, suddenly understanding the cause of the tirade we'd just witnessed. "You think that chile be another Tony Allen? He not ever gonna come in here in a dress! Why, Miss Hazel Marie, he all boy!"

"Yes," Hazel Marie fumed, "and I expect Mildred Allen thought the same thing when Tony was his age. I tell you, Miss Julia, this whole thing scares me to death. Lloyd's never had a constant male influence in his life. His daddy, well, we won't go into that, but you know. Coleman was so good with him. But now he's married, and even though he stays in touch, it's not the same. There's only one thing I see to do."

"Sit down, Hazel Marie, and calm yourself." I swung out a chair for her. "Pushing that child into activities he's not interested in is not going to help. You have to look at his talents and his aptitudes, and it seems to me that those indicate a wholesome masculine trend."

"Like what?" she asked, taking a seat and leaning her head on her hand. "Help me, Miss Julia, I'm so afraid I'm raising him wrong, I don't know what to do. All I could think of while we were at Mildred's is that one day I'd be bawling my eyes out over Lloyd and the way he turned out."

"Now you listen to me," I said, getting in her face as much as I dared. "You have to look at that child the way he is, not the way you fear he is. Now, I know he's not rowdy and boisterous and into sports and wrestling and such like. He's not even very muscular, but that's genes for you. But he is not girlish, and he's not interested in dolls or fixing hair or dressing up in your clothes. He has manly interests."

"Like what?" she asked again.

"Well, he's a wizard with that computer you got him. And he knows numbers and figures, and is ever so much help to me in keeping my records straight. He knows property values, and I wouldn't be surprised if one of these days soon he's going to get into buying and selling. He has an analytical mind, Hazel Marie, and he's smart as a whip."

"Everything you just said applies to any number of girls, and to you, too, Miss Julia," she said, startling me with the truth of her observation where I was concerned.

Lillian decided to add her two cents' worth at that point. "I still say that chile all boy. I oughtta know, 'cause I brung up three girls an' he nothin' like any of 'em. Now I give you, he don't act too much like some of them boys what show theyselves ever' chance they get, but you can thank the good Lord for that."

The kitchen settled into silence after Lillian's summary, as we all faced up to the dearth of masculine activities and attributes of the only male—young though he was—in the house.

"Maybe," I said, acknowledging my own

sudden concern, "maybe he just hasn't found the sport that suits him. Tennis, Hazel Marie, we ought to try him with tennis. Or swimming, or I don't know, horseshoes or something. A lot of people, I mean a lot of *boys,* aren't into team sports, and there's not a thing wrong with that. Maybe he needs a sport where individual talent can excel."

"That won't be enough," Hazel Marie said. "What he needs is somebody who'll show him what it means to be a man. If we're not careful, Miss Julia, all he'll know is us and tea parties and spring clothes and where hems will be next season."

"Well, I don't know what we can do about that, unless the three of us suddenly take up football or something."

She took a deep breath and said, "I know what to do about it. A mother just has to make sacrifices for her child, and that's what I'm determined to do."

My eyes popped open. "You can't be thinking of sending him to a military school. Hazel Marie, I beg of you, he is not the military type."

"No." She shook her head. "I couldn't bear to send him away. No, the thing to do is move back in with J. D. There's nobody more masculine than he is, and Lloyd loves him to death. You know, those few months when we lived with him, Lloyd was copying everything about J. D. He even copied that little swagger that J. D. gets sometime. No boy could live with J. D. Pickens and grow up to be anything but a real man." She pushed back the hair that kept flopping in her face. "I said I wouldn't live with him ever again until he was ready to marry, which looks like never, but for Lloyd's sake, that's what I'm going to do."

"Hazel Marie," I said, understanding her reasoning, but hating the thought of losing them to another round of illicit cohabitation. "Think about this carefully. Think about the kind of influence you'd have on that child, if you take up with Mr. Pickens again in open defiance of the conventions."

"All I know, Miss Julia, is that I'd rather Lloyd grow up and *live* with a woman, than grow up and *be* one."

I had to admit she had a point. Although I didn't say it out loud because I didn't want to encourage her to be a significant other rather than a wife and miss out on all the social and legal benefits of the marital state.

"Excuse me, Miss Julia, Lillian," Hazel Marie said as she rose from the table. "I need to think about this for a while."

She left and, as I watched her go, I felt for her, even though I thought that she had little to worry about where that child was concerned. Still, what did I know about raising children, particularly raising them in the way they ought to go?

"Miss Julia," Lillian whispered as soon as the door closed behind Hazel Marie. "That Mr. Pickens call while you gone, and he want to talk to you. He say not to tell Miss Hazel Marie, and for you to call him soon as you can when she can't hear you." She frowned at me. "What you got goin' on with Mr. Pickens?"

My spirits lifted at once, as I hoped Mr. Pickens had some good news for me. I got up and walked over to Lillian so I could whisper and not be overheard. "I'm sure it's about that Mooney woman, Lillian. I've employed Mr. Pickens to look into her activities, and we don't want Hazel Marie to know anything about it."

"Oh," she said, her eyes getting bigger. "I hope he run her outta town." Then she lowered her voice even more. "You gonna tell him he 'bout to have a boy move back in with him an' do everything he do?"

"Not for anything in the world. No, that's between him and Hazel Marie." I stopped and considered for a moment. "Although, I might mention the advantages he'd enjoy by having his own family, especially if it's blessed by both the church and the state."

"Uh-huh," she said. "I know that mean a lot to him."

Chapter 15

I tiptoed through the dining room, then part-way down the hall to check on Hazel Marie without alerting her. Then I crept up the stairs and into my room.

"Mr. Pickens?" I said when he answered his phone. "Julia Springer here. Hazel Marie's in her room with the door closed, and I'm upstairs with mine closed. What do you have to report?"

"Just the basics, I'm afraid. Monique Mooney—"

"Monique! What kind of name is that?"

"Beats me. It's just her name. I've checked the birth records at the court-house, and she was born in Abbot County fifty-one years ago. Father's name is, or probably was, Hoyt Mooney and the mother was a Lola Bennett Mooney, both from around Grovetown in the west of the county. Then I asked around—"

"Surely you didn't tell people why you were asking."

"Miss Julia," he said with the air of someone about half put out. "I know my job. Anyway, seems this Monique went to a county school, dropped out in the tenth grade, then some few years later took the GED and passed. I couldn't get a line on what she was doing before that, but sometime in the late sixties she married a William Wainright. No record on that in this county, but there is a record of a divorce. The record's spotty, but looks like the marriage lasted about two years. She married a Carl Simpson in 1983, when he was seventy-two."

"My word."

"Yeah, well, he died a year later. Then she went back to her maiden name. From what I've been able to find out, she worked off and on as a checkout girl in a couple of supermarkets, and she was on the night shift at a convenience store for a while. That's what people who knew her think they remember. Nothing that I could pin down, though. The only interesting thing I've found is that she worked as a teller in Mr.

Springer's bank for a couple of years or so in the late eighties."

"Oh," I moaned.

"I lose track of her in '89, but I located somebody who worked with her in the bank. A Millie Weston, who was also a teller, and a talker too, let me tell you. She told me there were rumors at the bank about Monique and a number of local men, but she only knew Mr. Springer's name for sure. She said everybody disliked her, because she got so much time off without being docked for it. Then it seems Monique left town in somewhat of a hurry—that's according to Millie—and the word is that she joined up with some sort of traveling show or carnival or something. I don't know how accurate that is, but I've not found anything else on her till she shows up here again with this Dooley character."

"Can you find out who the other men were? They need to take some of the heat, too," I said, hoping for a semblance of safety in numbers.

"No, that won't help you," Mr. Pickens said, infuriating me with his assumption that he knew what would help me. Before I could contradict him, he went on. "Their names aren't relevant to whatever she had going on with Mr. Springer, which is what we're concerned with. And I've pretty well confirmed that she did work in the bank, where she could've attracted his attention if he was so-minded."

"Oh, believe me, Mr. Pickens, he was so-minded. And I expect she was, too."

"Yeah," he said, "I'll keep looking around, asking questions and so on. This Millie Weston didn't have a lot of good to say about her. Seemed to think that Monique was a little on the loose side." He stopped then went on. "Well, what she said was that Monique was an out and out slut. I'm quoting her, because you know I don't use that kind of language."

I bit my lip, too intent on my concerns to respond to his usual inappropriate levity. I was finally able to ask the crucial question. "Mr. Pickens, I have to ask. Is there any record of her having a child?"

"No, and I should've told you that right off. I've checked county and state records and there's nothing on her having a child. That's not to say she never had one, because it looks like she traveled around a lot."

"Let us hope and pray she didn't go to another state and have one." I cringed at the thought of that woman claiming to have Little Lloyd's half-brother or half-sister, a state of affairs that would devastate him and divest him of his inheritance.

"Mr. Pickens? Why do you think this woman is letting rumors fly around about her lapse?"

"Her lapse?"

"You know, with Mr. Springer."

"Oh. Well, we don't know that she is. If there was gossip before she left, her coming back could be what's revving it up again. That Millie Weston, for one, didn't mind talking about her."

"Maybe so, but the Mooney woman isn't doing one thing to stop it. She should've known that coming back here would start the talk again. But it's as if she doesn't care about her own reputation. I tell you, Mr. Pickens, I don't understand people."

"Tell you what, Miss Julia, I'll keep looking, but I also want to get in closer. I'm thinking of applying for a job out there where they're building the theme park. Do a little undercover work."

"Oh, my. Is that a good idea? What if they find out who you are?"

"No reason for them to. They don't know me, and it's the only way to see what she's up to."

"You are a fine man, Mr. Pickens. And I say that even though you've been known to try my patience many a time. But I will be forever grateful to you if you can prevent this woman from destroying Little Lloyd's belief in his father."

"I have a stake in this, too, you know," Mr. Pickens said. Which was truer than he knew at the present time.

"Let me know, Mr. Pickens, because I want this over and done with as soon as possible. And I'll tell you something else. When you get through, you're going to have another mission, one that I know you'll be happy about. But it will involve a *heavy* responsibility."

"What?"

"You'll see. You just keep one thing in mind: responsibility. In the meantime, I'll be doing what I can to stop that woman's ugly talk. I have a few tricks up my sleeve."

He laughed. "I don't doubt it."

⌒⫘⌒

I was sitting in the living room after dinner, trying to keep my mind on the invitation list I was making out. You would think I'd be able to focus on something as important as that, but I found Rachel Claussen's name on it in three places. I marked out two of them, then went through the listing of physicians in the phone book to see if I'd left off any of their wives.

"Miss Julia!" Hazel Marie startled me as she suddenly flew into the room. "Guess what he's done now."

"Who? Tony?"

"No! That J. D. Pickens, who is the most uncooperative man who ever lived. Here, he's been begging me, *pleading* with me to move back in with him, and when I call him up and say I'm ready to do it, he's too *busy!*" She flung her arms out and glared at me. "His *client* needs him, as if Lloyd doesn't. I don't understand him, I just don't! I tell him what I've decided to do, *throwing* myself at him and expecting him to be over here in a flash to help me move. But what does he do? Says he'll be busy for a few days, maybe a week, and I won't hear from him until he's finished working for his *client.* I tell you, I'd like to know who that client is. Just who is so blamed important that he doesn't have time for me when I need him!"

I managed to keep my emotions from showing during this tirade. I was as much relieved to learn that he was on the job as I was fearful that Hazel Marie would find out who he was on the job for.

"Hazel Marie," I said, "I doubt a few more days will do much damage to the child's character. Besides, I will purely hate to see you go. I've grown accustomed to having you both around."

Hazel Marie smiled and calmed herself enough to sit beside me. "Now, Miss Julia, you know you're not going to have time to miss us. When you and Sam are married, you'll be so happy you won't even know we're gone. And, I'll tell you, it will be a relief to me to know you'll be with someone who'll look after you. I never told you this, but one of the reasons I left J. D. the first time was because I was worried about you being alone."

"Oh, Hazel Marie, that is dear of you. So thoughtful. But I thought the reason you

came home was because one of his ex-
wives showed up."

"That, too. What both of us ought to do, if
I could get some cooperation from J. D.,
and Sam could get some from you, is get
married. You to Sam, and me to that hard-
headed horse's behind. That would solve all
our problems."

"Don't count on it, for I'm not marrying
Sam." Tears sprang to my eyes, in spite of
myself. I blinked and looked away.

"You're not? Oh, don't tell me that. I
thought you were right on the brink."

"I was, but I stepped back."

"I don't understand. What do you have
against getting married?"

"Not a thing, Hazel Marie, for you. I would
like nothing better than to see you safely
married. But I've already had that experience, and I don't care to repeat it. Once you
do it, it keeps coming back on you." I patted her hand, deeply gratified that she had
worried about me. "Now, Hazel Marie, you
just let Mr. Pickens do his job, whatever
it is and for whoever his client is. The fact
that he's doing what he's committed to
do shows a healthy sense of responsibility.
Which is what you want to see in a man."

"Well, I know," she said, but without sounding as if she necessarily agreed with it. "But I'll tell you this: J. D. Pickens may not want to be a husband, but he's going to be a father, or he's seen the last of me. Lloyd *needs* him."

I opened my mouth to reply, but the doorbell rang and prevented my giving her whatever pearl of wisdom I was about to impart.

"Why, LuAnne," I said, as I opened the door and immediately tried to think of how to get rid of either her or Hazel Marie. If LuAnne had come to pass along more of what she'd heard concerning my husband and Hazel Marie's, well, whatever he'd been to her, I had to head her off. But I did my duty as a hostess and welcomed her as warmly as I could manage. "Come in, LuAnne. Hazel Marie, don't you have to pick up something at the cleaners?"

Hazel Marie frowned. "No'm, I don't think so. How are you, LuAnne?"

"Hi, Julia, Hazel Marie," LuAnne said, breezing in and handing me her jacket. "I'm glad you're both here, because I'm about to die to tell you the latest."

Oh, Lord, I thought, and wondered if I dared strangle her with her own coat.

"First off," LuAnne said as she bounced down on the sofa, "can you believe it about Tony Allen? What he's done to himself is just unheard of. Can you imagine what it's like for Mildred, being on the cutting edge of medical science?"

I breathed out in great relief. "Mildred's doing fine, LuAnne. Still and all, I don't think I'd mention 'cutting edge' to her, if I were you. And I might as well tell you now, Hazel Marie and I are giving a reception for Tony, to sort of re-introduce her to the town. You'll be getting an invitation in the next week or so."

"Really?" LuAnne's face lit up. "Oh, Julia, that's wonderful. I can't wait to see what he looks like. Listen, I've been wondering about something, and maybe you know. I know Tony got baptized long time ago, but what about Tonya? Won't she have to be baptized, too?"

"Oh, my goodness," Hazel Marie said, as the full import of the theological question hit her. "You're right, LuAnne. *His* name's on the church roll, but hers isn't."

"For goodness sake, you two," I said, not wanting to get tangled up with another sticky problem. "That's one thing I'm willing to let the pastor straighten out on his own. Although I will be interested to see how he handles it."

LuAnne hunched forward on the sofa. "Well, I'm going to ask him about it. Now listen, have you heard from Emma Sue?"

"Why, no," Hazel Marie said. She glanced up at me. "Have you, Miss Julia?"

I shook my head, as I continued to wrack my brain for a quick change of subject if LuAnne started springing Monique and company on Hazel Marie.

"Well, you will," LuAnne said, "because she's having several get-togethers next week and inviting a few church members to each one. I'm invited for Monday, and I was hoping you'd be going on the same day, but I guess not."

"What're these get-togethers for, Lu-Anne?" I asked.

"Oh," she said with a laugh, "I guess I didn't tell you that. They're to introduce Curtis Maxwell. You know, so we can get to know him on a personal basis? I'm real excited about it. He is so well-known everywhere, even written up in *Time* magazine one time. Why, he's been to the White House and everything." She leaned forward and lowered her voice. "I understand that he's advised the president on a number of occasions."

"Lord help us," I said before I could help myself.

"Well, now, Julia," LuAnne said, "Mr. Maxwell is a highly successful business-man. *And* he's a Christian. Who better to advise the president, I ask you. I, for one, am thrilled that our leader seeks advice from somebody like Mr. Maxwell. Some-body who stands for traditional family val-ues and who's made his money with the help of the Lord."

"LuAnne, for goodness sake," I said. "Hazel Marie showed me that *Time* article on him, and he's made his money on a pyra-mid scheme, where thousands work for him, funneling money to the top. How he gets away with it is a mystery to me. Now, is that really the kind of businessman you want advising the president or meeting at one of Emma Sue's get-togethers?"

"Oh, Julia, you are just so cynical," she said, waving her hand as if what I'd said was of no account. "Mr. Maxwell is a *Christian.*"

"Yes, well, I've known a number of Christians whose financial or political advice I wouldn't take in a million years."

"Then," she said with an edge to her words, "I guess you won't go to meet him."

"Of course I will. Why shouldn't I? I just don't expect to lose my head because he's talked to the president. Anybody with enough money can do that." Thinking, if that were my goal in life, I could send in a hefty enough check to be invited to a White House soiree, myself.

"Oh, and Julia," LuAnne said, standing as she prepared to take her leave, "you won't believe all the talk that's going around about that Mooney woman I told you about."

I could've smacked her, and it was all I could do not to. "LuAnne!" I said, right sharply. I put her coat on her shoulders and turned her toward the door. "We don't want to hear it."

"I do," Hazel Marie said. "Who's the Mooney woman?"

"Nobody, Hazel Marie." I opened the door and practically shoved LuAnne out. "I'll talk to you later, LuAnne. Thanks for stopping by."

I closed the door and turned to Hazel Marie, hoping to quickly repair the damage.

"That woman carries tales about people we don't even know. And I, for one, am tired of hearing them."

"Oh, I enjoy hearing what's going on," Hazel Marie said, but in an unconcerned way, "even when I don't know the people. It's all interesting to me."

This particular item, though, would be more interesting than she'd want, but I pretended none of it was of concern to me. "I tell you what, Hazel Marie, let's go shopping. And I do believe we have some cleaning to pick up."

If the mention of a shopping trip wouldn't distract her, I thought, nothing would. And it did, to my great relief.

Chapter 16

Emma Sue did call, inviting us for Thursday morning. Ordinarily it would've miffed me because it was so late in the week, meaning that she'd invited others before us. But I had too much on my mind to let such trivial matters concern me. Besides, she was probably saving the preferred guests for last, as I'd often done myself. But I told Hazel Marie that I'd never in my life heard of a preacher's wife having little get-togethers to introduce a visitor who had no intention whatsoever of joining the church.

"A visitor is lucky to get a phone call," I'd said. "But a party? The only thing I can say is that the roof on the sanctuary must be in worse shape than we know."

When we got to the Ledbetters' house that Thursday morning, I took in the long, ranch style construction, recalling the old

Victorian that had once been the manse, owned by the church and available to every pastor we'd had for some thirty years. It hadn't done for Larry Ledbetter, however, for he made it clear before accepting our call that he wanted a house of his own. And to that end, he'd asked for a larger salary and help with a down payment. So the old Victorian was now sold to a lawyer, who opened his office in it and complained about the heating bill, and the church owned no property at all, except what it was sitting on.

Emma Sue opened the door for us, smiling broadly in welcome. At the sight of her, I managed a greeting as Hazel Marie gasped behind me. And no wonder, for the woman wasn't wearing a lick of makeup in spite of all the efforts of Velma and Hazel Marie. She was back to the plain soap-and-water face that she'd presented to the world before her foray into the field of cosmetics.

"Don't look so surprised, Julia," she said. "This is the way the Lord made me, and it's been shown to me that his handiwork doesn't need anything artificial on it. Of course," she went on with a glance at Hazel

Marie's expertly made-up face, "I'd never criticize anybody who felt differently."

Of course she would, for she had in the past. But I'll say this for her, Emma Sue looked as happy as I'd ever seen her— glowing, in fact. Whatever she was doing to herself, it certainly hadn't come from the Clinique counter.

After ushering us in to join the ten or so church women milling around the living room and dining alcove, Emma Sue turned to greet a few more invitees who'd come up the walk behind us. Hazel Marie and I spoke to those already there and began to mingle with the small group. I could hear Emma Sue's excited voice urging her guests to have something to eat, to find a seat, to be sure and meet Mr. Maxwell. She'd never been a comfortable hostess, mainly because preachers and their families were more accustomed to being entertained than doing much of it themselves. But that's neither here nor there, for Emma Sue was thoroughly enjoying herself.

I poked Hazel Marie when I saw Norma Cantrell emerge from the kitchen, carrying replenishments for the table. "Look, Hazel Marie. What's she doing here?"

Hazel Marie whispered, "Maybe Emma Sue's keeping her away from the pastor's office."

I got another jolt when I saw Mayor Beebee circulating among the women, shaking hands and patting shoulders. He and Norma did not even look at each other, although I watched carefully to see if they'd give themselves away. Then I poked Hazel Marie again and whispered, "And what's he doing here?"

She whispered back, "I don't know. Maybe he came by to see the pastor. Except he's not here."

Emma Sue shooed us toward the group that was clustered around the Christian mover and shaker we'd heard so much about. To tell the truth, I was somewhat eager to see what he looked like. I expected him to be just as powerful in his person as he was in his reputation. Which just shows how wrong your expectations can be.

When the crowd parted, and Emma Sue introduced us, I was surprised to see a short, slender man who I wouldn't've given a second look on the street. But on closer inspection I saw he had that sleek look that only careful attention to one's grooming can give. He had brown hair that had been thin-ning until he'd had it surgically plugged. I know, because it was planted in rows on the top of his head. His eyes were hazel; his complexion clear and nicely tanned—all that jetting off to sunny climes, I imagine—and he had the sheen that Hazel Marie said came from facials and expensive creams made especially for men. Or *pour homme,* if you'll pardon the little French I know.

His hand was soft when he shook mine, and I was shocked to suspect clear polish on his nails. I couldn't help but wonder what Emma Sue thought about it. From all I could see, Mr. Maxwell had certainly not let the Lord's handiwork speak for itself. His suit and silk paisley tie were fine-looking, and I knew in a minute that I was seeing custom-made clothes. Although I do admit that it was probably the first time I'd ever seen any.

Mr. Maxwell was most pleasant, asking us about our interests, complimenting our town and our church, and, most especially, taking pains to praise Pastor and Mrs. Larry Ledbetter, especially Mrs. Ledbetter.

I didn't know what to make of him but, af-ter getting an eyeful of Emma Sue, from which I'd not yet recovered, I wasn't in any condition to pass judgment on her guest of honor.

Standing in the group around Mr. Maxwell, I happened to glance across the room, catching Louise Wortham and Peg Dolan eyeing me. They quickly turned away, then put their heads together to continue their whispering. I knew as sure as I was standing there that they were talking about the Mooney woman and wondering how much I knew.

I took Hazel Marie's arm and whispered, "Let's get something to eat to be courteous, then go home."

But right then, Emma Sue clapped her hands to get our attention. "Everybody! Everybody!" she called out, even before Hazel Marie and I could move to the table where coffee and finger sandwiches waited in vain. "Everybody find a seat. Curtis, I mean, Mr. Maxwell, has a few words he'd like to say."

We obediently found a seat on Emma Sue's sofa, a vaguely Victorian design that would've been much more appropriate in the manse that was now gone forever. Emma Sue's decor left much to be desired, which was what I thought everytime I visited her. Not being a critical person, however, I tried to overlook the framed embroidered slogans and Bible verses that hung on the wall, the cross-stitched pillows with more cute sayings and the crocheted doilies on the arms and backs of the sofa and chairs. There were a few dried wreath arrangements on the walls and a leather Barcalounger that didn't go with anything in the room. I declare, the room just cried out for something besides beige and brown to catch the eye. On the other hand, I expect a preacher couldn't very well afford to have color splashed all around. His wife would be talked about all the more.

"Ladies," Emma Sue said again. "I want to introduce Mr. Curtis Maxwell, the founder, owner, and CEO of Maxwell Household Products, which we all use and love. I know you're as honored as I am to have him with us, and just as eager to hear what the Lord has laid on his heart to say. Now, everybody, let's have a nice round of applause. Curtis, the floor is all yours."

Emma Sue glowed all the more when Mr. Maxwell stepped forward, took both her hands in his and thanked her for giving him this opportunity.

"Ladies," he began, looking very much at ease with every eye on him. "And Mayor Beebee. Let's give this fine man a hand." And he led the applause as the mayor took a bow. I clapped a couple of times, not wanting to appear discourteous.

Mr. Maxwell continued his little speech, pretty much repeating what I'd already heard about our town, our church, and our hostess. Then he got down to brass tacks. "Ladies, fellow-workers in the Lord's vineyard, I'm here in your lovely town, not only for the purpose of meeting you, especially those of you who are a part of the Maxwell Household Products family, but also to give my support to the fine group of people who are preparing to put Abbotsville on the map. The Lord has been gracious enough to bless me beyond my wildest dreams and, for a long time, my heart was burdened with the obligation to give back to him. But I didn't know how to do it, or where to do it. Then after much prayer and study, I knew I'd been touched by the Holy Spirit. He told me to return a portion of what I've been so abundantly given so that others might know his saving grace. Yes, I have received a call from the Holy Spirit, and he told me that the Walk Where Jesus Walked Christian Theme Park is a cause most worthy of my prayers and my support, and, my friends, yours, as well."

Mr. Maxwell paused to let his words sink in, a pause I needed so I could collect myself. At his mention of the theme park, my back had stiffened and my eyes had widened. If this was what we'd been invited to hear, I was mortally offended. Not only because I was trying for all I was worth to get rid of Dooley, Mooney, and company, and had no intention whatsoever of supporting them, but because Mr. Maxwell's paean of praise here in the Ledbetter house meant that the pastor had changed his tune since I'd talked to him. Now that he had his wife back the way he wanted her, why in the world would he get himself—and the church—mixed up in such a harebrained and risky venture? Especially after he'd warned me against getting involved?

But Mr. Maxwell wasn't through. He gave us a confident smile and said, "This effort has centered my life and given it focus, and I know it will do the same for you. I'm here to ask you to give the Lord a chance to change and bless your lives, just as he's changed and blessed mine. Now, I want to leave one thought with you: If you want the Lord to bless you with all the world has to offer, you have to honor him and give him a portion of what you have, no matter how small it might be. It's only in this way that he can pour out the blessings of heaven upon you. And he'll do it, believe me, for I am an example of what he can and will do. Now, I want to turn the floor over to the Honorable Clifford Beebee. Mayor?"

All through this testimony, if that's what it was, my back was getting stiffer and stiffer. I knew we'd been invited to meet Mr. Maxwell, an unusual occurrence at best, but I hadn't known that we were going to be subjected to a plea for money. And now we were going to get a dose of politics on top of that.

I started to get up and take my leave, but I was wedged in on one side by Hazel Marie, and on the other by Amy Broughton.

"I'll be short," the mayor started, and I almost laughed. He was already short enough. "Don't want to keep you ladies too long. I know you have to hurry home to fix lunch for your hard-working husbands." He paused to allow time for us to appreciate his thoughtfulness, although I'm here to tell you that Emma Sue was the only woman there who still prepared a midday meal.

After his little quip fell flat, the mayor pushed on. "I just want to add my two cents' worth to what Curtis has said, and urge you to support the Walk Where Jesus Walked Theme Park. It will be a fine addition to our fine town, but—you may not believe this—there're some in this town who are dead set against it. They're talking it down, saying it'll bring in riffraff and increase the crime rate and I don't know what all. Now, I ask you, would you call Christians who want to walk where Jesus walked *riffraff?* No, you would not. Do you think good Christian folk would be involved in a crime wave? Of course not. I'm here to ask you to throw your support behind these people who are going to make Abbotsville the Christian center of our fair state. Why, just think of it. Pretty soon, we'll have more hotels and motels, more restaurants, more gift shops, and more everything." By this time, the mayor's face was glowing as brightly as Emma Sue's, as he envisioned the economic stimulus the WWJW folks were going to give Abbotsville.

"Now, ladies," he went on, "when it comes time to vote, and the primary is coming up soon, I want you to remember which candidate honors the Lord and supports those who honor him." He stopped and smiled his vote-getting grin. "That's me, in case you don't know. And the one who would like to shut these good people down is my worthy opponent. Keep that in mind when you pull that lever."

Right that minute, I decided I'd cast my vote for the service manager of the Chevrolet dealership. No way in the world would I vote for a politician who stirred politics, money, and religion together. Give unto Caesar, I always say, but my religion is none of Caesar's business.

As we took our leave, the mayor and the moneyman stood beside Emma Sue at the door, giving each of us a last push toward supporting what they had their hearts set on. And making it clear that if you didn't agree with them, something was wrong with you.

"Miz Springer," the mayor said, taking my

hand in both of his, "I hope I can count on your vote."

"You can certainly count on my voting," I said and moved on.

Mr. Maxwell also took my hand and thanked me for all I'd done for the community and for the church. Emma Sue must've told him something about each one of us, because he didn't know me from Adam. Then he surprised me even more.

"I understand that you have been a great friend to my dear sister in the Lord," he said, and put his hand most familiarly on Emma Sue's shoulder. Then he took her hand and raised it to his mouth. He kissed it as she gazed at him in a state of rapture. "She and I are working together to get the WWJW park off the ground, and I hope we can count on your help, too."

"I'll think about it," I said, grabbed Hazel Marie's arm and got us out of there.

"Hazel Marie," I gasped as soon as we were in the car. "What is going on with Emma Sue? Did you see how she fawned over that man, and how he was buttering her up?"

"I sure did, but I just don't see the attraction. I mean, he's a dinky little thing, isn't he?"

"His looks aren't the point," I said. "She's a married woman, and married to a man of God. What's she doing hanging on another man? Lord, does Pastor Ledbetter know what she's doing?"

Then I answered myself. "I'll bet he doesn't. He may have changed his mind about those WW-whatever folks now that Mr. Maxwell has somewhat elevated them, but he can't know how Emma Sue's behaving. I can hardly believe it, myself, and, I'll tell you this, I do not appreciate being roped in under the pretext of a social affair to hear a plea for my money and my vote."

Hazel Marie turned the key in the ignition. "What I can't understand is why she's let herself go so bad. She looked good when I made her up, you know she did. Now, she's right back where she was before Velma got hold of her."

I bit my lip as Hazel Marie pumped the gas. "I expect it's all that holy talk she's hearing from Mr. Maxwell that's made her go bare-faced again. Anything to please him, although I don't know how it could, especially seeing all the artificial improvements he's made on himself." As Hazel Marie pulled away from the curb, I said, "Hazel Marie, I'm worried about Emma Sue. She could be losing her mind and, if she's not careful, she's going to lose her reputation, too."

Chapter 17

By the time we got home, I'd worked myself up into a state of consternation, and it wasn't helped one bit by the letter waiting in the mailbox.

"Look at this, Hazel Marie," I said, waving the offending form letter at her. "It's from the pastor, praising that little man we just met and, would you believe, urging us to support that crew out there on my property."

"Really?" she said, as unbelieving as I was. "I thought you said he didn't think much of them."

"I did, and he didn't. At least *then,* he didn't. But that was before that slick Curtis Maxwell hit town and put dollar signs in the pastor's eyes. That's what wealth will do, Hazel Marie, to the unsuspecting. It can give you more undue influence than you ought to have. But, listen, he can't know how taken Emma Sue is with Mr. Maxwell. It just doesn't stand to reason that he'd approve of that."

"Well, we could've been mistaken." Hazel Marie frowned as she always did when she was trying to figure something out. "I mean, maybe Emma Sue was just excited about having guests, and Mr. Maxwell, in particular."

"Didn't you see how she looked at him? And how he held her hands? And *kissed* one of them? Why, Hazel Marie, he put his hand on her shoulder in such a familiar fashion that I nearly lost my breath right there in front of them."

"I know," Hazel Marie said, "but he's a man of the world and, according to my magazines, those kinds of people do a lot of kissing and holding hands with each other. And it doesn't mean a thing. The only problem I see is that Emma Sue may think it does."

"Oh, my word," I said, sinking down into a chair. "The poor woman has been taken for granted so long she can't see what that man is up to."

"What's he up to?"

"Well, I don't know, Hazel Marie, except

it can't be anything good. First off, his whole business is based on something I thought was illegal and, second, he's hooked up with that WW-whatever group, and you know they're a fringe element. I mean, what is a man of means doing with the likes of them?"

Hazel Marie had no answer, nor had I. But I knew someone who might.

"I've got to talk to Sam," I said.

"Sam," I said as soon as he answered his phone, "I need to talk to you."

"Good, because I need to talk to you, too. Want me to come over?"

I thought for a second, then told him I'd come over there. "Latisha'll be home from kindergarten any minute, and we won't have a minute's peace when she gets here. I'll see you in a little while."

I told Lillian and Hazel Marie where I was going, then had to listen to Lillian reminding me that I'd had no lunch, which I knew better than she did.

When I got to Sam's house, he took me right back to the dining table where James, who managed Sam's house almost as well as Lillian managed mine, had laid out soup and sandwiches for both of us.

"Sit, Julia," Sam said. "We'll eat, then we'll talk. I have a lot on my mind."

"So do I, and it won't wait. I can't eat until I tell you, but I'll tell Lillian you offered me lunch. It'll relieve her mind considerably."

"Nothing can be as important as what I want to talk about," Sam said, "which is you and me. Julia, you're about to drive me around the bend. You won't even discuss why we shouldn't get married. If you'd give me a reason, I'd have something to work with."

I sighed and selected a sandwich. Nothing was going to do but taking up his concerns first. "Number one," I said, thinking that James made an excellent tuna fish sandwich. "I don't see why you want to risk messing up our friendship with marriage. You have James who does everything that a wife would normally do—cooking and cleaning and looking after your house."

"No offense, Julia," Sam said, smiling so that it was hard to take any. "But if I wanted a wife for those things, I'd be looking elsewhere."

"Why, Sam Murdoch, I'll have you know a woman doesn't have to do those things herself, she just has to see that they get done.

And that's what I do. But James doesn't need any supervision. He does fine all on his own."

"Ah, Julia," Sam said, leaning over the table toward me, "there're a few things that James can't do. Snuggle up on a cold winter night, for one thing. And he could never in this world entertain me like you do. No," he said, shaking his head, "I've given it serious consideration, but James is just not up to the job."

"Now you're teasing me."

"I can't help it," he said with a grin. "It's so easy to do."

"Well, save it, because I have some troubling matters to discuss. And they could have severe consequences." Of course, I had a much greater worry on my mind than what I intended to tell him, but I kept it to myself. Instead, I went on to tell him about Curtis Maxwell and how he was the unadvertised patron of the theme park. Then, I told him about Emma Sue and how she'd just glowed—in spite of being completely un-made-up—every time the man looked at her, to say nothing of when he laid hands on her.

"And, what's worse," I said, getting the

pastor's letter from my purse, "is that her husband has had a change of heart and is asking the church to get behind that group, too."

"I know," Sam said. "I got the same letter, and it surprises me that he'd support anything out of the denominational mainstream. It's not like him, even though he's pretty much at odds with the General Assembly half the time."

"But, Sam, that's what's so strange. The pastor told me straight out that he was leery of Dwayne Dooley and what he's doing. Now, when this Mr. Maxwell shows up in his jet plane, he's all of a sudden for it. And worse than that, his wife is acting like she's infatuated with the man."

I leaned my head on my hand, just overwhelmed with the thought of wheels within wheels, everything connecting to everything else and no way to stop any of it. And Sam was sitting there not looking anywhere near as up in arms as I was.

"Listen to me, Sam. You're not getting the seriousness of this. It all started with the preacher's secretary, who's been out cavorting with the mayor, but actually she has her eye on the preacher, whose wife is

didn't know the magazines Hazel Marie read. "If you ask me, Curtis Maxwell is leading Emma Sue down the primrose path, which could lead to her losing her reputation, her testimony, and her husband. And, I'm here to tell you, our church will not stand for a divorced pastor. Now, do you see why I'm so exercised by this?

"And furthermore," I went on, "the mayor, of all people, was there and he thinks the theme park is the best thing to happen to this town since he got elected. Oh, and I forgot to tell you. Norma Cantrell was there, helping Emma Sue. The mayor completely ignored her, and she ignored him. Now, doesn't that tell you something?"

"Wait a minute, Julia," Sam said, laughing in spite of the gravity of the situation. "You suspect Emma Sue and Maxwell because they looked at each other, and you suspect Norma and Beebee because they didn't?"

I waved my hand. "You don't understand these things, Sam. Courting can be done both ways."

"Well, now, that is a surprise. Hmmm, let me see. I've tried all the obvious things. Maybe I ought to try the silent treatment, like Norma and the mayor. You're right,

Julia, I don't understand these things, but all I want to understand is you."

I smiled in spite of myself. "I wish you luck, Sam, if that's what you want, because half the time I don't understand myself. Now, look," I said, putting my hand on his arm, which he immediately covered with his other hand, "we need to do something about this. I think you ought to talk to the pastor and find out why he's changed his mind about that theme park. And find out if he knows Emma Sue is making a spectacle of herself. And if he knows that he's getting the church caught up on one side of a political race, because I don't think a preacher ought to be meddling in politics, and it offends me for anybody to tell me how to vote, I don't care what the issues are. But I'm off the subject. I want to know why the pastor's up to his neck is this unlikely enterprise."

"I'd like to know, myself, to tell the truth."

"Well, then, ask him."

"I might just do that. Now, Julia, if you'll finish up your lunch, we need to talk about a wedding date."

I threw up my hands, almost losing the

sandwich in one of them. "You have a one-track mind, Sam Murdoch. I need your help, here—the whole church does. And I'm not studying anything else until this mess gets straightened out."

"I guess I'd better straighten it out, then," he said, but I wasn't sure that he was taking the matter with the seriousness that it warranted. He covered my hand again. "After that's done, will you talk to me about setting a date?"

"There're a lot more things going on than you know, so I can't promise anything at this point."

"Well, tell me what they are, and I'll take care of them, too."

I wished he could, but how could he, or anybody, protect a child from the repercussions of a philandering father? I opened my mouth to tell him about Monique Mooney, but I quickly closed it again. I couldn't bring myself to admit my double failure as a wife. The natural shame a woman feels when her husband makes it plain that she is an unsatisfactory wife made me keep my own counsel and my mouth firmly closed.

Besides, I was counting on Mr. Pickens

to come up with something that would dis-
credit the woman to such an extent that
nobody in their right mind would give her
the time of day.

⟨ Chapter 18 ⟩

For the next several days, it felt as if the whole town had closed down. People went about their business, and all was quiet. I had heard not one word from Mr. Pickens, and you'd think, wouldn't you, that he'd let his employer know what he was up to. He'd always been too independent for his own good, and I couldn't help but worry about him, out there with that straggly bunch doing who knew what.

And I hadn't heard from Sam, either, which was just as worrisome in its own way. Had he talked to Pastor Ledbetter? And would that open the pastor's eyes to the danger his wife was in? And, if it did, what would he do—lock Emma Sue up in a closet where she couldn't do any harm, or would he run Sam out of the church for being the messenger?

Lord, so much was going on in my mind that I could hardly stand the anxiety. I kept looking at Little Lloyd, wanting to bundle him up and get him out of harm's way. I was in such a state that I'd begun to think that a boarding school in Virginia would be the safest place for him. To all outward appearances, I was my usual serene self, but I was so distraught that it was taking all I could do to keep myself together.

It was with a great effort of will that I helped Hazel Marie address the invitations to our open house for Tonya Allen. I'd had them printed, and every time I looked at one I hoped to goodness it would do its part in sidetracking the gossip that lay heavy on my heart. But, even so, with what I already had to contend with, I was not in a party mood.

Yet once you go so far as to make out a guest list and have the invitations in hand, you might as well go through with the rest of it. I opened one invitation and read the handsome script:

Mrs. Julia Springer
and
Ms. Hazel Marie Puckett

request the pleasure of your company
at a reception
to meet Ms. Tonya Allen

then the date, time, and place, so they'd know when and where to come. I had, of course, telephoned Tony to be sure that he was willing to be put on display but, thank goodness, he wasn't at home when I called. Mildred assured me that he was thrilled, but I was just as glad that Hazel Marie answered the phone when he returned my call.

"Miss Julia," she said, "she was so nice and didn't sound at all like a man. At one point I thought she was going to cry, she was so choked up. She said she'd always thought the world of you, and she'll never forget what we're doing for her."

"They Lord, Hazel Marie," I said, "I hope this whole thing doesn't get out of hand."

"One thing's for sure," she said, "this party's going to be the talk of the town."

"That's . . . ," I started, almost saying *the idea,* but caught myself in time. ". . . the way it goes. You can't do anything in this town without it being hashed and rehashed.

You just have to let it roll off your back, like I do."

But the truth of the matter was that I'd lost my zeal for the idea of entertaining someone who had been one thing one day and another thing the next. But I purely did not know what else to do to distract the town from the news of Wesley Lloyd's latest escapade. The latest to come to light, that is, for who knew what, or who, else lay in the offing?

By the end of the week, responses to the invitations were coming in like I'd never seen before. Sara Bennett called and said she was supposed to have surgery to remove a plantar's wart on the bottom of her foot on the day of the party, but she'd rescheduled it so she could come. And Kathy Morgan put off going to see her new grandbaby in favor of coming to see the new woman in town. I'd never seen such enthusiasm for a party in my life.

So, with Hazel Marie's help and in spite of Lillian's grumbling that no good could come from such a wrongheaded excuse for a party—in many ways, she was more uptight about what was appropriate than I was—we made our plans. I ordered a centerpiece for the table from The Watering Can, and told them to fix arrangements for the two tole urns that would replace the girandoles on the mantel. Between the three of us, we planned the food we would serve, and Hazel Marie placed orders with Katie of Katie's Kuisine, who did lovely trays of finger sandwiches in spite being unable to spell. Lillian, relieved of the last-minute sandwich preparation, would do the sweets and make the coffee and tea. Hazel Marie volunteered to do a fruit tray, saying she could hardly mess up something that didn't need to be cooked.

"So that's it, I guess," I said as she and I checked our lists for the last time. "All we have to do now is wait for the day. I hope it doesn't rain."

Lillian said, "You better hope them ladies don't start faintin' on you when they see what they comin' to see."

Hazel Marie started laughing. "Maybe we ought to have an ambulance standing by, just in case." Then she frowned and went on. "We're not through yet, Miss Julia. What're we going to wear?"

"Oh, I don't know. Something nice and summery, I guess, if this constant rain doesn't cool things down too much. I hope the azaleas'll be blooming in the yard. They'll make it so much more festive, and we may need all the festivity we can get."

Hazel Marie dithered for days, trying to decide what to wear. She brought out her spring and summer clothes and tried on one after the other, worrying herself to death about it.

"I've got to have just the right thing," she told me. "I may have to shop for something."

"Why, you have things you've never worn, Hazel Marie," I said. "Nobody's going to be looking at us, anyway."

"I know, but Tonya will. You know he will, and he'll be dressed in the latest style. I want to impress him, so he won't think we're backwoods hicks."

I just threw up my hands. "He grew up here, Hazel Marie; he knows what we're like. And he'll be trying to impress us, not the other way around."

⁓⫯⁓

With all that going on in the house, you'd think I'd have my hands full and my mind occupied. But, no, all I could think of was when the other shoe would drop. No one, other than LuAnne, of course, had said a word to me about the Mooney woman, but I'd noticed some long, speculative looks aimed my way whenever I went to the bank or the post office. People were talking, I could tell, about me, but not to my face.

Nobody was telling me anything, which is usually the case when you're the main topic. I couldn't stand not knowing how far and how detailed the talk had gotten, so I gathered myself and went to see LuAnne.

I never liked going to her house, or rather to her and Leonard's condo. They'd sold their house in town a few years back, and moved up on the side of the mountain to a two-bedroom unit that was too cramped for the both of them, and even worse when they had visitors. Yet she was always extolling the virtues of condominium living, which I was not interested in hearing, having no plans to move into one, myself.

I'd called, of course, before wending my way up the twisting roads and parking in front of their home.

"Come in, Julia," LuAnne greeted me. "I'm so glad to see you, and I'm so excited about the reception you're having for Tony. I can't wait to see him. Or," she giggled, "is it her?"

"Everybody asks me that," I said, handing her my umbrella, "and I've yet to have an answer."

As we walked down the short hall to their living room, LuAnne whispered, "Leonard's here. I tried to get him to go off somewhere so we could talk. But he stays glued to the television, keeping up with the news, he says. You wouldn't believe what comes on that Fox channel, Julia. They'll say anything in the world on some of those programs. I'd be worried about him, except he sleeps through most of it."

Leonard roused himself from his recliner enough to speak to me, but it seemed such an effort for him to rise that I told him not to bother making it.

"In here," LuAnne said, guiding me through the dining area and into the kitchen, where she moved an ironing board out of the way. "Excuse the mess. I've been iron-ing curtains."

She closed the door behind us and pointed to a small table with a chair on each side of it. "We can talk in here. He won't hear a thing. Want some tea? I have Red Zinger."

"That'll be fine," I said, taking a seat at the table.

When we were both settled with cups of hot tea before us, I forestalled LuAnne's running commentary on the perils of living with Leonard, and said, "LuAnne, I have to know, and you're the only one I can ask. Have you heard any more talk about the Mooney woman and Wesley Lloyd?"

"Oh, Julia," she said, busying herself with stirring her tea. "I don't know whether to tell you or not."

"That means there is. So let's have it."

"I don't know why you want to know. It'll only upset you." She wasn't meeting my eyes, so I knew I'd have to drag it out of her.

"I'm not worrying about being upset, Lu-Anne. That man's already done all the damage he can do to me. It's Little Lloyd I'm concerned about. Now tell me, so I'll know what I'm up against."

"Well," she said, and scooted up in her chair, released from any bonds of conscience she'd had. "I heard that Monique and Wesley Lloyd used to go at it hot and heavy right there in the bank. I mean, right *inside* the bank. After hours, of course, with the blinds closed, but still. Can you imagine?"

"On the marble floor? That's hard to believe."

"No, in his office," she said, a smile playing around her mouth at the thought of it. "The way I heard it was that when the bank was dark and empty, he'd stay late or come back after everybody had left, I don't know which, and he'd leave the front door unlocked."

"My word. Leave the bank unlocked?"

"Yes, somebody said they liked the danger." LuAnne's eyes glittered. "Anyway, I heard that what he liked her to do was come in and lock the door behind her. Then she'd start taking off her clothes, leaving them in a row through the lobby and go back to his office, where she had to knock on his door and tell him she was the cleaning lady. Then she'd walk in, *stark naked*. Have you ever heard of such a thing?"

"No, and I don't believe it. How would anybody else know, if nobody was there but them?"

"Well, that's the thing, Julia. It's all coming from people who used to work at the bank.

Because, see, Monique told it on herself while it was going on. I mean, it would have to come from her, wouldn't it? Who else would know but Wesley Lloyd, and he sure can't tell."

"Oh," I moaned, wanting to hide my face, but refraining from it. "And in his office, which I decorated for him."

"That's not the only place. I heard that they used several other places, too, like the loan officer's desk and that big sofa in the lobby. Margaret Wood said she wouldn't ever put a foot in that bank again, she didn't care who owned it now."

I'd heard all I could take, and soon took my leave. I drove home in a daze, realizing that the gossip was getting worse and it wouldn't be long before some child at school told Little Lloyd what a lecherous old man his father had been. I decided, then and there, that if I didn't hear from Mr. Pickens soon, I'd have to try to track him down. And if he hadn't found a way to get rid of that loose woman, we might have to seriously consider sending the child off to school for his own protection. Lord, I hated to think of it. The thought of that sweet child in an Army uniform with his hair shaved off

and a fierce glint in his eyes from being
brain-washed into dashing blindly into danger on the orders of a bunch of big-talking
bullies who'd never picked up a gun in their
lives except to shoot at little birds, just
made me sick to my stomach.

Chapter 19

My nerves were acting up so bad, I would've quarrelled with a doorpost if it got in my way. I couldn't concentrate, and I couldn't sit still. Even Hazel Marie commented on my restlessness. "Uh-huh," she said, nodding as if she knew something, "you know what a young man's fancy turns to when Spring comes around, don't you? I wouldn't be surprised if a woman's fancy doesn't take the same turn. You better get Sam over here to straighten you out."

I just smiled agreeably, and let her think what she wanted to, but I thought it was the most foolish thing I'd ever heard. Sam hadn't done a thing to straighten out the pastor, as far as I could see, so how was he going to straighten me out? I knew, though, that he'd use a different method of straightening the pastor than the one he might use on me, but he seemed to be falling down on both jobs.

Not that I was longing for Sam, you understand, because I'd put him behind me as far as I was able to do. But the thought of Sam—of losing him or of getting him—kept my system in an unsettled state. My sleep was badly disturbed. My mind kept flitting from one thing to the next. I was hungry, and then I wasn't. Lillian said I was getting picky in my old age, and I thanked her to keep her opinions to herself.

It finally got to where I had to do something. So one morning I walked across the street to the church. By the time I went through the back door and into the Fellowship Hall under the sanctuary, I'd about worked myself up into a swivet.

It was Sam's fault. He was supposed to have talked to the pastor, who would then get Emma Sue out of the clutches of Curtis Maxwell, who would get mad and go home, leaving those theme park scoundrels including Monique Mooney high and dry with no money to carry on so they'd have to leave town, and, with Little Lloyd none the wiser, we'd all settle down and be back to normal.

Well, except for Tonya Allen, but you couldn't very well undo the kind of change she'd had.

After crossing the street to the church, I walked through the empty Fellowship Hall to Norma's office. I knew I'd have to put up with her officious questions but I was more than ready to do battle. I had right on my side, and I intended to let the pastor know that his wife was flirting with danger in the form of Curtis Maxwell. After all, the pastor himself had engaged me to help get Emma Sue back on track and, even though I could take no credit for her abandonment of makeup, he ought to appreciate my efforts and listen to me. I wanted Curtis Maxwell gone and, by the time I was through talking, I hoped the pastor would want him gone, too.

So I marched down the side hall to Norma's office, where she guarded the pastor from all who sought him. Her door was open, as it customarily was, and I walked in. Before I'd gotten inside the office good, I was hightailing it out of there, my breath coming in gasps and my heart pounding in my chest. I was almost run over crossing Polk Street on the way home, and it was all

I could do to get inside the house without collapsing.

"Hazel Marie," I called as I headed for the kitchen. She was sitting at the table, peeling apples with Lillian. They both came to their feet when they saw the state I was in.

"What's wrong?" Hazel Marie asked. "You look like you've seen a ghost."

"Worse than that," I gasped, trying to take a deep breath.

"Set yo'self down," Lillian said, grabbing my arm and leading me to a chair. "You gonna have a heart attack, you don't watch out. What's the matter with you?"

I leaned on the table, still trying to catch my breath. "Look at this," I said, and held out a quivering hand. "I've had such a shock." I patted my chest. "I may never get over it."

"Lord, Miss Julia," Hazel Marie said, concern written all over her face. "What happened? Did you fall? Did a car hit you?"

"No, but one almost did. Give me a minute and I'll tell you."

"She need something on her stomach," Lillian pronounced. "You eat, an' you feel better."

"Just some water, Lillian. I can't eat a bite.

But, wait, I want you to hear this. I don't know what in the world to do."

They leaned over the table, eager to hear my harrowing tale, whatever it might be.

"Well," I began, "you know I went over to the church to see Pastor Ledbetter, because I've been so concerned about Emma Sue. I was going to tell him how Mr. Maxwell seemed to be turning her head. In a nice way, of course. But, well, I never got the chance."

"Drink that water," Lillian commanded, so I did.

"I got to Norma's office," I went on, "and the door was open as it always is, but she wasn't there. I didn't want to see her anyway, so I started across the room to knock on the pastor's door, and you know there's carpet on the floor so nobody could hear me. Anyway, I noticed that the door to the pastor's office was ajar, so I thought maybe he was in there, and I'd just knock and see if he was. Well, I had my hand up to knock, and . . . I don't believe I can go on."

"Don't stop now!" Hazel Marie said. "What'd you see?"

"Not a blessed thing. The door was barely open, so all I could see was his bookcase.

But the lights were off in there, and just as I started to knock, I heard all this awful moaning and groaning. Oh, it brought me to a standstill, I tell you that."

"What you think it was?" Lillian whispered in an awe-filled voice.

"A better question," Hazel Marie said, "is *who* was it." Her face was tight with anger. She loved that church, in spite of her Baptist background.

"Well, at first I didn't know, but then I heard Norma giggle in a throaty kind of way and she said 'Wait, wait a minute.' Then she said . . . I don't believe I can repeat it."

"Yes, you can," Hazel Marie said. "What'd she say?"

"She said, 'Let me unbutton it.' Oh, that just mortifies me, I can't tell you how much. And he was groaning and just carrying on something awful. But he never said a word that I could make out."

"The Lord don't like that kinda messin' round in his house," Lillian said, her mouth tightening in disapproval. "He ain't gonna put up with it." Then she leaned in closer. "Who that man doin' all the carryin' on?"

"Well, it had to be Pastor Ledbetter,"

Hazel Marie said. "Who else would be in his office?"

"Oh, I hate to think it, Hazel Marie," I said, just swamped with a terrible feeling of loss. You want your pastor to have a spotless life, even if you can't claim the same for yourself. "Still," I went on, "it *sounded* like him, though I've never heard him groan before, so I don't have anything to compare it to. I can see him losing his head over money, but a woman? No. Especially with a woman who wears as much makeup as Norma does. She just cakes it on, and you know what a fit he threw when Emma Sue did the same. You'd think he wouldn't come near a painted woman."

Hazel Marie said, "I guess he changed his mind."

I nodded. "He's been doing a lot of that lately."

"But you've got to finish telling us," Hazel Marie said. "What'd you do then?"

"Well, I heard Norma say, 'Let me go lock the back door, so nobody can walk in on us.' I turned around fast, you better believe, because she was saying, 'Hold your horses, I'll be right back.' And just as I got to the door to the hall, she stepped right into her office, and I was caught. We both looked at each other, and I don't who was the more shocked. She pulled the door to the pastor's office closed and stood in front of it like a guard. And her face turned red as a beet, and her lipstick was smeared all over her mouth and the top button on her blouse was undone. And you know her top button is never very high, anyway. Well, we just stood there staring at each other, both too stunned to move, I guess. I know I was, although I'd've given anything to be able to sink through the floor. Then, all of a sudden, her face went dead white and she clenched her teeth and said, 'Why don't you learn to call before you come over here? We're not holding open house, you know.' And I was still so stunned, I couldn't think what to say, so I just said, 'Well,' real strong like, and left."

"Oh, it must've been awful," Hazel Marie said. "I wish you'd taken her down a peg or two, but I wouldn't't've known what to say, either."

Lillian was just shaking her head at the pity of it.

"I wasn't through, though. I was half-way out of the Fellowship Hall when I got my nerve back. I turned right around and marched into her office. I stuck my head in and there she was, sitting behind her desk, putting on more lipstick. 'Norma,' I said, 'if you ever lock me or any other member out of this church, you're going to be walking the street, which is just about what you're doing now.'"

Hazel Marie gasped, as a smile lit up her face. "You didn't!"

"I certainly did, and I hope she repeats every word to him. There's nothing worse than a cheating husband, unless it's a cheating preacher who ought to know better. And furthermore, I've thought of lots of other things I wished I'd said to her. I may go back over there and do it, too."

"You not goin' nowhere," Lillian said. "You already had more'n you can handle, so you gonna stay right here an' settle yo'self down."

"She's right, Miss Julia," Hazel Marie said. "There's no telling what a shock like that has done to your system."

"My system is fine. It's my nerves that're getting the best of me."

"I don't doubt it. Come on, I'll walk you

upstairs and you can lie down. I think you need to."

"Yessum," Lillian said, "an' I'll bring you a nice tray. You need something on your stomach."

I staggered to my feet. "Some Pepto-Bismol might not be amiss, either."

I declare, once you get images and visions in your head, especially of the noxious kind, it's next to impossible to get them out. I knew I would never be able to erase the picture of Norma and Pastor Ledbetter from my mind if I lived to be a hundred.

Chapter 20

Just as I got up to leave the kitchen, I heard Little Lloyd on the back stoop, coming in from school. I sat back down to hear about his day, trying as I did so to put that startling scene in the church out of my mind.

"Hey, everybody," he said, as Hazel Marie took his raincoat and bookbag from him. "Where's Latisha?"

"She off visitin' a little friend from kindy-garden," Lillian said. "She be home after a while. Set down now an' I fix you a snack."

"How was your day, Little Lloyd?" I asked, reaching over to pat his arm. It seemed that the more I worried about him, the more I wanted to touch him. And I am not a demonstrative woman, by any means.

"Some firemen came to talk to us," he said. "They brought their fire truck, and they let us climb all over it." He smiled as Lillian placed a plate of sugar cookies in front of him. "I might be a fireman when I get grown."

"We'll see," Hazel Marie said as she poured a glass of milk for him. "I remember when you wanted to be a garbage man."

"But if I was a fireman," he said, "I'd know what to do when somebody gets hurt. Like just now when I cut across the parking lot at the church."

He bit into a cookie as the three of us stopped and stared at him.

"What?" Hazel Marie said.

"Who'd you see get hurt?" I asked.

"Well," he said, dipping a cookie in his milk. "Nobody, really. I just thought he was."

I pulled my chair closer to him while Hazel Marie leaned on the table. Our sudden interest made him put down the cookie and look from one to the other of us.

"Did I do something wrong?" he asked.

"No, honey," his mother answered. "But we want to know what you saw. Exactly, Lloyd."

"Well," he said, "this man came out of the back door of the church just as I turned the corner, and he was walking real fast. I don't know who he was, but he had on a real nice suit and tie, and didn't look like he lived around here."

"Short, with a slender build?" Hazel Marie asked.

He nodded. "And funny-looking hair in the front."

Hazel Marie and I exchanged glances.

"Anyway," Little Lloyd went on, "he was wiping his face with a handkerchief, and it had something red all over it. I thought he'd cut himself. You know, shaving?"

"You thought he'd been shaving in the *church?*" Hazel Marie asked.

He shrugged. "It was just the first thing I thought of, but he didn't have any pieces of Kleenex on his face, so I guess not."

I leaned back in my chair, feeling an immense relief. "Then it wasn't the pastor," I said to Hazel Marie. "Unless . . ." I stopped, not wanting to say more in front of the child.

"No'm," Little Lloyd replied with a frown, not having been privy to our earlier speculations. "Nowhere near the pastor. Whoever it was crammed his handkerchief in his pocket when he saw me, and drove off in a big Mercedes. It was a rental. I know, because J. D. told me how to tell."

So it had been Curtis Maxwell who'd gotten Norma's attention as well as her makeup all over his face. Unless, I finished the thought I'd almost spoken, *unless* she was running them in, one after the other. It didn't at all surprise or distress me, though, to hear that Curtis Maxwell was a hypocrite in custom-made clothing. I'd learned long before this that the louder and more publicly a person talked about his faith, the more he probably had to cover up.

Lillian insisted that I go on upstairs and lie down. She said that I'd had more excitement than was good for me. I agreed with her, but I might as well have stayed up for all the rest I got. I could no more turn my thoughts from what I'd heard in the pastor's office than I could walk on water. Even though I was now certain that it had been Curtis Maxwell unbuttoning Norma's blouse, and not Pastor Ledbetter, I couldn't rid myself of the image of our rigid, straight-laced, by-the-book, critical, and judgmental pastor engaging in passionate congress with Norma Cantrell. Well, with any woman, if you want to know the truth, even his own wife. But that's what happens when your imagination runs wild on you, and mine kept putting Norma and the pastor together, even though I now knew better. Maybe I just wanted the pastor to take a fall to prove he was human. Of course he had proven it, at least twice, since there were two Ledbetter sons.

I sat up in bed, recalling some of the strange beliefs that I'd heard about. And one of the strangest was that conjugal activity had to be reserved for the purpose of procreation. That seemed a little harsh to me, although as far as I was concerned, I could take that activity or leave it. And while I was married to Wesley Lloyd, I'd left it more often than I took it. Well, that wasn't exactly true, for he was the one who left it. Still, it occurred to me that Pastor Ledbetter might well be one of those procreation-only souls, who was now so deprived that he didn't have the fortitude to resist a woman who threw herself at him.

That's it, I thought. That explains both him and Emma Sue. They'd denied themselves of marital comfort for so long that they were ripe pickings for anybody who came along offering temporary alleviation from distress. And that was why he'd been so disturbed by Emma Sue's pitiful attempt to make herself attractive—it stirred his loins, just as he'd said.

I came off the bed, confident that I'd found the explanation for the unnatural behavior of both the Ledbetters. But with all these thoughts about what takes place within and without marriage, my mind just naturally turned to Sam.

I needed to tell him what was going on, even if Pastor Ledbetter was as innocent as a lamb, which I kept reminding myself he just might be. But even so, he was guilty by association by virtue of the fact that a romantic interlude had occurred in his office where he prepared the sermons designed to tell us how to live godly lives.

Sam wasn't going to like that sort of goings-on any better than I did, but, Lord knows, I didn't need this on top of the constant worry over Monique Mooney. Yet something had to be done or, first thing you know, it would be all over town and people would be laughing at the pastor, his wife, and every Presbyterian in the county. Talk about ruining your testimony.

I slid into my shoes and, taking a sweater, went downstairs and out the door. As I walked the four blocks to Sam's house, I realized that he had certainly made himself scarce of late. No longer was he showing up at my door every time I turned around, and I wondered if he was trying the silent treatment I'd told him Norma and the mayor were engaged in.

If that's what he was doing, it was working. I missed him, although I could do without his constant harping on the subject of marriage. Once I made up my mind, there was going to be no un-making it. I walked along, trying to enjoy the first signs of spring on the way. Pale green buds with a hint of pink and red were on the azaleas, the forsythia was in full bloom, as were the early tulips and hyacinths. Birds twittered in the trees, then dashed down to the emerging grass to look for a meal. I noticed these things, but they didn't hold my attention as they might ordinarily have done. I had too much else on my mind.

Sam came to the door and welcomed me with a big smile.

"Julia," he said, swinging the door wide, "I was just thinking about you. Come on in."

"You may not want me, Sam, because I've come to jump all over you."

"Well, get on in here, woman, and start jumping."

I gave him an icy glare as I entered the hall. "You're as bad as Mr. Pickens, always taking everything I say the wrong way."

He laughed as he steered me to the leather sofa in his living room. I say living room, because that's where he did most of his living. But it was more of a study or a library, if you took note of the shelves of books around the walls, as well as the stacks of books and magazines beside every chair in the room. And, I daresay, he'd read everyone of them.

"Now," he said as he took his seat beside me, "what have I done to deserve to be jumped on?"

"It's what you *haven't* done that's the problem." I turned to face him, ready to let him have it. "Sam, if you talked to the pastor like you said you would, it didn't do any good. You'll have to do it again, because he's in bad need of some deep spiritual counseling. The man is headed straight to perdition, and something has to be done. Just listen to what I think I walked in on this morning."

And I told him what I'd heard coming from

the pastor's office while I was innocently standing in Norma's office. I must say that my account sobered him considerably, and for the first time he seemed to take my concerns with the seriousness they deserved.

"This is bad, Julia," he said, stroking his chin as he thought of the ramifications. "You're sure it was Ledbetter?"

"No, I'm not. I didn't see who it was, and all I can swear to is that there was a man in there. I know a man's voice when I hear it, even if it was only groaning and moaning. But I can absolutely vouch for the shape Norma was in. You should've seen her, Sam, she looked, I don't know, mussed up and, well, *aroused.*"

He cut his eyes over to me, a suspicious twinkle in them. "You'd know how that is, I take it?"

"I'm not dead, Sam. Who wouldn't, with lipstick all over her face and her blouse half undone. And I thought she was going to faint when she saw me. Guilty, that's what she was. She knew she'd been caught. And, let me tell you, she made sure that door was closed in a hurry so I wouldn't see who was in there. That's the only thing I can give her, she was protecting the pastor. Or whoever it was."

"Okay," Sam said, "let's think about this for a minute. You're not sure it was Ledbetter, are you? It could've been somebody else, right?"

"Well, yes, it could've been. Little Lloyd saw somebody who might've been Curtis Maxwell coming out of the church with certain evidence smeared all over his face. But it happened in the pastor's office, and nobody uses it but him. In fact, it stays locked when he's not there, so how could anybody else be using it?"

"But Norma has a key, doesn't she?"

"Well, yes, I guess she does. But, Sam, surely Norma wouldn't be so brazen as to have Mr. Maxwell in there. I mean, the pastor could've come sailing in at any time and caught them. She wouldn't risk her job just for a few minutes of . . . whatever it was. Would she?"

"I wouldn't think so. Although if she knew where Ledbetter was, knew, for instance, that he was tied up somewhere and wouldn't be back for a while, then she might." He stopped and studied the problem for a minute. "Look, Julia, the only thing we're sure of is that Norma was entertaining someone in the pastor's office."

"Yes, and not only on church property, but on church *time,* when we're paying her to be working."

"Right. Okay, that's enough to get her fired, if we want to pursue it. But, Norma's the least of my worries. I don't want us jumping to conclusions about Ledbetter. He knows he'd have a lot to lose, and not just his job, but his wife, his reputation, his standing in the presbytery, and his pension. I'm inclined to believe it wasn't him."

"Yes, and since talking with you, I guess I'm inclined to agree. It's just, well, I hate to admit it, Sam, but once I got that picture of the two them in my mind, I couldn't get it out." I stopped and considered the image for what I hoped was the last time. "I'm try-ing my best to substitute Curtis Maxwell in the picture, but you know how the mind works sometimes. It can run amok, or at least mine can. But I'm about to be con-vinced that it wasn't our pastor."

"I hope so, Julia. We don't want to con-demn an innocent man."

"Well, one thing is certain. Norma is not

an innocent woman. She was entertaining either Curtis Maxwell or Pastor Ledbetter.

"That brings me to Emma Sue. When you talked to the pastor, did you tell him about her and Curtis Maxwell? I can't tell you, Sam, how upset he was when she started using cosmetics. Although," I said, musing on Emma Sue's sudden about-face, "for some reason she's reverted to her former self. More's the pity, to my way of thinking. But you'd think he'd be beside himself with the way she's behaving around that man."

"No, Julia. I'm not going to talk to a man about his wife's behavior. That's just not done. I did bring up Maxwell, though, and immediately got a defense of the man that I couldn't break through. Ledbetter is certainly taken with him, and that's the reason he changed his mind about supporting the theme park. Sounds like anything Maxwell wants, Ledbetter wants, too. He said Maxwell is thinking of making a permanent home here, so Ledbetter's courting him for all he's worth."

"Why in the world would a man who could live anywhere want to live in Abbotsville? That doesn't make sense to me."

"Well, *we* live here," Sam reminded me.

"I tell you, Julia, I think all that's wrong with the pastor is that he's so impressed with Maxwell and so determined to get him in the congregation that he's lost all perspective."

My mind was churning with the complications that would arise if that jet-setting businessman could lead our pastor around by the nose. I didn't trust anybody who claimed that wealth was the reward for faith. What did that say about the thousands and millions of believers who didn't have two cents to rub together? Next thing you know, he'd be saying "Send *me* your money, and the Lord will return it to you a hundredfold," just like those television preachers rant about. I don't doubt that the Lord bestows material blessings on some, but it doesn't always follow that wealth indicates divine favor. If you think it does, you don't know many wealthy people.

"What're you thinking, Julia?" Sam interrupted the flow of thoughts that were running through my mind.

"I'm thinking I ought to move my letter and join another church. I am just so tired of one upset after the other, and all because of Pastor Ledbetter." I took a deep breath. "I'm tired of the church being a place of turmoil. It's not right, Sam. It ought to be a place of peace and quiet, where one can reflect on one's shortcomings, of which we all have a gracious plenty."

"I agree, Julia, but I think we need to hang in there. Ledbetter's eyes will be opened sooner or later, and he'll need some support. He's not a bad man nor a bad pastor."

"Well, I have a different opinion, and you would too if he'd tried to have you committed to a home for incompetents and take over your dead husband's estate, like he did to me. I won't forget that till my dying day. There's no telling where I'd be now, if it hadn't been for you and Binkie."

"I know, sweetheart," Sam said. "I'm not forgetting what he tried to do. He can be bull-headed when he thinks he's right, but we don't want to destroy him, do we?"

"I guess not," I reluctantly agreed. Then with a smile, I said, "I wouldn't mind embarrassing him to death, though."

"We could do that," Sam said, laughing. "I think what's happening now is that he's let Curtis Maxwell's wealth and personal charisma blind him to what's really going on."

"Don't talk to me about charisma! That word's been so overused, it doesn't mean anything anymore. But," I said, slowing down as I recalled something, "speaking of that, Mr. Maxwell did mention the Holy Spirit several times when he gave his little speech at Emma Sue's. Right there, I should've been on my guard. Sam," I said, grasping his arm in my agitation, "the man may have charisma, but it's more than that. He's *charismatic,* and maybe Pentacostal and Holy Roller, too. I'll bet you anything he speaks in tongues, and those theme park people are just the type to shake and shout and carry on, too. Oh, Lord," I moaned, covering my face with my hands, "Pastor Ledbetter's going to lead us into a *cult,* and you know we Presbyterians can hardly read the King James version, much less learn to speak a language that nobody can understand."

"Julia," Sam said, taking my hands and, I do believe, trying not to laugh. "I don't think we have to worry about that. You're jumping to conclusions and getting yourself all worked up. Let's just hang back for a while and see what happens. Chances are, Ledbetter'll come to his senses soon enough.

And," Sam shrugged, "if he doesn't, the session will tell him his ministry here is over."

"So," I said, taking back my hands, "we're just going to let Norma make a love nest in the church? And let Emma Sue and that smooth operator hang all over each other? Is that what you mean?"

"Not exactly. Look, I'll go back to Larry and tell him he needs to be more careful of what goes on in his office."

I jumped back in alarm. "Oh, no. Don't do that. He'll know it came from me. Because you know Norma told him I heard what they were doing."

"Not if it wasn't him doing it with her. Anyway, I think we ought to give him a chance to straighten out his own mess, don't you?"

"I guess, although he's never in the past been willing to acknowledge any mess of his own making. But he's sure been quick enough to notice anybody else's."

"Now that we've decided that, what about some of that jumping on you promised me? I'm all set, so you can start in anytime you're ready."

What in the world do you do with a man who has a one-track mind? But, being concerned with what could happen to him as a result of romantic deprivation, I acquiesced to a few minutes of personal interaction, all the while hoping that James wouldn't walk in on us.

Chapter 21

When I got home I found Little Lloyd and Latisha sitting on the floor in the living room, playing Old Maid. The game wasn't going so well, since, with only two players, they were defeating the purpose. It didn't help, either, that Latisha fell over backward, laughing, when Little Lloyd drew the Old Maid from her hand.

"You got her!" Latisha cried. "You got her, an' you better keep her, 'cause I'm not gonna be no old maid."

"You're not supposed to tell," Little Lloyd said as he rearranged his cards. "It's no fun, if you tell."

"Well," Latisha came back at him, "it's only me an' you, an' if she's not in my hand, I know good an' well she gotta be in yours."

Little Lloyd smiled as he glanced up at

me and said, "I can't fool Latisha. She catches me every time."

"Yeah," Latisha chimed in, "an' I'm gonna keep on a-doin' it, too." She moved over to make room and said, "Come play with us, ma'am. We'll let you be the Old Maid, 'cause that's what Great-Granny said you'd be if you don't marry that ole white-headed man what come courtin' you."

Little Lloyd hid his face behind his cards, trying not to laugh. For myself, I was so surprised that I hardly knew how to form an answer.

"I'm a widow, Latisha," I finally said, "so I can hardly be an old maid." Then thinking I'd been too short with her, but wanting to get her mind off that subject, I went on. "How're you liking kindergarten?"

"Well, it's all right, but that ole teacher don't do nothin' but make me color and color and color. I'm gettin' tired of it. I want to get my hands on that Play-Doh an' make me something."

Little Lloyd suppressed a grin and said, "Tell Miss Julia what you're going to do this summer."

"Oh, yeah," Latisha said, her eyes shining with anticipation. "My mama say she gonna take me to the beach, an' when I get there I'm gonna wear my new zucchini."

That stopped me. "Your new what?"

Little Lloyd doubled over, laughing, but he managed to get out, "Her new *bikini!* Latisha, it's a bikini, not a zucchini."

"I don't care what it is," she said, not at all abashed, "I'm gonna wear that thing, come hell or high water."

I threw up my hands and scurried up the stairs, having no desire to take on the rearing of another child. I could hear Little Lloyd's admonitions, which would make a bigger impression than anything I could say, anyway.

When I reached the peace and quiet of my own room, I closed the door and tried to soothe my edgy nerves. My worries always came flooding back when I took myself out of Sam's calming presence. When I was around him, the worst of my concerns just seemed to smooth out and stop agitating me. Sometimes, though, I could shake him because he was often *too* calming, always urging caution, saying "Let's wait a while." Wait, wait, wait and see what'll happen. But I didn't want to wait. I wanted to take the bull by the horns and *do* something. So I decided I would.

Determined to leave Pastor Ledbetter, Norma, and any and all trysts taking place in the church to Sam as much as I was able, I turned my mind to the problem of the Mooney woman. I didn't know exactly what I could do, since I'd heard neither hide nor hair from Mr. Pickens, but anything would be better than sitting around, going out of my mind with worry. Mr. Pickens should've been keeping me abreast of developments, but he was bad to go his own way in his own time, which, in my opinion, was no way to treat the one he was working for.

I tried his office number and his home number, but all I got at both were recorded messages. His voice on the home machine said, "Leave a message if you want to." On his office machine, he said, "J. D. Pickens Investigations. I'm out, you're on, so go ahead."

I'd never heard anything so unprofessional in my life, but that was Mr. Pickens for you. It all put me in a most unsettled state, wondering where he was, what he was doing, and how he expected to calm my fears by staying out of touch.

My continued indignation over Mr. Pickens's silence was broken by the ringing of the phone. I picked it up before Lillian did, and then wished I hadn't.

"Julia," Helen Stroud said, when I answered, "I hate to be the one to tell you, but I'd want to know if it was me."

"Know what?" But I thought I knew.

"Well, I had a board meeting for the garden club at my house last night, and Jackie Wright told us she heard at her bridge club that another one of Wesley Lloyd's ladyfriends is back in town."

At my silence, she hurriedly said, "I don't expect it's true. It's probably all mixed up with Hazel Marie, don't you think? Or if it is true, maybe Hazel Marie knows her."

"I doubt that, Helen," I was finally able to say. "Hazel Marie doesn't indulge in gossip and I, for one, would never bring up the subject to her. I hope you won't, either."

After assuring me that she would not, and I had thanked her for her concern, Helen ended her call. I hung up the phone, wondering why I had felt obliged to express gratitude for hearing gossip that cut so close to the bone. And the nerve of her, wanting me to ask Hazel Marie if she knew the woman!

Sooner or later, somebody *would* ask her, or some ruffian would taunt Little Lloyd, and what could I do then? I wiped my eyes and tried to calm my rattled nerves. All I could do was stand firm between them and the disastrous revelation of the truth.

That evening, while we were gathered around the kitchen table, the phone rang. Lillian answered it, said, "Uh-huh, uh-huh, uh-huh," then held out the phone to me. "It for you," she said, a worried frown on her face.

"Tell whoever it is that we're having dinner," I said, just so put out that people could be so rude as to call during the evening meal. Probably a telemarketer, who does it on purpose.

"No'm," Lillian said, that anxious look still on her face, "you better take this'un now."

"Oh, for goodness sake," I said, laying my napkin on the table and rising from my chair. "I do hate to have a meal interrupted. Excuse me, Hazel Marie, children."

I took the phone and said, "Yes?" in a tone that conveyed my annoyancce.

"Can you talk?" Mr. Pickens asked.

"Uh, no," I said, glancing quickly at the others who had politely stopped talking while I took the call. Or they'd stopped so they could hear who had called and why it was important. I turned my back to them in a vain effort to prevent them from hearing.

"Then listen," Mr. Pickens said. "I'm still out here, but we need to talk."

"Let me call you back," I said, being very careful not to say anything that would give anything away to those who shouldn't be listening, but could hardly help it. "We're at dinner." Trying to tell him that I was surrounded by eager and open ears.

"No, you can't reach me. You know how to get to Berea Church Road?"

"I think so," I said, becoming more and more aware of the pregnant silence behind me. I had to do something to lessen their interest. "Oh, yes, *LuAnne,* I do," I went on, coming up with the first name I could think of.

"What?"

"Never mind, *LuAnne.* Just tell me what you want me to do."

"There's a pull-off a couple of miles along Berea Church Road on the right. That's on the north side of the property out here. Park in there with your lights off, and I'll meet you about nine-thirty. Can you make it?"

"Why, yes, *LuAnne*," I said, thinking as fast as I could. "I believe I can. And you want me to bring Lillian with me?"

"Whatever," Mr. Pickens said. "Nine-thirty." And he hung up.

I kept talking to a dial tone. "Well, I don't know why it has to be done tonight, but I guess we can. All right. Then we'll see you in a little while." I hung up, took a deep breath, and prepared myself to carry off a little white lie that was absolutely necessary.

Taking my seat at the table while avoiding Lillian's eye, I said, "That was LuAnne. When that woman gets something in her head, nothing will do but everybody has to hop to."

"What did she want?" Hazel Marie asked. "Lloyd, pass Miss Julia the butter."

"She wants Lillian and me to help her hem up the dress she's wearing to our reception. And she has to have it done tonight, of all times."

"Oh, I'll help you do that," Hazel Marie said, perfectly aware that I didn't know one end of a needle from another. Besides, Hazel Marie was forever altering the length of her clothes and was an expert in the art of hemming.

I knew right then that I'd come up with the wrong excuse for getting out of the house. I had to think fast.

"Frankly, Hazel Marie, I'm surprised she didn't ask you in the first place, but I think she really wants Lillian to show her how to iron those linen curtains she's been having a time with. Lillian," I said, turning to her and trying to convey my need through my eyes, "you don't mind going, do you? And I certainly don't mean for you to iron them, just maybe show her how damp they need to be."

"No'm," she said, somewhat tentatively, "I don't mind."

"Good. Then, Hazel Marie, we'll leave the children with you, while we get LuAnne ready for our party." And I went on chattering about the coming reception, trying to distract Hazel Marie, while pretending that Mr. Pickens's phone call hadn't strung out my nerves. If he'd had news about Monique's imminent departure, surely he'd have told me then and there. His silence on the subject didn't bode well for our coming discussion.

{Chapter 22}

Lillian and I piled into the car about eight-thirty, on our way to LuAnne Conover's for all Hazel Marie and Little Lloyd knew. We were leaving an hour before Mr. Pickens's designated time, but if it'd been up to me I'd have left even earlier, before the sun went down and I had to negotiate in the dark. As it was, I knew I'd need all the extra time I could get to find the meeting place Mr. Pickens had specified. Besides, I believe in being punctual.

As soon as I closed my door and turned the key in the ignition, Lillian said, "Why you say it Miz Conover on the phone when you know it that Mr. Pickens?"

"Well, I certainly couldn't say it was him with Hazel Marie sitting right there."

"Yessum, first thing he say to me was 'Don't say my name,' an' I didn't."

"He understands that this whole expedition has to be kept under wraps, Lillian, and you know why. Of course, I hated to tell an out-and-out story about it, but if Hazel Marie'd known who it was, she'd've wanted to talk to him, and I tell you, I think he was calling in secret. He was very abrupt and quite specific about what he wanted us to do."

I turned the car in the direction of Lu-Anne's house, in case anybody was watching our departure. After a couple of blocks, though, I took a cross street and got us going in the opposite direction.

"It 'bout time you tell *me* what us gonna do," Lillian said. "Here you be drivin' all 'round, not goin' nowhere near Miz Conover's house."

"We're not going to LuAnne's house, Lillian. You know that wasn't her on the phone. I just made that up, and half the time I was talking to a dial tone, because Mr. Pickens gave me my instructions and hung up in my face."

I drove across town, then took the old highway south, knowing it would be a few more miles before we'd need to turn left on Berea Church Road. If I could find it.

"Well," Lillian continued, long after I'd thought the matter should've been over and done with, "if we not goin' to Miz Conover's, where are we goin'?"

"We're going out in the country on the north edge of the property where those theme park people are. Mr. Pickens is going to meet us there."

"Why we have to go in the dark? Seem like daytime be better, then we see where we goin'."

"Lillian, I declare, I don't know. I'm just doing what he told me to do, and I assume he knows what he's doing." I stopped for a minute, not at all certain about what I'd just said. "And I wanted you with me, because I'm not any happier about fooling around after dark than you are. Now help me look for Berea Church Road. It ought to be coming up pretty soon."

Lillian continued to mumble and I continued to reassure her. Although I wished I'd had somebody to reassure me. Turning off the highway onto the two-lane road took us away from streetlights and traffic into an area of farmhouses and empty fields. The occasional safety light high up on a pole spread a glow around clusters of house, barns, and sheds. But the farther in we got, the more densely the trees lined up on the sides of the road. It'd been years since I'd been out that way, and even then I'd gone in on County Line Road some way to the south of where we were. On this stretch of road I wasn't sure where my property line began or ended.

"Watch on the right side, Lillian," I said, slowing the car and peering through the windshield.

"What we watchin' for?"

"Mr. Pickens said there's a turn-off where we can pull in and park. He should've told me what a turn-off looks like, but I could hardly ask him."

I slowed the car even more, looking for a break in the trees and watching to see if any cars were coming up behind us. At least for the while, we were the only ones on the road, so I didn't mind creeping along to look for a place to turn in.

"Is this all yo' prop'ity 'long here?" Lillian asked.

"I don't know. It's somewhere around here. All I know to do is find a place to get off the road and park and wait. If he doesn't show, we'll know we're in the wrong place."

"Don't sound to me like anybody know what they doin'."

"Lillian, please. Don't remind me. I'm doing the best I can."

"Well, law, it seem to me you get better 'structions than what you got. I don't like this empty ole road. It real lonesome to me."

"Look," I said, relinquishing the wheel with one hand and pointing ahead of us. "See there, Lillian. See how the trees kind of dip in? That may be the place."

"Well, it look like *a* place, but whether it *the* place, I don't know."

"Let's try it," I said. "Open your door and see if there's a ditch on your side. I sure don't want to drive into one."

"Hol' this car still then," she said, as she unlocked and opened the door. "Lemme step out an' see can we turn in."

"Wait, Lillian!" I cried, grabbing her arm. Headlights were in my rearview mirror. "A car's coming. We've got to drive on."

"Law!" Lillian said, slamming the door. "I almost all the way outta the car. Halfway in an' halfway out, an' now I got to crawl back in."

I sped up, not wanting to draw attention to ourselves by being seen parked on a rural road at night. If a Good Samaritan was in the car behind us, he'd stop and offer help. And what would I have said our reason was for idling along, searching the side of the road?

So I drove on, trying to fix some landmarks in my mind for our return visit. I finally came to a crossroads and turned off, while the car behind us continued on. With my heart in my throat, I backed and forthed, and finally managed to turn the car around, ever fearful of dropping off into a ditch.

"Start watching again, Lillian," I said, as we retraced our steps. Or, rather, our tracks.

She mumbled something about it being on the wrong side of the road this time, and she couldn't see it so good.

We found it, though, and also found that others had been there before us. As my headlights lit up the semicircular clearing, I could see tire tracks, beer cans, McDonald's wrappers and I don't know what all strewn all over the place.

I pulled in and stopped the car. "Why don't you get out, Lillian, and guide me while I back over there behind those straggly pines? That way we'll be halfway hidden from the road."

"Lemme unlock this door, then, an' don't you run over me."

About half exasperated, I said, "I'm not going to run over you. Just look behind us, and be sure I don't hit a log or a stump."

She didn't like it, but she got out and directed the parking process. As I backed the car into a sheltered place, I could hear things crunch under the tires. Lord, if we had a puncture, we'd have to limp all the way home.

I switched off the engine and the headlights as Lillian crawled back in. "Law, it dark out here," she said.

"Maybe we'll see better in a few minutes," I said, as I hit the automatic door lock.

The locks thunked and Lillian levitated off the seat. "Oh, Jesus!" she shrieked.

"Lillian, I'm just locking the doors."

"Well, let me know 'fore you do it again," she said. "It nearly scare me to death."

After that, we sat in silence, while I worried that we were in the wrong place. Mr. Pickens could be waiting for us in some other pull-off a mile down the road. I knew what he'd be mumbling if we didn't show up, and I certainly didn't want to hear it. He might even worry about us, although that'd be a stretch for him.

The sounds of the night filtered into the closed car—the swish of tires on the road as the occasional car passed, rustles in the bushes that could've been the wind or something more sinister, the tick of the motor as it cooled.

"I don't like this," Lillian whispered. "It feel like something lookin' at us. No tellin' what be out there in them woods."

"I know," I whispered back, "and if Mr. Pickens doesn't come soon, we're going home."

"My mama," Lillian whispered, a tremble in her voice, "she say the wampus-cat, he walk back an' forth in the woods, lookin' for folks."

A chill shivered its way down my back, as I thought of some strange animal, its tail swishing as it slithered through the trees on its way to the car.

As the silence settled back around us, I began to feel more and more vexed with Mr. Pickens. There'd been no need to put us in this awkward situation. What if some teenage lovers showed up and we embarrassed them to death? Or they, us?

Lillian suddenly screamed bloody murder, almost stopping my heart. She shrieked again, pointing to the windshield with a wildly waving finger. "He lookin' at us!"

There, right in front of me, a man's face peered through the windshield. I thought I'd die on the spot.

Then he knocked once on the window, and I regained my senses. I unlocked the doors and Mr. Pickens slid into the back seat.

"Law!" Lillian cried, her voice two octaves higher than normal. "We thought you the bogey-man."

He grinned. "Scare you?"

"If you ever do that to me again," I told him, trying to catch my breath, "you'll be running for your life. And for the rest of your life, too."

Chapter 23

Mr. Pickens didn't look half his usual suave self. The brief glimpse I'd had of him, when the interior lights came on before he closed the door, revealed a plaid shirt, a beat-up leather jacket, and an unshaven face. The last named did not at all complement his black mustache that could've used a trim, but went well with his need of a haircut. There was also a noticeable lack of his normal use of an aromatic eau de cologne.

"What's going on, Mr. Pickens?" I asked, unbuckling my seat belt so I could turn sideways in the seat. "What've you found out?"

"First, how're Hazel Marie and Lloyd?" he asked, perturbing me for his delay in getting to the heart of the matter.

"They're fine. And, I remind you, it's for their welfare that you and I are engaged in this stealthy business, so get on with it. I don't know why we had to come all the way out here to meet you, anyway. You could've said everything you have to say on the phone."

"The telephone's off-limits," Mr. Pickens said. "Dooley says he wants the theme park to be revealed in all its glory, without any leaks beforehand."

"Well, my word," I said.

Lillian chimed in, "Miss Hazel Marie, she not too happy with you right now."

"It can't be helped, Lillian," I said. "She'll thank us for this later on. Now, Mr. Pickens, let's hear it."

"Right. Okay, I've not found out much, and I'm not sure there's much to be found out. Except Dooley runs a pretty tight ship. He's hired a few outsiders, like me, to help him construct what he calls the stopping places. The stable, a village square, the pool of whatever, and so on. Every one of us had to sign a statement of faith. Damndest thing I ever saw, too."

"I guess you signed it, since they hired you."

"Yeah, and lied through my teeth about most of it."

Lillian intervened. "You ought not be lying to the Lord, Mr. Pickens. He don't like it."

He reached over the seat and patted Lillian's shoulder. "I figured Dooley wasn't exactly the Lord, Lillian, so I don't think I'm in any danger. You'll pray for me, won't you?"

"Yessir," Lillian said solemnly, "I always do."

"Still," I said, "I'm not sure it was a good idea. I certainly don't want to be the cause of your spiritual downfall, Mr. Pickens. I mean, telling a story about spiritual things, well, you could suffer for it."

"Had to do it, or not get hired. Besides, I had my fingers crossed." His white teeth flashed in the darkness. "Anyway, this Monique Mooney is Dooley's woman. They share one of the trailers they're all living in. And," he said, somewhat ruefully, "the locals he's hired, including me, have to stay until everything's completed. That's part of our contract, and the reason I've been out of touch. We're all bunked in a trailer, too."

"Why, whatever for? Why can't you go home at night?" I asked.

"Too much time wasted going and coming, Dooley says. He wants us on the property all the time, mainly, I think, because he's hellbent on saving our souls. In spite of the fact that we all signed that statement where we swore our souls're already in good shape."

"Well, I say," I murmured. Then, "Will you be able to find out anything about the Mooney woman? I tell you, Mr. Pickens, we need to know what her purpose is, and whether she's encouraging talk about something that may or may not be true. I mean, either way, you'd think she'd be hiding her head in shame."

"I sho' would," Lillian said.

Mr. Pickens shifted uneasily in his seat. "I've not seen much of her, to tell the truth. Dooley keeps the men and women separate, even when we're eating or attending one of his never-ending prayer meetings. He says we have to keep our minds on higher things, and carnal thoughts will distract us."

"Under any other circumstances," I told him, "I'd say that was advice you should take to heart. But, right now, Mr. Pickens, you've got to get close to that woman."

"Never thought I'd hear that from you," he said, never losing an opportunity to misconstrue something I said. "But it won't be easy. While we're doing construction, the women stay in the trailers, making robes and sandals and such for the actors. And they're all actors. I think Monique's the Samaritan woman and Mary Magdalene, which sounds like typecasting to me, but they didn't ask me."

"Well, listen to this," I said, and went on to tell him about Curtis Maxwell and his financial interest in the theme park, as well as in our local elections. "So they have plenty of money and some political clout backing them up," I concluded. "And that Maxwell man has now got the church involved. It's an absolute mess, Mr. Pickens, and it all started when Mr. Dooley brought that crew to town."

Mr. Pickens grunted, then remained silent while he thought over my disclosure.

"So you see what we're up against," I went on. "And I need to know if you're willing to stay on a while longer. Anything you find out, Mr. Pickens, and I mean anything, might be helpful in running these people out of town—or at least discrediting them—before they take over completely."

"Yeah, well, you may have reason to want them gone. Dooley handles the money and he seems to have plenty of it. That's not sitting well with the rest of them. Anyway, I'll stay on a few more days. They're about to work us to death, though. But it's all that praying and testifying that's getting to me. We have a prayer meeting at the crack of dawn, one when we break for lunch, and another long-winded one after supper. And the food's not that good, either. I'm about sick of all this holy-roller stuff."

"Holy-roller?" I said, immediately perking up. "Are they speaking in tongues and shrieking and carrying on?" I would love to be able to tell Pastor Ledbetter that he was mixed up with a bunch of jabbering prophets who scream and faint and make short legs grow longer and operate on people without benefit of knives or anesthesia. He wouldn't put up with that for a minute.

"No," Mr. Pickens said, "at least, I've not seen anything so far, but there's a lot of 'Praise Gods' and 'Help me, Jesuses' going on. But then, I've not been to church in so long, that may be standard fare now."

"It sound pretty usual to me," Lillian said.

"Not for Presbyterians," I said. "Pastor Ledbetter's a dyed-in-the-wool mainline

Presbyterian, and he wouldn't get mixed up in such as that if his life depended on it. Why, one time an old man got carried away and yelled out 'Amen' right in the middle of a sermon, and the pastor had to have a long talk with him. He didn't open his mouth in church after that, and died soon afterward."

"Interesting," Mr. Pickens said, although he didn't say it with a great deal of sincerity. "I figure I can put up with being prayed over a little while longer. I've been trying to get close to one of the younger women . . ."

"Mr. Pickens," I said, with as much sternness I could muster, "that is not what you're here for. You need to settle yourself down, and not be cocking your eye at everything in a skirt. It seems to me that you could re-strain yourself long enough to complete your mission."

"Oh, don't get yourself in an uproar," he said, so dismissively that I could've smacked him. "I'm trying to get close to somebody who knows Monique and who'll talk to me about her."

"Oh. Well, if that's the case," I said, "all right. But you just mind youself and remem-ber who's waiting for you at home."

He laughed. "Gotta go," he said, as he

opened the door, "But don't worry about me forgetting Hazel Marie. I know a good thing when I see it."

"Wait a minute," I said. "Before you go, I want to ask you something." I stopped, wishing that I didn't have to reveal the matter that had troubled me from the minute I'd first heard of Monique Mooney. I closed my eyes and asked, "What does she look like?"

"Like somebody who's had a hard row to hoe," Mr. Pickens said. "Probably a good-looking woman when she was young, if you like dyed black hair and lots of makeup. Sorta theatrical-looking, which goes with what she's doing, I guess."

"Nothing to write home about, then?" I asked with a sense of relief that she was nothing like Hazel Marie. Or, I suddenly thought, me.

"Well," Mr. Pickens said with a grin, as he put one foot out of the car, "I'd write home about her figure. Nothing wrong with that."

"You have a job to do," I said with some asperity. "So you just keep your eyes to yourself while you're doing it."

He laughed, then slid back into the car, pulling the door closed. "One thing you could think about, Miss Julia. I'd gathered, even before you told me about Maxwell, that these people had a sponsor of some sort. That's how they've gotten this far. He's kept them on a pretty tight leash, though, and they're not too happy about it. They may've been promised more than they're getting."

"That is curious, Mr. Pickens," I said, thoughtfully. "Curtis Maxwell's been busy making a name for himself in town, talking this place up and drawing attention to himself in any number of ways. Not all of them to his credit, I must say." Then I veered off that subject, not wanting to go into the graphic details of Mr. Maxwell's behavior. "He tells us that the Lord gave him a mission to get this theme park off the ground, and he's dedicated to doing just that. He wants our help, of course."

"Huh," Mr. Pickens said. "From what I've seen, he needs a little more dedication. I was up on a ladder yesterday, nailing shingles on a roof, when Monique came flying out of a building where some of the women were sewing. She threw up her hands and said, 'I can't work with nothing, and I'm tired of trying.' And she went to her trailer. So what I'm thinking," Mr. Pickens went on, as he pulled himself close to the front seat, "is this. Why don't you pay her off? If she's fed up out here, she might be willing to move on if she had something to move on with. You wouldn't care about the theme park if she left, would you?"

"I wouldn't give it two thoughts if that woman was gone. But, Mr. Pickens, that's like paying blackmail. Only with the payer suggesting it instead of the payee. And what if she keeps coming back for more?"

"That could be a problem," he agreed. "But if you let me handle it, she won't be back. I guarantee it."

Lillian and I both turned to look at Mr. Pickens, wondering if he meant what we thought he did.

"I'll have to think about it," I finally said. "I'd do most anything to see the last of that woman before Little Lloyd hears about her. But, Mr. Pickens, I'm leery of starting a pay-off that might never end. And of getting you in trouble, if you have to enforce that guarantee you spoke of."

"Let me worry about that," he said, and got out of the car. "I'll be in touch." And without another word, he closed the door without slamming it and disappeared in the darkness.

"Wait!" I pushed open my door, almost blinding myself as I stumbled out into the dark, litter-covered ground. "Mr. Pickens, come back here."

"What?"

Lord, he was standing right beside me. I gasped, trying to still my pounding heart. "Don't do that!" I patted my chest, finally got my breath, and said, "I've thought about it, and I'll do it. Find out if she's open to a one-time, lump sum charitable donation to help her get started somewhere else. Make sure she knows it's a one-time thing, offered out of the goodness of my heart to help the downtrodden. In no way is it to be construed as a bribe or as blackmail." There, I thought, that'll solve my problem and clear my conscience, too.

I think he nodded. "Okay. It's probably your best bet, at least to get rid of her right away. I'll find out how much it'll cost you and make the arrangements."

He moved off, but I wasn't finished. "Wait. How will I know what to do?"

"I'll call you." And he was gone.

I crawled back into the car and fastened

my seat belt. "That man," I said, as I switched on the engine and the headlights. "He tries my very soul."

"Yessum," Lillian said, nodding. "He good at that."

{ Chapter 24 }

All the way home, I thought about what I had just done. Agreeing to finance Monique Mooney's departure put me squarely in the criminal column, if I understood the ramifications of blackmail. But it really wasn't blackmail, and if I kept telling myself it was charity, and not a bribe, I could go through with it. And the more I thought about it, the less I cared. If only she'd stay paid off, and not come back for more.

Then there was the talk that could still reach Little Lloyd's innocent ears. The best I could hope for was that it would die down with her out of sight and mind. Of course, a story as good as the one about her and my husband could just go dormant until somebody remembered and dredged it up again.

"Lillian," I said, "I know it's a sin to want

to wring your husband's neck, but if I could get at Mr. Springer, I believe I'd do it."

"Yessum, but you can't, so you do better to keep on lookin' after our little boy."

"I know. And that's exactly what I'm doing."

When we pulled into the driveway and walked into the house, we found Hazel Marie pacing the living room floor. She stopped long enough to listen to me go into a song and dance about the problems incurred in hemming LuAnne's dress. I needn't have bothered, because Hazel Marie had more on her mind than what Lillian and I had been doing or where we'd been doing it. Of course, if she'd known our true destination, it would've been a different story.

"Y'all, I got to go to bed," Lillian said, as she headed for the stairs. "It past my bedtime."

"Yes, run on, Lillian," I said. "I know you're tired after sitting on the floor, pinning and repinning that dress a dozen times."

She gave me a frowning glance, and I thought I'd better ease up on the LuAnne story. With her hand on the bannister, she said to Hazel Marie, "Both them chil'ren sleepin'?"

"Yes, I just checked on them and they're sleeping like logs. Good night, Lillian. Sleep well."

"Yessum, I aim to." And she went on up the stairs.

"Now, Hazel Marie," I said, taking a seat in one of the Victorian chairs by the fireplace. "I can see you're all up in arms about something. What's bothering you?"

"Why, the same old thing!" She flung out her arms as she took another turn around the room. "J. D. Pickens, of course. There's no doubt about it, Miss Julia. *Something*—I don't know what—is going on with him. There's something he's not telling me. He's being entirely too secretive."

Well, she'd certainly hit that nail on the head, but I had to steer her away from it. "He has to be secretive, Hazel Marie. That's the nature of his job. You can't blame him for keeping a confidence when that's what his business is based on."

She stopped and stood over me, her hands on her hips. "That's just the thing. I don't believe he's on a job. I don't believe he has a case or a client. And I don't believe he has to be out of touch. Anybody can get to a telephone, and he has a cell phone on him all the time. I know, because it's forever ringing at the most inopportune times." She whirled around, then narrowed her eyes. "He's hiding something from me. I know he is, because it's the only thing that makes sense."

This line of thinking had to be nipped in the bud, so I said, "I can't imagine why you'd think such a thing."

"If you knew him like I do, you'd know why. I can read him like a book. And if he was on a regular case, I wouldn't mind so much. But he's not. He's doing something else, and he doesn't want me to know about it."

I gripped the arms of my chair. "Be reasonable, Hazel Marie. What else could he be doing?"

She blew out a long breath, then ground her teeth. "He's seeing somebody, that's what. Why else would he put me off when I said we wanted to move back in with him? There's not a case in the world that would've kept him from running over here and getting us that very day. How long would it have taken? An hour? Less than that, even. Or he could've said he had to meet a client or something, and for me to just pack up and come on. But no, he said he'd be out of touch for a week or more, and for me to stay here."

"He just didn't want you and Little Lloyd to be by yourselves," I said, finding myself in the position of defending that world-renowned ladykiller. "Better for you to stay here until he could be at home with you."

"Yes," she said, frowning darkly, "so who is *he* at home with?"

"Oh, Hazel Marie, I don't think—"

"Well, I do. That two-timing rascal's got a woman over there, and it'll take him a week to get rid of her."

"Hazel Marie, really . . ."

She strode across the room again. "It's probably another one of his ex-wives, and he's too tenderhearted to kick her out."

"I never thought of Mr. Pickens as being especially tenderhearted," I mumbled, but she wasn't listening to my assessment of his cardiac functions.

"They take advantage of him, Miss Julia. You wouldn't believe. Remember that red-headed witch who showed up last year? That's typical, just typical! *Or,*" she flung out, "it could be some trashy barhop with a hard luck story who he just has to help. It could be anybody!" She stopped in the middle of the floor, frowning as she thought about it. "Whatever it is," she said in a low, dark tone, "I know a woman's involved."

I thought I'd slide right out of my chair onto the floor. Hazel Marie certainly knew her man. But I didn't want her to know the particular woman I knew he was involved with.

Maybe I should've told her right then that, far from being interested in another woman in the sense she feared, he was working hard in her interest and in Little Lloyd's. But I didn't want her to know about Monique Mooney, even though according to LuAnne everybody else did. I doubted that in my calmer moments, since LuAnne had been known to exaggerate on occasion. Still, Hazel Marie wasn't going to hear it from me.

"I'll tell you what, Hazel Marie, why don't you give him the week or so he asked for. Give him the benefit of the doubt, then see how he acts."

"But, Miss Julia, Lloyd *needs* him!"

"What about you?" I asked in an effort to shift the subject away from Mr. Pickens's apparent shiftlessness. "Do *you* need him, or is this just about that boy?"

"Oh, Miss Julia," she said, covering her face with her hands, "I *do* need him. I just feel so lost at the thought of him with somebody else."

Before I could respond, she straightened up and said, "And I'm not going to stand for it. He *promised* me . . ." She couldn't go on, so overcome with anger that she trembled all over.

"Listen, Hazel Marie, you need to put your mind on other things and give Mr. Pickens time to do what he needs to do. Our reception for Tony Allen is just days away, and that'll keep you well occupied. Then there're the Ledbetters and Norma Cantrell and Mayor Beebee and, let's not forget, Curtis Maxwell and his lipstick-smeared handkerchief. It's all about to worry me to death, Hazel Marie, and I need your help and your full attention, at least for the next few days."

"You know I'll help any way I can," she said in a more reasonable tone of voice. "If I can get what he's probably doing out of my mind."

"Don't go there, Hazel Marie," I warned, knowing better than I wanted to how the imagination could put tormenting pictures in your mind. "Block out Mr. Pickens, and think about Emma Sue and Mr. Maxwell and what they're doing. And think about Norma and the pastor and what they're doing. Or the mayor or whoever she's doing what with."

Then I stopped, fearing that I'd just added even more instances of cheating and betrayal to her mental repertoire.

"Trust, Hazel Marie," I advised, "is what you have to have. If you don't have that, you don't have much of anything. Take it from me, I know."

"I *do* trust him," she wailed. "I just don't know if I ought to. Maybe he's playing me for a fool, leading me on, making promises he won't, or can't, keep, lying to me. Oh, Miss Julia, I'm so mixed up. I love him, but he's so, just so, well, he just drives me crazy."

Well, of course that was it, wasn't it? I'd trusted Wesley Lloyd, never imagining that he was capable of such duplicity as he'd managed with Hazel Marie and with the Mooney woman and who knew who else. And that was probably part of Hazel Marie's problem now, having been involved with a cheating man, herself. She knew what a trusted man could get away with. But, far be it from me to bring that up. She'd figure it out for herself, if she hadn't already.

Then she surprised me. Turning to me, she said, "How much do you trust Sam?"

"I, well, completely, I suppose." Then I bit my bottom lip, thinking about it. "I can't imagine him deliberately deceiving me. He'd come right out and tell me if he found somebody else. At least, I think he would. On the other hand, if somebody really tempted him, he might be too blinded by the possibilities that he wouldn't give me a thought."

"Exactly," she said. "And that's what I'm afraid of with J. D. He's so easily taken in that he can't see when a woman is after him. Women just can't resist him."

"Well," I said, "I wouldn't go quite that far, although I will admit that he has a certain magnetism. Just like Sam, don't you think? Come to think of it, they're pretty much alike. Just look at us, Hazel Marie." I smiled ruefully. "Here we are, two grown women who ought to know better, and we're both embroiled with such irresistible men."

She laughed, making me feel that she'd come to terms with Mr. Pickens's unexplained absence.

"I know what we ought to do," she said, a smile lingering on her face. "We ought to tell them we're better off on our own. We can do without them."

I bit my lip again, looking away from her. A bereft feeling swept over me, for that's what I had told Sam.

"Yes," I managed to say, "there're a lot of things worse than living alone." Then, since I didn't want to get into the details of what those things were, I stood up and said, "We need to get to bed, Hazel Marie. It's late, and I'm tired. LuAnne wears me to a frazzle."

"Me, too, and I didn't even go with you." Hazel Marie yawned, then said, "I've been meaning to ask you something. Have you heard the talk about Dwayne Dooley and that theme park?"

"No-o-o, I don't think so," I said, trying for a disinterested tone, even though her question had brought me up short. "What've you heard?"

"Nothing much," she said, switching off a lamp as we left the room. "Just that they're really getting the park set up, and the strangest thing. When I was at the parent-teacher conference the other night, everybody was talking about how Mr. Dooley won't let the men and women out there have anything to do with each other. Keeps them separate all the time, except, of course, him and his woman." Hazel Marie laughed. "But isn't that the way it always is?"

"It would seem so," I said, shaken at how close Hazel Marie had come to hearing the rest, and the worst, of it. "But I wouldn't give the time of day to anything I heard about those people. Good night, Hazel Marie, I hope you sleep well."

"Yes, and both of us have sweet dreams, too." She smiled at me as she headed for her room, and I thought to myself that I'd do whatever was necessary to keep anyone from hurting her.

Chapter 25

I don't know how long I'd been asleep when the telephone blaring in the night scared me half to death. I snatched it up from the bedside table before it woke the whole house.

Befuddled with sleep, I croaked, "What?"

"*Julia,*" a woman's voice hissed. "Is that you?"

My eyes popped open, visions of wrecks on highways and late night heart attacks running through my head. "What?"

"Are you awake?"

"Give me a minute." I sat up in bed, preparing myself to hear of some tragic event. "Who is this?"

"*Emma Sue,*" she said, as if I should've known. "Listen, Julia, Larry hasn't come home."

"Oh, my goodness," I said, swinging my feet onto the floor and fearing the worst, ambulances and emergency rooms running through my mind. "What time is it?"

"I don't know. About three, I guess. I've got to do something."

"Of course you do. I'll go with you. Is he at the hospital?"

"Well, that's where he *said* he'd be. The Ewell family called him hours ago to come up and sit with them. But, Julia, that old man's been dying for months, so why would they need Larry tonight, and all night long, too? Besides, I tried to call him there, and the switchboard said he's not answering his page. So, see?"

"Uh, no, Emma Sue, I don't see. I thought he was hurt or sick or something."

"No, I'm the one who's hurt and sick." Emma Sue broke down then and began to cry. Before I could offer to come to her aid, she said in a muffled voice, "I'm going after him, Julia. I'm going to catch them red-handed, and I don't care who knows it. I've prayed about it till I'm blue in the face, and it just keeps on and on. It's time for some action, because I've put up with it long enough."

I rubbed my hand across my face, trying to come to grips with what she was saying.

Although after what I'd overheard in the pastor's study, I knew what she was talking about. "Emma Sue, it's the middle of the night."

"Well, I know that," she hissed, like I was dense for not understanding. "It's the best time to catch them. Julia, I need you to go with me. I'm scared to go by myself."

I grabbed the bedpost and pulled myself to my feet. "Where, Emma Sue? Where're you going?"

"To *Norma's.* Don't tell me you didn't know. She's been after him for the longest time, and now . . ." Emma Sue's voice broke, "he's *succumbed.*"

My heart thudded in my chest. Catch the preacher red-handed once and for all, with my own eyes? I wouldn't miss it for the world.

Then a smidgeon of reason intruded, as I had a sudden image of the kind of mess the church would be in if Emma Sue found the pastor with Norma. We'd never keep it off the six o'clock news.

Feeling obliged to offer a moderating comment, I said, "I'm not sure that's the wisest course you could take, Emma Sue."

"I *knew* you'd say something like that."

Emma Sue had to stop and cry some more. Then she got herself together and let me have it. "I don't know why you won't help me, Julia. You've been through this yourself, so you know how men can be, whether they're ordained or not. Every other member of the church would take Larry's side and think I'm crazy for even thinking such a thing. Julia, I tell you, I have only you and the Lord to lean on, and the Lord is leading me to save Larry from this perilous path he's on."

"Since you put it that way," I murmured, "let me get some clothes on."

As I threw on my clothes, I couldn't help but wonder why Emma Sue was so frantic over the pastor's possible waywardness when she, herself, had had eyes only for Curtis Maxwell ever since he'd hit town. But this was not the first time I'd marvelled over marital quagmires.

Feeling my way down the stairs in the dark, I got to the kitchen and turned on the light over the stove. I wrote a quick note for Lillian and Hazel Marie in case they arose before I got back, and put it beside the coffeepot. There was no easy way to explain what I was up to with Emma Sue, so I just wrote, "Out with a sick friend. Back soon," and left it at that.

I slipped out the back door to wait for Emma Sue, who had insisted on driving even though I'd offered to pick her up. Seeing headlights down the street, I hurried to the curb, noting as I went that we'd had another rain shower earlier in the night. Water stood in puddles in the yard and glistened from the streetlight on the boxwoods.

When Emma Sue pulled up, I got in the car, saying, "I hope you know what you're doing."

I'd gotten a glimpse of her when I opened the car door, and, now by the glow of the dashboard, I had a better look at her. She was in a bad way, breathing hard as her hands gripped the steering wheel. She'd taken no pains with her appearance, which wasn't unusual and entirely understandable given the time of night and the urgency of the mission. Her hair was standing out from her head, uncoiffed and unbrushed. There wasn't a lick of makeup on her face, which I no longer expected, except if I'd been out looking for a husband holed up with another woman, I would've tried to level the playing field. She had on knee-high rubber boots and a gray raincoat. As she moved to apply the brakes at a stop sign, I caught my breath at a flash of pink nylon where the raincoat gaped open.

"Emma Sue," I said, "what've you got on under that thing?"

"My nightgown," she said, as if it was the most normal thing in the world to be riding around in one's bedclothes. "You don't take time to dress when the Lord tells you to get up and get going."

Emma Sue's complacent words and calm demeanor were not stacking up with the way she was driving. She swung the car here, there, and everywhere, taking the corners and curves with an abandon that made me cling to the armrest and press my feet against the floorboard. I sat firmly strapped in the passenger seat, going back and forth in my mind about the wisdom of this enterprise. In spite of my shameful hope that Pastor Ledbetter would be caught in the act—it would serve him right—I reminded myself that Norma was more likely to prefer a successful businessman than a middling preacher, if she had a choice. Which meant that Emma Sue wasn't going to catch him, either red-handed or otherwise, but she was certainly going to embarrass herself in front of Norma.

"Um," I began after an especially vicious swerve onto a strip mall–lined thorough-fare, "Emma Sue, I expect deputies patrol through here occasionally."

"They won't stop us," she said with cool conviction, even as the tires squealed around another sharp turn. "The Lord is with us, Julia. You have to have faith. Let go and let God, I always say."

"My word," I gasped as I was slung against the door and my seat belt tightened up on me. "If that's the case, why aren't we home in bed?"

"I have to save Larry from himself," she said, giving me a quick glance, as if I should've known that. "No," she corrected herself, "I have to save him from Satan. That's what's going on here, Julia, we are wrestling against evil powers and principal-ities and wickedness in high places." Then she raised one hand, balled it into a fist and smacked the steering wheel hard enough to crack one or the other. "In the form of *Norma Cantrell!*"

Then, breathing heavily, she gained a semblance of control and said, "Of course,

I know she's being used, too, and I pray for her daily. We must love our enemies, Julia, you know that as well as I do."

I kept my peace, but believe me, I was offended at the lecturing tone she'd taken. *I* wasn't the one chasing down an errant husband with fire in my eyes.

Spurting us through an intersection just as the light turned red, Emma Sue hunched over the wheel and said, "Now, Julia, you stay out of this. All I need you to do is be a witness. He's not going to talk his way out of this one, I don't care if he's on his knees with her."

My Lord, I thought, she is convinced that he really is making free with Norma. In that frame of mind, there was nothing I could say that would deter her. Only the lack of proof, in the form of no pastoral visit to Norma in the dead of night, was going to convince her otherwise. Still, I thought I should try.

"Emma Sue," I ventured, "there's something I have to ask. How does Curtis Maxwell fit into all this? If you don't want to talk about it, I'll understand. It's just that, well, there's been some talk about your interest in him."

She slammed on the brakes, jerking me

against the seat belt, and came to a halt in the middle of the street. "Curtis Maxwell? How could you think such a thing! Julia, you know my marriage means more to me than anything in the world. Except the Lord, of course. And what do you mean, my *interest* in him? The only interest I have in Curtis Maxwell is gaining him as a member of the church. Besides, Larry said I should be nice to him, and that's what I've been doing."

"I'm glad to hear it," I murmured, taken aback at her vociferous denial of any wrongdoing or thinking. I wasn't sure that either Hazel Marie or I could've been so far off the mark in what we witnessed in her own living room, but now wasn't the time to point it out.

"Oh, Julia," Emma Sue said, suddenly beginning to sob as she leaned her forehead against the steering wheel, "I've been so wrong, you just don't know. I admit I had lustful thoughts in my heart, but not the way you think. I did want Curtis to join the church, but more than that. I wanted him to be interested in *me.* To show Larry, don't you see? To make Larry notice and see how Norma was turning his head. I was trying to bring him back into the fold. And now, this is my punishment."

As she dissolved in a flood of tears, my heart went out to her for the pitiful attempt she'd made to re-attract her husband. I was glad I didn't have one.

I patted her arm and mumbled, "Don't cry, Emma Sue, I'm sure it'll be all right."

She jerked upright and wiped her face with the heels of her hands. "No, it won't," she said, with all her former conviction. "Because Larry wanted me to entertain Curtis, wanted me to make him feel welcome. And all the time I was trying to please my husband, my husband was keeping me busy so I wouldn't find out what he was up to. That low-down, sorry excuse for a *Christian* husband, I'll show him! He preaches Judgment Day. Well, this is Judgment Night for him!" And she stomped down on the gas pedal and we went streaking through the quiet streets.

{ Chapter 26 }

We finally turned into the middle-class residential area on the far side of town where Norma lived. The houses were small, but well-kept in spite of their age. Light from the streetlamps pooled at each corner of the block, leaving the middle of the block where Norma's house was in the shadows. Most of the residents were sensible enough to be in bed, but an occasional light in one or two houses spoke of restless sleepers or early risers. Oak trees lined the street, interspersed with a few evergreens where, years ago, residents had planted their Christmas trees. Bicycles and plastic tricycles were parked or overturned in many of the yards and driveways.

Emma Sue turned off the car lights as we approached Norma's house, and cut across the street to glide up to the curb of the most immaculate house and yard on the block. The house—no more than a two-bedroom, one bath cottage, really—reflected Norma's obsession with precision. The foundation plants were absolutely symmetrical, pruned just so, and small, flowering plants lined the walkway that led to the railed porch. If I'd had the time and the inclination to count, I wouldn't have been surprised to find an equal number of flowers on each plant.

"We might as well go home, Emma Sue," I said, as I surveyed the dark house. "I don't see the pastor's car anywhere, and no lights are on. Either he's not here, or Norma's in bed."

"Maybe they're both in bed," she grated out, then calmed herself. "I didn't really mean that. I don't think Larry'd go that far, but he wouldn't be brazen enough to park in front of her house, either. Now, Julia, you just wait here. I'll leave the keys, just in case."

"What're you going to do?" I was feeling more and more edgy as she switched from pious utterances to explosive blasts of anger.

"I'm just going to knock on the door. Scripture tells me to turn the other cheek and give my coat to whoever needs it. But it doesn't tell me to give my husband to whoever wants him. I can't take this lying down, Julia. Larry's in mortal danger. From Satan, you know."

Well, actually, I didn't. I certainly would never downplay any kind of danger from Satan but, for my money, it wasn't the devil, but Emma Sue, that the pastor needed to fear. If he was there, which I was doubting more by the minute, in spite of having heard his—or somebody's—gasps of pleasure when Norma was having her way with him in his office.

Emma Sue let off the brakes and eased the car down to block the driveway, then she rolled down her window and gazed at the dark house. "His car may be in the garage," she explained. "And nobody's leaving until I get through with them."

She opened the car door and began to step out.

"Emma Sue . . . ," I started, wanting to make one last effort to slow her down. I needn't have bothered, for she was out of the car and headed across the yard to the front door.

"Well, Law," I said aloud to myself, "I can't

just sit here." So I got out and edged around to the front of the car, not only to be quick on my feet if things began to escalate, but also to hear better. Since I'd come this far, I didn't want to miss anything.

Crouched by the front fender, I looked up and down the empty street, then back at Emma Sue as she stepped onto the porch. She stood there in the shadows for the longest time, ringing, I assumed, the doorbell. I couldn't hear it, which meant the neighbors couldn't, either, for which I was grateful since Emma Sue must've rung the daylights out of it.

Finally she gave up and walked out into the yard. I breathed a great sigh of relief, figuring she'd satisfied herself as to the absence and innocence of both the pastor and Norma. At least, as far as this particular house was concerned.

But no, while I watched, she turned and slipped around the side of the house, headed toward the back.

"Emma Sue!" I called in a loud whisper. "Come back here!"

But she was gone, and all I could do was wait there on the dark street. I kept looking over my shoulder, for it all was so quiet that my nerves were about to jump out of my skin.

Then they did. I shrieked as the most ungodly racket commenced wailing and shrilling, and lights in Norma's house began blinking off and on; every dog in the neighborhood went crazy, barking and howling and baying, and house lights up and down the street flicked on.

I left my post by the fender and ran into the yard, my only thought to grab Emma Sue and get out of there. I got to the middle of the yard, thought better of it and headed back to the car, thinking to make a fast getaway. But I couldn't leave without her, so I headed back into the yard, yelling and waving my arms and dithering around. Not knowing what else to do, I flew back to the car again, all the time yelling my head off.

Then I saw her coming around the side of the house, arms chugging and rubber-shod feet pumping. Just then, the next-door neighbor yelled from his backyard, "What's going on over there!" And then he cut loose with a shotgun blast that peppered his yard and Norma's with leaves and twigs and a tire swing that bounced across the yard and out into the street.

I screamed bloody murder. "Don't shoot! We're leaving! Oh, my Lord, don't shoot!"

Emma Sue was panting hard as she sprinted across the yard. I flung open the door on the driver's side and stood back. She took a flying leap and went head first across the seat, as I tumbled in behind her. I swept her feet out of the way, and with trembling fingers, started the car.

"Move it, Julia!"

And I did, grinding the ignition in my haste and stomping the gas pedal so hard that the tires screeched on the pavement.

"Hurry, hurry!" Emma Sue yelled. "Don't turn on the lights, just get us out of here!"

We barreled down the dark street, houses lighting up as we passed, while that infernal wailing resounded behind us.

Emma Sue was on her knees by this time, looking out the back window. "Don't stop!" she yelled. "Keep going! Step on it, Julia!"

"I am! I am!" I yelled back, the wind whistling through the open window. "Where'm I going? How do I get out of here?"

"Turn here! Right here!"

I did, and felt the back end of the car slide out of control, the momentum carrying us across the intersection until a wheel bumped against the curb. I fought the steering wheel, moaning and praying as the car straightened out, and I hit it again. A number of right and left turns took us onto a main artery and farther away from the up-roar.

"You can slow down now," Emma Sue said, as coolly as if we weren't racing from a crime scene. She twisted around and sat in the seat. Her raincoat and pink nightgown were hiked up above her knees, and she jerked on them until she was as prim and proper as she usually was. "Turn on the lights, Julia, and drive like normal."

"Normal!" I cried, my voice breaking and my hands trembling on the wheel. "My Lord, Emma Sue, I'm a nervous wreck." But I slowed and drove sedately down the street that led back toward town. "What happened back there, anyway?"

"I guess I set off the burglar alarm."

Before I could answer, two sheriff's cars came flying toward us, light bars flashing and sirens wailing. My heart rate jumped up several notches, as I pulled over to the side of the road. I turned my head aside in case Coleman was in one of them. If he was and he recognized me, I'd be in more trouble than I cared to explain. But both cars blew past, one after the other, rocking us with the shock wave of their passing as they headed for Norma's house.

Looking around, I saw Emma Sue on the floorboard. "What're you doing down there?"

She slowly eased back up onto the seat, looking out the back window as the sheriff's cars turned into the subdivision. "Trying to hide," she said. "In case they're looking for two people."

"The Lord may be leading you, Emma Sue, but I'm all by myself, here. So don't be hiding behind me."

She waved her hand at me, dismissively. Then she settled back in the seat, and I carefully aimed us toward home and as far away as we could get. My nerves calmed down as we got farther along, but I was still in an unsettled state.

The silence stretched out as both Emma Sue and I caught our breath, for all I could think about was getting home, locking the door, and rejoicing that we'd escaped arrest and imprisonment. And rejoicing, too, that we'd not rousted the pastor out of Norma's bed. Although I admit to a twinge of regret, since that would've been something to see.

"I could wring her neck!" Emma Sue suddenly spat out.

"Who?"

"You know who! She booby-trapped that house, I know she did."

"It was an alarm system, Emma Sue, just like you said. But whatever it was, it was loud enough to wake both her and the dead, if either of them had been there. It certainly did her neighbors. What set it off, anyway?"

"I broke a window in the back door."

"You *broke and entered!* Emma Sue, that's a major crime!"

"Well, I only broke. I didn't get a chance to enter, so it's not much of one."

"They Lord," I said. "I'm glad you didn't get in. We'd've been caught for sure."

We studied on that for a while, as the blocks lapped away, taking us closer to home and safety. I was finally beginning to relax when she broke the silence again.

"There's one thing I want to know. If the alarm brought out the neighbors, but not Norma, that means she wasn't there, right? So, where is she? And where is Larry?"

Well, that was the question, wasn't it? I certainly had no answer, so I didn't attempt one. Although the Mountaintop Motel edged its way into my mind.

"At least," she went on, "I've done the Lord's bidding tonight, even if it didn't work out. He'll show me what to do next. You know, Julia," she said, then paused for a minute, "I don't believe in divorce, so I'll just have to pray to be able to live with this." She sighed long and deep.

"Under the circumstances," I started, then added a disclaimer, "if, that is, the circumstances are what you suspect, you might ought to reconsider what you believe in."

"But first," she went on, as if I'd not said a word, "I'll report him to the presbytery. Yes, that's what I'll do, make him publicly acknowledge his wrongdoing and stand in judgment until he's deemed fit to continue in the ministry. He'll think twice after that."

"I expect he will," I said, just to be saying something since she wasn't listening.

Then out of the blue, she asked, "Have you ever been fingerprinted, Julia?"

I glanced over at her, wondering why she

brought up such a subject. "No, I haven't."
Then I thought more about it. "Have you?"

"Well, yes, I have. When I was a teenager,
I worked a couple of summers as a coun-
selor at a Christian camp. Some money
went missing, and they fingerprinted everybody who worked there, which I thought
was a very unChristian thing to do." She
didn't say any more, although I was waiting
for it.

"And?"

"And," she said, "that means my prints
might be on file. And now they're all over
the front and back doors of Norma's
house."

"Oh, my word," I said, thinking I'd better
call Sam and Binkie as soon as we got
home. She was going to need a good
lawyer. Then I realized there was no need
for legal representation, which would only
bring her escapade out into the open for
everybody to talk about. "It's all right, Emma
Sue, you've been to Norma's under welcoming circumstances, so it's understandable that your fingerprints'll still be there."

"I guess," she said, somewhat pensively.
"They'll be fresh, though, so somebody'll
know."

"Well, there's not a whole lot you can do about it, so I guess this is one of those things you're just going to have to leave to the Lord."

"I just hope the police don't tell Norma."

Thinking to reassure her, I said, "I doubt she'd have you arrested. But if she tries to, you can just deny it till the cows come home. Nobody can prove otherwise."

"Oh, I couldn't do that. I mean, I wouldn't volunteer it or anything, but if the police ask me I'll tell the truth. I am a Christian, you know, Julia."

"So am I. But I'm not above staying out of jail any way I can. Now, Emma Sue, let me caution you about something. Don't, whatever you do, get it into your head that you have to confess to the pastor or to Norma what we've been up to. If your conscience starts acting up, just remember that I'm in this with you. And it's my firm belief that what those two don't know won't hurt them, whereas it'd play havoc with the two of us."

"I'll pray for both of us, Julia."

I grunted as I pulled up in front of my house. Unfastening my seat belt, I asked, "You going to be all right to drive home?"

"I'm all right." But she didn't sound it, and

she didn't look it, for she was making no effort to take my place behind the wheel. "I
just wish I knew where he is and what he's
doing."

"Go home, Emma Sue," I said as kindly
as I could. "You're tired and not thinking
straight. I'll bet the pastor is there, worried
sick about you. In fact," I went on, trying to
lighten her spirits, "you may have some explaining to do, yourself, coming in this time
of night."

"He'll not get an explanation from me. Let
him worry a little after what he's put me
through. But, Julia," she said, as if she had
to reassure me, "I will keep on praying that
the Lord will open his eyes to what he's
throwing on the wayside. Because I've been
a good wife to him. I have, haven't I?"

"You've been the perfect wife for him,
Emma Sue," I said, and a truer word I'd
never spoken. "And I think he's lost his
mind, and a whole lot of other things, if he's
thrown you over in favor of Norma Cantrell,
of all people. I just can't believe he'd be
taken in by a woman who has one of the
worst reputations in town."

"We mustn't talk ugly about our neighbors, Julia," she said in her prim minister's-wife voice. "It's not very nice."

I stared at her, my mouth open. "And, may I remind you, that neither is breaking into your neighbor's house!"

Then I opened the car door and left one parting shot. "Go home, Emma Sue, and do some more praying."

She shot me a glance that might've withered me if I'd been able to see it better. "Sometimes I wonder about you, Julia."

"No more than I do, myself," I assured her, knowing full well that I was the last one to ever know when the Lord was doing the leading, or I was doing my own. Emma Sue, though, bless her heart, never had a doubt in the world.

⁅Chapter 27⁆

By the time Emma Sue pulled away from the curb, and I had slipped into the house, feeling my way in the dark, I was so put out I didn't know what to do. Every time I was called on to help somebody, I ended up wishing I'd turned them down. Emma Sue just had no sense of the proper appreciation for efforts on her behalf.

Heaving a martyr's sigh, the first thing I did was crumple up the note I'd left for Lillian and Hazel Marie, and throw it away. Better they never knew what I'd been up to. I'd have to listen to Hazel Marie tell me a dozen times over that I could've broken a hip and been laid up for the foreseeable future, and Lillian would do nothing but mumble and fuss all day long. So I intended that neither of them knew how close I'd come to being handcuffed and incarcerated. I hated to think what they would've said if I'd had to call home for bail money.

As I crept up the front stairs, I heard Lillian going down the back staircase and Hazel Marie stirring around, getting the children ready for school. I headed to my bed, thinking that there were many benefits to being denied the blessing of a child of my own, and one of them was being able to sleep in when I needed to.

And I needed to after such a tumultuous night, but I would've slept considerably better if Lillian hadn't kept coming in to see why I was laid up in bed for half the morning. I finally straggled downstairs about ten o'clock, feeling the consequences of the night's escapade in every bone in my body. Being a criminal on the run was proving deleterious to my health and well-being in more ways than one.

As soon as I pushed through the kitchen door, I stopped short. Lillian was sitting at the table, crooning to Latisha who was curled up on her lap.

"Is she sick?" I asked, hurrying over to place my hand on the child's forehead as I'd seen so many mothers do. "She doesn't feel hot."

"No'm," Lillian said, smoothing Latisha's hair and holding her close to her ample bosom. "This baby missin' her mama, an' she feelin' kinda lonesome this mornin'. We gonna let that ole kindygarden pass us on by today."

Latisha did look subdued, as she snuggled against Lillian and slipped her thumb in her mouth.

"'Sides," Lillian went on, "she need her some new tenny pumps, so I thinkin' we go to the store an' get her some. That make you feel better, won't it, sweet baby?"

Latisha nodded, and I went to my purse, pulling out a couple of hundred dollar bills. I laid them on the counter and said, "Get her what she needs, Lillian. She can use some shorts and so forth for the summer, something to play with, too. Maybe some sandals, as well as tennis shoes."

Latisha pulled her thumb out with a plop, and said, "I want me some flip-flops for when I get to that theme park."

"Sh-h-h," Lillian said, rocking back and forth. "We get you some flip-flops. Miss Julia," she said, looking at the bills on the counter, "you don't need to do that."

"It's not a matter of need to, it's a matter

of want to," I said, as I poured a cup of coffee.

"I thank you then, an' I bring back the change."

"I don't want any change. If you don't spend it all today, just keep it until she needs something else."

"Yessum, I 'preciate it. Come on now, Latisha, le's us go get ready so we get back by lunch time."

"Don't hurry, Lillian. It'll take me all day to wake up. I don't know why in the world I slept so poorly last night."

"Well, I don't neither, but the same thing come down on Miss Hazel Marie. She take Little Lloyd to school, then come back an' hit the bed again. Y'all better not be gettin' sick."

I took my coffee into the living room, hoping the hot caffeine would jump-start my day. But the coffee wasn't working all that well, for before I knew it, I'd put my head back against the chair, struggling to keep my eyes open. It was all I could do not to succumb to the pull of sleep that would block out the worry over the Mooney woman and what she was up to and how much she'd demand from me. And now I had to add Emma Sue and Hazel Marie to my load of cares. Both of them were convinced that their men were running around. I could easily solve Hazel Marie's problem, and would when the time was right, but Emma Sue's was another matter. As far as I was concerned, a man who'd stay out all night and not be where he said he'd be, well, I'd have some questions for him, too.

As for Mr. Pickens, he was as innocent of the charge as such a man could ever be, but if he didn't soon get back and give Hazel Marie some peace of mind, there was no telling what she'd do. On the other hand, for *my* peace of mind, he needed to stay where he was until he found out what and how much it would take to rid me of the Mooney problem for good.

In spite of these conflicting thoughts running through my mind, my eyelids were getting heavier and heavier. If I could last until the afternoon, I'd feel justified in taking a nap. But one simply does not nap in the middle of the morning. So I tried to concentrate on my lists for Tony Allen's reception, hoping I had everything delegated and that it would all come together in a social function that would be memorable enough to displace the Mooney woman tales floating around at the garden club, over the bridge tables, and on the telephone lines.

With the muffled sounds of Lillian and Latisha leaving through the back door, my eyes began to close as the house settled into quietness. Just as I was about to drift off, the doorbell jerked me awake. Muttering to myself for not going up to the bedroom so I could ignore a visitor, I pulled myself up and went to the door.

"Julia," LuAnne cried as she rushed in before I could welcome her. Her hands were flapping and patting her chest, her face was contorted, and she could hardly draw a decent breath. "Oh, Julia," she gasped, "you're never going to believe it. It is just the worst thing in the world. I can't believe it." Then she peered at me. "You don't look so good. Are you sick?"

"Have a seat, LuAnne. No, just tired. Getting ready for the reception, you know. Would you like some coffee?"

"I can't think about coffee or anything else at a time like this. Let me get myself together." She took a seat on the sofa, as well as a few deep breaths, and went on. "Well, first off, have you heard that Curtis Maxwell might invite Emma Sue and the pastor to his beach house? They're going in his plane just as soon as the theme park is up and running. Is that not the most exciting thing you've ever heard? But, listen, that's nothing compared to what else I have to tell you."

"I do wish you'd stop going to Velma's so much, LuAnne. It just swarms with gossip and, frankly, I don't want to hear anymore about that woman."

"What woman?"

"The *Mooney* woman, the one you've already told me about."

"Oh," she said, waving her hand dismissively. "It's nothing to do with her."

"Oh, Lord, LuAnne," I moaned, holding my head, "don't tell me another of Wesley Lloyd's ladyfriends has popped up. I don't think I could stand it."

"No, nothing like that. This is about you."

"*Me?* What've I done?"

"Well, Julia, you know I don't like to carry tales," she said, as I did all I could to keep my eyes from rolling back in my head. "And I wouldn't do it for anybody but you, even though Leonard made me promise not to tell anybody. But everybody's going to know sooner or later, and I think you ought to know sooner than that."

I couldn't imagine what LuAnne's husband would know that needed to be kept secret. Actually, I couldn't imagine that Leonard would know anything, secret or not.

"What in the world is it? I'm doing nothing I haven't been doing for years."

"Well, but that's it. People are talking about you and you wouldn't believe the kind of speculation that's going around. Some of it's pretty funny, although you know I wouldn't laugh, but it's gotten so bad that the pastor and the session think something has to be done." She began wringing her hands, her eyes darting around the room in her agitation. "That's how I found out about it. Leonard's on the session, you know, and they've agreed that Pastor Ledbetter should go ahead and do it."

"Do what? Quit beating around the bush, LuAnne, and tell me what it is I'm supposed to be doing, and what the session has to do with it."

"Now, you know I don't really believe it. I know you, Julia, and I'm convinced everything is on the up and up. But you have to

admit that it doesn't look good. Appearances, you know."

I could've strangled her by this time, but I
took a deep breath and glared at her until
she looked everywhere but at me. I put
some grit in my voice and said, "I have not
done one thing that I'm ashamed of. Whatever you've heard is slander, pure and
simple."

"Well, I don't know whether it's true or
not, but it *looks* true, because it's about you
and Sam."

I stiffened in my chair. "What about me
and Sam?"

"Well, they're saying that he's over here
early and late, and who knows when he
goes home, and that what you're doing is
unbecoming to a big churchgoer like you.
Now, far be it from me to sit in judgment,
but it does look suspicious. For those
whose minds work that way, that is. See,
Julia, the session is concerned about how
shameful it is for you to carry on that way,
then come to church and Sunday school
acting all innocent and everything."

I came out of my chair like a shot. "I
am innocent! And, furthermore, LuAnne
Conover, I'll have you know that what I do or

don't do is nobody's business but my own. And Sam's." I paced back and forth, just so disturbed I could hardly stand it. "Everybody knows that Sam and I have been friends for years, and that's *all* we are. Don't people have anything better to do than meddle in the business of two honest and upright people like us? And discuss it in a session meeting! I tell you, LuAnne, Sam and I conduct ourselves in the most prudent manner possible. Why, we don't even sit together in church. How do people come up with such ugly talk?"

"I believe you, Julia," LuAnne said, somewhat tentatively. "I know you wouldn't do anything you shouldn't, but you have to admit that you and Sam have been awfully tight lately."

I turned on her. "Can't two respectable people keep company without the church getting in on it? I am just sick and tired of having to put up with gossip every time I turn around. And for no reason whatsoever."

She cut her eyes up at me, then said, "Well, everybody thinks you're all but married already, so why don't you go ahead and do it. That'd stop the talk."

I threw up my hands. "Of all the foolish reasons to get married, that one takes the cake." Then I leaned down and looked her straight in the eye. "I will get married *when,* and *if,* I want to, and not one minute before. And that minute is not here by a long shot, and I certainly don't aim to do it to please a bunch of gossiping busybodies on the session or anywhere else, none of whom can bear inspection, themselves. And you can tell all those people who have nothing more to do than talk about other people who live spotless, *spotless,* lives, that I said so!"

"I didn't mean to set you off, Julia," Lu-Anne said as she pushed back in her seat, getting as far away from me as she could. "I just thought you ought to know about it before Pastor Ledbetter censures you. In front of the whole congregation, which he said he might have to do."

I stared at her, my mouth falling open, so stunned that my mind went blank for a few seconds. Then it came back full force.

"Censure me! For *what?* LuAnne, do you mean to tell me that he intends to denounce Sam and me in front of the whole congregation? For being *friends!*"

"Oh, Julia, I know," she wailed. "It is just

awful, and I am sick about it. But it's not Sam and you. It's just you."

I whirled around, nearly stumbling in my agitation. "Just *me?* You mean Sam and I are supposed to be engaging in sinful acts, but I'm the one who's going to be blamed for it!"

"Well, you know the pastor takes the position that it's the woman who has to hold the line, and he doesn't think you have."

"That is pure defamation of character! How could he!" I turned back to her, my whole body quivering with the insult to my good name and the offense to every living woman. "What is he going on? Rumor? Gossip? How can he blame just me if what I'm supposed to be doing is being done with Sam! How can he do this!"

"Don't get so upset, Julia," LuAnne said, although she had begun crying in sympathy for the public exposure I was about to undergo. "You'll do yourself some damage if you keep on that way." She wiped her face and collected herself. "All I can tell you is what Leonard told me. Pastor Ledbetter says that when a member is involved in an immorality that becomes public knowledge—like the talk about you—then a formal reproof has to be issued. You know, like a court martial in church. I guess it's a reprimand, kind of, and a warning to be more circumspect in the future."

"Circumspect! That's what I already am!"

"I know you are, Julia. It's just that so much talk has come to the pastor's attention that he feels it necessary to deal with the scandal so that it won't become flagrant and of a continuing nature. That's what Leonard said the Book of Church Order says. He says you're supposed to cease and desist."

"And how," I demanded, "am I supposed to cease and desist when I haven't done anything to cease and desist *from?* What am I supposed to do? Get married for the sake of some old biddies? Or tell Sam to keep his distance so nobody'll get any salacious ideas? Am I supposed to cut myself off from the best friend I've ever had just to keep the preacher happy? Is that it?"

"That kind of hurts my feelings, Julia," she said. "I thought I was your best friend, but I know you're upset and I probably shouldn't've said anything, except I'd want to be warned, if it was me, so I could either stay home that Sunday or be sure to wear something nice. But you have to understand that the pastor can't ignore all those stories about how you're living in sin, and all the while looking down your nose at other people. Well, halfway in sin, since Sam's not actually living here." She paused. "Is he?"

By that time, I was so outraged that it was all I could do to hold myself together, I was shaking so. "No, he is not! *But Pastor Ledbetter?*" I shrieked. "That man dares to judge me? After what he's done?" Suddenly, Emma Sue's threat to report the pastor to the presbytery seemed an apt and fitting solution. It had, in fact, a certain retributive appeal. After all, he was in the process of condemning me for doing the exact same thing that Emma Sue thought he was doing. Only I hadn't, and he probably had.

My anger at the nerve of the man settled down to a smoldering fire, as my eyes squinched together and my fists tightened up so hard I thought they'd never come undone.

LuAnne sat up, her eyes lighting up. "What, Julia? What's he done? You can tell me. I won't tell anybody."

I glanced down at her, paying little mind

to her eagerness to know. "Let's just say he has no room to talk. Especially when it comes to the kind of thing he's accusing me of."

Her mouth fell open and her eyes nearly popped out of her head. "No! *Really,* Julia? Oh, my goodness, I can't believe this. Wait till I tell Leonard." She was all a-twitter with the juiciness of it. "But isn't that the way it always is? The ones who claim the high moral ground are bad to fall themselves, and hard, too."

"LuAnne, you've never said a truer word. That's exactly what's going to happen to Pastor Ledbetter. He's going to be exposed for everybody to see what he is—a hypocrite mired up to his neck in the sins of the flesh. He'll think twice about holding me up for public condemnation by the time I'm through with him."

{ *Chapter 28* }

I finally got LuAnne on her way, in spite of the fact that she wanted to stay and discuss, dissect, and dig into every aspect of what she'd told me and of what I'd told her. I admit to having a few qualms for spilling the beans about my suspicion that the pastor had fallen from grace with Norma within the confines of his office and possibly during the previous night, but there come times when you have to fight fire with fire. And, in my opinion, this was one of them.

My head was spinning, and it was all I could do to hold myself together as I stomped back and forth across the living room floor. The electrifying news that I might be publicly excoriated shook me so bad that I didn't know whether I was coming or going. Even Mr. Pickens and Monique

Mooney and the check I would have to write slipped to second place for a while.

I took another turn around the living room. It wasn't *my* fault that Sam couldn't keep his hands to himself, although how anyone could know about that was a mystery to me.

I rubbed my hands down my face, not caring if it loosened the skin, as Hazel Marie's magazines said it would. I was itching to get my hands on Pastor Larry Ledbetter and tell him that for his information I was the one who'd drawn the line and kept Sam on the other side of it. But do you think I was getting credit for managing my affairs in such an honorable way? No, I was not.

I leaned against the back of my chair, thinking of how I'd led my life in the most commendable manner, yet here I was being laughed at and whispered about. But what made me so mad I could hardly see straight was that I was being accused of something I'd not even had the benefit of. I mean, if you have to suffer the consequences of an imputed act, it seems to me that you ought to at least have had the enjoyment of it.

The phone rang just as I'd taken myself upstairs. I snatched it up, hoping it was Mr.

Pickens, but expecting to hear another report about my assumed misbehavior, and answered it sharply.

"Did I get you at a bad time?" It was Emma Sue, so I calmed myself down and assured her that she had not. "Did you see the newspaper today?"

"Just the headlines. Why, what's in it?" I asked, almost dreading to hear the answer.

"What we did," she whispered. "It was in the Police Notes."

"Our *names!*"

"No, just that they answered an alarm at Norma's address. And that no entry had been made, and no suspects were apprehended. It didn't say a thing about looking for fingerprints. I think we may be safe, Julia."

I let the *we* pass, for I hadn't touched a thing that belonged to Norma and had felt fairly safe all along.

"Now, Julia," she went on, "I want to ask you not to tell anybody what we did. Larry was at the hospital all that time, praying in the chapel. Which was why I couldn't reach him. I was wrong to suspect him, and I've asked God to forgive me."

"I'm glad, Emma Sue," I said, all too willing to forget that perilous night. "Life is so much easier without the burden of suspicion weighing you down." Emma Sue lived by platitudes.

"Yes, and I feel so much better now that I've given that burden to the Lord. I want to please him and my husband, so since neither of them approve of cosmetics, I've given them up for good. As you might have noticed."

"Whatever you think, Emma Sue," I said, although I was sorry to hear it, for properly applied cosmetics had done her a world of good.

"Yes, I've turned it all over to the Lord, though I think I ought to keep an eye on Larry, just in case. Don't you?"

After getting away from Emma Sue, the problem I was having with the pastor made me even more indignant. He might have authority over his wife, telling her what she could do and not do, but he had none over me. So I took myself off to Sam's house, intent on pouring out my troubles and seeing what he could do about them.

I found him in the yard along the side of

his house, raking up winter debris and spreading mulch. He stopped and smiled his great, welcoming smile when I walked up.

"Julia!" he said, as if I were just the one he'd been hoping to see. He wiped his sweating face with a handkerchief and took my arm. "Let's go up on the porch. I can't think of a better reason to quit work than to talk with you."

"You may not think so when you hear what I have to say."

"I'll take any excuse I can get for a chance to have you next to me." He smiled down at me.

We settled in the large white rockers on the porch, our hands side by side on the adjoining chair arms. He reached over and took mine, and I let him, for the warmth and comfort of him soothed my troubled soul.

"What's troubling you, sweetheart?" Sam said.

"Oh, Sam," I said, biting my lip and turning my head from him. "It's so embarrassing."

"Come on now," he said, cradling my hand in his, "if you didn't come over because you couldn't stand being away from me, tell me what brings you. You know you can say and do anything you want, Julia, and have no reason in the world to be embarrassed with me."

I wasn't too sure about that, for I am a modest woman and could think of any number of things to do with and say to Sam that would embarrass me to death.

"The fact is," I said, taking a deep breath that almost came out a sob, "well, I'm so upset I can hardly tell you, but the fact is, Sam, you have compromised me."

He cocked an eyebrow and viewed me with a hint of amusement. "Compromised you?" he said. "I plead innocent of all charges, though not from lack of trying."

"Guilt or innocence doesn't matter, as you well know. Just let one person raise the subject, and it begins to spread until it's taken as the Gospel truth." My voice trembled with the unfairness of it all. "I tell you, Sam, I am being accused of immodest behavior, and even though that kind of conduct requires two people to accomplish anything, it's me who's being held up for public scorn."

"Hold on a minute," Sam said, his amused expression suddenly replaced with a frown. "Who's accusing you, and who's holding you up for public scorn?"

"I just told you. Everybody in town, according to LuAnne. They're saying awful things about our conduct, accusing us of all manner of illicit activities, and . . . well, of doing things we shouldn't do," I said, unable to control the quaver in my voice. "And they're laughing and whispering and talking about us."

"Hmmm," Sam said, running his free hand over his mouth as he thought about this jolting news. "This is pretty serious, Julia. I don't want my girl blamed for something she hasn't done, even though I've been trying as hard as I can to get her to."

I snatched my hand away. "This is no time for levity. Everybody thinks we're practically living together, and," I stopped, so overcome with the shame of it that I could hardly go on, "Pastor Ledbetter wants to censure me in front of the whole congregation."

Sam's head jerked around so he could stare at me. "Censure you? For what?"

"For seducing you and leading you into the paths of evil with my irresistible charms, which I don't have any of in the first place."

"Oh, good Lord," Sam said, sounding

more disgusted than I'd ever heard him. "Of all the wrongheaded, misogynist thinking, this tops them all."

"Well, I don't know about that, but, Sam, you've got to do something. You've got to go see the pastor and tell him that it's all your fault. Because you know I haven't led you on or encouraged you into any kind of mischief or immoral behavior."

"I know you haven't," he said in all seriousness. Then he looked at me and smiled. "More's the pity."

"I'm going home," I snapped, snatching my hand away and jumping up from my chair. "I came over here to tell you that I'm not going to take this lying down and . . . Sam! This is no laughing matter, and if you think it is, you can laugh by yourself!" I jumped up from the chair. "I'm leaving."

"No, no, no," he said, getting up with me. "Don't go, Julia. I'm sorry. I shouldn't have laughed. It's just that when this town starts something, they always get it wrong. And I'm sorry that you're carrying the brunt of it. Would it help if I went around and told everybody that it's my fault?"

"I wish you would, but nobody'd believe you. According to the pastor—and you know those idiots on the session believe everything he says—it's the woman who leads the man astray so, in this case, I'm the one who's done the leading."

Sam lifted his eyes heavenward and said, "I only wish."

I spun away from him. "Now I *am* going home. I came over to warn you that sooner or later your reputation is going to suffer as mine already has, but if you don't care, I might as well leave."

"I care, Julia," he said, his face filled now with enough concern to gratify me. "Now listen to me." He put both hands on my shoulders and squared me up to face him. "There's not much we can do about gossip, but Ledbetter's another matter. First off, there has to be a trial, a questioning of some sort, before a censure can be pronounced. Censuring is the last resort, not the first. So either Leonard or LuAnne got it wrong, or Ledbetter's thrown over the Book of Church Order." He stopped and thought about it. "Something's going on, Julia. No way in the world would Ledbetter risk offending you and cutting off your contributions to the church unless he had somebody to take up the slack."

"Curtis Maxwell!" I cried, the whole picture suddenly becoming clear. "Sam, if that man joins the church, Pastor Ledbetter won't need my pledge envelopes anymore. And I guess the pastor is so sure of him that he's not worried about losing my tithes and offerings and over-and-above gifts."

"You may be right," Sam said thoughtfully. "But the idea of Ledbetter taking a step like this, well, it's pretty risky, considering what he might be engaged in himself."

"That's exactly what I told LuAnne."

He sobered at that. "You told LuAnne about him and Norma? Oh, Julia, I'm not sure that was a good idea. We don't know for sure who Norma was with."

"Don't remind me. I could've bitten my tongue off as soon as I said it, knowing how bad LuAnne is to talk. But, Sam, he's accusing me of something I haven't done, so why shouldn't he bear the brunt of something he might've done? Besides, his own wife thought he was playing fast and loose with Norma." And I went on to tell him about accompanying Emma Sue on a night raid that had proved nothing, but hadn't deterred Emma Sue from suspecting the worst at the time. "But now, after putting us both in such peril, she's convinced herself of his, if not Norma's, innocence.

"We could've been put in jail, Sam," I said, summing up the story, "if we'd been caught. The pastor would really have a reason to censure me then. Of course, he'd have to do the same to his wife, which I hope would've given him pause."

Sam put his arm around my shoulders and drew me close. If I hadn't been so perturbed by his quickness to laugh at our circumstances, I would've responded in a warmer manner. But I kept myself stiff as a board, although it was all I could do to stay that way. I just wanted to melt against him and hide my face from the world.

"Let me tell you something," Sam said, as he smoothed my back with his hand. "First off, you're not in jail and you're not going to jail. Second off, no one, not Ledbetter, not the session, not the General Assembly itself, is going to hold you up for any kind of censure, either public or private. Put your mind at rest, Julia, it is not going to happen, and you can count on that."

I could feel his chest and arms tighten up as he went on. "The more I think about it," he said, "the more determined I am to take

Ledbetter down a peg or two. And you can believe I'm the man to do it."

A warm shiver ran through me at the thought of Sam as my defender and protector—something I'd never had before. Wesley Lloyd would no more have taken a stand for me against the pastor and the session than he would've flown.

I was so overcome with Sam's commanding tone that all I could do was croak, "What're you going to do?"

"You just leave it to me," Sam said with considerable firmness. "Go on about your business, and let me take care of it."

"Well, but LuAnne said that everybody's talking about us. Can we do something about that, too?"

"Sure, we can. We get married, and that'll stop it once and for all."

I shook my head. "No, it won't. You know how this town is, Sam. First thing you know, they'll be saying we had to get married."

Lord, the man laughed so hard, I thought he was going to have a stroke.

"I mean," I protested, "they'll say we had to because the pastor made us. Now stop laughing."

But I had to smile with him, although

the thought of all the wasted years without him—years when the possibility of having to marry wouldn't have been a laughing matter—stabbed at my heart.

But you can't cry over spilt milk, as Lillian says, so I let the dark cloud pass on by and felt my spirits lift at having a share, late though it had come, in his great good nature.

Then he put both arms around me and rested his chin on the top of my head, and we stood pressed together right there on his front porch for all the world to see. And I didn't care at all.

"I'll tell you what," Sam said, his breath stirring my hair, "let's forget about the talk. Don't let it bother you, Julia. They're just jealous, and when they see how I cut Ledbetter off at the knees, they'll think twice about what they say."

I nodded against his chest, just so enveloped in the smell and feel of him that I would've agreed to almost anything he proposed.

"How're you going to do that?" I asked, picturing Pastor Ledbetter having to climb up on a stool to see over the podium.

"Don't you give it another thought. By the

time I get through, he's going to know he's been to the woodshed." Sam laughed. "I may mention the legal consequences of slander and false accusations. I expect I'll get his attention." Sam ran his hand down my back and went on. "Should've done it a long time ago, but he's gone too far this time. Can't let anybody upset my girl."

He made my knees weak, holding me so close and calling me his girl. Lord knows, my girlish days were over, although there was a place deep down where I was still a lost and lonely child. And Sam knew where it was.

{ *Chapter 29* }

That night, after the children were in bed, Hazel Marie and Lillian and I sat at the kitchen table, enjoying another slice of German chocolate cake before going up ourselves.

In spite of Sam's reassurances, I'd been brooding all afternoon on the tales running rampant throughout the town, and making myself miserable wondering why Mr. Pickens hadn't called. My nerves were so on edge that I'd not even been able to get the nap I'd promised myself.

I put down my fork and said, "I need to ask both of you something, and I want you to tell me the truth."

They looked at me, Lillian frowning and Hazel Marie nodding, as they waited to hear what I had to say.

I took a deep breath. "I want to know if

you've heard any gossip about Sam and me."

Lillian asked, "What kinda gossip?"

"If you have to ask," I said with some relief, "I guess you haven't."

"Oh," she laughed. "You mean *that* kinda gossip. Law, no, Miss Julia, don't nobody say nothin' to me 'bout you nor Mr. Sam. They know better."

Noticing Hazel Marie's silence, I peered at her. "What about you? Have you heard anything?"

"Well," she sighed, laying her napkin by her plate, "a little, but it's been going around for so long, I thought it'd about wore itself out."

"*How* long?" I was stunned. Here I'd been holding my head up high, confident of my spotless reputation, and now to find that people had been whispering and giggling behind my back for who knew how long, well, it just mortified me.

"I've not paid much attention, to tell the truth," Hazel Marie said, but her face belied her words. "And nobody's ever come right out and actually said anything. Just a comment here and there."

"What kind of comment?"

"Well, like 'I guess Sam's about moved in, hasn't he?' or 'Maybe Julia'll have better luck this time around,' things like that."

"And what do you say back?"

"Nothing. Just something like 'You'll have to ask them,' or 'That's Miss Julia's business.' Nobody's said anything to me lately. That's why I thought it'd died down."

"Well, for goodness sakes, Hazel Marie, I wish you'd told me, because it hasn't died down. It's spreading all over the place, even being discussed in the session, which Lu-Anne just had to tell me about. And now Pastor Ledbetter intends to make a public example out of me in front of the whole congregation, unless Sam can stop him."

"Oh, my word," Hazel Marie said, a shocked look on her face. "He can't do that. I've never heard of such a thing. Well, yes I have, but it was in a backwoods church where one of the deacons was caught feeling up a woman in a Holy Ghost trance. They whipped him right there in front of everybody. Scared me so bad, I never went back."

"Lord, Hazel Marie," I said when I got my breath back, "that's awful. I don't think the Book of Church Order provides for public whippings, but don't go telling that story around. I wouldn't want the pastor to get any more ideas."

Lillian stood up and began gathering our plates. She looked at me and said, "I tell you somethin' right now. I ain't never thought what mens and ladies do in they own house be bad as what folkses do when they start messin' in other folks's business. Nobody, not yo' preacher nor nobody, got no call to say you an' Mr. Sam be nothin' but pure as the driven snow."

Hazel Marie nodded emphatically. "As the driven snow. Amen to that."

Well, I wouldn't have gone quite that far, since I'd been known to harbor a few unseemly thoughts in the dark of the night, but their trust in my moral purity went a long way in easing my anxious mind.

"One good thing," Lillian said, as she walked over to the sink. "If all them folks so busy talkin' 'bout you an' Mr. Sam, they got no time for talkin' 'bout anybody else." A stricken look crossed her face as she realized she'd almost spilled the beans about Wesley Lloyd's double- or triple-dealing, right in front of Hazel Marie. Dishes clattered in her hands before she could get them in the sink. "I mean, folks skip around a lot when they get to talkin'."

I glanced at Hazel Marie, but the whole thing seemed to have gone over her head. She hadn't picked up on Lillian's near-slip, for she was concentrating on my problem.

"What I don't understand, Miss Julia," she finally said, "is why you and Sam don't go ahead and get married. You know you love him, and he just adores you. That'd fix it, and you wouldn't have to put up with any more talk."

"For goodness sake, Hazel Marie," I said, switching myself around in my chair. "That's exactly what Sam said, but I am not going to have it. I wouldn't marry him now for all the gold in Fort Knox."

"Why you be so bull-headed?" Lillian said, coming back to the table. "He a good man, an' that kind be few and far between."

"It'd be the perfect solution," Hazel Marie said, "and so romantic. I don't see why you won't."

"Because I don't want to give the gossipers the satisfaction, for one thing. Let them talk. I'll entertain Sam when and where I please and, who knows, I may decide to really give them something to talk about, and dare the pastor to do anything about it."

"Oh, Miss Julia," Hazel Marie said, her eyes glinting with mischief, "I wish you would. What would you do?"

"I'll have to think about it. Hold his hand in public, maybe."

Lillian started laughing. "Shoo. You got to do better'n that."

"I know," Hazel Marie cried. "Why don't you let somebody see you coming out of the Mountaintop Motel together? That'd do it for sure."

We ended up laughing about it, but deep down, I was still deeply disturbed. I didn't like being talked about, to say nothing of being laughed at. And I certainly did not like being thought of as a fallen woman and, even worse, being blamed for Sam's lapsed state.

As we prepared to go upstairs to bed, Lillian said, "I hope y'all got yo' ducks in a row for the party we givin' for Mr. Tony. It be here 'fore you know it."

"Oh, Lord," I moaned, "don't remind me. I hate to think of facing all those people, knowing what they're thinking. I wish we could just cancel and forget about it."

"You'll do fine," Hazel Marie said. "They're going to be so tickled to see Tony all decked out as Tonya that they won't give you a thought. And if you think it'll be bad for you, think about poor Mildred and what she'll have to face."

I patted her hand and gave her a grateful look as she took herself upstairs to bed.

"She's right," I said to Lillian as she put the last of our plates into the dishwasher. "I wouldn't change places with Mildred for anything in the world. I'll take what they're saying about me, which after all does come under the heading of *normal,* even if immoral, over their twittering about Mildred and her new thirty-something-year-old daughter. And, Lillian, you were right, too, about this being another topic that'll deflect the gossip from Wesley Lloyd and his ladyfriends."

"Well, Law," she said, wringing out a sponge. "I almost give it away, 'cause it be on my mind so bad. Miz Causey, my used-to-be next door neighbor, she call an' tell me they talkin' 'bout Mr. Springer an' that Walk Where Jesus Walked woman at choir practice the other night. I don't know why folks have to be diggin' up dirt all the time, 'specially when it likely hurt that little boy." She puttered around, wiping off the counters, window sills and stovetop. "Wisht they'd mind they own business, is what I wish."

"That's not likely to happen," I said, just done in by hearing that Wesley Lloyd's longago antics were making the rounds in another church. "Sleep well, Lillian. I'll see you in the morning."

I went to bed, so tired from the previous night's excursion and the day's exertions that I could hardly drag myself up the stairs.

I woke that Saturday morning with a renewed determination to protect Little Lloyd from the disastrous knowledge of his father's straying disposition. That, I told myself, was what I had to keep in the forefront of my mind, regardless of how my own reputation was suffering, and I didn't care how much it cost me. Well, of course, I did, but I meant within reason.

Then, too, I realized that if the child heard the tales about me and Sam, he'd be rightly disturbed, if he understood them. I had set myself up as an example to him of how one should live in a gracious and morally correct manner. Maybe he'd give me the benefit of the doubt, but even if he didn't, it wouldn't be as damaging to him as knowing about his father's goatish activities. Besides, I was an innocent party, and his father wasn't, which would surely count for something.

And, as I came out of bed, I smiled at a sudden delicious thought. Why not give the town something to really talk about? And let the boy take part in it? If he thought he knew all there was to know about Sam and me, he'd dismiss anything else he happened to hear.

Of course, my idea would give Pastor Ledbetter more ammunition against me. But, feeling energized at the thought of turning the gossip upside down, I decided to trust that Sam could put him on permanent hold.

To that end, I called Sam. When he answered, I said, "Sam, do you really mean all the things you've been saying to me?"

"Every word, Julia," he said. Then: "What things are we talking about?"

"About how you feel about me. Now, listen, if you want to back off, you can, but do it right now or forever hold your peace."

"Lord, Julia," he said, his voice full and rich. "I don't want to back off anything. Never did, never will. Are you saying you'll marry me?"

"No, I'm not. What I am saying is that I want some tangible expression of how you feel."

"Well, hell, woman. Let me put this phone down and I'll run over there and smooch on you all day long. Will that be tangible enough?"

"That's not what I had in mind."

"Tell me, and I'll do it. Anything in the world."

"Well, this is a little difficult to ask for, since it should be the man who offers it. But," I said, drawing a deep breath and plunging in, "I want you to give me a ring."

There was silence on the line, and I feared that I'd overstepped myself. "Now, Sam," I quickly said, "I don't want you to think I'm a golddigger or anything. It doesn't have to be expensive, but it does have to be big enough to be noticeable."

"Julia, you take my breath away. Of course I'll give you a ring, and would've done it long ago if I thought you'd accept it. Sweetheart, nothing would make me happier than to put an engagement ring on your finger."

"*Engagement* ring! I'm not talking about an engagement ring."

"What other kind is there?"

"Plenty of other kinds, because you know my position on getting married. No, what I want is a friendship ring."

There was another long silence on the line. Then he said, "A friendship ring, huh? Would that be like a pre-engagement ring or something?"

"I don't know what it'd be like. I just want something that'll knock a few eyes out and throw more fuel on the flame. They want something to talk about, so I'll give it to them."

He started laughing then and finally managed to say, "Well, I won't say I'm not disappointed, but I'll look at it as a step in the right direction. Tell me what kind you want, sweetie, and I'll take comfort in the fact that I'll have something wrapped around your finger."

"I don't care what you get, just so it's big enough to be noticed. But, Sam, don't spend a lot of money on it. And it doesn't have to be real, even. I just need it before our reception for Mildred Allen's new-born daughter on Tuesday, so don't piddle around making a decision.

"And one other thing. I want you to take Little Lloyd when you go to get it. That way, he won't pay attention to any rumors about us. He'll think the ring started them."

"Good thinking, Julia. See you in a little while."

We hung up with him still laughing, and me smiling at his reaction. I declare, he understood my devious designs better than I did, myself. As my smile spread wider, I realized that I wouldn't at all mind having Sam's ring on my finger, even if it didn't mean a thing in the world.

Chapter 30

Less than an hour later, Sam was at my door, eager to set off on his mission. He wouldn't take the time to come in and speak to Hazel Marie or Lillian, much less linger to hear me caution him about going overboard.

"This is man's work, Julia," he said. "Is Lloyd ready? We're going to have ourselves a time, picking out just the right thing."

"Now, Sam . . . ," I started, but he held up his hand.

"Not a word, Julia. Leave it to us."

Little Lloyd was full of excitement, readying himself in a few minutes for the unexpected outing with Sam. They left, whispering and laughing between themselves.

Latisha was disappointed she couldn't go, but that active little mind soon came up with another plan.

"Well," she said, parking her hands on her non-existent hips, "If I can't go shoppin' with them, I'm gonna go to that theme park y'all been talkin' about. That's what I'm gonna do, soon as somebody takes me."

"Hush, chile," Lillian said as she busied herself at the sink. "Nobody goin' to that place."

"I don't see why not." Latisha turned her big eyes up to Lillian. "I'm gonna ride one of them logs that come flyin' down a water-chute and throw water all over everybody." She bent over, laughing at the thought. "Great-granny, you gonna wet yourself all over. An' listen here, they got all kinds of rides and shows and Mickey Mouses and such as that. I got to get myself out there."

"Latisha," I said, "the theme park we've been talking about is a little different from the ones you're thinking of. I doubt you'd like this one."

"Well, I don't want no different one. I want the real thing. When can we go, Great-granny? I'm ready any time you are."

"Nobody gonna be ready any time soon," Lillian said, as she swooped her up. "I need you to help me with this here."

Lillian stood her up in a chair at the

kitchen table and gave her the job of counting spoons for our reception. As I made myself scarce, I could hear that little piercing voice going on and on, counting, talking, losing count, then starting over. At one point, she stopped counting long enough to tell Lillian some long story about her daddy who was living on an Army basement.

I couldn't help but smile at how she mixed up words. The child was an entertainment, if you were in the mood to be entertained. Which, at that time, I wasn't. I went upstairs to my desk to go over the lists for the reception, even though I'd lost my enthusiasm for it. My grand scheme to put Tonya Allen in the forefront of the town talk seemed unnecessary, now that Sam and I were occupying that unenviable position.

I tapped my pen against the side of my face, thinking how the speculations would really run wild, once I began sporting a ring. They wouldn't know what to make of it, nor would Pastor Ledbetter. Especially when no word of impending nuptials would be forthcoming.

Lord, as I thought about it, I wondered when people had time to take care of the necessities of life. Keeping themselves so busy talking and spreading rumors, when did they get their work done? If it wasn't the long-dead Wesley Lloyd and his paramours, it was Tony Allen and his remarkable trans-formation. And if it wasn't Tony, it was what Sam and I were up to on the sofa in my living room. Which was a wonder to me, because if you've ever sat on a Duncan Phyfe sofa, you know the style does not lend itself to any kind of energetic activities, much less amorous ones.

And if that wasn't enough to occupy my mind, another worry flooded in. Why hadn't Mr. Pickens called? Could the Mooney woman be in such a high spiritual state that she'd be offended at the offer of money? What would I fall back on then? Lord, I wanted it settled and over with.

I sighed and turned back to my lists, wondering if I had the stamina for a party. But, once you send out invitations, you're pretty well committed to going through with whatever you've invited half the town to.

"Miss Julia?" Hazel Marie came up the stairs to my room. She plopped down in the easy chair beside my front window. "Sam just called. They're on the way to Charlotte, so they're going to be late. He didn't want us to worry."

"Charlotte? Why in the world?"

"He just said they couldn't find what they were looking for in Asheville, and he knew he had to strike while the iron was hot." She smiled as if she knew something I didn't. "Now, what could he mean by that?"

"I have no idea, except he's making a mountain out of a molehill. I told him that I wanted a simple friendship ring, the selection of which should not entail a trip to Charlotte. He could've gotten something at Wal-Mart, for all the meaning attached to it."

"Well, I expect he's attaching a little more meaning to it than you are. You never let him give you anything except at Christmas, so now that you've asked for something, it's his big chance."

"You are such a romantic, Hazel Marie. I told him why I wanted it, and it's only to rub in the faces of the gossipers to prove I don't care what they say. It doesn't mean a blessed thing."

"Uh-huh," she said in a knowing way, which made me want to shake her. "Well, I expect you'll really be the talk of the town with Sam's ring on your finger."

"Let them talk," I said. "Now, Hazel Marie, if anybody asks you, you tell them that Sam and I have no intention of getting married. Tell them that we have a *relationship,* which is an overused word that doesn't mean what people think it does." I paused, thinking how the word had come to imply an intimacy that should be reserved for marriage, but often wasn't. "Because, when you come right down to it, you could say that I have a relationship with the mailman and the man who services my car. So you'll be telling the truth, but the way their minds work, it'll stir up a hornet's nest of speculation."

"You'll certainly stir up Pastor Ledbetter when that gets around," Hazel Marie said, a worried look on her face. "What if he does call you up in front of the congregation?"

"I'll just stand and walk out, not up. I've thought about it, Hazel Marie and, if Sam can't stop him from publicly humiliating me, I'll just move my letter. Maybe to the Episcopal church. They'll be glad to have me."

Lillian and Latisha were long in bed, but Hazel Marie and I waited up for the shoppers. She'd gone to the window half a dozen times, hoping to see Sam and Little Lloyd turning in. By this time, though, I, too, was becoming concerned, since it was after eleven and long past the child's bedtime. Sam's, too, for that matter.

"Hazel Marie," I said, putting aside the newspaper I'd read all the way through without becoming any more informed than I already was. "Try not to be so anxious, you'll make yourself ill. You know Sam'll take care of him, and I'm sure they'll be here any minute. Though why they had to make that three-hour trip, I don't know."

"It's awfully late," she said, peering again through the window. "I just hope they're not stranded on the side of the road somewhere. Believe me, Lloyd is not leaving this house again without a cell phone with him."

"I expect they had dinner and left after that. So they're not very late at all." I wouldn't tell her, but Sam was going to hear from me for keeping that child out till all hours of the night.

"Oh, here they are!" Hazel Marie cried,

and almost tripped in her haste to get to the door.

Little Lloyd barely got inside before he was scooped up and hugged by his mother. Sam came in close behind the child, while they both tried unsuccessfully to hide their beaming expressions.

As Hazel Marie almost smothered him, Little Lloyd grinned over her shoulder at me and said, "We did some major shopping today. Just wait till you see."

"Don't let the cat out of the bag yet," Sam told him, as he did a little grinning of his own. He looked so good that I was tempted to give him the same kind of welcome Hazel Marie was giving Little Lloyd.

"Oh, that's right," the boy said. "Mama, it's time for us to go to bed. Say good night and let's go."

"But I want to hear about your trip," she said.

"I'll tell you in the morning." Then pulling her down so he could pretend to whisper in her ear, he gave me a laughing glance, and said, "Mr. Sam said we had to go to bed."

"Oh," Hazel Marie said. Then, "*Oh!* Now I get it. Good night, Sam. Thanks for taking

Lloyd with you. Good night, Miss Julia, and I mean a *real* good night."

Little Lloyd, still beaming with their secret, started toward the stairs, then turned back. "Thank you, Mr. Sam. I enjoyed going with you." And he shook Sam's hand, while I looked on with pride at this exhibition of good manners. Then he and his mother left, and Sam and I were alone.

"Well, Julia?" Sam said, with a lift of his eyebrows.

"Don't *'well, Julia'* me. What do you mean, staying out this late?" But I didn't really care, since they were safely home. I smiled at him. "Well, never mind, now that you're here. Have a seat, Sam. Is it still raining?"

"Just a little drizzle coming up the mountain." He settled himself on the sofa and patted the space next to him. "Come sit with me, Julia, while I figure out the proper way to present a friendship ring to my sweetheart."

"Oh, Sam, there's no proper way about it. But I'll just sit over here till we're sure the others are asleep."

"They know to leave us alone. Now, come

on over here. This thing's burning a hole in my pocket."

So I did, but with some trepidation, not knowing what he had in mind or in pocket.

"Julia," he said, as he pulled out a small brown sack that looked as if it had come from a dime store, "I'd like to get on my knees . . ."

"Don't you dare!"

". . . but I'm afraid I couldn't get back up." He smiled at me and pulled a tissue wrapped object from the sack. "And of course, being fully aware that this is merely a friendship ring, I'm not sure kneeling is in order, anyway."

"It certainly is not. And you're making too much of this, Sam. Just get on with it."

He unwrapped the ring and held it up in front of me. Then he put his other arm around my shoulders. "Julia," he said, his voice steady and sincere but his eyes were twinkling with humor. "It would please me more than I can say to see you wear this ring as a token of our deep and enduring friendship."

Lord, my breath caught in my throat, and I thought I might pass out. Not from what he said, since that was nothing particularly new, but at the sight of that dark blue stone, set in sterling silver and surrounded by glittering zircons. It looked real enough . . . well, to be real.

"Oh, my goodness, Sam," I managed to say, "it's beautiful. Just perfect, in fact, and I know it'll fool some people who wouldn't know a diamond from a diamonique."

Actually, it was going to create a sensation, since the thing was remarkable for size and sparkle. It went beyond anything I had envisioned and, if I'd not been dead set on showing the town how little I cared what they said about me, I would've refused it. The thing was gaudy, if you want to know the truth, and not at all like the sedate and classic pieces in my jewelry drawer.

"I'm sure it will, sweetheart," Sam said, then lifted my left hand to place it on my finger.

I quickly switched hands, holding out my right one. "Mind yourself," I said.

With a laugh, he slid it on my finger, and clasped my hand. "I'll take either hand I can get."

I closed my eyes and, for a moment, allowed myself to feel the thrill of belonging to this man, while at the same time sadness filled my heart because it just wasn't expedient to make that belonging permanent. In that sense, a ring made of paste, no matter how beautiful, was the perfect symbol of what was between us.

But even as a symbol, it was a knockout. I held my hand up to admire it. "If I didn't know better," I said, wiggling my fingers to see the ring sparkle in the lamplight, "I'd be fooled, myself."

"That's the idea," he said. Then, at my quick look, he added, "You wanted it to look real, didn't you?"

I nodded and smiled with pleasure. Then Sam said something else, and I kept smiling and nodding. But after that, what he said and what he did are best left untold.

As I readied myself for church the next morning, it was all I could do to keep my heart from jumping out of my chest. I didn't know which was sending jolts of adrenaline through me more—the dazzling ring on my finger or the prospect of showing it off for the first time. It made me feel warm all over whenever I looked at it.

Hazel Marie noticed it the minute I walked

into the kitchen for breakfast. She gasped and grabbed my hand, turning it first one way, then the other. "Is this what Sam gave you? Oh, Miss Julia, it is drop-dead gorgeous. Look, Lillian." And she dragged my hand, with me trailing along, over to wave it in front of Lillian.

"Get a load of this, Lillian," Hazel Marie said. "Have you ever seen anything like it?"

"Not in all my born days," Lillian said, reaching a finger out to touch it. "That thing 'bout blind me with all them sparks flyin' off."

Little Lloyd looked up from his cereal bowl. "I helped pick it out."

"I know you did, honey," I told him, "and I appreciate it. But you both about went overboard. I wanted big and gaudy, and I certainly got it."

Latisha piped up. "If it was me, I'd marry that big ole white-headed man, and get me some more rings. I wouldn't care if he was old as Methuslum."

As we laughed and Lillian continued to admire the ring, Hazel Marie suddenly demanded, "You know what it's a copy of, don't you? Princess Diana's ring, that's what!"

"Oh, hardly," I said, smiling with pleasure at their reaction. "It does look nice, doesn't it? Even though I'm not much of a jewelry person, I'm quite pleased with it."

"Well, you ought to be!" Hazel Marie said. "I mean, those are killer diamonds and that sapphire! If that's a friendship ring, I'll eat it."

"Oh, Hazel Marie, it's just glass in a sterling setting. They can do lovely things with artificial gems nowadays. Not like it used to be, when anything that wasn't real looked like it came out of a Crackerjack box."

"It look pretty real to me," Lillian said. "Though it so big an' sparkly, I wouldn't care either way."

"Me neither," Latisha said. "What you grinning for, Lloydy Lloyd?"

Little Lloyd took a great interest in his cereal bowl. "Nothing."

"Miss Julia," Hazel Marie said, "that ring is real, I'll bet you anything. Take it off and I'll show you."

I slipped it off and gave it to her. She turned it to the light and squinted at the underside. "Look at this," she said. "Right there, it says p-l-a-t. You know what that means? Platinum, that's what. And, believe me, they don't put glass in platinum."

I had to sit down to stop my head from spinning, at the same time wanting to wring Sam's neck for playing such a trick on me. "How much do you think he paid for it?" I asked, as I looked at the ring again, fearing now to wear it. "Little Lloyd? Did Sam pay a lot for this?"

He ducked his head, hiding a smile. "I'm not supposed to tell."

"Ten million dollars!" Latisha cried.

Hazel Marie shook her finger in my face, and said. "How much it cost is not for you to know or even think about. Sam gave it to you because he wanted you to have it. Now you put it on and enjoy it. It's certainly going to start people buzzing. Nobody'll miss that thing."

She was right. If I had wanted to attract attention, this was going to do it. I reached over for the ring and slipped it on my finger again. I'd wear it to church, let it accomplish its purpose, then have it out with Sam for going so far above and beyond the bounds of friendship.

{Chapter 31}

By the time we were making last minute preparations to walk over to the church for Sunday services, I had myself worried sick about losing the ring. Lord, if Hazel Marie was right, I was carrying around a chunk of money on my hand. And, to tell the truth, I was having second thoughts about displaying it in the brazen way I'd planned to do.

So I decided to wear gloves, then had the most grievous time getting the right one on. Kidskin gloves are just not made to fit over large stones. I managed, however uncomfortably, to hide the ring until we were settled in our usual pew.

Finally, I could stand it no longer—it was either do or die, and I decided to do it. So, during the anthem, I took off my gloves. Then, without thinking, my right hand went up of its own accord to smooth the hair on the back of my head. In the pew behind us, Amy Broughton gasped, and I heard her husband grunt as she poked him. I straightened the collar on the back of my suit jacket to give them a good look, then so very nonchalantly, I grasped the pew in front of us with my right hand and pulled myself forward to whisper a greeting to Helen Stroud and her husband, Richard, who bought and sold real estate right and left. As she turned to acknowledge me, she cupped her hand around her mouth and whispered, "I can't wait for your party." Then her eyes fell on the ring and her mouth dropped open. I just smiled and sat back.

I looked across the aisle and saw LuAnne and Leonard in their usual places, and thought about ways to run into them after the service. If anybody could spread the word about Sam's gift, she could. And I didn't intend to tell her, or anybody, that it was only a friendship ring—what it signified was between Sam and myself. I knew they'd make note that I was wearing it on the wrong hand for an engagement, but they'd also notice that my left hand was bare, waiting perhaps for a transfer from one to the other.

I tried to put my mind on the service, but Hazel Marie on one side and Little Lloyd on the other kept picking up my hand to admire the ring. None of us had the right attitude for a worship service, I'm sorry to say. But then, it's not every day that one receives such a momentous token of friendship.

After all the usual rituals—the congregational hymns, the responsive reading, the anthem, the collection, and the pastoral prayer—that led up to the sermon were over and done with, I settled back, determined to keep my mind on what Pastor Ledbetter had to say. Even though he made me mad half the time, I felt it my Christian duty to listen intently to the sermon in case he said something profound. Not like some who gazed wide-eyed at him while their minds were a million miles away or others who valiantly fought sleep or others who lost the battle.

I stiffened in my seat when Pastor Ledbetter stood up in his black robe and, after issuing a welcome to all newcomers, said, "It is my great honor to turn the pulpit over today to my friend in the Lord, Curtis Maxwell."

As Mr. Maxwell ascended the steps to the

pulpit, dressed in another of his tailor-made suits, I thought to myself that if I'd known he was giving the sermon, I'd have stayed home.

Looking out over the congregation with the ease of an accomplished speaker, Mr. Maxwell let the silence grow. Then he held up his notes and tore them in two. "I am going to speak to you from the heart," he said, "because it's burdened with the need I see as I travel across this great country. To meet that need, Christian men and women must stand together, spiritually, emotionally, and financially."

With that, he had my attention and then some. He was a good speaker, I'll give him that, for there were no hesitations, no repetitions, and not one lame joke. This was a man who was accustomed to giving sales talks, for that's exactly what he gave.

"My friends," he said at one point, "the Lord has blessed Abbot County, this church, and each one of you by seeing fit to make this community the home of the Walk Where Jesus Walked Christian Theme Park. He has given you a great opportunity, but where there is great opportunity, there is also great responsibility. It is incumbent upon each one of us to support by our presence and our gifts what the Lord has so graciously given for our benefit and for the increase in tourist trade."

I glanced across the aisle at Emma Sue, who was sitting in her usual pew on the right side, second row from the front. The woman was entranced by every word that issued from Curtis Maxwell's mouth. She sat there, as plain as she'd ever been, gazing raptly at the man she'd told me was only a candidate for membership in our church. That wasn't the way it looked to me, and I shook my head at the unseemliness of it, wondering if anybody else had noticed this inappropriate display of adoration. Whatever her purpose was, it didn't look good in my opinion. Emma Sue was playing with fire, being so openly receptive to Mr. Maxwell's attentions. And what would happen if those attentions flared up? She'd get burned, that's what.

Then Mr. Maxwell got to the highlight of his sermonette: The theme park was having a Pre-Grand Opening this coming Saturday night, with a special invitation to all the churches in the county.

"Now, don't expect the theme park to be

completely finished," Mr. Maxwell said, his smoothly barbered face all aglow, "because it won't be. But enough has been done to make you want to take an active part in completing this great project. In fact, the Pre-Grand Opening will be an old-fashioned tent meeting, and it will prove to be a blessing to each one of you, I promise you that."

Uh-huh, I thought to myself, they need more money to finish the thing, and that's the reason for a Pre-Grand Opening. Well, I thought, I was willing to write a check, but for a better cause than a slap-dash replica of the land of Palestine. And that brought Mr. Pickens's continuing silence to mind. How was I going to pay that woman, if he didn't let me know something?

Mr. Maxwell went on and on in a similar manner and, if he mentioned Maxwell Household Products once, he mentioned them a dozen times. I was surprised, when the service was finally over, that he wasn't surrounded by people clamoring to buy bathroom deodorizer.

I was so offended by the use of our pulpit for a marketing spiel, that I herded Little Lloyd and Hazel Marie out one of the side doors. I didn't want to speak to the man or to his black-robed sponsor. And, as far as showing off my new ring to LuAnne or anybody else, that could wait till Tuesday at our reception for Tony Allen.

As we walked down the sidewalk beside the church on our way home, Hazel Marie, having noticed my spiritual discomfort, ventured to say, "At least he was a good speaker, don't you think?"

"All the more reason to beware of him," I said. "He has a twofold agenda, it seems to me. One is to drum up contributions to that rag-tag group out there on my property, and the other is to sell his less-than-satisfactory cleaning products." I stomped on down the sidewalk, so full of outrage that Hazel Marie had to skip to keep up with me. "And possibly one more thing, and that is to create enough mischief to turn Emma Sue's head further than it's already been turned," I said as we climbed the porch steps. "Did you see how she was looking at him? If the pastor didn't notice it, he must be blind."

As Little Lloyd opened the front door for us, he said, "I didn't notice anything. How was Mrs. Ledbetter looking?"

"Oh, my," I said, biting my lip. I kept forgetting that the child understood more than

I often gave him credit for. "She was looking quite well, Little Lloyd. She's trying to take care of herself a little more, and that's all I meant. Now, run upstairs and change your clothes before we have lunch."

As he ran upstairs, I turned to Hazel Marie. "I'm sorry that I so often speak without realizing how much he takes in. I shouldn't've let fly like that."

"Oh," she said, as we both headed to the kitchen. "He doesn't pay that much attention. Don't worry about it."

We placed our pocketbooks on a side counter and commenced removing dishes from the refrigerator. Lillian always prepared enough for Sunday lunch on Saturday, and all we needed to do was heat it up. She and Latisha would soon be home, since their services lasted a little longer than ours.

"Miss Julia?" Hazel Marie said tentatively. She was at the sink, filling a pan with water for tea. She set the pan on a stove eye and turned to me. "I've been thinking."

I looked up from setting the table, immediately on my guard. Whenever Hazel Marie said she'd been thinking, I knew to prepare myself. "What about?"

"Well, you know how worried I am about

Lloyd growing up without a strong male influence and you know how unlikely it is that J. D. is going to provide that on a permanent basis, so I've been thinking that I ought to look around a little."

"Lord, Hazel Marie, in this town there's nowhere to look. Mr. Pickens is the choice by far." Which, I thought but didn't say, indicated the level of available men in Abbot County.

"Well, I know he is, but if I can't pin him down to making a family for my boy to grow up in, then I might as well give up on him."

I didn't say anything for a few minutes as I tried to figure out how I felt about this sudden about-face. I liked Mr. Pickens and Little Lloyd practically worshipped him, a fact that elevated the man in my opinion. On the other hand, Mr. Pickens was so free and easy and uncommitted and irresponsible that he would drive any woman crazy. Hazel Marie might be better off to look for another fish in the sea.

"That's interesting, Hazel Marie," I said, trying not to take sides one way or the other. "Mr. Pickens is a fine man after his fashion, but I can see that he'd be hard to live with."

"Live with! I can't even get him on the

phone!" Hazel Marie slammed the oven door shut, then walked over to lean on the counter. "Little Lloyd needs a father who is respected and successful and someone he can look up to, and someone who can help him get a good start in life."

"I don't know anybody like that around here," I said as I put the butter dish on the table. I smiled at her. "You have anyone in mind?"

"Yes, I do. Curtis Maxwell."

I dropped the cover on the butter dish. "Hazel Marie! You don't want that man! Why, he's a hypocrite of the first order, going around selling household products in churches and sponsoring that fringe group out yonder. How can you think such a thing!"

"He has a lot going for him," she said, a smile pulling at the corner of her mouth. "Lloyd would have all the advantages."

"He already has advantages," I snapped back, refraining from mentioning where they came from. "Hazel Marie, you can't be serious about this."

She laughed. "No, I just wanted to see what you'd say."

"Well," I said, fanning myself with a place mat, "don't scare me like that again."

"I am serious about one thing, though." She straightened up and stood with her hands on her hips. "I'm giving considerable thought to looking some place other than J. D. Pickens."

"One more week," I said, recalling the announcement of the big Pre-Grand Opening of the theme park for the following Saturday and hoping he'd have Monique paid off and on a Greyhound bus by then. "Give him one more week, Hazel Marie. I think he'll be here eating us out of house and home by this time next Sunday."

She frowned at me. "Do you know what he's doing?"

Before I could answer—not that I wanted to—Lillian's car drove up and we heard her and Latisha heading for the door.

"We could go to Six Flags," Latisha said, as they came inside. She was still on her favorite subject. "They got them flags over just about every state in the world. I think we ought to go to a theme park *some*where, don't you?"

"I'm with you, Latisha," Hazel Marie said. "I've been wanting to go for ever so long, and one of these days we're just going to pack up and go."

"I'm not studyin' goin' nowhere," Lillian said, reaching for an apron. "Le's us get something on the table, so I can start makin' my pecan tassies. We got to have I don't know how many dozen for our party."

That was the end of the conversation concerning Hazel Marie's lifestyle choices, for which I was thankful. But, before she let her fancy run far afield, I had to get Mr. Pickens back, lest she ruined her life and turned Little Lloyd into a world-wide jet-setter.

{ *Chapter 32* }

For the rest of the time leading up to the day of the reception, I didn't let Hazel Marie out of my sight. Determined to give her no time to think of replacing Mr. Pickens, I kept her hopping. She and Lillian and I had given so many teas, coffees, receptions, and open houses that each one of us knew what had to be done, and we went about doing it— dusting, straightening, arranging flowers, polishing silver, and all the other last-minute preparations necessary for the critical eyes of our guests.

I knew she was still calling Mr. Pickens and getting his answering machines, which meant that she had not given up on him entirely. And whenever she was out of earshot, I was doing the same, hoping to get him back to defend his rights. It just frustrated me something awful that there was no way to reach him. He needed to know how dangerously close he was to losing what he was out at that place trying to protect, and I needed to know how big a check I had to write. There was only one way to get to him and, though I hated the thought of doing it, I knew I had to.

"Hazel Marie," I said, walking into her room where she was trying to decide which of her outfits would compare favorably with Tonya Allen's New York couture. "This is the last thing I want to do, but I think I ought to go to that Pre-Grand Opening Saturday. I want to see what they're doing on my property, and if I don't like it, which I probably won't, I'm going to evict them. Now," I said, hurrying to forestall any help from her, "it's not necessary for you to accompany me. I'll ask Sam to go, so you and Lillian and the children can rent a movie and make popcorn. Or something."

"Oh, Miss Julia, I want to go," she said, which was exactly what I had not wanted to hear. She laid another dress on the bed and stood back, considering it. She looked up at me. "Let's all go together. I haven't been to a tent meeting in a long time. There used to be a lot of them, and somebody always got filled with the Holy Spirit, and people got healed and everything. A lot of stuff happens that you never see in a downtown church."

"That's what I'm afraid of. I'm not sure it would be conducive to Little Lloyd's spiritual growth to witness such a spectacle." I stopped, bit my lip and thought about it. "I'm not even sure it'll be conducive to mine."

"I'll talk to him about it before we go," she said, turning back to her closet. "It'll be good for him to know that people worship in different ways."

"Well, I don't know, Hazel Marie. Train up a child in the way he should go, you know, and to me that means not giving him a choice until he's old enough to make the right one. Well," I said, seeing that her mind was centered more on choosing the right dress than on shielding that child from deviant influences, "maybe we won't have to worry about it. Maybe it'll rain Saturday and wash the whole thing out."

But later that night, I found myself downright eager to get out to that place. It was after midnight when the telephone beside my bed jarred me awake. Scrambling to get it, all I could think of was that Emma Sue was on the rampage again.

"It's me," Mr. Pickens said. "Just listen, because I don't have much time." Then he told me Monique Mooney would accept a sum of money that made me gasp. But, quickly recovering, I realized it wasn't as much as it could've been if she'd known my net worth.

"Agreed," I said, "on the condition that she never set foot in this county again. You told her that, didn't you?"

"I did, and she knows she'll have me to deal with if she comes back looking for more. Here's the way we'll do it. She wants to be part of the opening program Saturday night, so you come, too, and bring the check. I'll meet up with you when it's over, and get it to her."

"Can't we do it before then and be done with it?"

"No, that's the way she wants it. She's going to leave right after the program without telling Dooley a thing." He laughed quietly. "I'm going to drive her to the bus station, so I'll know she's gone."

"You don't know what a relief it is to hear

that. I'll be there, Mr. Pickens, and I hope we've seen the last of her."

And before I could express my heartfelt gratitude, he said he had to go and hung up. I slept until the children clomping up and down the stairs woke me the next morning, and it was the best night's sleep I'd had since Dwayne Dooley came ringing my doorbell.

Tuesday, the day of Tonya's coming-out party, dawned bright and clear for a change. It was a perfect day for the entertainment of the year. The caterer arrived, bearing trays piled high with finger sandwiches of all shapes and sizes, cheese straws, cheese balls, fruit slices, tiny cream puffs, petit fours, cookies, and tarts, as well as concoctions for the chafing dishes. Lillian's pecan tassies were arranged on one of my best silver trays, and two thirty-cup urns of coffee perked on the counter, while tea steeped on the stove. Hazel Marie brought in the silver service to await the hot beverages, while I placed flowers around the punch bowl gracing one end of the dining room table. It would be filled with an ice ring and ginger-ale punch. Not spiked, of course.

Hazel Marie had finally settled on a simple, A-line dress of pale pink silk faille. "I wanted something classic," she said, "and pink is so good this year." She fastened the strand of pearls I'd given her around her neck, and pinned on a pearl and diamond brooch that she'd bought for herself. As she turned for my viewing, I had no doubt that she would hold her own with anything Tonya Allen would wear. Of course, I would've chosen a more decorous pair of shoes, but she told me that sandals with three-inch heels and ankle straps were the height of fashion, which made me wonder if she'd break her neck falling from that height.

I'd been so taken up with all the worries on my mind that I'd hardly given a thought to my own party ensemble. I knew that The Ring, as I'd begun to think of it, would lessen the attention paid to anything worn on the rest of my person, but it also made me want to wear something that was equal in grade and quality to such an outstanding piece of jewelry. I mean, would you wear diamonds and sapphires with a house dress? Well, Hazel Marie would, but I wouldn't. So

I ended up with an off-white crepe with long sleeves and a high neck. The Ring stood out like the North Star against it, especially since I was careful to hold my hand just so.

"Hurry, Miss Julia," Hazel Marie called from the bottom of the stairs. "Mildred's coming up the walk, and Tonya's with her! At least, I guess that's who it is."

They were thirty minutes early, an entirely proper arrival time for the honored guest and his mother. I rushed to greet them with Hazel Marie, more anxious than I'd let myself admit to see the results of a gender reassignment.

Lord, I'd never have believed it. Tony was a Tonya, if I'd ever seen one. In the midst of greetings among the four of us and while Hazel Marie pinned a corsage on Tonya's shoulder with trembling hands, I looked carefully at Mildred, fully expecting to see the ravages of her grief.

"Oh, Julia," she gushed, her eyes shining as she embraced me, "Tonya and I have been so looking forward to this. You are just the sweetest thing, and I'll never forget what you're doing."

Well, it certainly seemed that she'd forgotten her previous sorrows. She let her eyes linger proudly on Tonya, who was telling Hazel Marie that she looked fabulous, winning Hazel Marie's heart on the spot.

Mildred leaned close and whispered to me, "Can you believe it, Julia? I have a beautiful daughter and never even knew it."

I nodded, trying not to stare at our guest of honor, but unable to turn my eyes away. Tonya looked as if she could be Tony's sister. His twin sister, in fact, which might not've been far off the mark. Tony had never been a large boy, always small for his age, and that stood Tonya in good stead now. She was beautifully dressed in a smart silk tweed suit and high heels similar to those that Hazel Marie wore, although I must say that pumps would've hidden those bony feet better than sandals, no matter how high the fashion. Tony's blonde hair color seemed little changed, with maybe a few added highlights—which I'd learned to recognize from Hazel Marie's use of them. Tonya's coiffure formed a smooth cap on her head, with wings that followed, and hid, the contours of her somewhat angular jaw. Full bangs emphasized her delicate features

and covered a hair line that might've revealed her former masculine orientation.

From a distance, Tonya Allen would
attract the eye of any indiscriminate man,
of which I knew a number. She was
well-dressed, with bosomy curves that sur-
passed even Hazel Marie's. It was only
upon closer inspection that you might wonder at the large wrists and feet, and, Lord
help us, the hint of an Adam's apple.

While taking in Tonya's appearance, I led
her and Mildred to seats in the living room
where we would visit until the other guests
arrived. Hazel Marie could hardly contain
her fascination, as she hung on Tonya's
every word. And there were plenty of them,
for Tonya had retained Tony's bubbling personality. She chattered away, completely at
ease as she laughed in that tinkling way I remembered so well, flapping her hand to
draw in a listener, and reaching out occasionally to touch Hazel Marie.

I did my best to engage Mildred in conversation, but both of us were too enthralled
with Tonya to pay much attention to each
other. Mildred was gazing at her with pride,
and I with amazement.

Then Tonya gracefully rose from her chair,

walked over to me and, with the ease of an accomplished guest, took my hand and thanked me for honoring her.

She patted my hand and said, "You are so dear to do this for me, Miss Julia. My New York friends said I shouldn't come home, but I knew I could count on the graciousness of Southern ladies like you."

A stab of shame struck me, as my far less-than-commendable reason for honoring her flashed in my mind. But I pulled myself together and said, "It's a pleasure to have you in my home." After all, we Southern ladies learn the art of graciousness from having to deal with eccentrics of one kind or another for most of our lives.

Tonya, still holding my hand, eased herself onto a chair next to mine. "You don't know how many times I've recalled how Mother and I used to visit right here in your living room. It looks so different now, so light and fresh. You've redecorated, haven't you?"

"Why, yes," I said, pleased that she had noticed. "Hazel Marie was ever so much help with the color scheme."

Tonya leaned over to whisper, "Mother told me that you and Hazel Marie had developed a warm friendship, and I can see why—she is charming. But a lot of credit must go to your kind heart and generous nature, especially after the inauspicious start the two of you had."

I struggled, because of the increased shame I was feeling, to reply in equally complimentary terms. But I didn't have to.

"Miss Julia?" Lillian stood in the doorway, her eyes locked on Tonya while she got my attention. "'Scuse me, but Miz Ledbetter on the telephone for you."

"Oh, for goodness sake," I said, getting up from my chair. "I've asked Emma Sue to pour, so she should be here, not on the telephone. I hope nothing's happened to her."

Excusing myself, I hurried after Lillian into the kitchen where the caterer and an extra server were embellishing the sandwich trays with sprigs of parsley.

I picked up the phone and said, "Emma Sue, where are you? If you don't hurry, everybody'll be here and I'll have nobody to pour."

"You'll have to get somebody else, Julia," she said, and I could tell by her strangled voice that she was crying, which was nothing unusual, but still.

"What's wrong, Emma Sue? Are you sick?"

"No, I'm not sick, just disappointed. I hate to let you down like this, especially at the last minute, but I won't be able to pour." She stopped as a flood of tears overcame her. "I can't even come."

"Why?" I demanded. "Emma Sue, stop crying, and tell me what's wrong."

"Well," she sniffed. Then I had to listen to her blowing her nose. "Well, Larry doesn't want me to, and Curtis agreed that it wouldn't look right for me or any other church member to be there. They said, as Christians, we shouldn't associate with anything unnatural."

I could hardly control my blood pressure, which shot straight up at the very idea. It wasn't enough that Pastor Ledbetter made decisions for his wife, he was now letting a perfect stranger in on the act. I wanted to shake Emma Sue for going along with it.

"Now, listen, Emma Sue," I said, controlling my temper with some effort, "Tonya Allen may be unnatural, but that's no reason for you to be impolite. And I'll tell you another thing, she is just as pleasant as she can be and there's not one thing unnatural-looking about her. In fact," I went on, unable to refrain from getting in a jab, "if he didn't know better, Curtis Maxwell, himself, might invite her to fly off with him on his jet airplane."

"Oh, Julia, I don't think so," she said, as I tried to keep from grinding my teeth at her literalness. "But that's not the only reason, and I just hate to tell you this." She broke down then, and I had to wait until she got herself under control again. "Larry said . . . oh, I know this is hurtful, but he said I shouldn't associate with you, either."

"What!"

"Now, Julia, don't get upset. It's only till you get your personal life straightened out, although I haven't seen anything wrong with it, myself. Are you and Sam really, well, you know, jumping the gun?"

It was all I could do not to blow my stack. "We are not jumping anything, and I resent the implication. You know me better than that, Emma Sue, and if you don't, well, what I do within the confines of my own home is nobody's business." I had to stop to get my breath, visions of what I'd risked for her when she was tracking her wandering husband springing to mind and churning my stomach.

Then I collected myself, recalling my intention to rattle the town's cages good. "You might mention to the pastor, if he needs something to confirm his baseless suspicions, that Sam has given me a very expensive ring to seal our . . ." I stopped, considered and discarded the word friendship, then very deliberately said, "our *relationship*." Because, nine times out of ten, what did having a relationship mean, except having relations? Let Pastor Ledbetter chew on that for a while.

"I knew you'd be mad," she said in a subdued tone.

"You couldn't be more right," I said, and started to slam down the phone. Then, on second thought, I went on. "But not at you, Emma Sue. Just at people who're more interested in my personal life than their own, which is what they ought to be looking after. And you know what I mean, or at least you ought to."

She was silent for a few seconds, then she said, "Larry's not going to censure you, Julia. He just gets righteously indignant when he thinks people aren't living right.

Then he calms down. I wish you'd talk to him, Julia. You could make him see that you're not doing anything wrong. At least, I don't think you are. Then we could keep on being friends in public, just like we're still friends in private. Pray about it, Julia, and talk to him."

To my amazement, it was as if her fear that the pastor had become a man about town had never been. But, with the caterers and servers standing around listening to every word I said, I could hardly remind her.

Becoming aware of the commotion in the living room as more guests arrived, I said, "I have to go, Emma Sue. Thank you for your advice, but I have a party to attend to."

I hung up, then stood leaning over the phone, trying to get my wits about me before facing people who didn't mind being my public friends. And from the noise emanating from the front rooms, there were plenty of them.

So I straightened up, put on my party face and, seething inside, went out smiling to greet my guests.

The noise level increased as soon as I pushed through the door into the dining room. A quick glance assured me that Hazel

Marie had the front door well in hand, welcoming each guest as if she'd been born to it. Tonya stood beside her as Hazel Marie made the introductions. Of course, almost everyone had known Tony all of his life, but fresh introductions were called for in the present circumstances.

Ladies were coming up the walk and crowding onto the porch, squealing greetings to each other and appraising each other's apparel. They gently pushed toward the door with expectant looks on their faces, as they awaited their turn to come face-to-face with what, on the face of it, was the biggest scandal to hit the town since Wesley Lloyd's theretofore unknown son and heir became known.

I edged into the dining room, speaking to a few as I went, trying hard to appear above any speculation about either my husband's affairs or my own suspected one with Sam. Looking around the crowded and noisy rooms, I felt vindicated by the outpouring of the town in response to my invitation. Tonya Allen, in spite of the pastor's edict to avoid associating with her, was doing exactly what I'd hoped for. She was drawing them in like flies to honey and, because of it, nobody would care two cents what else Wesley Lloyd had done. Or so I hoped, because, upon closer inspection, I noticed one or two clusters of whisperers in the corner of the living room. I saw them look at me, then huddle their heads together again.

I took a deep breath and plunged into their midst determined to hold my head up, come what may.

{ Chapter 33 }

"Julia!" LuAnne shrieked, as she whirled away from a group of women and flew at me with open arms. "There you are. I was beginning to wonder if you'd show up at your own party." She gave me a hug as if we didn't ordinarily see each other several times a week, then she grabbed my hand and said, "Let me see that thing. I've heard all about it. My word, Julia, that is a *rock!*"

Then she turned back to the room and called, "Everybody, come see Julia's ring. You won't believe it."

They gathered around me and passed my hand from one to the other with appropriate expressions of admiration and wonder. More than a few eyes viewed it with envy, which filled me with pride of possession, I'm sorry to say.

"I didn't know Sam Murdoch had it in him

to pick out something like that," someone said. "Much less give it away."

"Oh, it's gorgeous," Kathy Morgan said. "You're so lucky to have a ring like this and Sam, too."

"What does it mean, Julia?" Amy Broughton asked with a sly smile. "Are we going to have an announcement soon?"

Tonya Allen grasped my hand, turned it this way and that, and said, "Honey, it is absolutely stunning. Listen, you all, if a man gave me something like this, I'd just love him to death."

That comment momentarily quietened things down, as the ladies glanced at one another. Not a one of us could escape the uncomfortable image of a ring-giving man and a surgically altered Tonya loving on each other.

"Ladies," I said, mindful of my hostess duties to smooth over any awkward moments, "please go to the table and help yourselves. Helen, would you mind pouring? Emma Sue has been unavoidably detained."

The rest of the morning entertainment went remarkably well. I had already cautioned Hazel Marie to help me watch for any little gathering of cliques in corners where Tonya might be discussed in whispers. I wanted her talked about later, not while she was a guest in my home. For the time being, Hazel Marie and I had an obligation to protect her from snide remarks and lifted eyebrows. "We have to mingle like we've never mingled before," I'd told Hazel Marie. "Keep things moving," I'd said, "and let's make sure that every woman here speaks to Tonya face-to-face. I don't want anybody to go out of here with some sort of misplaced pride in having socially shunned him. I mean, her."

And that's what we did, thrilling Tonya with the way they all flocked around her. I'd never seen anybody enjoy a party so much, although, as I recalled, Tony had always loved being the center of attention. And, if they'd admit it, the other guests enjoyed her, for Tonya sparkled as she handed out compliments to everyone, and delighted us with stories of the New York fashion world.

At one point, Hazel Marie whispered to me, "That's a *Chanel* suit she's wearing. Can you believe it?"

At another point, Hazel Marie, even more breathlessly, whispered, "I think there's something going on with her and Calvin, don't you?"

"Surely not," I whispered back, as I motioned to the server to pass a tray of sandwiches around the room. "This town might bring itself to accept a woman taking the place of a man, but not *that.* I mean, Tony may be mixed up physically, but Mildred would just die if he got mixed up romantically."

"Well, I don't know," Hazel Marie mused. "I've seen Calvin, and he's real good-looking."

She moved off to talk to someone else, leaving me with my mouth open. Lord, I'd be glad to get Mr. Pickens back in circulation before Hazel Marie cast her eyes even further afield than Curtis Maxwell.

As I moved from one cluster of women to the next, always keeping my eye on the table to be sure the trays were replenished, I made sure to keep the conversations on the thrilling topic of either Tonya or The Ring. I intended those women to have so much to think and talk about in the coming days that any other escapades Wesley Lloyd might've engaged in would be rele-

gated to the bottom of the list to die a natural death as he had, himself.

Norma Cantrell, who'd been uncommonly
standoffish during her brief visit, as indeed
she should've been given what I knew
about her, edged up to me as some of the
guests prepared to take their leave. "Did
Sam really give you that?" she asked. When
I smiled and nodded, she said, "Does it
mean what I think it does?"

"One never knows, does one?" I said with
a knowing smile that I couldn't restrain. I
was surprised, to tell the truth, that she'd
had the nerve to even show up for the party,
much less speak privately to me. I'd never
again be able to look at the woman without
recalling the moans of passion stemming
from the pastor's office, and I knew she
knew I was doing just that.

But she had the gall to look me in the eye
and say, "People're going to talk if it's not
an engagement ring. And if I were you, I'd
avoid giving any more reason for rumors to
fly around."

"You should take some of your own advice," I said, in spite of the fact that she was
a guest in my home. We glared at each
other for a few seconds but, heedful of the

rules of hospitality, I gave way first. I took a deep breath of resignation and said, "I'm glad you could come, Norma. It's been an education to meet the former Tony Allen, hasn't it?"

She agreed, and it seemed we had bridged the gap. At least, until she could get back to the church office and tell the pastor that I was sporting a rock as big as Gibraltar, obvious proof that liberties had been taken and more could be expected.

Finally the last guest left after wringing my hand at the door and assuring me that she'd had a wonderful time. That constituted the usual effusive farewells, but this time I thought they meant them. They'd never had so many exciting items to ponder, discuss, and take home to further embroider with each repetition.

I shut the door and turned back to the living room where Mildred and Tonya, who'd stayed till the bitter end as they should've, were waiting with Hazel Marie.

"Julia," Mildred said, "this was a wonderful party. Everything was beautiful, the food was delicious, and the flowers perfect. I'm so glad we did this. Now everybody will be kind to my sweet Tonya." With an adoring look on her face, she reached over and patted Tonya's knee.

Tonya leaned back in a corner of the sofa, tired from the constant chit-chat required of the center of attention. Men just don't realize how much a social function can take out of you. You're just drained when they're over.

Tonya looked up at me and said, "This was the most fun I've had since I became a real woman." Then she grinned wickedly.

I had to laugh, although that was as tasteless a comment as I'd ever heard. "Well, you were certainly a success," I said, taking a seat across from her.

Mildred smiled, but wagged a cautionary finger. "Manners, Tonya," her mother admonished. "Let's remember our manners."

"Oh, everybody just loved Tonya," Hazel Marie said, still enchanted with this new woman. Or maybe with her Chanel suit. "I think everybody had a good time."

As Mildred gazed lovingly at her daughter, Tonya patted my ring-bearing hand and said, "I can't thank you enough, Miss Julia."

"We enjoyed it, too," I said, smiling with the satisfaction of having thrown a successful party, as well as at the fact that it was over. "And, you know you'll be getting more social invitations, now that acquaintances have been renewed. I hope you'll be staying in town a while longer."

A mischievous look glinted in her eyes as she glanced at her mother. "Actually, I hadn't planned to stay this long, but home seems to have a special attraction for me now."

Mildred sighed. "Tonya, special attractions come and go, as any woman worth her salt can tell you. You need to give yourself time to know what you really want."

"Oh, Mother," Tonya said, teasingly. "A girl has to have a little freedom to look around before she know what she wants."

If I'd had any doubts that there was still the scandalous Tony Allen inside that altered exterior, I had them no longer.

Hazel Marie, taking a cue from Mildred's discomfort, suggested that Tonya go with her to the kitchen. "We want you to take some things home with you," she said. "I'll bet there's a pile of sandwiches left, and I know Lillian has plenty of pecan tassies. We want you to take the centerpiece, too."

They left the room, chatting together like

old schoolmates, while Mildred and I stayed where we were.

"Mildred," I said, "I am proud of you. You and Tonya seem to be on such good terms and enjoy each other so much. I'll be honest and say that there was a time in my life when I probably wouldn't have understood, but now I know there's more than one way to skin a cat." That hadn't come out exactly as I'd meant it to, so I tried again. "I mean, more than one way to get a daughter. Who would've ever thought I'd get one the way I got Hazel Marie?"

"That's so true," Mildred agreed. "When you look at it that way, we've both been blessed in having such lovely daughters." She sighed, then went on. "I wish Horace could see it that way. He is just beside himself and so angry that he won't even speak to Tonya. He says it's a sin and a disgrace what Tony's done to himself, and he wants to kick him, I mean her, out of the house."

"That's too bad," I said, wondering how Horace expected to do that without Mildred's cooperation. It was family money that Horace used for his investments—Mildred's family's money, that is.

"Yes, it is," Mildred replied, in her placid

way. "I think everybody ought to learn to get along. Lord knows, that's what I try to do. Although," she said with a heaving sigh, "I keep thinking of all the things we've missed by Tony doing this so late in life. I mean, if this had happened when he was young, he could've made his debut and everything. That way Tonya would've had more experience with young men. And not taken up with my yardman, like she's done."

"Probably so," I murmured, just to make some response to keep up my end of the conversation.

"Well, I'm going to take your advice," Mildred said, gathering up her purse as I wondered just what it was that I'd advised. "You said I should hold my head up and defy the gossips, so if Tonya decides to stick with Calvin, that's just what I'm going to do."

I searched for something comforting to say, but couldn't find anything. Mildred was bearing up better under such a prospect than I could've imagined. At the moment, though, all I could think of was how such a shocking union would explode in the town. Couple that with a pay-off to Monique, and I wouldn't have to worry about lingering idle talk getting back to Little Lloyd. Nobody would be interested in talking about a man who'd been dead for years when there was something so much more recent and of such breath-taking import to talk about. I smiled to myself, thinking that life was good again and that a few other people might soon be joining Tonya and me on Pastor Ledbetter's list of disassociates.

As if she'd read my mind, Mildred said, "I know it would be a sensation in town if that happened. But, you know, while I was in bed recovering from Tony's operation, I listened a lot to a preacher on the radio." She smiled in a satisfied way. "I've taken everything he said to heart."

I frowned. "What did he say?"

"Well, he reminded me that everything that happens to us is part of God's plan. And he said that by grace we are enabled to accept what we can't change."

I put a spiritual expression on my face and nodded. "Very true, Mildred."

Mildred got to her feet and called toward the kitchen, "Come on, Tonya. We better go." Then she leaned toward me and lowered her voice. "He said something else that's really helped me. He said we should always look on the bright side, and the bright side where Calvin is concerned is that at least he's not a Baptist."

Well, for the Lord's sake, I thought to myself, if that was the only bright spot she could find, she was certainly scraping the bottom of the barrel.

But I said, "Look at it this way, Mildred. You missed Tonya's debutante parties, but you can look forward to her wedding. Even if you don't approve of her choice. Mothers don't have much say in that anyway, even under the best of circumstances."

"Oh, you are right, Julia," she said, her face lighting up. "And, you know, when Calvin changes from those filthy overalls and work boots, he can look quite presentable." She clutched my arm in sudden inspiration. "Just think what a tuxedo will do for him."

"If you're thinking that way," I said, somewhat dryly, "you might want to raise his salary."

"Well," she said gaily, "I've supported Horace all these years, what's another one?" Then, turning her head toward the kitchen, she called, "Tonya, let's go. We have plans to make."

As the door closed behind them, I realized how impressed I'd been with Tonya. Say what you will, a pleasant aspect and good manners can overcome a multitude of otherwise questionable qualities.

{Chapter 34}

The telephone rang all afternoon and most of the following day with first one then another of our guests calling with their thanks for the lovely party. Everyone spoke in guarded terms about Tonya at first, then gradually began to express delicious enjoyment of the scandal. I let them, for wasn't that the reason for the party in the first place? But, since I'd used Tonya for my own less-than-admirable purposes, I countered some of the more scathing comments with compliments on her appearance, her sweet disposition, and her lovely manners.

Several callers went around Robin Hood's barn trying to find out more about Sam and me, but I neither confirmed nor denied, letting them draw their own conclusions. That's the way to foster more gossip, in case you're interested.

Sam called every day and came over whenever he had a mind to, which was almost too often for me. I needed time to think and to nurture the right kind of gossip, since the Mooney woman's departure was still some days hence. Actually, though, Sam's visits helped keep things stirred up. Whenever someone called, I could truthfully cut the conversation short by saying that he was at the door.

He'd come in, try a few liberties if no one was around, and say that he had to check on his investment in the future. That's what he called The Ring, although I'd made it perfectly clear that it signified no more than an amicable association of congenial companions, and that I planned to return it as soon as it accomplished its purpose. He laughed every time I brought that up. It's a fact that when men lay out good money for something, they think special privileges go along with the purchase price.

"Sam," I said, later in the week when I was trying to divert his attention from my person before one of the children came in and caught us, "I need an escort for tomorrow night."

"I'm your man. Where're we going?"

"To that Pre-Grand Opening thing they're having."

His eyebrows went up. "Why, sure, Julia, if that's what you want. But it surprises me."

"Well, don't think I want to go for any spiritual edification, because I don't. I doubt I'd get any from that bunch, anyway. No, I want to see what they're doing out there. And . . ." I stopped and looked away, a cloud of uncertainty sweeping over me.

"And what, Julia?" Sam turned my face to his. "Tell me, sweetheart."

So finally I did. I just let it pour out—the talk about Monique Mooney and Wesley Lloyd and what they'd done on the loan officer's desk and in Wesley Lloyd's office and on the marble floor of the bank lobby, as well as the dreadful ramifications for Little Lloyd if any of it got back to him. I told him how I'd finagled to distract the talkers by honoring Tonya Allen, and was now getting credit for being kind and broad-minded and tolerant, when all I'd been was devious and self-serving. And, on top of that, she'd written the sweetest thank-you note and sent flowers, too, so that I was even more ashamed of myself. I told him about Pastor Ledbetter being so hypocritical as to shun me, and making Emma Sue do the same, which wasn't as bad as being censured but was bad enough. I told him about engaging Mr. Pickens and how he was now locked in out at that place, while Hazel Marie was turning her eyes to other possibilities, the thought of which turned my stomach, and how I needed to get to Mr. Pickens and going to the Pre-Grand Opening was the only way I knew how to do it.

But I didn't tell him about the eye-popping check I'd already written or what I planned to do with it. Sam might mean the world to me, but he didn't have to know what I did with my money.

"My Lord, Julia," Sam said after listening to this outpouring of concern. "You've been carrying a heavy load." He pointed a finger in my face. "Don't do that anymore. When something worries you, I want to know about it. Understand?"

I nodded, feeling an immense relief just to get it said and shift the burden a little. Although, Lord knows what he could do that I couldn't.

"Now, listen," he said, "put Larry Ledbetter out of your mind. I had a talk with him and, believe me, he got the message. You might say he now has a thorough understanding that censuring you is not the best idea he ever had."

"Well, that's a consolation. Even though he's put disassociation in its place. But I can live with that since I wasn't planning to have anything to do with him, either. And at least it doesn't include a public dressing-down." Then recalling how set in stone Pastor Ledbetter's decisions usually were, I asked, "How did you manage to change his mind?"

Sam smiled. "Don't worry about it. I just showed him the error of his ways, and he got the message. I expect he's trying to save face now by telling Emma Sue to keep her distance from you. That'll last about as long as his fascination with Curtis Maxwell."

"That man's like a spider, Sam, sitting back and weaving his webs. And I wish you wouldn't use the word *fascination* in the same sentence as the Ledbetters and Curtis Maxwell. It's too close to the truth where Emma Sue is concerned, in spite of her denial that anything's going on between them. Lord knows, we don't want to imply that there is. There're enough infelicitous couplings going on already." I forgot myself for a moment and leaned my head against his shoulder. He tightened his arm around me until I straightened up at the sound of the children's voices in the kitchen.

"But back to Curtis Maxwell," I went on. "I'm convinced he's behind everything that's happened. Well, except for Tonya Allen. I doubt he had anything to do with her."

"No, I expect he didn't." Sam's eyes crinkled at the corners. "So you want to go to the tent meeting? Okay, we'll go. We'll find Pickens and check the place out at the same time."

"There's another problem, Sam. Hazel Marie's planning to go, too, and take Little Lloyd. I'd rather she not see Mr. Pickens out there, so I've done everything I could think of to dissuade her. But she's determined. I think she's expecting the Holy Spirit to descend, and she doesn't want to miss it."

"We'll watch out for her. And him. But Pickens will probably be more than ready to get back to something normal. And if I know him, he'll take Hazel Marie's mind off whatever she's got it on." He rubbed his hand over my arm, taking my mind off what I'd had it on, too. "And," he said, "I'm just as curious as you are to see what they're doing out there. I know you're not interested in politics, Julia, but you know Mayor Beebee's hooked his wagon to them. I have a feeling that this special meeting is an indication the whole project's in trouble. Which means he is, too."

"That wouldn't bother me."

"Me, either," Sam smiled. "But I like to keep my hand in and see which way the wind's blowing."

"Why don't you run for mayor, Sam? You'd do a better job than anybody who's running now, although Mr. Denby's a good mechanic from all I hear. It doesn't follow, though, that he'd make a good mayor. But you would."

"Well, I'll tell you, Julia. I'd consider throwing my hat in the ring, except for one thing. A politician needs a wife. How could I campaign on family values if I don't have a family?"

"Oh, you," I said, smiling at the way he could turn any subject at all back to his preoccupation with my single state.

So it was settled. Sam and I would go to the tent meeting and, in spite of all my suggestions of better things for her to do, Hazel Marie was planning to go, too. I tried to talk her out of it, not wanting to witness her castigation of Mr. Pickens if she saw him out there. But she was so eager to go, that all I could hope for was that he'd be on a ladder somewhere out of sight, still nailing shingles.

Then, to make matters worse, Hazel Marie talked Lillian into going, which meant that both children would be part of our entourage instead of staying home, far from baleful influences.

And wouldn't you know but LuAnne called with word that everybody was excited about the meeting, and now that Pastor Ledbetter and that soap salesman had urged attendance, they'd all turned into sheep, willing to do anything they were told. So Dwayne Dooley was going to have a full house but, if I knew the temper of my fellow church members, he wasn't going to have a full collection plate. Oh, it would look full, but a dollar bill from each attendee wouldn't amount to much, even if three hundred people showed up. And there'd be some, like me, who wouldn't give a red cent.

{ *Chapter 35* }

Convinced that the Walk Where Jesus Walked people were nothing more than swindlers in sheep's clothing, I had myself worked up to the boiling point by Saturday evening. I *knew* they were not what they purported to be, and Monique's willingness to fill her bank account proved it. I so wanted to broadcast that fact all over town, but of course I couldn't. I could only hope that when she hightailed it out of town, Dwayne Dooley and the rest would soon follow. Then I'd be rid of them all, binding lease or no binding lease.

Even though it grated on me to finance that woman's departure, I had to do it. After all, if I'd not been so pleased to get a return from unused property, they would've never set up shop here in the first place. I owed it to the naive and unsuspecting Abbot

Countians, to say nothing of Little Lloyd, to protect them from what I'd made possible.

"Miss Julia," Lillian said, as she pulled a tee shirt over Latisha's head, "how long you think this meetin' gonna last?"

"I have no idea. As long as it takes to ask for money and to collect it, I guess."

Lillian glowered at me, shaking her head at my cynicism. "You be better off, you not 'spect the worst outta people you don't even know."

"Lillian," I said, snapping my pocketbook closed after making sure the check was in it, "I may not know all those people, but I know one. And you do, too, because I told you about her and the reprehensible stories going around about her."

Latisha turned her large eyes up at me. "I been hearin' my teacher read all kinds of stories here lately, but I don't b'lieve she got to that kind yet."

"And let's hope she won't ever," I said, realizing anew that I had to watch what I said around inquisitive children. "Where're Hazel Marie and Little Lloyd? Sam'll be here any minute, and we'll have to go."

Before Lillian could answer, Little Lloyd came into the kitchen with his mother right behind him. He looked so neat and put-together in spite of his casual attire—khaki shorts, a polo shirt, and tennis shoes. Hazel Marie wore long pants with a matching cotton sweater, so neither of them looked as if they were going to a worship service. Which was just as well, because they weren't.

"Think it'll rain again?" Little Lloyd asked, glancing out the window at the low clouds, glowing at the edges from the setting sun.

"I hope not," I said, looking over his shoulder, expecting to see Sam to come driving in. "But let's take some umbrellas just in case."

"I think we'd better," Hazel Marie said, as she distributed umbrellas from the stand to each of us. "Miss Julia, I'll take everybody in my car and let you and Sam have some privacy in his."

"I'm in no mood for privacy," I returned. "Still, it would be crowded with all of us in one car. You can follow us, Hazel Marie, and we'll park close to each other and go in together." I took my bottom lip in my teeth, worrying anew about exposing Little Lloyd to the unknown doctrine of a vagrant preacher with no seminary degree. "I'm still not sure these children ought to go. I'd stay home with them, but . . ." I stopped. I couldn't stay home, and I couldn't say why.

"Oh, no," Hazel Marie said, as Lillian looked up in surprise. "You have to go, Miss Julia. It'll be fun for all of us to go together. If it's anything like I remember, you'll have a great time. If they don't get too carried away." She stopped and frowned. "Well, if they do, we'll just get up and leave."

"All right, then," I conceded. "But, believe me, I am not above walking out if I don't like what I hear. I don't care who it embarrasses. So be warned."

Lillian winked at Little Lloyd and said, "We jus' make out like we don't know you."

Hearing Sam's car turn into the driveway, we gathered our things and hurried out. Sam's face lit up when he saw me approach, a wondrous thing that still amazed me. What in the world did he see in an old and cranky, no-nonsense woman like me? Of course, I was not without a few virtues to my credit—honesty, for one, and level-headedness and moral rectitude, in spite of what my own pastor thought. On the other hand, I'd never known, or known of, a man who had virtue as his number-one requirement in a woman, so that still left me at a loss to explain what attracted Sam to me.

Ah, well, I thought, as I gave Sam a tight smile and slid into his car, why question a good thing?

"You ready for this, Julia?" Sam asked, as he backed out of the drive.

"As ready as I'll ever be. Now, Sam, be careful how you drive. Hazel Marie doesn't know the way, so we don't want to lose her."

"Yes, ma'am," he said, cutting his laughing eyes at me.

"You," I said, smiling in spite of myself.

But the closer we got as we drove the several miles south of town, the more distressed I became. How would I recognize the Mooney woman? What would I do if I did? How would Mr. Pickens find me, and how would he get the check to Monique without anyone seeing? And what if Hazel Marie saw him drive off with a strange woman who had a suitcase with her? Surely he'd know the peril he was in and be doubly careful.

Sam drove past the state road that Lillian and I had taken the past week to meet Mr. Pickens, but I didn't point it out. We drove several miles farther on, turning at last onto the road that bordered the south edge of my property.

"Lord, Sam," I said, struck by the straggly trees that lined both sides of the road, "there's nothing out here but trees and scrub. I ought to buy some more acreage before developers discover it. In fact," I went on, vaguely recalling a list of properties in Binkie's possession, "I think Little Lloyd has a tract in here somewhere."

Sam nodded. "You know, I believe he does."

"Then I ought to buy up enough to tie in with his, wherever it is. It'll be worth something some day."

"Good idea," Sam said, making me preen a little by taking my business acumen seriously. "I'll check the plats and see where the lines are."

As we drew nearer to the theme park, we joined a line of cars waiting to turn in. I was startled to see a ten-foot-high chain-link fence along the road for several yards before opening at a gate where gravel had been spread to cover the mud.

"Why in the world would they enclose this place with a fence?" I asked. "Can you imagine what it cost to fence in twenty acres?"

"I doubt it's all the way around," Sam said, as he pulled into the drive. "And, remember, they'll be charging admission when they open it to the public, so they'll need a fence."

"They better not be charging admission tonight."

Sam grinned, drove through the unattended gate and swung to the left, where a young man was motioning to parking places. We were not the first by any means, for the muddy, thinly graveled area was thick with many more cars than I'd expected to see. In spite of being there myself, I had hoped for a poor and discouraging turn-out.

"Just wait, Julia," Sam said as I reached for the door handle. He opened the door on his side and looked down at the treacherous footing. "I'll come around and help you out. This place is a swamp."

I looked at my white lace-ups with a sinking feeling. They were going to be ruined, but there was nothing for it but to follow through. By the time we met up with Hazel Marie and Lillian and the children, we were all picking our way through the rutted and soggy parking lot toward another gate in another fence. Lillian kept mumbling about how somebody ought to put down more gravel, and Hazel Marie moaned about her high heels that kept sinking into the mud. Latisha wanted to run ahead but Lillian kept her close with a firm hand. Little Lloyd eyed the darkening sky, predicting just as darkly that we were in for more rain.

At the next gate, there was a woman handing out what I took to be programs of the order of service, but which turned out to be something else. She directed us down a gravel path toward a large mustard-colored tent just visible through the few pines they'd left standing. I pursed my mouth at the sight of so many stumps, indicating the number of trees they'd taken down. *That's one thing against them,* I thought to myself, determining to count the offenses.

"Look, Miss Julia," Hazel Marie said, pointing at a shed to the right of the path. It was a three-sided construction made of un-planed planks with a roof of straw. Bales of hay were stacked inside, surrounding what looked like a horse trough.

"It's the manger!" Little Lloyd said, proving that he had a more imaginative mind than I, for it looked nothing like what one would expect to find in a sun-baked desert country.

"I didn't know they had pine boards in Palestine," I sniffed.

"Look beyond it," Sam said, and we all stopped to wonder at two walls standing alone. Although I shouldn't say exactly standing, but they were evidence that some attempt had been made toward authenticity by using mud bricks. Most of the walls had melted in the heavy rains, so they were hardly more than two piles of glistening mud.

Latisha said, "I don't see one of them logs I been wantin' to ride, an' I been lookin' everywhere."

"I tole you," Lillian told her, "that this not the kind of theme park you got on yo' mind. This a *religious* theme park, an' they don't have no logs. 'Cept what they cut down."

People were passing us on the path, some of whom spoke and others stopped to shake hands. They seemed in a gala mood, eager to hear and see what they'd been talking about for so many weeks. We followed the crowd toward the tent, taking note as we did of the small buildings in various states of construction on each side of the path.

The children were entranced, I think because the place looked like a toy village, and they would've loved to've gone in and out of the carpenter's shop—I could tell because of the Ace Hardware saws hanging on the walls, a replica of the Upper Room where a table waited if anybody had the nerve to climb the rickety stairs, and the net-covered boat anchored at the pool of Siloam or the Sea of Galilee, I didn't know which.

"My word, Sam," I said, "this place is pitiful looking. Curtis Maxwell hasn't been as generous with his contributions as we've been led to believe. No wonder they're having us all out here."

When we got to the tent with its rows of chairs borrowed from both funeral homes, I noted with some relief that the ground had a heavier layer of gravel than the path and the parking area. Yet mud still oozed where shoes and boots had trampled as people made their way to seats. The light breeze that blew through the open sides of the tent was damp and chilly. The heavy canvas sagging overhead was held up by a series of slender metal poles on the edges and interspersed at various crucial spots in the interior. I pulled my sweater closer and began to worry that the children didn't have enough clothes on.

The place was almost full and, to my dismay, the only vacant seats were down toward the front. I would've much preferred to be near the back where it would be easier to leave if I took a mind to, but no, we had to sit only a few rows from the improvised stage, which was a couple of feet higher than the auditorium. A lectern, equipped with a microphone, stood empty and waiting in front of a semicircle of folding chairs for visiting dignitaries.

As we got ourselves settled, I looked around, saw LuAnne, and waved to her. Taking note of those present, I saw any number of my fellow Presbyterians, a large contingent of Baptists and Methodists, a sprinkling of Lutherans, and more than I could count of people who never darkened the door of any church. What they were doing there, I couldn't imagine, unless it was to see the show or perhaps to find something that was unavailable in a mainstream church. For which I was firmly grateful.

Leaning close to Sam, I whispered, "I don't want Hazel Marie to know he's here, but have you seen Mr. Pickens?"

"No, and I've been looking. Maybe I ought to wander around, see if I can find him."

"Don't leave me now," I said, linking my arm in his. "But let's keep looking. I want him to know where we are." And to that end, I craned my head to scan the audience to see if I could spot him.

Then I leaned across Little Lloyd and said, "Hazel Marie, the Allens are here, even Horace who looks none too happy to be seen with his new daughter. Look over to your left."

She craned around, then quickly turned back to me. "My word, Miss Julia. That's Calvin with them! No wonder Mr. Horace looks so put out."

I couldn't believe it, but there Calvin was, sitting beside Tonya, as if he belonged there. He was as well, or better, turned-out as any man there. I confess that I wondered if Mildred had been responsible for his pinstriped suit and regimental tie. But perhaps he had his own good taste.

"There're the Strouds and the Brough-tons," Hazel Marie said, drawing my attention away from the Allens. "Looks like just about everybody's here, except Binkie and Coleman. I don't see them."

"It's too damp for the baby," I said. "Or maybe they couldn't get a sitter." Whatever the reason, Coleman and Binkie seemed to be the only ones with good sense, and I wished I'd had no cause to be out, either. I leaned over to Hazel Marie again. "Do you see Emma Sue?"

"She's right over there in the front row." And so she was, studying her program and looking neither to the left nor the right, getting herself into a frame of mind suitable for a preacher's wife at a religious service.

I followed her lead and looked at my program, only that wasn't what it was. Instead, it was a list of supporters of the Walk Where Jesus Walked Theme Park. Mayor Beebee headed the list, followed by several businesses advertising themselves as American-owned, then there were two columns naming the churches and their pastors that had signed on.

"Look at this, Sam," I said, leaning toward him. "Take note of the churches that aren't on here as sponsors. The Catholic church, for one, and none of the Episcopal ones. And I don't see the downtown Methodist church, either. Nor the Lutheran. In fact," I went on, gathering steam as I ran my finger down the list, "the only mainline churches on here are the First Baptist and the First Presbyterian.

"Does that tell you something?" I demanded, poking my finger at the offending sheet. "What is Pastor Ledbetter thinking of, aligning himself, and us, with something that all the dignified churches wouldn't touch with a ten-foot pole? And look at this," I said, outraged at the sight of blank lines at the bottom for name, address, and the amount of money one promised to give. "It's a pledge card!"

Sam started to reply, but all of a sudden a band located on the side of the stage started playing. There was a piano, two trumpets, an electric guitar, and a set of drums, and the noise they put out grated on my nerves something awful. As a Presbyterian, I was accustomed to a pipe organ playing classical music I didn't know, with the occasional piano joining in for congregational hymns or playing alone when the youth choir sang.

But this band had nothing if not rhythm, and before I realized it, people in the audience began to stand in scattered groups, and as others joined them, they began to clap in tune to the music. It was infectious, I give them that, but you won't catch me getting into the swing of things with something like "Bringing in the Sheaves."

Some people began to sing, and others gradually added their voices, as a number of men filed onto the makeshift stage. I recognized Dwayne Dooley right off in spite of his suit and tie and his, Lord help us, white socks. Several others crowded in behind him, including Pastor Ledbetter, who looked a little bewildered at being there; and Mayor Beebee, who waved to the crowd; and Curtis Maxwell, who brought up the rear.

By the time they'd all trooped in, each one standing, with his hands clasped in front as men are wont to do, by the chairs lined across the stage, most of the people in the audience were singing their hearts out, getting louder and happier by the stanza. Pastor Ledbetter was always complaining that Presbyterians didn't sing like they should, but this should've shown him that if he'd select hymns that somebody knew, they'd get sung.

Nonetheless, the whole revival atmosphere affronted me, unaccustomed as I was to jarring music and joyful singing and hand-clapping and arm-waving and body-swaying in what claimed to be a religious setting. You could look around the audience and pick out the Presbyterians by their unbending discomfort in the midst of such enthusiasm.

As I stiffened in displeasure, Sam took my hand and rubbed his thumb across the back of it, somewhat easing my seething emotions in spite of my aversion to public displays of affection.

He put his mouth next to my ear, which was the only way he could be heard in all that racket, and whispered, "Let's just see what happens."

I nodded and squeezed his hand, thankful that somebody with a sense of decency and order was there with me.

{Chapter 36}

The service pretty much followed your basic evangelistic tent meeting format—several more hymns, all with a driving beat that loosened inhibitions to the point of scandal to my way of thinking, prayers from first one preacher then another asking for generous hearts to see this beneficial project through to completion, thanks given at length by Dwayne Dooley for help already given and for help pledged in the future, and of course the passing of the collection plates—*twice,* to my utter outrage, in case anybody was moved to increase their contribution.

And if I'd heard the supremely smug and self-confident words, 'the Lord will provide,' one more time, I was going to send that collection plate winding. The Lord may, indeed, provide, but he does it through the pockets of everyday working people, and, in my opinion, it was past time for them to get a little appreciation.

I was once reprimanded and corrected by a preacher for my custom of referring to the receiving of money in a church service as the collection. It's the offering, he'd said. Maybe so, I thought, but whatever was being offered was also being collected, so what it was called depended on which side of the plate you were standing, or sitting.

Then Mr. Dooley introduced Curtis Maxwell, who didn't need an introduction since he'd already visited every church in the county, talking up the theme park and his washing powder. We had to listen to it all again, but finally Mr. Maxwell nodded at Mayor Beebee and with a wink at the audience, said, "I know you're all going to vote right. And remember, the more you give to God, the more he'll give to you." Which just tore me up, knowing that whatever money was collected wasn't going to God at all. Dwayne Dooley looked nothing like him.

As the service proceeded, I felt the legs of my folding chair sink unevenly into the muddy ground. I ended up sitting on a slant that threatened to slide me off completely. That was another reason I clung to Sam's arm. Besides that physical uneasiness, I was becoming more and more concerned about Mr. Pickens. What if he didn't show up? How would I get the check to the Mooney woman?

What if this motley crowd was growing something illegal in the back acres of the property, hidden by scrub pines and under-growth? What if Mr. Pickens, with his nose for criminal activity, had discovered it and they had him locked up somewhere?

Lord, I wanted to jump up and call Deputy Coleman Bates and tell him to get one of those sharp-nosed dogs out here to sniff out the evidence.

Just as I started to tell Sam my sus-picions, he nudged me and nodded his head toward the side of the stage. "There's Pickens."

I breathed out in relief, for there he was indeed, standing in the back row of a group of what looked to be local handymen, hired as he had been to help with the construc-tion of the park. But from the looks of what they'd done, none of them had been any handier than Mr. Pickens when it came to town planning and carpentry work.

I glanced over at Hazel Marie, but she'd

not seen Mr. Pickens and it suited me not to draw her attention to him. I was going to have a hard enough time explaining my silence as to his whereabouts, when she discovered he'd been working for me all along. No telling what kind of disruption she'd cause if she saw him now, although she might not've even recognized him. He blended in with the group he was with in his work clothes and muddy boots. He needed a haircut worse than the last time I'd seen him in the back seat of my car, and all I can say is that he was downright scruffy looking.

"As soon as this thing is over," I whispered to Sam during another interminable prayer, "I'm going to meet with Mr. Pickens and tell him to pack up and get out of here." And, though I didn't say it, arrange for him to finalize the business matter with Monique Mooney. I clutched my pocketbook where the check lay in wait.

Sam nodded, and I bowed my head again, trying to remember enough of the Twenty-Third Psalm to recite to myself so I wouldn't have to listen to more of what I'd been hearing for the past hour.

Then when I thought the thing was surely

drawing to a close, Mr. Dooley introduced the mayor and we had to listen to a bunch of campaign promises that had nothing whatsoever to do with a mayoral race in a small town in North Carolina.

"You know my stand on homeland security," he said, leaning on the lectern and frowning in a serious manner. As he continued on in like manner, I tuned him out and expressed my displeasure by conspicuously consulting my watch on several occasions.

By the time he finished, I thought my eyes would never come down out of my head. Of all the presumptuous tirades I'd ever heard, that one took the cake. All a mayor of Abbotsville ever did was moderate the council meetings, cut a few ribbons, and get his picture in the paper. If those piddling duties had anything to do with homeland security, prescription drugs, or the economy, I'd eat them.

Surely, after that, I thought we'd be dismissed, but no, Mr. Dooley claimed the lectern again and announced that, in all fairness, the good people of Abbot County deserved to know more about the staff of the theme park and the way they'd dedicated themselves to the Lord's work.

"We're not theologians," he said, which hardly came as a surprise. "We're not sent out and supported by any denomination. There're no ordained preachers among us, nor any pseudo-intellectuals who think they have all the answers. We're just plain folks, like you, who've lived hardscrabble lives and who have, by grace, come out on the other side." He paused, bowed his head, and shook it, as if in sorrow, drawing out the moment like an actor. "I'm just a sinner saved by grace, lifted up out of the mirey ground, and set on a firm foundation." One of my chair legs sank another inch in my own bit of mirey ground.

"I was a drunk!" Mr. Dooley suddenly shouted, startling me as I tried to adjust my seating. "They say it's a disease, a sickness. But I tell you, it's nothing but sin. I was a fallin'-down drunk. I lost my job, my family, and my good wife who couldn't take it anymore. I lost everything to the evil of liquor and, I tell you good folks, Satan was in every swallow I took. And, believe me, I took me a lot of swallows. Satan had hold of me good, but listen to me because I been there and I know, there's somebody stronger than he is. Look at me now, clean and free of that depraved craving. So whatever's houndin' you, whatever's latched onto your back, grace can free you for good, just like it's done for me." He took out a handkerchief and mopped the sweat from his face.

The whole thing mortified me. I didn't need to hear a tale of shame and misery, and I didn't know why he felt compelled to demean himself in such a way. It seemed to me that his current manner of living should've been testimony enough without giving the unseemly details of his former fallen state.

"I'm ready to go," I whispered to Sam. "I've had all of this I can take."

But, Lord, I spoke too soon, for Mr. Dooley turned to the row of men behind him and introduced Pastor Larry Ledbetter, who looked surprised to be called upon. I thought I'd die of embarrassment for my pastor being identified as part of such an undignified service. But he gathered himself, went to the lectern, gave a short and sweet altar call, and an invitation to anybody who answered it to join our church. Then he sat down.

The expression on the pastor's face reminded me of someone who'd walked through the wrong door. He looked as if he was having second thoughts about what he'd gotten himself into. But I didn't have long to ponder the pastor's discomfort, for Mr. Dooley then introduced Skeeter McKenzie, and it took me some little while to get over hearing such a name being applied to an ordained minister, even if he was pastoring a splinter church out in the county.

Preacher Skeeter went on for some little while, spending an inordinate amount of time on the benefits of home-schooling, which I had a hard time connecting to the needs of the theme park.

Apparently, Mr. Dooley did, too, for he edged Preacher Skeeter aside and took the microphone. He turned and beckoned to someone out of my line of sight. "And now," he said, "here is the helpmate of everyone involved in the Walk Where Jesus Walked organization. She is our backbone, our encourager when things get dicey, and the one who keeps our eyes on the prize. We couldn't do this without her. Monique, come on out here. Folks," he said, turning to the audience, "this is Monique Mooney, who grew up here in Abbot County, and believe me her testimony is going to fill you with Holy Ghost grace and make you shout for glory."

I reared back in my chair, feeling the back legs sink down further. My breath caught in my throat, as every system in my body practically shut down entirely. I grabbed Sam's hand and clamped down on it. For there she was—the woman who threatened Hazel Marie's peace of mind and Little Lloyd's idealized, though painfully incorrect, view of his father.

She came striding out onto the stage like she'd done it a million times before, looking for all the world like Loretta Young, if anybody remembers her. Lord, my mouth dropped open at the sight. The woman was tall, with the lush figure that Mr. Pickens had referred to. She wore a form-fitting lavender dress that flared at the knees, ending in a short train. A matching cape swirled around her as she headed for the microphone. Her hair was as black as any dye Velma could've come up with. It lay full on her shoulders, framing a heavily made-up face that would surely earn Pastor Ledbetter's disapproval.

But, beneath that dramatic exterior, I thought I discerned a woman who was trying too hard to appear at ease. Her eyes, flitting this way and that, betrayed her, as did her trembling shoulders. I felt a stirring of pity, but quickly restrained it as I recalled the damage she could do.

After giving Mr. Dooley a fleeting smile, Monique leaned into the microphone and looked out at the audience. When she began speaking, I was struck by her husky voice and her slow, deliberate delivery.

"Dwayne has nothing on me," she began as she gripped each side of the lectern. "My life has been a long and perilous journey into the depths of sin. For many long years, I poisoned my body with liquor and Virginia Slims. I wore seductive clothing and brought many a decent man down. But by the leading of God through Dwayne, I have been slain in the spirit and delivered up into joy."

Well, that was a striking beginning, and she had the attention of every person there. The only thing was, I didn't see any evidence of the joy she said she'd been delivered into. There was no smile, no holy glow, no sign of happiness. And I soon found out why.

"When I heard," she went on, "that we were being led to Abbot County, I knew that the Lord was showing me what I had to do. My friends, it's not enough to be convicted of our sins. It's not enough to realize how far short we come from the glory of God. It's not enough to ask him for forgiveness, which he is ever gracious to grant. No, there's more that has to be done before the Holy Spirit is able to cleanse our filthy bodies and turn them into temples fit for his indwelling. Yes, before He can come in and fill us with his powerful presence, we have to ask forgiveness of all those we've hurt and wronged and spiritually damaged. And that's what God is leading me to do tonight."

Thunder rolled in the distance, but nobody paid any attention to the threatening sound. Every eye in the place was glued to the woman before us. If I could've moved from the paralysis that gripped my limbs, I would've left right then and there.

Chapter 37

Stretching her long, white neck, Monique threw her head back and stared at the top of the tent. "Lord," she prayed, her hands lifted high in supplication, "free me from the burden and the wages of sin, and make me whole again. Work on these good people, Oh, Lord, so that they will look with compassion upon this poor, prodigal daughter set back down in their midst. May they find it in their hearts to forgive the wrongs I perpetrated on so many, who didn't even know I was alive."

Then she bowed her head, swinging her shoulders so that the cape fluttered around her. She stood that way for a few seconds, while the rest of us waited out this dramatic moment. My breath was coming in little gasps, hardly daring to think what this woman would say next. One minute I wanted to snatch up Little Lloyd and run out of the place, and the next I was telling myself that surely she wouldn't give chapter and verse of her unabridged book of life.

I glanced over at Little Lloyd to see how much attention he was paying, and was reassured when I saw him whispering with Latisha. I felt no call to admonish them as I would have done in a normal church service.

Monique finally got through praying, and began to testify.

"Like the Samaritan woman with all the husbands," she began, "I took what did not belong to me. Mrs. Allen," she said, lifting her head and peering out into the audience. "Mildred, I think of you as my sister in the Lord, I ask you now to forgive me for my trespass against you."

Everybody turned to stare at Mildred, whose face registered nothing but astonishment and embarrassment for being singled out in such a way. She turned this way and that, trying to see if there were another Mildred Allen who was being put on the spot. Tonya, sitting beside her, gaped in equal astonishment, while Horace on the other side of Mildred shrunk down in his seat, his hand

covering his face. Calvin just looked confused, probably wondering what kind of
family he'd gotten himself into.

People all over the auditorium looked
at one another, whispered together and
shrugged shoulders in wonderment at
Monique's words. Then, in the ensuing silence, she went on to make her meaning
perfectly clear. "I once—no, several times—
knew your husband, Mildred, in what is
called the biblical sense, but there was
nothing spiritual about it. The guilt now
weighs heavily on me, and I beg you to lift it
off with your forgiveness. And there were
others . . ."

Every eye there was fastened on Monique, as her words rang out in the open-
mouthed, breath-holding silence. I felt every
drop of pity for her drain away, while the full
meaning of her words sunk in.

"I don't want you to think," Monique went
on, "that I limited myself to those who belonged to faithful wives. Dwayne," she said,
turning to Mr. Dooley who gave her a weak,
but encouraging, smile, "while I'm going
good, I might as well get it all said. You were
thrilled when Curtis offered to finance your
dream, but you don't know why he did. He

did it because he wanted me, and I wanted to keep the money rolling in. But Curtis," she said, rounding on Mr. Maxwell, who was sitting behind her. His face reddened and his eyes darted from side to side, looking for a way out. "Not enough has been rolling in, so I've had to make a different arrangement."

Even as I wondered where that left Dwayne Dooley, a piercing scream cut through the heavy air, raising the hair on the back of my head. Norma Cantrell came out of her chair and, pushing her way across those sitting in adjoining seats, she scrambled toward the aisle, screaming, "You promised me! You promised me!" Emma Sue swiveled around, staring at Norma, her face lighting up as Norma publicly acknowledged the focus of her interest, which most assuredly was not the pastor.

Mr. Maxwell came to his feet and began to edge toward stage left.

"The Holy Spirit is working now," Monique cried out in wonder, as she leaned closer to the microphone to be heard over the stir she was causing. "I can feel him here among us."

Something certainly was working among us, but I wouldn't've bet on how holy it was.

But Monique was swept away with the power of her testimony, letting it pour out with no heed to the agitated murmuring of her audience. "There were others whose marriage vows I trampled upon," she said, raising her voice over the disturbance Norma was creating as she headed for the stage. "Mrs. Richard Stroud, Helen, your husband was weak and I used that against him. Forgive me, I beg of you. Mrs. Amy Broughton, Mrs. Mayor Beebee, Mrs. Wesley Lloyd . . ."

Lightning flashed, throwing the surrounding trees in bright relief, as I sprang to my feet and clapped my hands over Little Lloyd's ears. Thunder crashed above our heads, as a sudden downpour of rain drummed on the tent canvas. I crushed the child to me, almost smothering him in my effort to block out that wretched woman's words.

As the full import of Monique's confession took hold, the audience became more and more agitated. People came out of their seats, as tumults broke out in first one place, then the other. Someone threw a chair, another crashed into a pole, loosening the support of the whole tent. The rain-filled canvas dumped a cascade of water over everybody on the right side. I heard a shriek from Mildred and saw Helen deck her husband with her pocketbook.

By this time, Norma had bulled her way up onto the stage, brushing against the podium as Monique grabbed the teetering microphone. Mr. Maxwell jumped off the back of the stage, heading for the hills with Norma, screaming like a banshee, right on his heels. Gladys Beebee lifted her skirts and leapt onto the stage. She pushed Mr. Dooley out of her way and went straight for the mayor. He cringed away from her, his arms held protectively around his head, as she slammed him over and over with her umbrella. The preachers on the stage scattered in various directions, losing every ounce of dignity they'd ever had trying to get out of the line of fire.

Mr. Dooley grabbed the microphone from Monique, causing an awful screech in the sound system. He yelled at the top of his voice. "People! People! Please, this is a testimony! A sister, convicted of sin and standing before you asking forgiveness. Everybody! Let's sing a hymn of praise." He swung around to the band and waved his hand to get them started. "'Leaning on the Everlasting Arms,'" he yelled, announcing the selection as loudly as he could. The band commenced blaring forth as he lifted his voice in a crowd-calming effort: *"Lean*ing, *lean*ing, safe and secure from all alarms . . ."

But nobody was listening, much less singing. The audience erupted from one end to the other, as even those wives who'd not been named cut loose with threats and questions and accusations. Fights and screams were breaking out all over the place. All I could do in the midst of the uproar was hold Little Lloyd close and pray that he'd not put two and two together and come up with a footloose father. Sam was beside me, his arms shielding us from flying objects, urging a quick retreat. Hazel Marie sat in shocked silence, her face as white as a sheet. Lillian was aghast, her eyes wide and her mouth open. Over the rising din, I heard Latisha say, "I don't like this place, Great-Granny. It don't look like a theme park to me."

In a flurry of motion, Mr. Pickens suddenly appeared in the row behind us. He leaned over, took Little Lloyd from me and lifted him over the seat. With the boy clinging to him, Mr. Pickens touched Hazel Marie's shoulder and said, "Come on, sweetheart. I'm getting you out of here."

She climbed over the seat and fell against him, so glad to see him that she hugged him and the boy in his arms. The three of them pushed their way to the aisle and the last I saw of them, they were halfway to the exit.

"Let's go, Julia," Sam said, with one arm around me, and the other reaching out to Lillian. People everywhere pushed and shoved and shouted over the racket the band was making. Mr. Dooley had given up on leading a congregational hymn, for the alarms just kept on piling up.

We got to the aisle, but it was so full of the seething crowd that we were stopped cold. In the meantime, Mr. Dooley and Monique, herself, had come down into the audience, trying to bring some semblance of decorum back to the proceedings. Things had gotten far out of hand, as old scores were being settled in the midst of legitimate marital discord. I could hear the two of them yelling for quiet, and at one point, Mr. Dooley shouted out to the band,

"Stop that infernal racket!" Which didn't speak highly of his spiritual state.

The turbulent crowd squashed me against Sam and somebody stepped on my foot. I made my discomfort known by lashing out with my pocketbook, freeing up a little space around us. Sam leaned down and picked up Latisha and I grabbed Lillian's hand and pulled her out into the aisle.

"Stay together now," Sam yelled out, and we began to push through the churning mass before us. At one point, I was able to look back at the stage. Pastor Ledbetter, who'd not retreated from the fray like the other preachers, had Emma Sue locked in a most unministerial embrace. In all the years he'd occupied our pulpit, it was the first time I'd seen him treat her in any way other than in a formally condescending manner. In fact, as you may remember, I'd often wondered how they'd managed to produce the offspring they had, and this glimpse of them clasped together in a public forum satisfied my curiosity.

With Sam herding us all together, we finally gained the path leading from the tent. I searched the crush of people around me, looking for Little Lloyd and Hazel Marie, but

I couldn't see them. Hoping that Mr. Pickens had gotten them safely away, I clung to Sam's arm to maintain my balance as we were pushed and shoved and jostled along on the muddy track.

The rain had slacked off, although sprinkles from the sky and the trees continued to fall around us. Yet, hardly any unbrellas were unfurled. Some, like ours, had been left behind, and others had so many ribs broken from their use as weapons that they wouldn't open.

We all rushed out, rudely knocking into each other as we slipped and slid in the mud. There was no speaking, no greetings, no rehashing of the recent shameful events, as we ducked our heads and hurried away from the scene of such a decidedly unsanctified service.

Nobody, not us nor any of those who brushed past, was interested in the various half-built structures that were intended to carry our minds back into another time and place. Instead of walking where Jesus walked, we were running where Jesus would've never set foot—unless it was to take a whip to the money-changers as he'd done once before.

I almost stumbled when my shoe got stuck in a particularly soupy spot, and had to hold on to Sam while Lillian helped me regain my footing. That was about the last straw, for I was so full of fury over that woman's lurid confession that I could hardly see straight. And running through the fury was the fearful certainty that Little Lloyd had understood exactly what Monique meant when she listed his father among her conquests.

Why in the world had I allowed that child to come to this place? After all my plans and strategems to protect him, I'd marched right into the lion's den and brought him with me.

Just as I thought I'd have to sit down and cry with the futility of it all, I felt someone tug at my sleeve. Turning around, I came face to face with Monique Mooney, herself. It was all I could do to get my breath.

"Mrs. Springer," she said in that husky voice, causing people to stop and stare, "It looks as if you and I will have to complete our arrangements on our own." While I tried to find my voice, she looked around at the spectators. "We'd do better to find a more private spot." Then she smiled at me. "Perhaps you'll give me a ride to town afterward, since Mr. Pickens seems to have flown the coop."

I stared at the woman, stunned at her boldness and lack of sound judgment. If she'd had any sense at all, she wouldn't have come within ten miles of me.

I opened and closed my mouth several times, trying to work up the effort to speak. Finally I was able to. "Let me explain something to you, Miss Mooney. Our arrangements just got completed in there!" I flung my hand back toward the tent. "That so-called testimony of yours did nothing but broadcast exactly what I wanted to stay dead and buried. The idea! Dredging up things better left unknown and unsaid. And for that matter, *undone!*"

"My testimony was important," she said, lifting her head in defiance. "I was led by the Lord to give it."

"Well, maybe he'll give you a ride to town. I certainly won't." I opened my pocketbook and extracted the check made out to her. "See this?" I waved it in front of her. "It's going right back where it came from." I stuffed the check back into my pocketbook and snapped it closed, as Monique's mouth fell open.

Lillian edged in close, mumbling behind me, "We better go on home now, Miss Julia."

I shook her off and leaned in on Monique. Through gritted teeth, I said, "You were supposed to keep your mouth shut and *leave.*"

Sam put a hand on my arm, but I paid no attention, so steamed up that I wanted to lash out even harder. From the looks of her, Monique was just beginning to understand that she'd lost her ticket out of town and anywhere else she wanted to go. She pulled herself together and stared down her nose at me. If she could've breathed out the fire that reddened her face, I would've been fried to a crisp right then and there.

Her eyes began to take on a peculiar glitter, and very deliberately she widened, then closed them. Turning ever so slightly toward Sam, she arched her neck so that her face was right under his. Then she opened her eyes in a slow, soulful manner so that she was gazing fully into his.

Sam's eyebrows went up, as he took a step backward. Latisha, still in his arms, pointed at Monique and said, "That black-headed lady got something wrong with her. She looking like this." Latisha pulled down her mouth and squinched up her eyes, mimicking Monique's moony-eyed expression.

Sam, ever the gentleman, turned away to hide his amusement. I thought at first that he was entertained by Latisha, but when his laughing eyes found mine, I knew it was Monique he found so funny.

I smiled in return, feeling something cold and hard inside begin thaw and shrink. Monique, and her like, had no power over a rock-solid man. She could turn her face up to his and give him all the come-hither looks she could muster, and he'd stay steadfast and true. Right at that minute, I knew I could trust him to keep his head and any vows he made, regardless of the temptations strewn in his path.

But Monique was so confident of her own charms that she'd not noticed how flat they'd fallen. She shifted her gaze back to me, while a knowing smile lifted one corner of her mouth.

I gasped, shocked to my soul, for the shameless trollop was letting me know that she was still proud of, and willing to prove, her ability to beguile any man within range.

In spite of the trust I was now willing to put in Sam's fidelity, I lost every bit of control I'd ever had. "You wicked woman!" I shrieked, barely aware of the avid faces that surrounded us. "Do you know what you've done? Do you know who you've damaged? Of course you don't. All you thought about was your own wretched sins and trotting them out for us to see. Or to admire. Was that it?"

I stopped for breath, preparing myself to tell her that she could have Wesley Lloyd if, considering his present state, she still wanted him. But I was unceremoniously pushed back.

Mildred Allen barreled in front of me, breathing hard and panting with the effort. "Stand aside, Julia," she said. She leaned right into Monique's face and said, "You dare humiliate me! Well, let me tell you something, confession may be good for the soul, and you may feel better for telling everything you know. But, believe me, nobody else does."

Then she hauled off and slapped the fire

out of Monique, rocking her back on her heels.

Then Mildred turned away and, head held high, left with a parting shot. "Now at least, *I* feel better."

As Mildred stomped off, Tonya threw me a concerned glance and hurried after her. "Manners, Mother, manners," she cautioned, as she caught up with her mother and put an arm around her.

Chapter 38

I was never so glad to see anything in my life as I was to see Sam's car and climb into it. The rain began to come down harder, and all over the parking lot people were diving into cars, slamming doors, and turning on lights. Motors roared to life and wheels churned up clots of mud, splattering it over fenders and anyone passing.

"We'll wait till it clears out," Sam said, turning to make sure that Lillian and Latisha were safely in the back seat with the doors closed. He smiled at Latisha. "You okay, little girl?"

"Yessir, I'm fine. I think I had a pretty good time, seeing something I never seen before."

"Nobody ever seen nothin' like that," Lillian said, mopping the rain from her face.

"That the world's worst tent meetin', I do believe."

"Well," Latisha said, sounding put out with the world, "don't look like I'm ever gonna get to a real theme park."

"Yes, you will, Latisha," Sam said, looking at her through the rearview mirror. "You've started me thinking. Let me look into it, and find one we'll all enjoy."

"Count me out," I mumbled, as I leaned against the window and huddled up in my sweater, just so heartsick about the events that had just transpired that I could hardly stand it.

Sam put his hand on my arm and said in his quiet and comforting way, "Julia, it's all right."

"No, it's not. I've never let my temper get away with me like that. I guess I made a spectacle of myself." I gave him a weak smile, as he patted my arm. "At least I didn't slap her like Mildred did. But, believe me, I wanted to."

"I tell you one thing," Lillian said, "if they's ever a woman need slappin', that one did."

"Thank you, Lillian," I said, as I searched for a Kleenex in my pocketbook and tried to pull myself together. "Sam," I went on, clasping his hand, "did I embarrass you to death?"

"Not a bit of it, Julia," he said. "You've never embarrassed me, but you do keep me hopping, wondering what you'll do next. Tell me, though, what was that check you were waving around? Or is it any of my business?"

"It was Mr. Pickens's suggestion," I said, then realized I was shifting the blame. "But I was only too happy to act on it. I was going to make a charitable donation and hope Binkie could take it off my taxes. Thank goodness, I didn't waste my money. That woman is a menace, and not to be trusted."

Sam just shook his head, but I saw him smiling. "When you and Pickens get together, everybody better get out of the way."

I managed a laugh, feeling suddenly better. If Lillian approved and Sam appreciated my entertainment value, why should I care what anybody else thought?

"My Lord," I said, wiping my nose as daintily as I could, "can you believe what that woman said right up on stage with a microphone, and half the town listening? How could she do such a thing?"

There was silence in the car as we marvelled at Monique Mooney's lack of shame. I watched the rain streak down the windshield, cringing inside at what Little Lloyd might have understood from her rantings. After all my care and concern to protect his innocent admiration of his father, I had miserably failed. Even though we all come to learn, sooner or later, that our parents aren't perfect, I'd have preferred that the child learn about his considerably later, when he was better able to understand a roving eye. Although, I must confess, as advanced in years as I am, it's still beyond my understanding.

Sam rubbed his thumb over my hand. "He'll be all right," he said. "Pickens is probably halfway home with them by now."

I couldn't help but smile at the way he could read my mind and know what was troubling it.

When we arrived at the house, Lillian immediately took Latisha up to bed, while Sam and I went to our customary place on the living room sofa.

I was still in a daze from the enormity of

that woman's arrogant disregard for the feelings of other people. Not, you understand, that I thought the men she'd been involved with deserved to have their secrets kept. Not a bit of it. As far as I was concerned, their names could've been printed in the newspaper and scrolled across the bottom of CNN, and they wouldn't have come close to getting their just desserts. But what about Mildred and Helen and Amy and even Norma—Lord, what about Little Lloyd and Tonya and all the other children who'd just been told that their fathers had not only lusted after that black-headed witch, but had slaked that lust?

My insides knotted up at the thought.

"Why, Sam?" I asked, leaning close to his warm side. "Why did she think she could get up there and broadcast her darkest deeds and think that people would just calmly listen and forgive her?"

Sam patted me with the hand that was draped across my shoulders. "I wonder, myself. Maybe she thought she could right a few wrongs. The only problem is, when we think we have to get ourselves right at the expense of others, well, let's just say that no matter how sincere you are, it can't excuse a lack of common sense."

"I don't think she was sincere," I said. "I think she liked the attention. You know— 'Look at me. See how bad I've been.' And, Sam, she caused an all-out riot! I wouldn't be a bit surprised if there're not a few divorces in the works right this minute."

The telephone rang, and I hurried to the kitchen to answer it before it woke Latisha. Sam followed me and, as I picked up the receiver, he gave me a quick kiss on the cheek and said, "I have a few things to look into tomorrow, but I'll see you later in the day."

I waved him off, turning my attention to the telephone.

"Miss Julia?" Hazel Marie's voice had a low and disconsolate tone to it. "Lloyd and I are going to stay over with J. D. We'll be home Monday."

Not a hair on my head turned at this blatant announcement of their sleeping arrangements. I had more important things on my mind. "How is Little Lloyd, Hazel Marie? Did he understand what that woman said?"

"He understood enough," she said, still

subdued. "Enough to ask questions I didn't have it in me to explain." She took a deep breath that ended in a sob. "Oh, Miss Julia, I'm so sorry for all I've done to hurt you. All this has just opened my eyes to what I put you through."

"Stop that right this minute! You don't have to turn yourself inside out for me, Hazel Marie. That's all in the past, and it's going to stay there. You keep your mind on one thing: we have Little Lloyd and, I'll tell you the truth, I don't care *how* we got him." I took a deep breath of my own. "Where is he? What's he doing now?"

"He's out in the carport with J. D. They're sitting out there in the dark, and J. D.'s talking to him. He said," she stopped and I could hear a smile in her voice, "he said they had man-talk to discuss, and I was to make myself scarce."

The smile didn't last long, because I could hear her sniffling. "He's a good man, Hazel Marie," I said. "I'm glad he's explaining it to the child. I, for one, wouldn't know how to start."

"Me, either."

Lord, the next day the whole town was stirred up even more, so much so that hardly anyone attended church services. I know I didn't, not wanting to hear another word about the previous night's events. But from what I did hear, even those who had not been at the tent meeting expressed their outrage, fearing, I suppose, that the next thing on Monique's agenda would be a tell-all book, complete with a television interview. From the anxious telephone calls and visits that I received, no one seemed to think Monique had reached the bottom of her list by a long shot. Yet at the same time, I was reassured by the number of people who expressed admiration of me for telling her off, and especially of Mildred for hauling off and slapping her. I can't tell you how many said they wished they'd had a chance to smack her silly, too.

I'm here to tell you, though, I couldn't understand how any woman would take up a career in seduction. If what had happened to Monique Mooney and Norma Cantrell was any indication, there was mighty little future in it. Why they'd want to flit from one man to another was beyond me. One had been all I could handle and, as we all know, I didn't do too good a job of it.

But there were a few good things that came of Monique's testimony. Before the day was out, Helen Stroud was driving around in a brand-new convertible, and Amy Broughton had the diamond tennis bracelet she'd been wanting. I don't know what kind of peace offering Mildred Allen received, but Horace got moved downstairs to a room of his own, and he suddenly exhibited a little more understanding of Tonya's divided loyalties.

Some folks said that Norma had caught Curtis Maxwell deep in the woods behind the tent and let him have it. But others were sure he'd escaped her clutches by hiding out all night in the Upper Room. Either way, he was gone by morning, lifting off in his jet plane without a hello, good-bye, or a fare-thee-well.

Emma Sue, from all I heard over the telephone and from drop-in visitors eager to discuss Monique's revelations—and to see how I was bearing up—seemed to profit the most from the can of worms that had been opened. After LuAnne told me that Norma was taking some personal time away from her desk in the pastor's outer office and that Emma Sue was filling in for her, I got Emma Sue on the phone.

"How are you?" I asked, not knowing exactly how to approach the subject I most wanted to talk about.

"A burden has been lifted," she said, sounding so pious I could hardly stand it. "Oh, Julia, I've been so mistaken about Larry, you just wouldn't believe. There's no way in the world he'd look at another woman, so it was Satan who led me to distrust him. Well, and the way Norma acted didn't help."

"No, I guess not," I said, still suspecting that Norma had had an eye on the pastor until a better prospect in the shape of Curtis Maxwell happened along. "Anyway, I'm glad you've straightened things out, Emma Sue. Suspicion is a terrible thing to live with, although there was a time in my life when I could've used a little."

"Oh, I never really suspected Larry," she said, stunning me with this sudden revision of events. "It was always Norma who worried me. She was the one I suspected, and I wasn't wrong about her, just wrong about the one she was after. How in the world could she ever think that somebody as sophisticated as Curtis would be interested in her? But I'm not going to talk about her, because I've forgiven her for what she put me through."

"That's good of you, Emma Sue."

"Oh, and Julia, you'll never guess," Emma Sue went on. "Larry's been shown that cosmetics aren't so bad, after all. The Lord spoke to him this morning while he was shaving, and told him that there was no harm in gilding the lily, so to speak. And," she stopped and giggled a tiny bit, "I reminded him that it's possible to be both sexy and saved. Don't tell anybody I said that."

"I wouldn't dream of it," I said, thinking, *My word, maybe the pastor does have a guilty conscience, if he's letting Emma Sue get away with that.* And, if his conscience was bothering him, I hoped to goodness he'd have a little more compassion for other people because of it—especially people he wanted to shun for no reason in the world.

I got off the phone as soon as I could, shaken by Emma Sue's blithe conviction of her husband's innocence. She might no longer suspect him, but there would always be a little niggle of doubt in my mind. There was still the question of who'd been passionately moaning over Norma in the pastor's office. It had probably been Curtis Maxwell, but it could've been the mayor, or the pastor, for all Emma Sue—or I—knew. But then, after my experience with Wesley Lloyd, I'm just slightly inclined to believe the worst.

Hazel Marie got home late Monday morning, but she didn't stay long. "I thought it better not to send Lloyd to school today," she told me. "I'm just dropping him off with you, so I can get a few things done in town."

I kept my thoughts to myself, but I couldn't keep my mouth from tightening up. Of all the times to go shopping, this was not one of them. I needed her at home where we could discuss Little Lloyd's eye-opening experience, not off on some frivolous expedition for new shoes.

After she left, I kept watching the child, hoping with all my heart that what he'd learned from Monique and from Mr. Pickens had not turned his life upside down and against me. To my great relief, he seemed the same as ever, except for the one time I caught him giving me a long look. Probably trying to figure out where I fit in, vis-à-vis his mother and father. But he quickly smiled when he caught my eye and went on upstairs to play with Latisha. There's something to be said for basic family values—which I had constantly instilled in him—even when that family is as uncommonly constructed as ours.

That afternoon I was in my bedroom, trying to study my daily devotions. My mind kept sliding away, though, as I relived the moment when Sam made it plain that he preferred me to Monique Mooney, even though my first husband had not.

My first husband. I smiled at the thought, because that meant I was thinking about a second one. Glancing down at the ring on my finger, I had an even better thought: It could be that I wouldn't have to give it back.

I put away such idle musings, when Lillian came halfway up the stairs and called to me. "Mr. Sam comin' in the door, an' Miss Hazel Marie with him."

"Well, for goodness sakes," I said, closing my devotional book and preparing to go downstairs. "How did those two hook up together?"

"Maybe they jus' happen to get here at the same time," Lillian said, as she left.

I hurried downstairs to find Sam and Hazel Marie in the living room, both of them smiling in a secretive way. Beaming, if you want to know the truth, which I felt most inappropriate under the circumstances.

Hazel Marie jumped up as soon as I appeared. "Miss Julia! You'll never guess what's happened."

"Lord, don't tell me any more bad news," I said, sitting by Sam on the sofa and, without thinking a thing about it, taking his hand. "I've had enough of it."

"Oh, this is not bad news. You tell her, Sam." Hazel Marie could hardly restrain herself, she was so full of something she was about to pop. "Then I want to tell her the best part."

"Okay," Sam said, his eyes almost dazzling me with their shining. "I get to tell you that Mayor Beebee has withdrawn from the race." Sam had to stop and laugh. "Citing personal reasons and saying he wants to spend more time with his family."

"Well, I never," I said, recognizing the trite

excuse used by politicians in trouble. Then I laughed. "I don't know whether Gladys'll be glad to hear that or not. It's been a blue moon since he's spent any time at all with her."

"Oh, but that's not all," Hazel Marie said, as she waved her hands excitedly. "You'll never guess what Sam and Binkie found out. And I'm the one who thought of it, although Sam almost beat me to it."

"What is it? I declare, Hazel Marie, you're acting like it's the greatest thing that ever happened."

"It just about is!" She finally settled herself on the arm of the sofa, her face shining with expectation. "You know the property that you leased to the WWJW theme park folks? Well, it's not yours. It's Lloyd's!"

"What?" I was confused. I looked at Sam. "What is she talking about?"

"The boundary lines out there aren't properly staked," Sam said with some satisfaction. "Nobody checked the plats in the courthouse, so Dooley's built on land that doesn't belong to you."

"But," I said, not daring to get my hopes up too far, "I signed a lease."

"Yes, but," Hazel Marie said, as she

fidgeted with excitement, "you can't lease land that's not yours. Don't you see, Miss Julia, that lease is not worth the paper it's printed on."

"Well, for goodness sakes," I said, sinking back into the sofa. "And all this time I've been beating myself up for letting those people in, and they weren't even supposed to be there in the first place."

"Hazel Marie put us onto it," Sam said, always eager to give credit where it was due. "She remembered looking over a list of Lloyd's properties, and thought some of his acreage was pretty close to where they're building."

"Yes, and I got Binkie and Sam together this morning to figure it out." Hazel Marie could hardly sit still, which didn't help the stability of the sofa arm. "And sure enough, your property line is some two hundred yards away." She leaned down practically in my face. "They're building on Lloyd's land, and we've already sent the sheriff to tell them they have to vacate immediately!"

I rested my head on the back of the sofa, just stunned at this turn of events. Even though the theme park looked to have come apart at the seams due to Monique's urge to broadcast her dark deeds, I didn't doubt Dwayne Dooley's ability to put it back together again. But with this astounding news, he'd have to put it together somewhere else. After the events of the previous night, there wouldn't be a soul in Abbot County who'd lease a foot of ground to him. Too many wives were up in arms.

"Why, Hazel Marie," I said, putting my hand on her knee as a sense of peace swept over me. "I didn't know you had a head for business."

She wrapped her arms around her shoulders, and beamed in wonderment. "Me, *either.*"

{Chapter 39}

Ever since Sam started all his serious talk about marriage, he'd kept me up past my customary bedtime and that night was no exception. He lingered on well after Hazel Marie, feeling exceptionally pleased with herself, left for bed.

"Did she really think of that all on her own?" I asked Sam. Not that I wanted to take anything away from Hazel Marie, but it hardly seemed the sort of thing she would ordinarily concern herself with.

"She did," Sam said, nodding. "I'd wondered about it when I saw where they'd built, but Hazel Marie was positive they were across the line. None of us wanted to get your hopes up, though, until we confirmed it. And Hazel Marie wanted to surprise you, so she called Binkie and me, and we all went to the courthouse this morning to look at the plats."

"I declare, Sam," I said, sighing as I sat in the far corner of the sofa, "every time I think of that WWJW crew, I could just whip somebody."

"Let it go, sweetheart," Sam said. "They'll be out of your hair before long, and you can give some thought to me. Now, why don't you come on over here next to me? You're about to wear me out, having to chase you down all the time."

"Oh, for goodness sake," I said, not moving an inch. "If you want to sit by me, just do it and quit moaning about having to exert yourself."

Laughing, he did just that, and I settled into what had more and more become my special place in the crook of his arm. It felt especially comforting, now that my fears about his trustworthiness had been put to rest.

After a minute or two of silence in which I became increasingly aware of his heartbeat and the rhythm of his breathing, I thought it wise to say something. "If Dwayne Dooley leaves those pitiful buildings behind, I think I'll talk to Little Lloyd about setting up a park out there. Not a theme park," I quickly added. "But a park where children can play."

"That's a fine idea," he said, his breath ruffling my hair while his hand slid up and down my arm.

"I'll see what he says," I whispered against his shirt. My arm crept around his waist, as I rested my head on his chest and molded myself against him.

"You'd better say something, Sam," I said presently. "I'm about to fall asleep."

I could feel him smiling against my forehead. "You could fall asleep here every night, Julia, if you just would."

I let myself think about what that would be like, surprising myself with how desirable it now seemed. Far from giving the whole marriage business short shrift, as I'd been doing, I realized that the thought of nightly snuggling with him held some decided attractions. Even though I had good reason to abstain from another marriage, this one just might be worth the risk. After all, nothing of this magnitude carried either a lifetime or a money-back guarantee.

But first, he needed to know the ground rules. So I laid them out for him.

I straightened myself, took a breath, and said, "You might as well get this straight right now, so there won't be any confusion on the subject. I am not going to put up with any messing around in any shape or form. If you ever get it into your head to do any, you just let me know and I'll pack your bags."

Sam's face turned serious in a hurry. "What're you saying, Julia?"

"I'm saying this: if the Monique Mooneys of the world start looking good to you, you can have them. I won't stand in your way. In fact, I'll divorce you so fast it'll make your head spin." I crossed my arms across my chest so he'd know I meant business. "Even though I don't much believe in divorce."

"You'll never have reason to worry about me, Julia."

"Well, you just keep that in mind. I've had more than my share of marital discord, and I don't intend to put up with any more of it."

"I promise, you won't have to. Do you think, after all the trouble I've had courting you, that I'd throw it all away? Not on your life."

"It's not my life that's in question, here," I said, deciding I could do a little teasing of my own. "It's yours that's in mortal danger."

Sam grinned and drew me back against his chest. "I'll take my chances, if you'll take a few with me."

"I'm thinking about it," I said, smiling. Then I sat up, overcome with a sudden vision of what lay before me. "Oh, Sam, if we did it, think of all the turmoil and upset and confusion a big wedding would cause. And it would have to be big. We know everybody in town."

Sam's face lit up, along with his eyebrows. "You're sounding mighty serious here, Julia. Are you?"

"I might be, if I wouldn't have to walk down an aisle and have everybody holding their breath to see if I'd make it."

Sam threw back his head and laughed, while I continued to enumerate my objections to the act of marrying. "And what about all the rigamarole we'd have to go through? Invitations and lists and flowers and parties and I-don't-know-what-all." I paused, picturing in my mind such inappropriate celebrations. "Can't you just see me at a wedding shower, opening gifts that neither of us needs while everybody watched? Sam, I tell you, I am not going to go through all that foolishness at my age."

"You don't have to, sweetheart. Just say the word, and I'll fix it so it'll be nice and private."

"You don't know Hazel Marie," I said, frowning darkly. "There's no way in the world she'd let us do something small and quiet. You remember how excited she was about Binkie and Coleman's wedding. She could hardly contain herself, and I know she and Lillian would just blow everything all out of proportion."

"How about this, then? We'll swear Ledbetter to secrecy and do it in his office. Then if Hazel Marie wants to throw a big party, she can."

Alarmed, I untangled myself from his arms. "No, no, a thousand times, no. If I have to be married by Pastor Ledbetter, I just won't do it. That man thinks we've already been up to something, Sam, and I'm not about to let him think he's pushed us into legitimacy. Besides," I went on, my eyes narrowing at the thought of all I had against my own pastor, "he's the one who was hellbent to hold me up for public condemnation. So, if you want him to do the honors, you'll have to trade me in."

"Oh, Julia, I wouldn't trade you for anything in the world. You make me happy, woman." From the looks of him, he was speaking the truth, and it just warmed me all over to know I was the cause of it. I thought I might kiss him pretty soon.

"Now, listen," he said, "I thought you'd want to have Hazel Marie and Pickens, and Binkie and Coleman, and Lillian and certainly Lloyd at a small ceremony, either here or at my house or in the pastor's office. It certainly suits me to bypass Ledbetter, but we'd never hear the end of it if we asked another minister in town. We'd offend not only Ledbetter, but the whole church."

"I wouldn't care if we did," I mumbled, as I twisted my friendship ring around my finger, just about ready to call the whole thing off. It was getting too complicated, what with wondering what I would wear and if a hat with a veil was appropriate and how binding a marriage would be if the bride had malice in her heart toward the presiding minister.

"It's too much trouble," I said, deciding I wasn't going to have it. "Let's just keep on like we're doing, and not fiddle around with anything else."

"Oh, no," Sam said, firmly enough to

make a shiver run up my back. "You're not backing out on me now.

"Come on," he said, standing up and urging me with him. Before I knew it, we were through the dining room and into the kitchen, heading for the door.

"What're you doing?"

"I'm getting married and so are you."

"Tonight? Sam, have you lost your mind!"

"Get your sweater, sweetheart, we're going to tie the knot tonight."

Then he whispered something that made me lose my composure completely. We stood together, laughing there in the kitchen, as I gave in to the joy that swept through me, his suggestion taking my breath away. He drew me close again and told me in wondrous detail what he had in mind. I stepped back from him in amazement. It was so outrageous that I laughed until he had to hold me steady.

"A *theme* park?" I sputtered, hardly believing him. "And at Pigeon Forge, Tennessee? Sam, I have had my fill of theme parks near or far, and I'm not about to get married in or near one."

"But it's just the thing," he said. "You'll love it."

"No, Sam," I said, trying to stop laughing, but having little success. "We can't, we'd never live it down. How did you come up with such a thing?"

"Latisha gave me the idea. Come on, and I'll let you ride the log flume. And, listen, we won't have to worry with a big wedding and all the trappings. Just think, no need to make a reservation, much less send invitations. They welcome walk-ins, Julia. And listen to this, you won't even have to get out of the car. There's a Drive-Thru Special for sixty-nine dollars."

"Sam," I said, choking with laughter at the thought of eloping on the cheap, "that is the tackiest, most tasteless thing I've ever heard! Hazel Marie will just die if we get married at Pigeon Forge. And Latisha! My goodness, I can't go to a theme park without taking that child."

"Maybe after a little honeymoon time, we'll call them all to come over and join us. Now, Julia, I know that an all-night wedding chapel doesn't exactly fit with tradition as you know it, and it's not at all what I had in mind for us, but think about this: You'll be my wife by sun-up tomorrow. Do you really want to pass that up?"

Well, no, I didn't, as the thought of it made me weak inside. "Well," I murmured against his shirt, "when you put it that way, and since we're not inviting Emily Post . . ."

I felt him laugh against my hair. Then he put a hand on each side of my face and tilted it up so that we were only inches apart. "I want to marry you, Julia. I want to share your life, and make you happy as long as I live. I don't care how we get married, just so we do."

Happiness filled my soul, and set all the nerves in my system tingling. I banished every thought of what was appropriate and what was correct and what was traditional, along with every concern of what people would say. There was nothing in my mind but the desire to hold on to this man and, if it took flying off with him to Pigeon Forge or wherever he wanted to go, that's what I would do.

"That's all I care about, too," I said, and joyfully sealed my fate.

"I'm taking that as a yes." He opened the back door. "Come on, sweetheart, let's hit the road."

"Wait, wait just a minute. I have to leave a note. If I'm not here when Lillian and Hazel

Marie get up, they'll have every law enforcement agency in the state looking for us."

"They'll have to do better than that, because I'm taking you across the state line. We'll have it done before they know you're gone."

"I need to pack something," I said, as more and more practical matters came to the fore.

"We'll buy what we need. Now write your note, and let's go before I change my mind."

"Oh, you," I said, snatching up a pad and pen with trembling hands and laughing, in spite of myself. If life with Sam was going to be this good from now on, I had surely made a fine match—at least for once in my life.

Leaning over the table, I hurriedly scribbled a note, so excited and happy I hardly knew what I was writing. This is what Lillian and Hazel Marie would find the next morning:

Have gone to Pigeon Forge to find an all-night wedding chapel. Sam says it's swarming with them.

Wonder how he knows? Will call soon.
Love to all,

Sam took the pen from my hand and scrawled *Mr. and Mrs. Sam Murdoch* across the bottom. Then, with my hand in his, we ran out into the night.

Well, actually we just walked fast, since neither of us was quite as spry as we once were.